A R Points: 16.0
Reading Level: 4.7

FiVE KINGDOMS

CRYSTAL KEEPERS

FIVE KINGDOMS

CRYSTAL KEEPERS

BOOK 3

Brandon Mull

ALADDIN

NEW YORK LONDON TORONTO SYDNEY NEW DELHI

ALADDIN

An imprint of Simon & Schuster Children's Publishing Division
1230 Avenue of the Americas, New York, NY 10020
First Aladdin hardcover edition March 2015
Text copyright © 2015 by Brandon Mull
Cover illustration © 2015 by Owen Richardson
For information about special discounts for bulk purchases, please contact Simon & Schuster Special Sales at 1-866-506-1949 or business@simonandschuster.com.
The Simon & Schuster Speakers Bureau can bring authors to your live event. For more information or to book an event contact the Simon & Schuster Speakers Bureau at 1-866-248-3049 or visit our website at www.simonspeakers.com.
Cover designed by Jessica Handelman
The text of this book was set in Perpetua.
Manufactured in the United States of America 0215 FFG
2 4 6 8 10 9 7 5 3 1
This book has been cataloged with the Library of Congress.
ISBN 978-1-4424-9706-1 (hc)
ISBN 978-1-4424-9708-5 (eBook)

FOR LIESA, MY GUIDING STAR

CHAPTER
1

BUTLER

The sky was getting bright, but the sun had yet to rise as Cole carried his saddle pad to his horse. He tossed it over Ranger's back, but the quilted pad fell through the horse to the ground.

Cole whirled. "Dalton?"

His friend stood a short distance away, arms folded, leaning against a tree trunk. "Not bad?"

Cole picked up the saddle pad and shook off the dirt. "Really good, actually." He swiped a hand through the horse, feeling only a vague, cobwebby sensation. "That looks perfect."

"I moved Ranger last night after you conked out," Dalton confessed. The illusionary horse disappeared.

"Couldn't sleep again?" Cole asked.

"I tried," Dalton said. "I couldn't shut down my brain. It took some time."

"Dalton!" another voice called. Taller than Cole and Dalton by a few inches, though not much older, Jace stormed over to them, his deeply tanned face flushed. "Where's my saddle?"

Dalton cracked a smile. "Isn't it over there?" he asked, pointing.

Cole followed his finger to where Jace's saddle leaned against a mossy log.

"Ha-ha," Jace said. "I already tried to grab it."

The saddle vanished.

"That's two really good seemings at once," Cole said. "How long did you maintain them?"

"Since right before you two got up," Dalton said. "Fifteen minutes or something."

Jace huffed. "Good for you. Maybe you and Skye can set up your own dazzle show. Now where's my saddle?"

Dalton looked around innocently, then craned his head back. Cole tracked his gaze up into a tree where a saddle straddled a high branch, and a laugh spurted out before he could hold it back.

"That better not be real," Jace threatened. "I'll drop it on your head."

The saddle disappeared.

"Three seemings at the same time?" Cole asked.

"It's over by that stump," Dalton said, nodding toward the one he meant.

As Cole watched, the scarred old stump melted away to reveal Jace's saddle. "Four," Cole said. "And they all looked great."

Dalton shrugged.

"Nice waste of time, Dalton," Jace complained. "We're on the run."

"You'd do the same thing if you could work seemings," Cole said.

"I'd make you two walk off a cliff," Jace said.

"You'd kill us?" Dalton exclaimed.

"Into a lake," Jace said. "I'd get two of the highest screams ever."

"We'd cannonball in and make two of the biggest splashes ever," Cole said. "Then we'd come for you."

"I'd be pretty scared," Jace said with a snort. "You guys better hurry up and get ready. We're moving out."

Cole turned to reach for his saddle, but Dalton restrained him. "Wait for it."

Jace hoisted his saddle pad and saddle together, marched over to his horse, and flung them onto its back. The saddle fell through the illusion to the dirt. Jace turned and glared.

"Pick up the pace!" Dalton called. "The horses are this way. We're heading out!"

Dalton grabbed Cole's saddle pad and Cole claimed his saddle. They walked together toward where Dalton had moved the horses. Cole glanced at his friend. They had come to the Outskirts together from Mesa, Arizona. When they arrived, they knew nothing about this world. They'd never heard of shaping or the High King or even knew that a place like the Outskirts was possible. A slave trader had kidnapped dozens of kids visiting a neighborhood haunted house on Halloween and brought them to a bizarre new world. Shortly after their arrival they were marked as slaves and scattered across the five kingdoms. They started out alone—strangers in a strange land.

But they were gradually figuring things out. Cole had managed to find his best friend, and Dalton had some crazy strong abilities.

"That was amazing," Cole said. "But why go after Jace so hard? He's a hothead. You're going to get punched in the face if you don't watch out."

"He hid my saddle yesterday," Dalton replied. "If he wants to make jokes, he has to take them too."

"I didn't hide your saddle," Cole said.

"I didn't want to make him the only target," Dalton said. "I know you can take a joke."

"Right. Because we're friends and we get each other. Jace could be a different story. I'm not sure you want to tangle with him."

"Whatever," Dalton said. "We can't let him think he's Mr. Big Shot. So if Jace teases—we tease him back."

"I get standing up to him," Cole said. "But is it smart to prank him?"

"What's the worst he could do?" Dalton asked. "I mean really. Retaliate somehow? If he does, I'll get him again. It'll save us trouble down the road."

"What about when we leave Elloweer?" Cole said. "You won't be able to make illusions in Zeropolis."

Dalton sighed regretfully. "That'll stink. But all the more reason to get him while I can. If he respects me, he'll back off."

"Or he'll tease you harder until you cave," Cole said.

Dalton shrugged. "I won't give up."

"It's risky," Cole said.

"It's more risky to let him bug me whenever he wants," Dalton replied. "Wait and see."

They reached Cole's horse.

"You first," Cole said.

Dalton laid the saddle pad across the animal's back. "This one's real."

Cole swung the saddle onto the pad. "You better mount up too."

"If Jace is my biggest problem before we leave Elloweer, I'll be grateful," Dalton said, walking away.

Cole gave a nod. "I can agree with that one."

Shortly after sunrise the Red Road came into view, interrupting the wilderness like a wound. Bordered by maroon curbs, the avenue of seamless red pavement began abruptly and extended to the edge of sight, the only evidence of inhabitants in the otherwise untamed landscape. Cole, Dalton, Mira, Jace, Skye, and Joe had avoided serious trouble since parting from Honor and the former Rogue Knight on their way to Zeropolis. Cole hoped that drawing near to Trillian wouldn't end their peaceful streak.

He looked to Skye, who considered the road warily. He understood her hesitation. The Lost Palace, longtime prison of Trillian the torivor, awaited at the end. As the new Grand Shaper of Elloweer, Skye was about to ask Trillian to become her teacher.

Cole did not envy her. One of the most feared and dangerous beings in the Outskirts, Trillian had been caught off guard by a team of mighty shapers and locked away long ago. Had they failed to imprison him, the torivor probably would have brought the entire Outskirts under his control.

Only a few weeks had passed since Cole first visited the

Lost Palace and witnessed Trillian's enormous power first-hand. Inside his prison, the torivor could rearrange reality almost without limits. Not only had Trillian invaded his mind, but Cole had risked his life and freedom to rescue Mira's sister Honor from captivity.

As a rule, the people of Elloweer stayed far from Trillian's domain. Nobody wanted to risk crossing the torivor or the members of his Red Guard, which was exactly why Joe had suggested their little group of fugitives should accompany Skye to the Lost Palace on their way to Zeropolis. Since Skye had official business with Trillian, Joe had been willing to gamble that the nearness of the torivor posed a lesser threat than traveling through more populated regions.

Cole's eyes strayed to Mira, astride her dappled mare. There was no question that her father, the High Shaper, desperately wanted her back. After stealing the shaping powers of his five daughters, Stafford Pemberton had faked their deaths and tried to hold them prisoner. With help from their mother, the daughters had escaped and survived in exile, never aging after their powers were taken.

Not only Mira had regained her power—her sister Honor had as well. The High Shaper had first sent legionnaires to apprehend Mira, and then sent his secret police, the Enforcers. He now had to be more frantic than ever to find her. Since defeating Morgassa, Cole hadn't seen any agents of the High King, which suggested that the strategy of heading toward the Lost Palace was working.

"Do we ride on the road?" Skye asked, having stopped

only a few paces from where the red pavement started.

"We don't really need to hide that we're coming," Mira reasoned. "Hopefully Trillian will be satisfied to learn he'll have a new Grand Shaper to train."

"I don't know," Cole said. "Trillian was pretty interested in you and Honor. He can sense people on his road. Is it smart to let him know you're near?"

"Good point," Jace said, sitting tall on his horse, his face serious. "Last time, Trillian let you go because he wanted us to stop Morgassa. He might try to retake you and keep you this time."

"He'll have more Morgassas to fight if we don't stop my father and his shapecrafters," Mira said. "Trillian can read our thoughts. He'll know how important it is we find Constance and my other sisters."

"Will that matter as much to him?" Dalton asked. "Morgassa was a direct threat. He thought she might be able to take him out. Will he care about problems in other kingdoms?"

"I can tell you one thing," Skye said. "I won't work with Trillian if he tries to hold you."

"He might not care," Cole said. "He can probably find ways to train you whether or not you're willing, Skye. I've met him. The guy can get inside your mind and take over your dreams. Inside his prison, he can do pretty much whatever he wants. He might be more than happy to capture us no matter how we feel about it."

"We can't afford to make ourselves easy targets," Joe said, the only other adult in the group besides Skye. "Taking

7

the road might be a little smoother, but Cole's right—we don't need to let Trillian know we're around sooner than necessary."

"We traveled beside the road last time," Mira said. "It wasn't too bad."

The conversation ended there. Joe and Skye started to parallel the road, and the others followed.

Dalton brought his horse alongside Cole. "Seems like we were just here."

"It really does."

"Minimus was with us last time," Dalton said. "I wish we had a knight or something."

"I'm glad he's with Twitch," Cole said. "The bully who took over Twitch's village won't know what hit him. But if we're wishing, I'd want Twitch here too. He's saved my life more times than anyone."

Dalton nodded. "If trouble comes, Skye and I can hide us with seemings."

"Hiding is probably our best bet for now," Cole said.

"At least until you find your power again."

Cole forced a smile, but he didn't love the reminder. Not long ago Cole discovered he had the ability to energize magical items from Sambria so they could work in Elloweer. But right before Morgassa died, she had sunk her fingernails into his sides and somehow used shapecraft to separate him from his power. Just after he had learned to recognize and access the ability, it had vanished.

"We have the masks," Cole said.

"Only as a last resort," Dalton said. "Callista warned

that the more we use them, the harder they'll be to take off. Plus, she's no longer around to help if something goes wrong."

The masks that Callista had given them for their battle against Morgassa could transform them into powerful animals. Looking back at his time as a mountain lion, Cole recalled the experience through a dreamlike haze, running across many miles of Elloweer in a tireless sprint. Dalton was right about the danger—neither time he removed the mask had been easy.

"Last time we were animals, most of us got badly injured," Cole said. "Jace and I almost died. We might be just as hurt if we put the masks back on."

"Only one way to find out," Dalton said. "Not that I'm in a hurry to test it."

"Once we make it to the Lost Palace, we'll leave the masks with Skye," Cole said. "They won't work in Zeropolis, and they're too powerful to leave randomly stashed someplace."

"After that our only defense will be my seemings and Joe," Dalton said.

Cole looked ahead at Joe. How old was he? Thirty? He hadn't seemed like an amazing warrior or anything, but he was certainly brave and scrappy. Joe had come to the Outskirts from Monterey, California, but Cole didn't know much else about his history.

"Think Trillian will give us trouble?" Cole asked.

"We'd be dumb if we didn't expect it," Dalton said.

They spent the day with the road on their left, veering closer or farther as obstacles arose. As night fell, they made camp. Bedullah, a large orange moon, eased up into the sky, outshining the nearby stars.

Cole noticed Mira standing apart from the camp, her eyes on the heavens. He walked over to her. "This is the biggest moon, right?"

She glanced his way. "Bedullah is the biggest I've seen. It doesn't show up very often. It makes all the stars fainter. An even bigger golden one used to appear sometimes."

"Are you looking for your sisters' stars?" Cole inquired quietly, referring to the heavenly markers that Mira's mother sometimes used to show her daughters' locations.

"Every night," Mira whispered back. "Just in case."

"Can't be easy with the stars and moons always changing," Cole said.

"It isn't. Their stars are always the same color and brightness, but they can be in any direction, and they show up against a different backdrop every night."

"I don't get how the Outskirts have such different skies every night."

"What's not to get?" Mira asked, her eyes skyward.

"On Earth the stars have regular patterns," Cole said. "One moon circles us. Here the stars can be anywhere. You have over ten moons that show up when they feel like it. Where do they hide the rest of the time? What kind of universe shifts around during the day into something else?"

"The heavens here have always been erratic," Mira said. "It's just how it is. It'd take somebody smarter than me to explain why."

"Any luck with the stars?" Cole asked.

"No," Mira said.

Cole studied the sky. He had no idea what to look for. Mira kept the specifics of the stars a secret. If anybody ever learned about the celestial lights occasionally used by Harmony Pemberton, it could prove fatal.

"Not seeing the stars is a good thing," Mira said. "It means my sisters are safe."

"It also means Constance will be hard to find," Cole replied.

"Then we'll look hard," Mira said. "Hopefully we'll find more of your friends, too."

Though Cole had found Dalton, he had only crossed the path of one other person who was kidnapped from Mesa with him—a girl named Jill. He had offered to rescue her, but she had been too scared to try to escape her position as a slave at a confidence lounge, where she helped create illusionary disguises so people could exchange secrets anonymously.

There were still so many people to find! He worried most about Jenna, his friend who had also been his secret crush for years. When they were separated, he had promised to find her but hadn't uncovered any clues yet. Would he finally track her down in Zeropolis?

"Who goes there?" Jace shouted.

Turning, Cole saw a form racing toward their camp. Though it was hard to catch all the details in the mellow orange moonlight, the shape of a man glided hurriedly forward, his feet a few inches off the ground.

Drawing his Jumping Sword, Cole raced back toward the center of camp, where the ghostly figure was heading. One foot got caught against a stone, and he went down badly, twisting away from his blade to avoid slashing himself.

By the time Cole was back on his feet, the figure had come to a stop before Skye. Dressed in a dark suit, the balding man stood with stiff posture. Cole trotted toward them with Mira a step behind.

"Jepson?" Skye exclaimed.

"The very same," the butler replied, smoothing a hand down the front of his jacket. "Your mother sent me to you."

Cole halted not far from Skye. Though Jepson appeared tangible and solid, Cole knew he had no substance—he was a figment, a living illusion created by an enchanter. The stuffy man served Skye's wealthy mother. Joe, Jace, and Dalton joined Cole and Mira.

"How'd he find you?" Cole asked Skye.

"He's bound to mother and the person who will inherit him," Skye said. "He could find either of us anywhere."

Jepson gave Cole a superior glance then faced Skye. "Do you wish to converse in front of these . . . people?"

"Absolutely," Skye said. "Is mother all right?"

The butler's brow crinkled, and his lips quivered. He used a long sniff to collect himself. "Sadly, she is not." His eyes squinted shut, and he shook with sobs. It took a moment before he straightened up and continued. "You must help her. Lady Madeline has been abducted by a vile ruffian called the Hunter."

Skye gasped, putting both hands over her mouth. "No!"

Cole had never met the Hunter but knew about him—an Enforcer who had been chasing them since Sambria. In his pursuit of Mira, the Hunter had captured the slavers Ansel and Secha back in Carthage to wring information from them. The Hunter had a scary reputation. Evidently the trail had led him to Skye's home.

"Your mother ordered me to find you," Jepson said.

Skye dropped her hands. "Before or after the Hunter seized her?"

"After," Jepson said. "The Hunter would gladly exchange your mother for a child called Mira. An escaped slave, it seems."

Skye's gaze took in the moonlit landscape. "Were you followed?"

"Not to my knowledge," Jepson said. His distress won out again as he wrung his hands, tears glistening in his eyes. "There is no time to waste. What do you know of this Mira?"

"He was followed," Joe said, gripping the hilt of his sword.

"You see something?" Dalton asked.

"The Hunter wouldn't miss such a golden opportunity," Joe said. "If he sent a homing pigeon, it didn't come alone."

Rattled, Cole squinted into the moonlit dimness beyond their encampment. He saw the shapes of trees and shrubs and the empty expanse of a brushy field, but no movement.

"Is there any chance you were followed?" Skye asked the butler heatedly.

"I suppose," Jepson replied. "I had no orders to take precautions against such measures. My concern is the safety of Lady Madeline."

"Get to the horses," Joe said, hurrying away from the conversation. "Saddle up. We may already be too late."

They scattered. Cole rushed to his horse, flopped the saddle pad in place, heaved the saddle on top, cinched it, then hopped on one foot while hastily poking the other one at the stirrup. After several clumsy misses, Cole got his foot in place and mounted. Nearby, Dalton fumbled with the straps of his saddle as his horse stamped restively. Cole jumped down and joined his friend, securing the straps while Dalton held the bridle and calmed his horse.

By the time Cole was back on his mare, the others had mounted up as well. Jepson waited nearby, unruffled by all the urgency.

"Go back and check the way you came," Skye told the butler. "Try to mislead anyone following you. Take them as far from us as possible."

"You are not yet my mistress," Jepson reminded her. "My instructions are to—"

"Doesn't matter," Joe interrupted, pointing.

Partially screened by shrubs and trees, at the far side of the brushy field, mounted shapes bobbed in the dimness. It took little more than a glance to see that the shadowy forms were riding hard in their direction.

"Enforcers," Cole said, a jolt of panic coursing through him.

"Lots of them," Dalton added.

Cole counted at least seven or eight. In Sambria they had encountered three Enforcers and defeated them. But last time Cole and his friends had better weapons and managed to surprise them. There were more Enforcers this time, and they looked ready to fight.

"Ride for the Lost Palace," Skye urged. "Use the road. Jepson, you've served their purpose. Go home!"

The others turned their horses and started riding hard toward the Red Road. Cole tugged the reins and nudged with his heels, but his horse held perfectly still. He kicked a little harder only to discover that the sides of his mare felt hard as a rock. A quick hand to the horse's neck revealed the problem.

His mount had turned to stone.

CHAPTER
2

RED GUARD

rying to collect his panicked thoughts, Cole slid off the stone horse, keeping the petrified animal between himself and the oncoming riders. His previous encounter with Enforcers had taught him that they had shaping abilities. In Elloweer that meant they were enchanters, capable of creating illusions and changing living things. Cole recalled the soldier, Russell, who had survived an encounter with Morgassa because an Enforcer had turned him to stone.

That explained the fate of his horse.

Dalton and the others were racing out of sight. The other horses all appeared to be fine. Cole was glad they were getting away but terrified at being left behind. Would his friends notice he wasn't with them? How long before he became the next statue?

Everything went dark. Cole blinked and strained his eyes, but there was absolutely no light. He could hear the thundering approach of the mounted Enforcers.

Fear threatened to suffocate him. Fighting the impulse

to run blindly, Cole battled to stay calm. The sudden blackness had to be some sort of illusion. He kept a hand on the stone horse to retain a sense of his location. The Enforcers pounded nearer.

When they had fought Morgassa, wearing the animal masks had prevented her from working changings on them. If a mask could frustrate Morgassa, it should provide plenty of protection from the powers of some Enforcers.

Reaching out in the blackness, Cole felt the saddle. None of the gear had turned to stone, which made sense, since changings only worked on living things. The mask was in a saddlebag on the other side of the petrified horse. To get it would mean exposing himself to the oncoming riders. Would the darkness hide him, or could they see through it? Maybe it wasn't darkness. Maybe he had lost his sight.

Cole ducked under his horse and blindly fumbled open the saddlebag. He yanked out the mask and hesitated for a second.

The last time he wore the mask he had been terribly wounded by Morgassa. He had abandoned the mountain lion form on the brink of death. Might the mountain lion have recovered somewhat? Could it already be dead? What if the mountain lion form was still horribly injured? If that was the case, Cole supposed he could quickly take the mask off again.

As he placed the mask over his face, a flurry of disorienting sensations overwhelmed him. Cole tipped, spun, and grew.

Suddenly Cole stood on four paws. He felt balanced, and calmer. The new form was familiar and most welcome. With his heightened hearing and smell, Cole knew the position of each of the oncoming riders. Their mounts smelled peculiar.

Cole could sense they had been changed. No natural horses were so large and strong.

It felt as if his previous injuries had never occurred. No soreness lingered. Cole supposed that made sense—when wearing the mask, *he* was the cougar. It didn't exist elsewhere. The wounded mountain lion had been erased the instant he removed the mask. When he put the mask back on, it had changed him into a healthy mountain lion, not a wounded one. That meant he could heal any injury to his cougar form simply by taking the mask off and replacing it! He wished he had known that when they fought Morgassa.

Cole's first instinct was to attack the riders. But what about his friends? They needed to know the masks were safe to use. Jace's wolf and Skye's bear had been badly wounded as well. If they hesitated to put on the masks, the Enforcers might work changings on them.

Powerful paws pulling at the ground, Cole bolted after his friends, thrilled by the rapid acceleration. He rushed ahead low and fast, muscles churning. No regular mountain lion was this large and strong. No ordinary mountain lion was this fast. Cole knew from experience that he could maintain a full sprint all day without tiring.

Cole swiftly exited the dark patch and once again could add sight to his other senses. Glancing back, he saw a black sphere that reflected no moonlight concealing his stone horse and the surrounding area. The Enforcers rode hard, but despite the impressive speed of their enhanced mounts, Cole was faster than them. Leafy forms of shrubs and trees whipped by as he plunged forward through the gloom.

Before long, Cole reached the Red Road. Benefiting from a head start, his friends galloped away on the smooth pavement. All except one. Dalton had halted his horse and was looking back. He waved when he saw Cole.

Cole dashed to Dalton. He was glad his friend had noticed him missing, but stopping his horse had put Dalton in greater peril. The Enforcers were close behind.

"Put on your mask," Cole cried. "It's your best protection."

Dalton started digging in his saddlebag. Cole did his best not to notice how tasty his friend and his horse smelled.

With the Enforcers closing in, Cole sprinted past Dalton. It didn't take him long to catch up to the others. The Enforcers would soon overtake their ordinary horses without much trouble.

"Use the masks!" Cole called. "Our animal forms aren't hurt!"

Looking back, Cole saw a dark sphere where Dalton had been. Cole slowed and was about to turn back when a huge bull charged out of the blackness.

Cole let his friend catch up, then rushed to rejoin the others. While still riding, they were putting on their masks. Tumbling from her horse, Skye became a huge, shaggy bear. Jace transformed into an enormous wolf. As Mira reached into her saddlebag, her horse slowed and turned to stone beneath her. Cole and Dalton stopped to stay with her.

Mira put on her mask and dropped to the ground as a bighorn sheep. After reining in his horse, Joe was the last to change form. He hadn't worn a mask before, so he used Twitch's eagle.

Everything went dark again. Growling, Cole spun to face the Enforcers. Sound and smell told him exactly where the nearest horse was charging. Attacking low, Cole dove into the legs, biting down with his powerful jaws and swiping with his claws. The large mount was moving at great speed, and though legs and hooves crashed into Cole, making him flip and slide, the mutant horse got the worst of it, pitching forward violently onto the pavement. The rider went down hard, armor clanging and scraping against the Red Road, and Skye fell upon him savagely.

In his wolf form, Jace took out the next horse much as Cole had done. Before the rider could rise, Dalton came at him with his horns lowered, goring and trampling him.

Cole rolled over and crouched for another attack, but the other riders were swerving off the road. Six remained on their mounts, fanning out. Strange tingles sparked across his hide, and Cole realized that changings were being cast against him and failing. As expected, the changing caused by the mask was too potent for other changings to take hold.

Something lanced into his side, and Cole swiveled to discover a crossbow bolt protruding from his ribs. By the sudden difficulty in his breathing, Cole knew it had punctured a lung. He let out an angry yowl, noticing as he did how easy it was to switch from his human voice to his cougar growl. Skye let out a roar as well, deeper and more rumbling than Cole's.

The darkness lifted, revealing that all of the Enforcers had bows or crossbows trained on them and were firing at top speed. An arrow hit Jace in the neck, and two already protruded from Skye. In his eagle shape, Joe soared upward, flying out of range.

Skye tore off her mask, and immediately stone walls appeared between the horsemen and their targets. Cole knew the stony seemings were intangible, but at least they would make aiming difficult. He dodged to the side and pulled off his mask. His world spun and flipped, and he returned to two legs, but no sooner had he become himself again than he replaced the mask, passing through another whirlwind of sensation to emerge as an uninjured mountain lion.

Beside him, Jace did likewise. Still in her human form, Skye retreated down the road on foot. "Run!" she called. "Make for the palace."

The Enforcers rode forward through the stone walls, and Skye covered their heads with wooden crates. They batted futilely at the illusions. Cole lingered, ready to attack again.

Mira crouched near Skye, allowing her to climb aboard. Once Skye had mounted, the big ram took off down the road. Cole felt more tingling as additional changings failed to alter him. Their remaining horses turned to stone. Deciding to forgo more attacks and follow Mira, Cole turned on the speed, exhilarating in the stretch and pull of running as a cougar. Jace and Dalton sprinted beside him.

Skye put on her mask, rolling off Mira to become a bear again. A glance back told Cole that as soon as Skye replaced her mask, the illusionary crates had dissipated. Skye could only maintain seemings while in her human form.

Once again the Enforcers took up the pursuit. Cole

pushed to his maximum speed, his paws slipping a little on the smooth pavement. The Enforcers charged after them, gradually losing ground.

Up ahead, four mounted Enforcers rushed onto the road. Two of them held a flaming net between them, barring the way. Another readied a huge bow, while the fourth leveled a lance at them. But Cole didn't smell the horses, or the Enforcers, or the fire, though he heard it crackling.

"Fakes!" Jace shouted.

"Seemings," Skye agreed.

The closer Cole came to the Enforcers, the more certain he became that they had no scent. He and his friends barreled through the insubstantial Enforcers and continued down the road. Dalton laughed, Jace gave a quick howl, and Cole let out a snarling roar.

A rearward glance showed the Enforcers even farther behind, allowing Cole to wonder where the chase might end. Would they take the Red Road all the way into the Lost Palace? Putting themselves back into Trillian's power could prove more dangerous than fighting the Enforcers. What if the gates at the end of the road were closed? That would force a showdown unless they veered off to one side and kept running. Might Trillian send help? What if the help he sent turned into even bigger trouble?

Settling into a steady sprint, Cole let his worries get swallowed by the joy of running. Something about being a mountain lion made it much easier to tune out fear. He wasn't fleeing in terror—it felt like a race, and he was confident that he could keep stretching his lead.

"Why run?" Jace complained, dashing at Cole's left. "They want a fight. Let's give it to them."

"I feel the impulse too," Dalton said from the other side. "My bull side wants to turn around and plow through them."

"It's not just my wolf side," Jace replied. "We could take them."

"They have pretty good aim with those bows," Cole said. "They didn't miss many shots until Skye put up those walls."

"It would be harder for them to shoot us if they were dead," Jace growled. "They're made of meat. Let's eat them."

Cole didn't want to admit how tempting that sounded.

"Keep running," Skye called back from a few paces in front of them. "These Enforcers will give Trillian something to worry about besides capturing us."

"Nobody is going to capture us with these masks on," Jace said.

"Remember the sky castle rules," Mira said. "Don't fight when you can run. Why risk arrows bringing us down if we can get away?"

"She's right," Cole said.

"Whatever," Jace said. "Is it bad to hope we get cornered?"

"It's not healthy," Cole said, though he also felt the strong urge to fight. What if Skye returned to her normal form and raised some illusions so they could attack out of hiding? The Enforcers would be down before they knew what hit them.

The conversation ended. They ran onward in silence, the rumble of hoofbeats receding.

In the moonlit distance the Lost Palace rose into view. The skeletal castle looked like it had barely survived a bombing raid, but Cole knew that for anyone who passed the front gate, the charred building became a shimmering wonder of pearl and platinum. Cole had never figured out whether the real version was the scorched ruin or the fairy-tale palace. Maybe they were both seemings.

"Riders," Mira said.

Peering ahead along the road, Cole counted at least ten riders approaching, shrunken by the distance. "Another illusion?" he asked.

"They're pretty far off," Skye said. "I think they're real."

"Red Guard or more Enforcers?" Dalton asked.

"It's hard to recognize color in the moonlight," Skye replied. "They seem to be coming from Trillian's prison."

Joe came swooping back from the direction of the Lost Palace. "Red Guard!" he called. "Twelve of them."

"Think they're here to help?" Dalton asked.

"If not, it's their funeral," Jace said.

"Leave the road when they get near," Skye said. "If they ride past us, we'll know they're after our foes."

Cole had heard that the Red Guard were dangerous, though on his previous visit to the Lost Palace he had only seen a few people besides Trillian. But that proved nothing. Other members of the Red Guard could have been out on assignment, or they could have been hiding.

Running at top speed, Cole watched as the galloping riders rapidly drew closer. Still charging hard, Skye led Cole and the others off the road as the riders came near. With hardly a glance to the side, the riders raced by them, except for a woman who slowed her chestnut stallion to a stop.

Coldly beautiful, she gazed down at Cole and his friends as they also came to a standstill.

Cole recognized her. It was Hina, the woman who had escorted him around the Lost Palace.

"What are your intentions?" Skye asked.

Hina turned and looked down the Red Road, where her fellow guardsmen were about to engage the Enforcers. She waved a hand, and the number of guardsmen suddenly tripled.

"Are any of them real?" Cole asked.

"Eleven," Hina said, her voice calm and rich.

"Should we go help?" Jace asked.

"Not necessary," Hina assured him.

Just before the clusters of horsemen collided, Hina made a curt gesture, and for a moment the Red Road beneath the oncoming Enforcers flapped like a towel in the wind. All but one of the Enforcers went down in a calamitous tumble as the Red Guard reached them.

Cole watched as the Red Guard cut down the single Enforcer who remained mounted and wheeled to engage the fallen ones. It was hard to catch many details. The skirmish ended quickly.

"You know why I'm here?" Skye asked Hina.

"Naturally," the silver-haired enchanter responded. "My master welcomes you. He laments the passing of Callista, but believes you have the potential to surpass her in many ways."

"The others in my party have business elsewhere," Skye said.

"We know," Hina said. "He'll allow it. He would like the other heiresses to come out of hiding. I will accompany your friends to the edge of Elloweer, where Zeropolis begins."

"You?" Mira challenged.

"The masks will enable you to elude your pursuers and get to Zeropolis," Hina said. "But someone must bring the masks back. They are too valuable to leave Elloweer."

Nine of the Red Guard came trotting back down the Red Road. One pair of riders held a dark-armored captive between them by his arms. The injured Enforcer jogged alongside the horses, struggling to keep up. A second pair held another prisoner. First one of the Enforcers stopped jogging and let them drag him, then the other.

"We lost two men," Hina said. "But we gained two captives. My master is studying their minds. Upon finding you, they sent three of their number back to report. The messengers split up and rode hard. This was one of many search parties. They did not expect to find you here. Had they known, they would have sent more men."

"Seemed like a lot," Cole said.

"The Hunter has learned respect for you," Hina said. "As has the High King. Many resources are now bent on finding Mira and bringing her in. This was a relatively minor show of force."

"You can hear Trillian from out here?" Dalton asked.

"As long as I remain on the Red Road," Hina said.

"What of my mother?" Skye asked. "Have they information about her?"

"She lives, so far as these men know," Hina replied. "Trillian suggests that the best thing you can do to help her would be to let your companions take the chase to another kingdom. The farther away Mira goes, the less relevant your mother becomes."

"I wish I could see her," Skye said. "Get a message to her."

"You will," Hina said. "All in good time."

"Does Trillian really want us to find the other princesses?" Jace wondered. "Or does he just want the masks?"

"Both," Hina replied. "The masks are the greatest legacy left behind by Callista. Those in her home must be protected as well. And my master wishes you well on your journey. With the masks, crossing Elloweer should be quick."

"You want us to wear the masks until we reach Zeropolis?" Cole asked.

"My master insists upon it," Hina said. "Reinforcements will come searching for you. The speed afforded by the masks will baffle them. They are your best chance of shaking the Hunter off your trail for a time."

"Does Trillian know much about the Hunter?" Cole asked.

"Not directly, but he knows of him," Hina replied. "The Hunter is among the most competent Enforcers. He now has knowledge of your whereabouts, which would normally be enough for him to ensnare you. But he doesn't know about the masks."

Joe landed on a nearby limb. "The Enforcers sent some riders back," he reported. "I tried to chase them and got shot in the wing. I took the mask off and put it back on, and they gained a lot of ground on me, splitting up. I don't think I can stop them alone."

"No matter," Hina said. "The information they bring to the Hunter will mislead him. Using your masks, we'll reach Zeropolis inside of four days."

"We?" Joe asked.

"We'll fill you in," Mira said. "Looks like Hina is coming with us."

"We should make haste," Hina said. "Skye? Do you mind if I borrow your bear?"

BORDER

The next days passed in a trance of constant motion. Having assumed the form of a bear, Hina led the way. Cole lost all desire to speak, focusing instead on the terrain beneath his paws, the smells and sounds of the wilderness, and the rapture of tireless running.

The sun rose. The sun set. Moons traversed the sky as the stars reeled. Cole dashed over boulders, splashed through rivers, knifed through forests, and raced across plains. Diverse landscapes came and went.

Joe scouted above them, ranging far and wide on his inexhaustible wings. But Cole wasn't sure the eagle's vigilance was necessary. Hina seemed to have a sense for avoiding danger. She knew which passes would take them through the mountains, what routes among the reeds would avoid the mires, and where the rivers could be safely forded. Maybe it was sharp instincts, but Cole suspected she had roamed Elloweer extensively and knew the most remote paths.

From start to finish they never saw or smelled a human,

let alone a human settlement. No threatening predators crossed their way. Of course, Cole suspected there weren't many predators who would be in a hurry to tangle with a huge mountain lion, wolf, bear, ram, and bull racing along at unreal speed.

At first Cole felt urges to eat or drink out of habit, particularly when they crossed a clear brook or he smelled a tasty deer. But as he denied those urges to keep running, he realized they were remembered needs, not current ones.

And then they stopped.

It was a grassy glade sheltered by surrounding trees. The sun shined high overhead. Hina pulled off her mask, transforming from a bear back into a beautiful woman.

"We have reached the edge of Elloweer, not far from Post 121," Hina reported. "This is the destination Joe requested shortly before we departed. Please remove your masks."

Cole paced instead. It was strange to stop running. Offputting. It was even stranger to think of reverting to human form. What was the hurry? He sensed no people or human settlements nearby. Couldn't they proceed as animals a little longer?

Dalton was not a bull anymore. Joe landed and removed his eagle mask. Mira became a person instead of a bighorn sheep.

They all looked so small and vulnerable. Defenseless. And strangely appetizing.

"Come on, Cole," Mira said. "Take it off."

Cole thought about speaking, but it seemed burdensome. His mouth felt too lazy to form words. Instead he yawned.

Then he inhaled the scents of the surrounding forest: old wood decaying, a family of possums, the dung of an elk, leaves and brush and dirt and stone.

His eyes strayed to distant peaks. Why stop here? He could keep running. His many problems felt distant while running.

"Lose the mask, Cole," Jace said. "Don't let it beat you."

When had Jace removed his mask? Cole remembered not wanting to take his mask off before. Long ago. He had given in and removed it. Should he again? Or had that been a mistake?

If he removed the mask, Hina would take it away. How he would miss being a mountain lion! The strength, the speed, the alertness. He could spend his whole life like this. Perhaps this was his destiny.

"Don't forget Jenna," Dalton said. "Don't forget our friends. We have to find them and get home."

Cole blinked.

Jenna!

Of course, she was lost, a slave. He had to help her! That was why he had run through the wilderness—to get to Zeropolis in the hope of finding her. And to help Mira find her sister Constance.

Why was he waiting? He couldn't remain a mountain lion. People needed him. He had a greater purpose.

Not without some regret, Cole reached up and pulled off the mask. He reared back, giddily whirled, and abruptly stood on two feet with the mask in his hand.

As the leonine instincts lost their grip, he realized how

close he had been to losing himself in the mask. Even now, restored to his true form, he felt tempted to put it back on.

The rest of the group stood in a semicircle, staring at him. "You okay?" Dalton asked.

Cole swallowed. It was good to focus on his best friend. His mind felt clearer. He really had been at the brink of running away for a moment. He held out the mask toward Hina. "I'm better now."

Hina came to him and accepted his mask. In the sunlight, her silvery hair looked almost metallic. Her beauty was so flawless that it looked crafted. Maybe it was, Cole realized. Changings? Seemings? Who knew?

"This is where I leave you," Hina said. "We're at the border near your desired outpost."

"I saw Post 121 from the air," Joe confirmed. "When I tried to fly that way, I bumped against a barrier. Felt hard as stone."

"You can't leave Elloweer with these masks on," Hina said.

Staring at the stacked masks in her hands, Cole frowned slightly. He had used his power to make the Jumping Sword and Jace's golden rope work here in Elloweer. Did his power have the potential to make the masks work elsewhere? There might be an unseen boundary, but what if he took off the mask, crossed the border, recharged it, and put it back on? Cole felt for his power, even just a hint of it, but came up empty. Since he couldn't access his ability, there was no way to experiment with the masks.

Cole considered the hold the mask had started to have on

him. He had felt so content as a mountain lion that he hadn't wanted to return to his real life. It seemed sort of silly now, but just a few moments ago, he had been ready to run off into the wilderness. Callista had warned that the more they used the masks, the greater power the animal forms would exert over the wearers. Maybe not having the masks anymore was a good thing.

"I ranged widely across this area and saw no enemy activity on the Elloweer side," Joe said. "We seem to have given the Enforcers the slip for now. I'm sure the Zeropolis side will have the standard patrolmen to deal with."

"Would you like me to wait here a day with the masks?" Hina asked. "In case you need to retreat?"

"I don't know how much longer I can wear the mask without staying a wolf forever," Jace said. "I can tell Cole was feeling the pull too."

"We all were," Mira said. "But if it's between getting caught and using the masks again, I'd find a way to fight off my sheep instincts."

"We'd appreciate knowing you were here for a day," Joe told Hina. "I have no plans to come back this way, but if we get discovered, retreat might become our only lifeline."

"This time tomorrow?" Hina asked.

Shading his eyes, Joe squinted at the sky. "Could we say sundown tomorrow? By then I should know if we can get transportation into the city."

"I will wait until sundown tomorrow," Hina affirmed. "If I do not hear from you by then, I will assume you've gotten safe passage into the city."

"Post 121 isn't the city?" Cole asked.

"It's an outpost of the city," Joe said. "There are currently one hundred thirty-eight outposts in operation, connected to the city via monorail. Sometimes the outposts grant access to resources like mines or forests. Sometimes they serve as a way station when traveling to other kingdoms."

"What does this outpost do?" Cole asked.

"It isn't far from a salt pan where minerals are harvested," Joe said. "It's also near Elloweer, obviously, and the small town of Eastmont. I suggested this outpost to Hina because it's farther north than necessary. From the Lost Palace, the nearest outpost would have been 93. We could have strayed a little to the south to Post 88, or north to 76. Or even farther north to 84. Keep going northeast after 84 and you end up here—Post 121. Not the most likely destination."

"Is there any sense to the numbers?" Jace wondered.

"It's the order the outposts were added," Joe replied.

"I don't get something," Dalton said. "Is Zeropolis the city or the kingdom?"

"Both," Joe said. "The city is the kingdom. The outposts are extensions of the city. When people in Zeropolis talk about the city, they mean the huge cluster of buildings in the center of the kingdom where most people live. I think the intent is for the city to one day fill the kingdom. The city is huge, but nowhere near that goal. Maybe someday. For now, using the monorails can get you to most areas of the kingdom."

"When you say monorails . . . ," Cole said.

"I mean monorails like we have back home," Joe said. "But more advanced than any I know about. More like bullet trains. Zeropolites do amazing things with magnetics. And they can store energy in crystals. It's so efficient. No fossil fuels required. They energize the crystals with shaping, and create many of their materials using shaping as well, so the majority of their technologies aren't transferable to other kingdoms, or back to Earth, either."

"I'm not from Outside," Jace reminded everyone. "What's a monorail? What do you mean by magnetics?"

"Have you seen a magnet?" Joe asked. "It sticks to certain metals?"

"I've fiddled with magnets," Jace said. "They had some at Skyport."

"So you know they can attract or repel each other," Joe said.

"Right. Sometimes they snap together. But when you face them a certain way, there's a spongy invisible force that keeps them apart. You can push them around."

"Exactly," Joe said. "Now imagine a vehicle like the auto-coach, except much longer, suspended on a magnetic cushion, and propelled by magnetic forces as well. It rides on a long, elevated track. That's a monorail."

"Sounds slick," Jace said. "Is it fast?"

"Like you've never seen," Joe assured him.

"What now?" Cole asked. "Do we just walk over to the outpost? You said something about patrolmen. What's Zeropolis like?"

"Yeah," Jace agreed. "Give us the lowdown. I knew some stuff about Elloweer. But I don't know much about Zeropolis."

"I still have my slavemark," Dalton reminded everyone. "Will that cause trouble?"

"We'll all need identification cards," Joe said. "The government in Zeropolis loves IDs. None of you have been to Zeropolis before, am I right?"

Everyone but Mira shook their heads.

"I went once as a kid," Mira said. "I might have been five. I remember riding the monorail. And the tall buildings."

"Were you issued an ID card?" Joe asked.

"I don't think so," Mira said. "I was with Mom and Dad."

"Not letting your identity leak is essential," Joe said. "If you were issued an ID, the checkpoints have access to it, but they need to know where to look. They don't have biometrics to help them."

"Biometrics?" Cole asked.

"You know, fingerprints, iris scanners, facial-recognition software," Joe explained. "Those advancements might be coming, but they hadn't hit when I left. All a troublemaker would have to go on is a seventy-year-old picture of a five-year-old. Miracle Pemberton is supposed to be dead. We'll make up fake names for all of you, just in case word of us has spread. Considering you're all minors, and outsiders coming to Zeropolis for the first time, I should be able to get fresh IDs for all of you."

"What about my mark?" Dalton reminded him.

"You'll play the role of our slave," Joe said. "Technically we should have papers to prove ownership, but that sort of detail gets missed all the time. If it comes to it, we'll try a bribe."

"Do you have an ID?" Jace asked.

"I've got three," Joe said. "A luxury of having friends in the Unseen."

"Fake IDs?" Cole checked.

"One is authentic," Joe said. "Two are false. Top quality. The real one is no good to me anymore. As long as nobody has combed through the millions of other ID photos on record to find the duplicate faces and flag the false names, I should be fine. Wanted members of the Unseen get away with it all the time."

"What should my name be?" Jace mused.

"Something you'll remember," Joe said. "Something that'll roll off your tongue."

"Drop the *J*," Cole said. "Be Ace."

"Too close," Jace said.

"Maybe Face?" Cole went on. "Or Vase. Or Outer Space."

"Your name is going to be Black Eye if you don't watch it," Jace threatened.

"Then you're going to be Mr. Overreactor," Cole replied. "Or maybe Sore Fist."

Joe pulled out a couple of ID cards. Dark blue and metallic, they looked about the size of driver's licenses and had different pictures of him. One had a mustache.

"Should I be Harvey Michaels?" he asked. "Or Walt Boone?"

Cole held out a hand. "Let me see one." Joe placed an ID in his palm. Cole found the thin card heavier than it looked. The name Walt Boone was printed in silver letters above a long number sequence. A fancy insignia in the upper corner looked like three overlapping moons behind a tall, slender building.

"Sweet 'stache," Dalton said, checking out the ID. "Be Walt."

"If I'm Walt, then Cole, Jace, and Mira will be my niece and nephews. We'll all be Boones to keep it simple."

"And who am I?" Dalton asked.

"The slave," Jace said. "Rupert."

"I vote you name yourselves," Joe said. "We should get going. You can think about it while we walk."

"We still don't know much about Zeropolis," Jace argued. "I don't want to go in blind. What if somebody questions us?"

"Security is loose in the outposts," Joe said. "Things aren't as organized. If somebody gives you trouble, just be vaguely honest. You came from Elloweer and don't know anything. We won't have much to worry about until we try to board the monorail."

"Unless the Hunter sent a message to watch for us," Mira said. "Don't forget, he nabbed Ansel, who drew pictures of Cole, and probably the rest of us too. Our faces could be public knowledge."

"It's possible," Joe said. "I just don't see Enforcers working directly with local authorities. They seldom cooperate with legionnaires or guardsmen. They prefer to operate quietly."

"What's the shaping like in Zeropolis?" Jace asked.

"Their shapers are called tinkers," Mira said. "They shape useful materials. They manipulate energy. And they use those resources to create all sorts of things."

"The pros call themselves technomancers," Joe said. "They can replicate just about anything we had in the world I came from. And they do lots of things we can't."

"Computers?" Cole asked.

"Yeah, but they limit access to some of that stuff," Joe said. "They don't always push as far as they could. Some supercomputer went haywire a long time ago. It trashed the city. They don't want a repeat. Also, the Grand Shaper, Abram Trench, worries about keeping control, so he heavily restricts the use of lethal weapons and communication devices."

"What's a computer?" Jace asked.

"It's a machine with lots of abilities," Dalton said.

"It can almost think," Cole added.

"It's like a really complicated abacus," Joe deadpanned.

"This place sounds strange," Jace said.

"To you most of all," Joe agreed. "For Dalton and Cole, some parts of it will almost feel like home. Can we go? I'd like to get settled and plan for tomorrow."

"Okay," Jace said.

Mira went to Hina. "Thank you for guiding us here," Mira said. "And for waiting around in case we need to escape."

"I'm on an errand from my master," Hina replied. "I would not disappoint him. I wish you good fortune in finding your sister."

Joe extended an arm eastward. "This way, right?"

"Correct," she said.

They started walking with Joe in the lead. Cole fell in beside Dalton.

"Cole," Hina said. "A word?"

They all paused. Cole looked back at her, feeling slightly suspicious. What did she want? What if she put on the bear mask and kidnapped him? Trillian had shown interest in his abilities, and Hina had all the masks now. There wouldn't be much the others could do.

"It'll just take a moment," she assured him. "You can catch up."

"Okay," Cole said, with a nod at Joe.

The others started walking, but Dalton lingered.

"What is it?" Cole asked, taking a couple of steps toward Hina.

"My master has a message for you," she said.

"Okay."

"When you stood on the Red Road, he could sense that your power is blocked. He wanted me to tell you that it may not be easy, but you can get it back. I was asked to recommend that you accept none of the apparent limits to shaping here in the Outskirts. And he wanted me to convey that although your current focus is to get home, the Outskirts may not survive without your help."

For a moment Cole forgot to breathe. How could the fate of the Outskirts depend on him? It was absurd, right? This place was his prison. It would be hard enough to find his friends and get home. Maybe impossible. What game was Trillian playing?

Cole glanced over at Dalton, who could hear the conversation. His friend raised his eyebrows.

"That's all?" Cole asked.

"Yes," Hina said.

Cole gave a disbelieving laugh. "How am I supposed to save the Outskirts?"

Hina gave a slight bow. "I have shared his message."

"Okay," Cole said, suddenly wishing he could speak to Trillian again. Why would the torivor leave something so important so unexplained? Did Trillian want to lure him back to the Lost Palace? Might he have good reason to do so? Did the torivor know techniques that could help him regain his lost ability? How sure was Trillian that the Outskirts needed his help? Was it just a manipulation? Was it because Mira needed him? "Thanks."

Hina sat down cross-legged, the masks on her lap.

Cole jogged away with Dalton, hurrying to catch up to the others as questions continued to occupy him.

POST 121

No marker announced the border between Elloweer and Zeropolis, but Cole knew they had crossed when electric tingles raced through him and his ears popped. "Feel that?" Cole asked the others.

"Yep," Dalton said, rubbing his ears.

"Welcome to Zeropolis," Mira said.

"I didn't feel squat," Jace said.

"Nobody ever accused you of being sensitive," Cole said.

"I didn't feel much either," Joe said. "Maybe a little tickle."

In a corner of his mind, Cole had wondered if the crossing might help undo the changing Morgassa had worked on him before she died. Was it unreasonable to hope that whatever blockade she had raised to divide him from his power would be destroyed by leaving Elloweer? But as he searched inside, he still found no hint of his ability. His power remained out of reach.

"Weird," Dalton said. "I can't make a seeming."

"Did you expect to be the only exception?" Jace asked.

"No," Dalton said. "It just cut off so suddenly. I can still feel my power. It's there. But if I try to make a seeming, I can't even manage a spark. It's frustrating."

Jace pulled his little golden rope from his pocket. "Is it kind of like having a really cool weapon that no longer works?"

"Pretty much," Dalton said.

"I think we all get the feeling," Jace said.

The trees thinned and prairie land came into view. As the group exited the forest, there was no missing Post 121. The outpost was much larger than Cole expected. He had pictured an isolated monorail stop with a few buildings and some mules. Instead, the community spread across the prairie for quite a distance, a windswept jumble of low, fenceless structures.

The strangest dwellings looked almost like playground equipment—tubes and globes of colored plastic joined together in odd combinations. There were also boxy apartments made from concrete blocks, flimsy shacks composed of tin panels, earthy structures of adobe and plaster, patchwork pavilions of weathered hides, log cabins, canvas tents, and shanties cobbled together from scraps of wood and metal. The styles varied at random. With few trees or bushes in view, the only landscaping seemed to be the natural dirt and brush of the prairie.

Above the sprawling mishmash of haphazard architecture, the monorail track and station stood out as the glaring landmarks of advanced civilization. Shining like polished platinum, the lofty track overshadowed the chaotic neighborhoods, its metallic whiteness gently curving away into the distance, supported by pillars at regular intervals. The station also looked very modern, a lustrous construction of glass and metal.

Besides the monorail track and station, not many structures in town surpassed two stories. Joe explained that the large, weathered, egg-shaped building was the power facility, where the main energy crystals for the outpost were housed. He also mentioned that the two cylinders on the hillside were water towers. A few windmills of varied design poked up here and there. Cole's favorite kind of looked like an upside-down eggbeater.

The closer they got to the outpost, the more vehicles came into view. One looked like a cross between a dune buggy and a monster truck, rolling around on swollen tires. Another was a motorcycle with wheels as wide as overturned barrels. A spiderlike contraption prowled around on slender legs, while the driver sat atop the body yanking levers. Some vehicles had treads like a tank. The roads Cole saw were rough pathways carved by frequent travel. Without decent roads, he supposed the vehicles needed to be hardy.

"It looks like people made stuff out of whatever they could find," Dalton said.

"True enough," Joe said. "The outposts only get materials from the city by monorail. Anything else they make themselves. The tinkers can get pretty creative."

Cole glanced back at the woods, where Hina waited unseen. He wondered if he would ever make it back to Elloweer. Not for some time, he decided, since he knew

Jenna wasn't there, and he had already rescued Dalton. He might have to go back one day to free Jill. And if he got totally stuck finding a way home, it might be worth risking another conversation with Trillian.

"We'll have to change our money," Joe said. "Some of the outposts will do business with ringers, but once we hit the city, it's all credits."

"Like credit cards?" Dalton asked.

"Kind of," Joe said. "Your credits are linked to your ID card. It's one of the instances where the Grand Shaper allows computerized communication. I think he does it so he can freeze anyone's money whenever he wants. It's a powerful control tactic."

"Then we should keep some ringers just in case," Jace said. "We can always transfer more to credits later."

"You're thinking like a survivor," Joe complimented

"Don't jinx me," Jace said.

Cole patted his chest, where he had tied his ringers. They jangled softly. It was a convenient way to store the little rings that served as coins in the Outskirts. As a group, they had a lot of money. Before parting with the Rogue Knight, he had restored all of the ringers he had taken from them when he robbed the wagon train. It meant they should be able to afford some comforts in the city.

"I want to get a spider car," Dalton said. "That thing is cool."

"Too wobbly," Jace said. "I'll take one of the big ones with the treads. What powers them?"

"The same source that powers most of Zeropolis," Joe

said. "Harmonic crystals. Also called dynamos, juiced crystals, energy crystals—whatever the name, they're crystals that can store and share vast amounts of energy."

"Electricity?" Cole asked.

"That's one way to picture it," Joe said. "I sometimes think of it that way to help me relate. Like electricity, the energy from the crystals can be used to generate heat, motion, light—all sorts of effects. It could be converted into electricity, but that's not usually useful, because it's already in a purer state. Less volatile. And it doesn't need wires."

"Wireless electricity?" Dalton exclaimed.

"That's the idea," Joe said. "Once harmonic crystals are linked, they can share power with one another across great distances. Most of the crystals in Post 121 are linked to the power facility, where sparkers keep a central crystal juiced."

"Sparkers?" Jace asked.

"Tinkers who specialize in generating energy," Joe clarified. "It's a form of shaping."

"This place is weird," Jace said.

"You'll like some of the conveniences," Joe promised.

Cole fell into step beside Mira. "You seem quiet."

"Huh?" she replied. "Oh, I was thinking about Costa. My only memories of Zeropolis are as a kid. Everything seemed so big and fancy. Foreign. It's intimidating to think of finding Costa there. The city is enormous."

"The outpost is bigger than I expected," Cole said.

"Maybe. But just wait. The city is by far the biggest in all the Outskirts."

Cole thought about that. Even compared to the cities

back home, Carthage had been impressive. So had Merriston. He wondered how Zeropolis would compare against major cities like Phoenix or Los Angeles.

"I wish Honor were here," Mira murmured.

"She'd be a big help," Cole said.

"Not just that," Mira said. "I've waited sixty years to see her, then once we finally find each other, we hardly get to spend any time together."

"She's looking for Destiny," Cole reminded her.

"I know," Mira said. "It's important to find Tessa. Honor is doing what she always does—her duty. And I'm glad she's doing it. It just would have been nice to see her for a while. Imagine if right after you found Dalton he had to take off."

"I get it," Cole said. "That stinks. I'm sorry."

"It's not your fault," Mira said. "I get it too. Sometimes you do what you must. I just miss my sisters."

"We'll find Costa," Cole said. "That's something you can look forward to. Maybe this time you won't have to split up right away."

"Wouldn't that be nice?" Mira said wistfully. "What if we weren't the mascots for a revolution? What if we were just a normal family?"

"You might never know," Cole said.

Mira gave him a sharp glance. "Too true."

They began to pass some of the buildings at the fringe of the outpost. The people they saw didn't pay them any mind. Cole was surprised to see a guy wearing blue jeans and a denim jacket.

"Is that guy in jeans?" Cole asked Joe.

"Yeah," he replied. "They make synthetic denim in the city. It's everywhere. They do plenty of things their own way here, but they borrow a lot of ideas from Earth."

"Are there many Outsiders?" Dalton asked.

"That could be part of it," Joe answered. "I've met several. But they also have ways of keeping tabs on our world. Some people in Zeropolis can connect to our Internet."

"The Internet back home?" Cole asked in astonishment.

"They call them thruports," Joe said. "Technically they're illegal. But I know some of the government people use them. And so do some of the Unseen."

"I could e-mail my family?" Dalton asked.

"You could," Joe said. "But they won't open it."

"How can you be sure?" Dalton countered.

"I've tried," Joe said wearily. "I tried and tried. It never worked."

"Who were you trying to reach?" Cole asked.

Joe bit his lower lip. "You remember I told you I left Zeropolis for a reason? I volunteered to go warn Mira?"

"Yeah," Cole said.

"The person I e-mailed most ties into that," Joe said. "You deserve the whole story. What happened could make this more dangerous for all of us. And I learned some things you ought to hear. But not here. Later. For now, let me go change some money to credits. I'll buy us some clothes that won't stand out so much in the city. You guys go check out Gizmo Row."

"What's that?" Jace asked.

"Every outpost has one," Joe said. "They're named after

the big one in the city. Gizmo Row is where the tinkers peddle their inventions. Some of the stuff can be useful, and in an outpost near the border, some of the tinkers might be willing to trade in ringers. It should help you kill some time and start to get a feel for Zeropolis. It's also a place where strangers fit in just fine. Just don't buy anything too expensive. And don't let them take you into a back room. We don't want black-market gear. Not now at least. All we need is to get arrested for buying restricted tech before we even reach the city."

"Okay," Dalton said. "Where do we find it?"

Joe pointed over some of the nearby rooftops. "See the sign on that pole sticking up over there? Blue circle with a sun in the center? That marks Gizmo Row. Head that way. I'll go over to the monorail station and see if I can find a place to turn some ringers into credits. It'll also give me a chance to make sure my fake ID works."

"What if you get nabbed?" Dalton asked.

"It should be fine," Joe said. "I've used Walt Boone before."

"If he gets nabbed, we'll bust him out," Jace said.

"Well . . . ," Joe said. "I appreciate the loyalty, but only if you find a real opportunity. Our top priority is keeping Mira safe. Second is finding Costa. If it comes to it, I want you kids to leave me behind. I wouldn't be able to stand the thought of you getting into trouble trying to help me."

"Let's just try to stay out of trouble to begin with," Mira said, giving Jace a stern look. "That means not creating any of our own."

"Don't look at me," Jace said with a smirk. "I don't start fights. I end them."

"You heard me," Mira said.

"Once you get there, don't leave Gizmo Row," Joe said. "I'll come find you."

"Unless you get arrested," Dalton said.

"Right," Joe said. "Unless I get arrested." Turning, he started toward the monorail station.

Picking up his pace, Jace marched toward the Gizmo Row sign, following a narrow footpath. Mira caught up to him. Cole and Dalton walked together.

"Think we'll find Jenna in Zeropolis?" Dalton wondered.

"I can only guess," Cole said, looking around. "You know all the kids who were sent with you to Elloweer, so she's not there. I started out in Sambria, but never really searched it. She could be in any kingdom besides Elloweer. That means we have a one in four chance she's in Zeropolis."

"Unless she stayed in Junction, between the kingdoms," Dalton said.

"You all went there at first," Cole said. "Did anybody stay?"

"Not that I know of. I'm just trying to cover all the possibilities."

"Hopefully some of Joe's contacts here can help us," Cole said. "Maybe they can search for her ID card or something."

"It would be nice to catch a break," Dalton said.

Up ahead, Mira laughed at something Jace had said, patting him on the arm.

"He's in heaven right now," Cole said.

"Jace?"

"He has the biggest crush on her."

"She's pretty great." Dalton paused. "Does it make you think of Jenna?"

Cole inhaled sharply. He usually tried to downplay his feelings for Jenna in front of Dalton, though his friend seemed to see through it. "Yeah. Not that it really matters how I feel about her. She's my friend. She was kidnapped. I want her safe."

"What if tomorrow we find out Jenna isn't in Zeropolis? Do we stay and help Mira, or do we move on to the next kingdom?"

Cole groaned. "I don't know. Who's going to help us in the next kingdom?"

"What if Joe and Mira teach us how to contact the Unseen?" Dalton asked. "What if they give us a note or something that lets us get help from the rebels anywhere? Wouldn't that be faster than sticking with them?"

"Maybe," Cole said, feeling torn. "Why are you asking now? Because of that message from Trillian?"

"Don't tell me you haven't been thinking about it," Dalton said.

"I have. I don't know. The guy is scary, but it doesn't mean he's wrong. Supposedly he can't lie. Maybe my help really is important to the rebellion. I've saved Mira before. What she's doing matters to this whole world. Her dad is a monster. And his shapecrafters keep building actual monsters. If Mira and her sisters can't defeat him, this whole world could be doomed."

"You care about Mira," Dalton said.

Cole felt unwanted tears sting his eyes. "Of course I do! I care about everybody. I care about her and Twitch and Jace. I care about Jenna and the other kids who got kidnapped with us too. I think me, you, Mira, and Jace make a good team. My first choice would be to find the others with their help. And to help Mira along the way."

"And save the entire Outskirts," Dalton said.

"Maybe," Cole replied softly. "Especially if that means helping Mira."

"It's nice to have friends," Dalton said. "But it gets us into trouble. Her dad cares a lot more about finding her than he does about us. And helping her find her sisters leads us into ugly situations."

"So we abandon her?" Cole said.

"I don't mean we leave her stranded and friendless," Dalton said. "She has Joe and Jace. I'm sure wherever she goes she'll find other people to help her, like Skye. People with more skills than we have."

"I don't know," Cole said. "My power was looking pretty useful before it got blocked. Trillian seemed to think it would be crucial."

"Are you going to let him plan your future?" Dalton asked. "Didn't you almost get killed the last time you visited him? Didn't he try to take you prisoner?"

"You think he's wrong?"

"I think it's easy to say you can't lie. What proof do we have? He's an evil menace they locked up years ago. People avoid him like the plague. He could be telling the truth, Cole. I'm just not in a hurry to believe him."

Cole thought about it. "I don't know either. He might have just been trying to control me."

"What if we find Jenna tomorrow?" Dalton asked. "Let's say we also have a way home. Do we go? Do we try to find all the other kids first? Do we wait to help Mira?"

Cole had fretted about similar questions. "I honestly don't know. I'd hate to ditch the other kids. I'd hate to run out on Mira."

"It'll be hard to find all of them," Dalton said. "I don't even know them all. And sure, this world has problems, but so does ours. That doesn't mean I rush out and join the army or the Peace Corps so I can personally solve everything. We're still just kids."

"You're saying if we get the chance, we should leave?"

"I'm wondering what you think," Dalton said.

"I want to help Mira unless it makes no sense to stay with her," Cole said, feeling the truth of the words as he spoke them. "And I'm going to keep looking for Jenna. I'll save the other choices for when I actually find Jenna and a way home. Maybe when the time comes, Mira will be fine, and leaving won't be a big deal. Or maybe we'll never have the option to go home. Who knows?"

They emerged from the footpath onto the widest road they had seen. Shops and stalls lined both sides of the street. Other merchants sold from carts or off blankets.

"Welcome to Gizmo Row," Jace said over his shoulder.

The shops all had open fronts, inviting customers to step close and inspect items or have them demonstrated. The street wasn't packed with people, but a decent crowd of customers moved up and down the rows of storefronts, browsing, buying, and haggling. Cole noticed a lot of denim—jeans, shirts, skirts, and jackets. He wondered if he could find some jeans for himself. Did denim count as a gizmo?

One of the nearest shops looked full of strange aquariums. Closer inspection revealed that they were various types of water purifiers. Most were made from a mix of metal, plastic, and glass.

An older man with a curled mustache grinned from behind a counter at the front of the store. "Water is life," he said, with a faint accent that Cole couldn't place.

"Don't you guys have water towers?" Cole asked.

"We do today," he said. "For this I give thanks. Tomorrow?" He gave an indefinite shrug. "I hope so. For the sake of the children. Pause to consider—those towers only provide for the post. What if you go on an excursion?" He patted a small machine. "This condenser will strain water out of the air." He pointed at another. "Feed this device mud, and cool, clear water will emerge. How can one put a price on such magnificent functionality? Such security against drought? Such profound peace of mind?"

"I bet you found a way," Cole said.

"For you, a special price," the man replied, stroking one of his smaller purifiers. "One hundred and fifty credits. I lose money on this. You make me a pauper. But it would pain me if you perished from thirst. I sell it to you as charity."

"We don't need purifiers," Jace said, coming up behind Cole and tugging on the back of his shirt. "Come on."

"Who is this prophet?" the man asked Cole. "How does he know there will be no need for clean water? Would he be so kind as to speak my fortune? Perhaps reveal how I will meet my end?"

"It's a hunch," Jace said.

The man gave a nod. "May your hunches guide you to prosperity. Consider mentioning my wares to your parents."

"Will do," Jace said as he and Cole left the store.

"A purifier could come in handy," Cole said once they were out of earshot.

"If we were *walking* to the city," Jace replied. "I have no plans to get lost in the wilderness here. Keep in mind, most of this stuff will fall apart if we take it out of Zeropolis."

Cole, Jace, Mira, and Dalton moved along the row of shops. One place specialized in vehicle-repair tools, including a variety of jacks. Another shop featured lamps and other decorative lighting. A third had advanced tools like power saws and welding gear. Cole avoided getting close enough for the merchants to engage him.

Until they reached the shop with the robots.

"Whoa!" Cole exclaimed, his feet carrying him into the roomy store without much thought.

"Seriously?" Dalton asked.

Robots large and small moved around the area. Some rolled on wheels; some mimicked animals or insects; a few walked upright. They were mostly made from metal and glass.

A humanoid robot toddled up to Cole, all brassy metal and transparent panels. It was slightly taller than him and had a bronze mask for a face, with lights behind the eyes.

"How may I serve you, master?" the robot asked in a female voice.

"You tell me," Cole said. "What can you do?"

"I can cook over three hundred meals using standard equipment," the robot said. "I serve. I clean. I answer doors. I can handle all your domestic needs, freeing up your time for other pursuits."

"Can you fight off robbers?" Dalton asked.

"I can sound an alarm and get in the way," the robot replied.

"Can you sing?" Cole asked.

"I can be taught," the robot replied. "It would require some minor upgrades."

A husky man sauntered up to Cole. He wore jeans, a white shirt, a denim vest, and what looked like a leather baseball cap with mud flaps on the back. "Don't tease the domestic bots, kid," the man said.

"What if I might buy it?" Cole asked defensively.

"You'd start by needing around eighteen thousand credits," the man said.

"What's that in ringers?" Cole asked.

"Ringers? You from out of kingdom?"

"You're right by the border," Cole said.

The man shook his head. "Kids are talkers these days. They love to yap. I don't take ringers, boy, but ten credits is roughly one copper ringarole. You're looking at about four platinum."

Cole had much more than that but knew it would be foolish to reveal it.

"Why so much glass?" Cole asked.

The man huffed. "Boy, that is grade three bonded crystal. Harder than most alloys, and energy friendly." He huffed again. "Glass would shatter. I'd like to see you try to break a plate of grade three. That would be comedy."

Jace stepped in front of Cole. "How much for your hat?"

The guy scowled. "You cracking wise?"

"No," Jace said in his most sincere voice. "I'm absolutely serious. I'd buy it right now."

Weighing the reply suspiciously, the man brushed the bill of his cap. "Not for sale. I've had this hat for years. Too much sentimental value."

"Where'd you get it?" Jace asked.

"Ordered it in from the city," he said. "Place called Headgear. Synthetic leather with a waterproof sealant."

Jace gave a nod. "Thanks."

"Do you have anything we might be able to afford?" Dalton asked.

The man took a deep breath. "This is a bot shop. Nothing here comes cheap. It all depends on what you have to spend."

"What about that little crab-looking guy?" Dalton asked, pointing at a robot skittering around on a countertop in controlled bursts of motion.

"Does that look like a plaything to you?" the man asked. "That's a workbot. Tinkers use it to track energy flow in vehicles and other systems. It can find and repair damaged panels on a magroad. You'd be amazed by the energy surges it can withstand, the extreme temperatures that fail to bother it."

"We're sorry to trouble you," Mira said, tugging at Dalton.

"Kids love bots," the man said, waving a hand. "I get it. I don't have any toybots here. Some of the junkers on the row may have some. I can't vouch for the quality."

Cole, Dalton, and Jace followed Mira out. She walked briskly down the road.

"What was the hurry?" Cole asked her quietly. "That place was cool."

"Other shoppers were listening in on your conversation," she said. "You were drawing attention. That's not the goal right now." She glanced over her shoulder. "We're being followed."

Cole turned and saw a grungy guy in denim overalls coming toward them from the direction of the robot shop. He waved when Cole met his eyes and jogged to catch up.

"I don't know your faces," he said, his friendliness sounding a little forced.

"We're from out of town," Jace said.

"Your folks are letting you wander?" he asked.

"They trust us," Cole said. "You want something?"

"I'm Wilcox," the guy said. "I overheard you asking about bots. You kids have ringers?"

"Our parents might," Jace said.

Wilcox lowered his voice. "I've got a shop next street over. There's some great stuff down on the lower level. Want to check it out for your folks? Bots. Gadgets. Hard to find items. Really fun. Great deals."

"Why aren't you at your shop?" Mira asked.

"Everybody comes to Gizmo Row," Wilcox said. "I watch for clients here."

"Are a lot of your clients kids?" she asked.

Cole was glad she had called him on it. The guy gave off a shady vibe.

Wilcox frowned. He tapped Dalton on the shoulder. "Noticed this one's a slave."

"Our slave," Mira said.

"Mouthy for a slave," Wilcox said. "Saw him talking up a storm in there. You have IDs? Papers?"

"None of your business," Jace said.

"Isn't it?" Wilcox asked, cocking his head.

"Is there a problem?"

Cole breathed a sigh of relief to see Joe step up behind Wilcox. Joe didn't look pleased. Wilcox turned to look at him.

"Hey, Dad," Mira said.

"No problem," Wilcox said. "The young ones were pestering Chuck in the bot shop. I thought they might enjoy some of my toybots."

Joe narrowed his eyes. "So you were asking about identification? Who are you?"

Wilcox gave a smile and a shrug. "Just a fella looking to make a few credits. Good afternoon." He ambled away casually, hands in his pockets.

"That was good timing," Mira muttered.

"Looked like it," Joe said. "He was running some sort of scam. There's plenty of that in Zeropolis. Maybe I shouldn't have left you alone. Anyhow, I've got a bunch of credits on my card, and I know where we're going to stay tonight. We'll catch the monorail in the morning."

Chapter
5

GWEN

Joe booked a pair of adjoining rooms on the second floor of a big inn made of concrete blocks. One room contained four narrow beds, the other two. All of the beds had mattresses that looked and felt like the mattresses Cole remembered from back home, though a bit thinner. A couple of cowhide rugs softened up the cement floor.

"An actual faucet," Dalton said, standing by the sink. "With hot and cold running water."

"A toilet too," Cole added.

Dalton twisted on a faucet and let water run over his hand. "What a miracle."

"The showers are in a common area down the hall," Joe said. "They have one washroom for men and another for women. But in the city, we'll have showers in our rooms."

"Sweet," Cole said. "This might be my favorite kingdom."

They had gathered in the room with four beds. Mira would sleep in the other one when the time came.

Joe sat on the edge of one of the beds, hunched forward,

hands folded. He cleared his throat. "It's time I tell you my story."

Cole perked up. "Why you wanted to get away from Zeropolis?"

Joe nodded. "That and more. As long as we're together, the mess I made for myself here could affect us all. Cole, Dalton, in a lot of ways, we're in the same boat. I tried to get back home, and you deserve to hear about the problems involved." He rubbed his thighs and chuckled. "I hardly know where to begin. Some people know pieces of this, but I haven't told all of it to anyone."

"You're from Monterey?" Dalton prompted.

"Right," Joe said with a smile that was almost a grimace. "That's a place to start. I'm, what, thirty-four now? I was thirty. I worked as a paramedic, and occasionally as a studio musician."

"You were in a band?" Cole asked.

"Yeah, a few, when I was younger. Later on I just helped out when other people needed stuff recorded. Guitar mostly. It was fun work. I did most of it in the Bay Area. A little in LA."

"You can shred on guitar?" Dalton asked, impressed.

"If shredding is required," Joe said. "That hasn't been the handiest skill here. Knowing some first aid helps at times."

"Like with Sultan," Cole said.

Joe winced. "I wish I could have handled that better. I'd never worked on an arrow wound."

"I wasn't criticizing," Cole said. "At least you did something."

"Have you guys been where he's from?" Jace asked.

"Monterey?" Dalton clarified. "I haven't."

"Me neither," Cole said. "Don't they have an aquarium?"

"A famous one," Joe said. "And a lot of natural beauty. Great coastline. Nice bay."

"How'd you end up here?" Jace asked.

Joe clapped his hands together. "It's a painful story. But it's part of what I need to tell you. Let's see . . . I was engaged to be married. Gwen Saunders, the love of my life. Our wedding was coming up. We were about ready to send out invitations. Her family had some money, so it was going to be at a fancy country club. Some of my friends were lined up to provide live music. It would have been awesome."

"What happened?" Cole asked.

"I was walking by the ocean one evening," Joe said. "I was lost in thought. Feeling grateful, mostly. Gwen is amazing. It's ridiculous. She's so smart. A lawyer. The kind you don't want working against you. She's beautiful. We both love music. Especially some of the oldies. Anyhow, the air in front of me opened up, and before I knew what was happening, I got sucked through to here."

"The air opened up?" Cole asked.

"It was a Wayminder," Joe said. "I wasn't part of her plan, apparently. Just a mishap. She wanted to cross over to the Outside, and I was in the wrong place at the wrong time."

"Did you ask her to send you back?" Dalton asked.

"You bet," Joe said. "And she told me the same thing you guys have heard. Once we cross to the Outskirts, we can return home temporarily, but we can't stay there. And those who know us best forget us the most."

"Gwen?" Mira asked.

"Bingo," Joe said. "I ended up in Zeropolis, and my fiancée forgot she ever knew me."

"You're sure she forgot?" Cole asked.

Joe scrunched his nose. "I'm sure. There's more to the story."

"How did a Wayminder bring you to Zeropolis?" Dalton asked. "I thought their shaping worked in Creon."

"Or Junction," Cole said. "Like when we came through."

"Their shaping messes with time and space," Joe said. "The time manipulation only works in Creon. They open ways by tweaking space. That works best in Creon, but it can be done all over. A Wayminder could explain it better, but I think they can borrow space from Creon wherever they go."

"That's right," Mira confirmed.

"The Wayminder felt bad," Joe said. "She tried to make it right."

"She was a girl?" Jace asked.

Joe nodded. "Sallanah. When I came through the way she opened, I broke her concentration and the way closed. She couldn't open a new one right there, so we moved. She sent me back as soon as she could—within four hours of me crossing over. She got me close to where I had departed from. I ran to my car, drove to Gwen's place. She answered the door . . . and looked at me like a total stranger."

Cole's insides twisted. He imagined getting a look like that from his mom. Or his dad. Or his sister. Is that what the future held? He glanced at Dalton. Based on his friend's expression, the same worries were attacking him.

"Sallanah had warned me what to expect," Joe said. "Since I'd only been in the Outskirts a short time, I kind of hoped the side effects wouldn't take hold. I said Gwen's name, and she asked if she knew me. I told her my name but got a blank stare. It was right out of a nightmare. The more I tried to talk, the more I hinted at details I knew about her, the more uncomfortable she became. Before things got out of hand, I walked away."

"Did you get sucked back here?" Dalton asked.

"In less than two hours," Joe said. "After Gwen, I went to visit a good friend who also had no memory of me. I called in to work. Nobody knew me. I found a place to park my car and just sat there, trying to think. I felt like I was losing my mind. For a good while I couldn't stop laughing. Not healthy laughter. Before too long, the air over the passenger seat started to ripple. A way opened up and I was back in Zeropolis."

"That's the worst," Cole said.

"Not yet," Joe said. "The worst is coming. Sit tight. Sallanah came and found me not long after I returned to Zeropolis. She apologized again, and explained that I was stuck in the Outskirts. She helped me get a freemark, an identity card, and a place to stay. She gave me some money. I was in a daze at the time. I couldn't appreciate how lucky I was to have someone to orient me."

"Are you still friends?" Dalton asked.

"Not really," Joe said. "In theory, I guess. I wasn't overly nice to her. In spite of her help, she had kind of ruined my life. Looking back now, I can at least appreciate how she tried to make up for it. I don't think she's in Zeropolis anymore. My understanding is she returned to Creon."

"You got stuck here," Jace said. "Then what?"

"I found a hospital," Joe said. "Since I'm a paramedic, they became very interested when they learned I was from Outside. They hired me, and we taught each other some techniques. The medical care in Zeropolis is pretty good. Some of their technology surpasses what we have back home, though our medicines are more advanced."

"How'd you get involved with the Unseen?" Cole wondered.

"Gradually," Joe said. "I began to notice how controlling the government is here. I could never shake the hope of finding a way back to Monterey. You meet a lot of people as a paramedic. I kept my eyes and ears open. I started to hear about thruports that could connect to our Internet back home. When I met the right people, I started asking questions. Within a couple of years, I connected with some members of the Unseen who helped me get online."

"That's so weird they can get our Internet," Dalton said. "Are we even in the same universe?"

"It takes help from a Wayminder," Joe said. "Under normal conditions, a Wayminder can only hold a way open for a limited time. But some can open tiny ways for a really long time. The Wayminder opens tiny ways near a wireless router in our world, a tinker makes gear to pick up the signal, and before you know it, they're online. Some tinkers even own routers in our world and pay the access fees and everything."

"Did you try to contact Gwen?" Mira asked.

"What do you think?" Joe replied. "Nonstop. She never opened a single e-mail from me. None of my friends or family did either. I went through some of my obscure contacts and tried them. Sometimes I'd hear back. We'd make idle chitchat. I never tried to tell anyone where I was. I knew how it would sound."

"That must have been so frustrating," Cole said as his hopes of e-mailing his family crumbled. This story was creating a dark, anxious pit in his stomach.

"Still gets worse," Joe said. "See, I know the password for Gwen's e-mail. She had mine, too. She never changed it. So even though I couldn't contact her, I could peek at her life. I could see the e-mails I sent, sitting there unopened. She opened everything. Even half of the spam. But nothing from me."

"Man," Dalton said.

"Bummer, right?" Joe said. "I'd check up on her from time to time. Meanwhile, the more I learned about the Unseen, the more I believed in their cause, and the more involved I became. I began to understand how completely Abram Trench wants to control life in Zeropolis. And I came to realize the tyranny of the High King. If I was stuck here, I wanted to help this world become the best it can be. I mean, slavery? Are you kidding me? As a fringe benefit, the Unseen gave me access to thruports so I could keep peeking at my world."

"Because thruports are illegal," Dalton said.

"The Grand Shaper does all he can to shut them down,"

Joe said. "But the Unseen are well organized here. I had good access."

"How'd it get worse?" Jace asked.

Joe sighed. "About six months ago, I started to notice some of Gwen's e-mails taking a turn for the worse. I can read her pretty well. I know how she gets when she's frustrated. She's type A—works hard, plays hard, and takes things hard. She internalizes every little failure. I helped balance her out there. I helped her have fun. I helped her shake stuff off. We'd listen to music, or I'd play my guitar, or we'd get Italian, or we'd ride bikes along the coast. She was going into a downward spiral like I'd never seen. It wasn't clear in most of her e-mails—mainly the ones to her sister, and hints in the messages to her mom."

"Did you feel bad spying on her?" Jace asked.

Joe rubbed his face. "Well, yeah. But it was my only form of contact. I couldn't resist. As time went on, I realized that she felt alone. Maybe it's the romantic in me, but I thought maybe even though she couldn't remember me, a part of her was grieving my absence."

Suddenly Cole was fighting back tears. Were his parents like that? Could they feel something was wrong, even though they had forgotten him? Were they depressed without knowing why? Even if it caused them pain, Cole couldn't help hoping that some part of them deep down remembered him. He had to believe there was some hidden refuge of memory that might be wakened somehow.

"That must have been difficult," Mira said tenderly.

Staring at the floor, Joe folded and unfolded his arms. "It

wasn't a picnic. The longer I watched, the clearer her sadness became. I couldn't take seeing Gwen like that, unable to help her. It led to a crazy, stupid plan."

"What?" Cole asked, fascinated.

"I decided to bring her here," Joe said.

"Did you do it?" Dalton asked. "Did it make her remember you?"

"I'm getting there," Joe said. "I checked with a Wayminder. Not Sallanah. She was long gone. He told me that bringing Gwen here wouldn't make her remember me. But Gwen fell in love with me once, right? I'd woo her again. I'd fix the emptiness I saw in her. And maybe fill the void inside of me."

"But she'd be stuck here too," Cole said.

Joe nodded, rubbing his hands together. "I thought that through. If you're not a slave, and you live quietly, keep your head down, it isn't so bad here. We could live fulfilling lives, especially if we had each other. What I had with Gwen was epic. Whether or not she could remember me, I knew we'd figure it out. I convinced myself that if given a choice, Gwen would want to be with me. So I hired the Wayminder. My plan was to kidnap my fiancée and bring her here."

"How'd that work out?" Dalton asked.

Joe winced. "Could have gone better."

"Tell us," Cole urged, completely hooked.

Gazing down at the floor, Joe wiped a hand over his face. "I knew it was a risk. That she might see me as a villain. But I thought we could overcome that. She was still Gwen, right? And I'm still me." He fell silent.

"It went badly?" Mira guessed.

"Imagine this. We open a way to the street in front of my fiancée's apartment. Ex-fiancée? Anyhow, I knew she was bad at locking the back door, and sure enough, I hop the fence into her little yard and find it open. I creep across her kitchen in the dark and up the stairs. It's all way too familiar. Almost like I never left. I'm going quietly. I know that to her I'll seem like a burglar. By the light coming through her window from the street I can see her sleeping. She's so pretty. Without the worst luck ever, she would have already been my wife. We would have been married for years."

Joe folded his arms. "There I am, in her room. I just have to get her down the stairs and out front to the way. She's no weakling, but neither am I. I was sure I could get her there."

"But," Cole inserted.

Joe grimaced. "But there she was, snug and safe in a city without slaves, a place where she was free to live however she chose. How could I take that from her? Take away her home. Her family. Her job. Her life. Without permission."

"What a nightmare," Mira said.

"I couldn't do it," Joe said. "I wasn't just worried about her *thinking* I was a villain. I knew in that moment that if I took her, I would *be* a villain. However much I loved her, however much she once loved me, I had no right to drag her here. So I left. I came back through the way empty-handed."

"She's still there?" Cole asked.

"And I'm still here," Joe said. He smirked. "The next time I tried to check up on her using a thruport, I got caught. City Patrol raided the place. The guys running the thruport got taken away. It was my first offence. I got probation. It's what wrecked my true ID. The City Patrol is aware of me now. It makes me less safe to travel with."

"You used your fake ID today without trouble?" Jace asked.

"Yeah, it went well," Joe said. "We should be all right to take the monorail tomorrow. How backward is a place where it would have been legal for me to kidnap Gwen and bring her here, but I'm not allowed to browse the Internet? I could have made Gwen my slave without any legal trouble."

"This is why you wanted to leave Zeropolis?" Mira asked.

Joe nodded. "I got depressed. Really low. I knew I'd never see Gwen again. I was on probation. I was done with Zeropolis. I needed to get away. I went to the Unseen and told them I wanted a mission as far from the city as possible. I'd done some good work for them. The right people trusted me. That was when they let me know about you, Mira, and sent me on a mission to warn you about the legionnaires coming for you."

"You went straight from that to this?" Mira said with concern.

Joe flashed a tight smile. "This was exactly what I needed. Something to lose myself in. I threw myself at the danger. Part of me didn't mind the idea of dying. But I keep surviving. And now fate has brought me back here."

"What are you going to do?" Cole asked.

Joe gave a grim chuckle. "I've been pondering that long and hard ever since I learned we'd be coming here to find Constance. I think I just keep helping you kids. Focus on the work. Do I still miss Gwen? Take a wild guess. I'll miss her until the day I die. I know Cole hangs on to hope that there might be a way to get home. I'm open to that, but I don't dare to hope for it yet. I don't think my heart could take another disappointment. But I won't tell you to give up. If you find a way, please take me with you."

Cole's throat felt thick with emotion. It was hard to feel hopeful after hearing Joe's experience. "Trillian told me that there might be ways to change how things work here. It kind of makes sense. Pretty much everything else can be shaped. I'm not giving up until we try every option. We'll bug the Grand Shaper of Creon. We'll find out more about shapecraft. We'll go back to Trillian if we have to. We'll figure something out."

"Man, you guys really hate it here," Jace said.

"It's not our home," Dalton said.

"No, but it's my home," Jace replied. "And I've lived most my life as a slave. So I get not loving it."

"I admire your optimism, Cole," Joe said. "I know you really mean to tackle the impossible. I'll help however I can."

"First thing *I'm* going to try is getting some sleep," Jace said. "Those days as a wolf are catching up with me."

"We're all tired," Joe agreed. "Sorry for the long story."

"Don't apologize," Mira said. "It was brave and generous of you to share it. We'll do our best to help you."

"Sorry about Gwen," Cole said. "That's really rough."

"No worse than what you boys are going through," Joe said. "You were ripped away from your families. I can only imagine what that feels like at your age."

Cole didn't trust his voice. Dalton wiped at his eyes. Cole tried to ignore the pitying looks from Mira and even Jace.

"Thanks for telling us what we're up against," Cole managed.

"It doesn't paint a pretty picture of our chances to return to our normal lives," Joe said. "But you deserve to know."

"We always knew it would be hard," Cole said. "I sometimes suspected they were bluffing about people forgetting us. I wondered whether we'd really get pulled back here if we made it home. I wanted it to be propaganda. A trick to keep us here. That hope made your story kind of disappointing, but it's good to know the truth. We just have to find a way to change how it all works. Somehow we'll do it."

"We start by surviving tomorrow," Joe said. "Let's get some sleep while we can."

CHAPTER

6

MONORAIL

The monorail station was a spacious, modern structure of steel and crystal. After walking through the front doors, Cole almost felt like he was back in Arizona at some public building—tile floors, powered lights, service counters, people waiting in line. It could have been the lobby of an airport.

"IDs first," Joe said, leading the way.

Cole was now dressed in jeans and a brown shirt. The others all wore new clothes too. Joe wanted them to look like true Zeropolites.

They got in a fairly short line at a counter marked IDEN-TIFICATION. Joe had explained that the city government used the monorail stations to provide services for the outposts. More than just transportation and shipping, the stations provided banking, processed identifications, registered vehicles and property, recorded complaints, and housed a modest garrison of patrolmen.

When their turn came, Joe and the kids approached the

counter together. Joe handed his ID card to the older woman on duty. She looked at it, held it under a bluish light, then scanned it into a machine. Staring down at her screen, she looked perplexed for a moment, glancing quickly at Joe.

"Is there a problem?" he asked.

Cole's gut clenched, but he tried to look calm.

The woman gave a small smile. "Your mustache in the photo threw me off."

"I miss it sometimes," Joe said, rubbing his upper lip.

"You look better without it," she whispered loudly. "How can I help you today, Mr. Boone?"

"I'm traveling with my two nephews, my niece, and their slave. They're all first-timers in Zeropolis, so they'll need IDs."

"Okay," she said, fingers rattling on a keyboard. "Do they have any identifying paperwork from Elloweer?"

Joe shook his head. "I'm sure you know how badly organized they are in Elloweer when it comes to records."

"All too well," she said. "I deal with the sloppy results every day. Do you have papers for the slave?"

"He's marked, of course," Joe said. "But we don't have papers."

The woman behind the counter looked at Dalton. "Are these your owners?"

"Yes, ma'am," he replied.

"Very well," the woman said. "There's a two-hundred-credit processing fee for minors, and a six-hundred-credit fee for slaves."

"Use my card," Joe said.

"The fees double without papers," she said.

"I understand," Joe replied.

The woman held his card under a scanner. "Okay." She smiled at the kids, her gaze taking them in. "Have you ever been to the city?"

"No," Mira said.

"Are you sure you want to go there?" she asked playfully.

"Yes," Cole said.

"Very well," the woman said. "I need to take individual pictures, then I'll need your names along with the correct spellings."

She gestured for Cole to come around the counter, so he did. He stood on a mark, stared at a lens, and smiled. It didn't feel too different from school photos.

"Name?" she asked.

"Bubba Boone," Cole said. "B-U-B-B-A."

As Cole watched, Mira went on record as Shannon Boone, Jace became Hampton Boone, and Dalton became Kevin son of Mark. Cole was the first kid to receive a dark green ID card. He hefted it, stroking the metallic surface with his thumb. "Why isn't it blue like yours?" Cole asked Joe.

"You're under sixteen," Joe said.

Jace and Mira accepted their cards. Dalton got his last. It was bloodred.

"Slave color?" he asked, holding it up to the lady behind the counter.

She gave a curt nod, then looked beyond him. "Next."

Joe herded Cole and the others over to a nearby wall. "Wait here while I buy tickets," he instructed.

As soon as he walked off, Jace turned to Dalton. "I'm thirsty, slave boy," he said. "Fetch me a drink."

Dalton scowled.

"Don't make a scene, Kevin," Jace warned. "We all have to do our part."

"Yes, Your Highness," Dalton said.

"I'm not royalty," Jace explained. "Master will do."

"Knock it off," Cole said. "It isn't his fault he wasn't around when Declan changed our bondmarks to freemarks."

"Wasn't my fault I had a bondmark to begin with," Jace countered. "If our slave just stands around all the time and never serves us, how realistic does that look? It's safer for him and for us if he plays the part."

Cole could tell Jace enjoyed bossing Dalton around, and he was probably getting in some retaliation for the hidden saddle, but it was hard to argue against his point. They wanted to blend in.

"It's okay," Dalton said. "Do you want a drink, Mira? Cole?"

"Sure," Mira said. "Thanks."

"Won't that be a lot to carry?" Cole asked.

"I'll manage," Dalton said.

"Don't forget to hold any doors open for us," Jace said. "Be the first to stand, the last to sit. Treat us like masters. Work to keep us comfortable. Anticipate our needs. And try not to jump into any conversations free people are having."

"Aren't you getting carried away?" Cole said.

"I was a slave for a long time," Jace said. "Believe me, I know how they're supposed to behave."

"Thanks, master," Dalton said with some sarcasm. He walked away.

"How is he supposed to find drinks?" Cole wondered. "He doesn't have any money."

"A good slave would figure it out," Jace said.

"I understand playing our roles," Mira said. "But, Jace, you don't have to enjoy it so much."

Jace chuckled and stuffed his hands in his pockets. "I'm just grateful to be free."

"I'd think that would include some empathy for those still stuck as slaves," Mira said.

"We're just pretending he's our slave," Jace reminded her.

"But we're not pretending he's a slave," Cole said. "He's been a slave since he got here. His bondmark is real."

"Sometimes you two are unbelievably boring," Jace said, turning his back on them and shuffling a few steps away.

A few minutes later, Joe returned with Dalton behind him. Joe held a can of soda. Dalton carried four others. He handed one to Cole, another to Mira, and a third to Jace.

Cole inspected the orange can. The word "POW!" slanted across it in thick yellow letters. It had a pull tab just like the soda cans back home. Cole popped the top and took a sip. The bubbly liquid fizzed in his mouth and down his throat. It tasted sweet, the orange flavoring enhanced by a hint of vanilla.

"That's not bad," Cole said, licking his lips. "I haven't had a soda since I came here."

Jace squinted at the top of the can, first pressing the tab down, then picking at it. Mira held her soda unopened as well.

"Having trouble, master?" Dalton asked.

"I'm waiting for you to do your job," Jace said.

Dalton held out a hand, accepted the can, and demonstrated how to use the tab to pop it open. He handed it back to Jace. After seeing the example, Mira popped her own can open. Dalton opened his as well.

"We have tickets?" Cole asked, taking another sip.

"We're officially going to town," Joe said. "The monorail leaves in about fifteen minutes. We should get aboard."

"Will our swords be a problem?" Jace asked.

Joe held up his travel bag. "Both are in here. Primitive weapons like swords should be okay. They don't really screen for weapons here. Not like on flights back home."

Joe led them to a line waiting to pass through a door in a high crystal wall. A pair of patrolmen flanked the door, one checking IDs and tickets, the other watching the line. They wore gray-and-black uniforms with padding over the chest and on their limbs. Dangling from their shoulders by a strap, each man had a tubular weapon that looked like a miniature rocket launcher.

The line moved steadily. Cole shuffled forward beside Joe.

"What are those weapons?" Cole murmured. "Little bazookas?"

"No," Joe said softly. "Those are trapguns. Most of the weapons used by patrolmen stun or entrap. You'll get gummed up by quicktar, or stuck to webby nets. Nonlethal, but very effective. There isn't usually much violence in Zeropolis. Crime happens quietly here."

Joe stopped talking as they drew near to the door. Cole

clutched his ticket and his ID card. He thought about how he would hand over the ticket and ID card if he wasn't a wanted fugitive. He decided to act calm and polite, maybe a little distracted.

Joe held out his card. The patrolman scanned it with a device, glanced at his ticket, then waved him along.

Upon reaching the patrolman, Cole fretted about making too much eye contact. Or too little. The patrolman took Cole's card and scanned it, then waved him through. Cole didn't look back to watch the other kids, but soon they were all together beyond the crystal wall.

Up ahead, three elevators shuttled people up to the level of the track. Elaborate compartments of crystal and bronze, the elevators were not hidden within a shaft. Each had an operator and could fit roughly ten passengers.

"They look kind of old-fashioned," Dalton observed, beside Cole.

"They're fast though," Cole replied. He noticed Jace watching the elevators climb and sink. He looked both excited and a little uncertain. "Ever ridden in an elevator, Jace?"

"Nope," Jace said.

"Me neither," Mira added.

"They call them senders here," Joe mentioned. "Like 'ascend' and 'descend.'"

After a short wait, Cole and his four companions entered a sender with a few other people. The operator raised a lever, and the compartment surged briskly upward.

When Cole exited the sender, the monorail came into

full view. Long and sleek, the streamlined train was composed of silvery metal and crystal tinted such a dark blue that Cole could only barely see the forms moving inside.

"Bonded crystal?" Cole asked.

"Very good," Joe said. "They use it a lot here. Those elevators were made of bonded crystal and some sturdy alloy. Maybe renium. The crystal for the monorail is grade two, tougher than steel. The train moves fast—over three hundred miles per hour."

Cole and the others joined the crowd making for one of the many doors of the long train. More patrolmen stood on the platform, trapguns dangling within easy reach. A conductor at the door to the monorail quickly checked tickets as people entered. Cole boarded after Joe, flashing his ticket to the conductor, then following Joe down the central aisle of the train.

From inside the monorail, the tinted glass didn't look nearly so dark, though everything outside had bluish tones. People were settling into the cushioned seats at either side of the aisle. Much as when he had walked into the station, Cole felt a sense of home. This monorail was too modern to fit his experiences in the Outskirts. It was too much like boarding the light rail in Phoenix or getting on a plane.

Joe led them down the aisle to the end of the car, through a set of doors, and along another aisle until the seats gave way to private compartments on either side, each with its own door. Checking his ticket, Joe opened the door of a compartment where two cushioned benches faced each other. The far wall was all window.

"Our own room?" Cole asked.

"We're not poor," Joe said. "I thought a little privacy would be nice."

Joe and Dalton sat on one side, leaving Cole, Mira, and Jace on the other. With the door shut, they could almost be alone on the train—only the faintest noise of other passengers moving around or conversing reached them.

Looking out the window at the platform, Cole watched other passengers approaching the monorail. The crowd thinned until only a few patrolmen remained.

A soothing female voice came from a speaker in the ceiling. "Now departing Outpost 121. Next stop, Outpost 45. Please keep your tickets handy and enjoy the ride."

The monorail began to slide forward, starting off so gently that it was difficult for Cole to determine when the motion began. Smoothly and steadily they picked up speed. They left the station behind, and the low buildings of the outpost blurred beneath them. Cole leaned his head against the window to enjoy the foreground streaming past.

The monorail reached terrific speed, but inside their compartment Cole could feel no motion. When he closed his eyes, they could have been standing still.

"Are we even moving?" Cole asked. "It's almost like the outside scenery is fake!"

"The monorail is well designed," Joe said. "It floats on a magnetic cushion and is extremely aerodynamic."

"I've never imagined anything like this," Jace asked. "I can't believe the speed!"

"When do we get off?" Dalton wondered.

"Sixth stop from now," Joe said. "Hanover Station. We'll stop at two other outposts, then pass a few stations in the city."

"How long?" Dalton asked.

"We have to go more than a thousand miles," Joe said. "Including the stops, we should arrive in just over four hours."

Cole gave a low whistle. That was fast!

"Do you know how to find the Unseen?" Mira asked.

"I've been gone for a while," Joe said. "They change location a lot to stay ahead of the patrolmen. We'll hit a gaming hub called Axis. Cole or Dalton would call it an arcade. Some of the CKs should be there. The Crystal Keepers. They're a gang of gamers who help out the Unseen. They'll know how to help us get in touch with the leadership."

"Think we can find a thruport?" Cole asked.

"Probably, once we reach the Unseen," Joe said. "We'll get their help in finding Constance and ask about your slave friends."

"And I'm going to find out about Headgear," Jace said. "I want a hat like that robot guy had."

Joe snapped his fingers. "Whoops, I meant to put some money on your ID cards. We'll have to do that once we get to the city."

Somebody tapped on the door. Joe opened it to reveal a conductor. "Tickets, please," the man said.

They handed over their tickets. The man passed a handheld scanner over them, then returned them. "Thanks for riding the monorail," he said, tipping his hat. Then he backed into the hall and closed the door.

Cole leaned back on his bench. It was comfortable, the cushions a nice blend of soft but firm. He hadn't slept well the night before. He had been excited to see the city, and he had kept thinking about his parents not missing him.

Cole was in the corner by the window, so he leaned his head against the glass. In that position, he could feel the slightest hint of vibration against his skull. It was kind of soothing.

His thoughts turned to Jenna. Where was she now? Was she comfortable? Scared? Was she expecting a rescue? Was she trying to free herself? What if she had made a successful escape? Could she be on the run too?

Hopefully there would be answers in a few hours after he reached the city and the Unseen. What if they traced her ID card and instantly found her? What if he would see her later today? Or tomorrow? The hope seemed too greedy, but he knew it was possible. She had to be somewhere.

Gazing far out the window toward the horizon, Cole lost the sense of their speed. But when he glanced down at the nearby prairie streaking by beneath them, his appreciation was reawakened.

Feeling drowsy, Cole experimented with shutting his eyes. When he woke up, he found that the monorail was inside a station. Jerking away from the window, Cole saw the others eating sandwiches.

"I wondered when you'd join us," Dalton said around a mouthful. "This is the first stop in the city."

"We got you food," Mira said, handing Cole a wrapped sandwich.

"How much longer?" Cole asked.

"The monorail doesn't go as fast inside the city," Joe said. "About half an hour."

Cole unwrapped his sandwich and started working on it. The bread was a little stale, and the cuts of chicken inside it a little dry, but the tangy sauce was good, and he was hungry.

As the monorail slid out of the station, Cole watched eagerly out the window for his first view of the city. What he saw delighted him.

He had expected nonstop buildings. And yes, there were some serious clusters of skyscrapers spaced about, tall and elegant, mostly made of metal and crystal. But there were also open areas. Big parks and lakes. Neighborhoods with yards. Mansions with grounds. Huge, low buildings topped with gardens.

Even from the vantage of the elevated track, the city stretched as far as he could see, which led Cole to suppose it might continue well beyond what lay before him. Vehicles zoomed along the dark roads crisscrossing the city. Were they cars? He couldn't see tires. Were they hovering? They all shared a similar design, though the colors varied. It was hard to discern all the details from up high, moving quickly.

"Next stop, Canal Station," announced the soothing female voice from the speaker in the ceiling. "Please remain in your seats when we stop while the City Patrol arrests a suspect. The all clear will be announced once the suspect is in custody. Walt Boone, please submit quietly."

WELCOMING COMMITTEE

Joe immediately tried the door to the compartment. It was locked. He jiggled the handle roughly, but it only moved a little, and the door had no give.

The compartment was silent as Joe slid back into his seat. He looked ill, his face oddly blank. "Okay," he said softly. "Okay. Okay."

Cole banged the side of his fist against the window. It made no sound. The vault door at a bank might have shown a similar indifference to a punch.

"We're not getting out through the window," Cole said, hoping to jump-start Joe.

"No," Joe agreed. "It would take serious tools." His eyes darted, but Cole wasn't sure he was seeing much. "They must have flagged my ID after all, but let me board. That kind of patience isn't how City Patrol normally works. I should have gone with my gut. The woman at the ID counter seemed a little flustered at first. We've made one stop in the city so far. I bet a bunch of patrolmen got on. Now they're taking me off."

"What can we do?" Mira asked.

Joe clutched the sides of his head. "A private compartment was a terrible idea. We're stuck here until they come for us."

The monorail began to slow.

"I should have spaced us throughout the train," Joe lamented. "We should have sat near exits."

"Would have, could have, should have," Jace said impatiently. "What do we do?"

Out the window, the view of the city was replaced by the inside of a building. Signs on the wall declared it CANAL STATION. People milled on the platform. The monorail slowed even more.

Cole's mind raced. What could they do? They had no time! They were trapped!

"We let the welcoming committee take us," Joe said hurriedly. "They'll be ready for trouble. It's the wrong time to resist. I'll comply. They'll focus on me. Come quietly, but move slowly. Stray as far from me as you can. After we're off the monorail, I'll make a run for it. Scatter. Don't stay together. Don't use your ID cards. They're all tied to me now. Jace, keep my travel bag, if you can. All of you make your way to Axis. Leaf Street, near Hanover Station. Across from Zenith Park. Crystal Keepers."

The monorail had eased to a stop. The compartment door opened. Two heavily built patrolmen filled the doorway.

"What's the problem?" Joe asked politely.

"Joe MacFarland, you're under arrest," one of the patrolmen said.

"May I ask the charges?" Joe asked.

The patrolman grunted. "Not now. Come with us."

"I'm not sure what I've done wrong, but I'm all yours," Joe said.

"The false ID is a start," the patrolman said, glancing around the compartment. "Who are the kids?"

"Relatives of a friend," Joe said.

"You're the only adult present?" the patrolman asked.

"That's right," Joe said.

"We'll have to bring all of you to HQ," the patrolman said. "Step out into the hall. Joe first." He backed away from the doorway, allowing room to exit.

After a quick glance at Cole and the others, Joe rose and passed into the hall. The patrolman who had been speaking leaned back into the compartment, all business. "You kids stay with us."

"Why do we have to come?" Jace complained.

"Let's cut the chitchat," the patrolman said. "You're with a wanted criminal. Hurry up."

The patrolman backed out the door. Cole waited while Jace grabbed the travel bag and exited, then watched Mira and Dalton exit as well. What would it mean to go to HQ? It would get ugly fast if anybody figured out Mira's identity. What if the Hunter caught wind of it?

Cole took his time leaving the compartment. They had to try to get away. Maybe by going slow, he could create some space for himself.

Out in the central aisle, Joe stood with his wrists bound in front of him and a patrolman on either side. With his wrists tied and so many patrolmen around, would he even get the chance to run and make a diversion?

Once Cole exited the compartment, the lead patrolman gave a nod, and the procession started down the aisle toward the exit. Cole only had one patrolman behind him, so he tried to dawdle, crouching to tie his shoe, but the patrolman stayed with him.

As he advanced up the aisle toward the exit, Cole wished for his power back. If he could energize the Jumping Swords and Jace's golden rope, the odds of escape would immediately improve. But searching desperately inside, Cole perceived no trace of his power.

Accompanied by patrolmen, Joe stepped off the monorail. Other patrolmen followed.

The soothing female voice spoke again over the loudspeakers. "You may now exit the train for Canal Station. Thank you for your cooperation."

Passengers began to rise from their seats and move into the aisle, forcing the patrolman ahead of Cole to pause. Cole flattened himself against the seats at one side of the aisle to allow an older woman to pass. He stayed there, hoping the patrolman behind him might pass him as well, but the patrolman nudged him to continue.

Cole stepped down from the train onto a bustling platform. Some people were boarding the train, others getting off. Looking compliant, Joe stood some distance away with four patrolmen. Jace, Mira, and Dalton were moving in Joe's general direction, while also doing a decent job of spreading out.

Joe briefly met eyes with Cole. Then he bolted, racing down the platform toward the front of the monorail. All of the patrolmen reacted. Most reached for their trapguns, then seemed to think twice about using them on the crowded platform.

Though caught flat-footed, the patrolmen who had stood with Joe took off in pursuit, weapons in hand. Joe turned and raised his bound hands. In them he held a silver tube that Cole remembered from Skyport. Joe had pointed it at the legionnaires when he joined the fight to help Mira escape. Nothing had happened.

This time it worked.

A narrow jet of white material fountained from the end of the tube, staying in a focused stream until it hit the patrolman nearest to Joe and expanded into a dense cloud of foam. The foam only sprayed for a few seconds, but Joe managed to heavily cover two patrolmen and lightly got a third.

The rich lather made Cole think of shaving cream, but as the men coated by the substance slowed down, it became clear that the foam was rapidly hardening. One patrolman tipped over, trapped in a pillowy cocoon, his arms encased in front of his chest, his legs stuck together above the knees. The foamy husk helped break his fall. Another patrolman froze up while wiping the lather off his face. Only his upper body was covered, but he ended up with one hand stuck over his eye, and the other against his neck. A third patrolman had his hand bound to his weapon and his elbow to his side by a large, creamy glob.

Joe kept running, brushing by others in the crowd. As

people saw him coming and made room for him, he swerved toward them rather than accepting the open space. Cole realized that Joe was using the crowd to deny the patrolmen a clear shot.

Cole also abruptly realized that he was unsupervised.

People were still going in and out of the monorail through the door he had just exited. The patrolman who had accompanied him was running after Joe, just like all the others. Taking his ticket from his pocket, Cole turned and boarded the train.

No conductor monitored the door. After stepping aboard with his head down, Cole turned away from the private compartments where he had ridden with his friends. He didn't want to walk by the same people who had watched the patrolmen march him off the monorail.

Moving down the aisle, Cole raised his head and tried to appear casual. Anxiety boiled inside of him. He expected a patrolman to call out to him at any moment. He walked through two cars before choosing an empty seat in a vacant row with a view of the platform. He wasn't sure if the seat required a certain ticket, but he figured he could act really polite and move if somebody called him on it.

Peering out the window, Cole found it mostly looked like business as usual on the platform, though a few people had paused to stare toward the front of the monorail, necks craning, presumably watching the chase. Joe had been sprinting while Cole walked, so unless he got caught right after Cole stopped watching, he was probably a good distance down the platform. Cole couldn't see him from his seat and didn't want to make a show of looking.

Could Joe still be running? Did he have any chance of getting away? There had been a lot of patrolmen present, but if the crowd interfered enough, maybe it was possible. The distraction had sure worked. Cole hoped Dalton, Jace, and Mira had also taken advantage of the opportunity.

Cole silently willed the train to move forward. He didn't think any patrolmen had seen him return to the monorail, but he couldn't be sure. With the patrolmen chasing Joe, how much would they care that the kids who were with him had scattered? Would they bother to search the area?

The nearest exit door slid closed, and the monorail glided forward. The soothing woman came on over the loudspeaker. "Sorry for the delay. Next stop, Rockford Station."

As the monorail picked up speed, Cole watched out the window, hoping for a glimpse of Joe, trusting the tinting to hide his face from any patrolmen outside the train. Toward the end of the platform, Cole saw a group of patrolmen gathered around a pair of people pinned to the ground by a ropy mass of gray webbing. Due to the increasing speed of the monorail and the presence of the surrounding patrolmen, Cole only caught a quick glimpse of the people beneath the webs. But he knew one of them had to be Joe.

The train passed beyond the station, and once again Cole could see the sights of the city. But his gaze dropped to his lap. He felt guilty for escaping while Joe paid the price. He knew Joe wanted him to flee, but he still felt miserable. Why couldn't Joe have gotten away? What would the patrolmen do to him?

Cole stewed about his other friends. He assured himself

they must have escaped. He couldn't be the only one who had made it. Joe had led the patrolmen on a good chase. He had made it a long way down the platform. Dalton, Jace, and Mira should be long gone.

From his current seat, Cole could see no patrolmen aboard the monorail. If he could make it past Rockford Station to the next stop, he could get off as planned and make his way to Axis. The others who got away would go there too. Then maybe they could contact the Unseen and figure out how to help Joe.

Or maybe none of the others had escaped. Maybe Mira would be discovered. Maybe he had seen the last of his friends.

Maybe he was alone.

AXIS

Cole stepped off the monorail at Hanover Station, the fourth stop inside the city. The bustling station had a high ceiling and an enormous platform. Cole flowed with the crowd of disembarking passengers toward a wide stairway. Off to one side he saw senders as well.

It felt strange to be alone. He had traveled as part of a group for a long time. There had been others to rely on. When Joe was with him, he hadn't worried about navigation at all. Now he felt the true enormity of the city.

He was an outsider. He didn't know the places or the customs. He needed to fit in. He couldn't afford to draw attention. For the moment, that meant staying with the crowd.

Two patrolmen wandered the platform, trapguns dangling from straps over their shoulders. Cole avoided paying special attention to them, and they returned the favor.

As he reached the top of the stairs along with a funneling mass of other people, a hand clamped down on his shoulder from behind. "You're coming with me."

Cole jumped and turned, breaking the grip, and was ready to dash down the crowded stairs before he recognized Jace. "Not a great time for jokes," Cole said hotly.

"Seems like the perfect time," Jace replied. "It's the best I've felt all day."

They started walking down the stairs together. As angry as Cole felt at being startled, he was also relieved. At least somebody else had slipped away. He wasn't completely on his own. Cole noticed Jace still carried the travel bag. "Good job keeping the bag."

Jace glanced over. "Did you expect me to leave it? My golden rope is always in my pocket, but I didn't want to lose the Jumping Swords and whatever else Joe stashed in this."

"How'd you get here?" Cole asked in a hushed voice.

"How do you think?" Jace replied. "On the monorail."

"Did you see what happened to the others?" Cole asked.

"A little," Jace said. "What do you know?"

"Not much," Cole said. "After Joe ran, I realized the patrol guys were distracted, so I hopped back on the train. As we pulled out of the station, I'm pretty sure I saw Joe glued to the ground by giant webs."

They reached the bottom of the stairs and walked out into a spacious lobby. The black tile floor darkly reflected the people walking on it.

"When Joe ran, I saw you get back on the monorail," Jace said. "Mira took off toward the nearest stairway. Dalton went diagonally to a different stairway. I headed along the platform in the opposite direction Joe had run. As I moved toward the back of the monorail, I decided you had a good idea, so I climbed aboard. The doors closed before long."

"Did you see what happened to the others?" Cole asked.

"Looked like they got away down the stairs," Jace said. "I was stupid. I should have found some other stairs and stayed with Mira to help her. I watched as best I could, and didn't see any patrolmen tailing them. They all went after Joe."

"Did you see him go down?" Cole asked.

"He was too far away and the station was too crowded," Jace said. "Since I went to the back of the train, I was farther from him than you were. When the monorail pulled out, I saw a couple of guys stuck to the floor. The way the patrolmen had gathered around them, it must have been Joe."

Cole and Jace exited the station through a pair of double doors. Outside, a wide sidewalk gave way to a glossy, black street composed of tightly fitted panels. Heavy traffic zipped up and down the street, the cars hovering roughly a foot above the ground. They were all rounded like Volkswagens, but a little longer and sleeker. The windows were tinted almost as much as the monorail's, keeping the drivers and passengers mostly hidden from view.

Watching the hover cars zoom along, Cole flinched as they swerved aggressively, weaving in and out of close gaps. Time after time, right when a crash seemed inevitable, the vehicles corrected enough to avoid the collision. Cole had thought driving on the Arizona freeways looked intimidating, but that was nothing compared to this!

Along the edge of the street, at intervals, dark gray boxes sat atop metal poles. They looked kind of like parking meters, except nobody was parked. A woman approached a pole box and held up her ID card. A green light flared to life atop the box. Seconds later one of the hover vehicles glided to a stop near the woman. The door facing the sidewalk opened. Peering inside, Cole saw that the vehicle was vacant. No driver.

"Check it out," Cole said, nodding toward the lady getting into the car. Without a driver, there was room for six passengers—three in the front, three in back.

"I am," Jace replied.

The woman held up her ID card to a sensor inside the car. The door closed, and the vehicle darted away, deftly blending in with the rest of the traffic. As Cole and Jace continued to watch, more cars were summoned to pole boxes, while others stopped to drop off passengers. The hover vehicles accelerated briskly and braked abruptly, all without touching the ground or causing a wreck. They were almost totally silent except for the air whooshing around them.

"I think it's completely automated," Cole said.

"Fancy word," Jace said.

"There aren't any drivers," Cole rephrased.

"I noticed," Jace said. "How could that work?"

"It must be computers," Cole said. "Machines. Like the robots we saw."

They stood watching the frenetic parade of near misses. Even when an accident looked certain, it didn't happen.

"This many cars should be causing a traffic jam," Cole said. "It's a cool system. I've never seen anything like it."

"Me neither," Jace said wholeheartedly. "Should we go?"

CRYSTAL KEEPERS

"I wish I had an ID card with credits on it," Cole said. "I'd love to go for a ride."

"You heard Joe, right?" Jace checked. "We need to ditch our IDs."

"I heard him," Cole said. "I was just wishing."

"Might be smart to get moving," Jace suggested. "Who knows if those patrolmen are searching for us? We should get away from the station."

The reminder helped snap Cole out of his fascinated trance. Just because they had made it a couple of stations away from where Joe got arrested didn't mean they were safe. There would be time to pay more attention to the amazing technology of Zeropolis later.

Tearing his gaze away from the interweaving parade of hover cars, Cole noticed the park on the far side of the road. Tall trees presided over neat hedgerows, wide walkways, lush lawns, and splashing fountains. Beyond the borders of the park, Cole could see a variety of buildings.

The street was much too busy to cross without making a scene. Cole wondered if the vehicles were programmed to avoid a person on the road, or if they'd just mow him down. He didn't want to be the guinea pig for that experiment.

Picking a random direction, Cole followed the sidewalk, Jace at his side. Before too long they came to a flight of stairs that gave access to a pedestrian tunnel under the road. "Should we cross?" Cole asked.

"Sure."

They started down the steps. "Look," Cole said, pointing

97

at a sign. "Zenith Park. Joe said Axis is across the street from there."

"Then it could be on this side of the street," Jace said.

"What street did he say Axis is on?"

"Leaf?"

"Is this Leaf Street?"

"Do I seem like a local?" Jace complained.

Cole waved at a young guy coming up the stairs. "Excuse me. What street is this?"

"Grant," the guy said.

"Which way is Leaf?" Cole asked politely.

"Far side of the park," the guy said, not slowing.

Cole picked up his pace. "Thanks."

He and Jace passed through the pedestrian tunnel, then climbed the stairs at the far side. They emerged into the park. The sun was getting low but wouldn't set for a couple more hours. Cole could smell the nearby lawn. Birds twittered in the trees. It was too pretty of a day to be on the run from patrolmen. Frisbee golf seemed more appropriate.

"This feels too much like home," Cole said.

"You live in a park?" Jace asked.

"I mean everything. This city."

"Your home is like this place?"

Cole studied the buildings beyond the perimeter of the park. Some were skyscrapers. Some were apartments. Some looked like banks or museums. There was a nice variety. It all felt modern.

"Where I'm from is way more like this than Sambria or Elloweer," Cole said. "We have public parks and big cities.

We have trains and even some monorails. We have tall buildings. We have cars, but people drive them."

"You drove one of those?" Jace asked, pointing back at the road.

"I wasn't old enough," Cole said. "My dad drove. He let me steer a couple of times, but not on busy streets."

They strolled toward a plaza with a multitiered fountain at the center. After spouting up in the middle, the water flowed from level to level in a series of broad cascades.

"Must be nice to feel at home," Jace said.

"I don't know," Cole replied. "I've never been alone in a big city like this. That much is unfamiliar. Some of the technology is pretty different from what I know. And back home I was never a wanted fugitive."

Jace took a deep, cleansing breath. "Cities are the place to be. You can find so much without going very far. Places to eat. Things to do. Sights to see. People to meet. And this is the biggest city in the Outskirts."

"Which can also mean lots of bad guys," Cole said. "Lots of people who want to find us. Lots of criminals. Lots of danger."

"It can also mean lots of places to hide," Jace said. "Crowds to blend with. Bargains to make. Allies to find. Don't be such a wimp."

"Sorry if I'm not doing cartwheels after the patrolmen took Joe," Cole said. "Makes the city seem a little less safe. I'm sick of being chased."

"Then you're hanging with the wrong crowd," Jace said. "Mira's going to be chased until her dad is off the throne. And that day is a long way off."

"Duh. I'm not new here. But so far, we've never been in a city long before we're running for our lives."

"It looked bad back there," Jace admitted. "But we're in the clear now. Be glad we got away. Joe pulled off a great diversion. I'm pretty sure Mira and Dalton escaped too. It'll take them longer to get here without money. The monorail took us a good distance from Canal Station. But sooner or later they'll turn up, then we'll figure out how to help Joe."

"I hope so," Cole said, though he didn't feel very optimistic. None of their powerful items worked here. How were they supposed to take on a huge police force like the patrolmen? Their only chance was if the Unseen could aid them.

With its name inscribed in flashing neon on the side of the building facing the park, Axis was not tricky to find. Cole and Jace took a pedestrian tunnel under Leaf Street and emerged near the front doors. Checking up and down the bustling road, Cole noticed trees lining both sides as far as he could see.

"Let me take the lead in here," Jace said.

"Why?" Cole replied. "Because you have so much experience with arcades?"

"We might have to look streetwise," Jace said.

"I wasn't a prince in my world," Cole said. "I know how to stand up for myself. And I've been to places like this."

Jace shrugged. "I like the confidence. Let's go."

Cole led the way through two sets of doors and into the sprawling arcade. The high, black ceiling almost made it seem as if the room extended up into a starless sky. Cole wondered how the room could look so dark when there were so many lights pulsating in a wide array of colors. The gaming hub wasn't too crowded, with only about half the games occupied and short lines for the more popular attractions.

Some aspects of how the games were arranged reminded Cole of his world, but there were also many differences. None of the games within view used a video screen. He saw elaborate pinball machines, complicated ring tosses, diverse shooting galleries, and many games where balls were rolled or thrown. A good number of the games were larger than any he had seen back home. Several required the participant to enter a spacious cube with clear walls.

"This place is unreal," Jace said with reverence.

Cole nodded. How would they know who belonged to the Crystal Keepers? Would it be written on their T-shirts? Who could they safely ask? "Do we just roam around?" Cole wondered.

"Yep," Jace said. "Keep your ears open. Watch for clues. We'll find who we're looking for."

They wandered over to a clear cube labeled KNOCKOUT!, where a kid in a helmet and padded vest fought a heavily padded robot. Not much more than a cylinder with two long arms and a glowing face near the top, the robot was anchored to the ground and wielded a cushioned club in each hand.

As they watched, Cole realized the boy was trying to use his own padded weapon to strike five targets on the robot without getting hit. He used his club defensively to block blows, then lashed out at the targets when he had an opening. When he hit a target, it lit up.

After connecting with the third target, the robot sped up. The kid strained to block the more aggressive attacks but got whacked in the side of the head and then thumped on the chest.

The illuminated targets went dark, the lighting within the cube dimmed, and the robot laughed mechanically, raising both arms in victory. The boy went to the door and it opened up, freeing him from the cube. He handed his padded bat to the next player in line, who was already wearing a helmet and vest. The new player entered, displayed his ID card, and the door closed.

"Looks like you pay with your ID," Cole said.

"Isn't that how you pay for everything here?" Jace said. "Too bad our cards will probably alert patrolmen if we use them. Plus, we're broke."

"I still have a bunch of ringers," Cole said.

"Me too. But even if we could change them to credits, we can't risk using our cards."

"Think you could take out the robot?" Cole asked.

Jace gave a small snort. "In a heartbeat."

Cole couldn't help thinking it was easy to brag since they didn't have any way to try the game. The second kid didn't last long, striking only one target before getting pummeled. Cole wondered how he would do against the robot. It was pretty quick.

Jace led the way to another game. A glitzy sign above the cube dubbed it PRIZE HUNTER. Inside the cube, a weaponless girl in a helmet and puffy vest crouched in a corner. In the center, a robotic cylinder with twenty padded arms twisted and flailed. An additional three dozen mechanical arms reached down from the ceiling. About half the arms held slender cushioned weapons. The other half clutched prizes ranging from candy bars to stuffed animals to electronics.

"What's she doing?" Cole asked.

"Picking her moment," Jace said. "Looks like the game can't reach her there."

The multijointed arms raised and lowered, stretched and bent. Suddenly the girl raced out of the corner. After dodging a couple of arms, she reached for a bag of peanuts. Her fingers brushed the bag, but she failed to take hold of it. A padded arm struck her across the back. She went down, and the lighting in the cube dimmed. The arms stopped moving.

The girl got up and exited. Nobody was waiting for the next turn. Jace hustled over to the girl, who looked about their age.

"You wanted the nuts?" he asked.

"Kind of," the girl said. "Stupid thing is rigged. It's impossible to win."

"You have to grab a prize before you get hit?" he asked.

"You can take as many hits as you want until you get knocked down," the girl said.

"Want me to get you some nuts?" Jace asked, rubbing his hands together.

The girl paused. "If you want."

"I don't have any credits," Jace said. "I'd need to borrow your ID."

"Yeah, and then run off with it," the girl said. "Get lost." She walked hurriedly away.

A girl who must have been a couple of years older than them approached. She had a dark, stylish haircut with the tips dyed red and wore a mostly black outfit that hugged her trim physique. About the same height as Jace, she was a few inches taller than Cole. "You bothering her?" she asked.

"I was going to win her some prizes," Jace said.

"Win some for me," the girl replied.

"You have to cover my game," Jace said.

The girl rolled her eyes. "You'll win me prizes using my money? No wonder she took off! Are you guys posties?"

"Huh?" Cole asked.

"You know, from the outposts," the girl said. "New to town. What are you trying to pull?"

Cole didn't like her attitude. She seemed to think she was pretty awesome. "Maybe we're con artists trying to seem oblivious."

The girl folded her arms. "If so, you're doing a perfect job."

"Bet on me," Jace invited. "I'm a good investment. But I keep every third prize."

"If you win them at once," the girl replied. "Otherwise I keep everything."

"Sure," Jace said.

"Fine, I'm curious," the girl said. "It's ten credits per game. You get one try."

"Where do I snag a helmet?" Jace asked.

The girl groaned. "You really are from the posts!"

"Maybe," Jace replied. "But I'm here now."

She walked them over to a bin with helmets and padded

vests and helped Jace choose some. They returned to the Prize Hunter game to find the cube still empty.

The girl held out her ID. "I need your card as collateral."

Jace handed it over. The girl glanced at it. "You just got this today."

"Maybe," Jace said, glancing at her card, "Luri."

"You're not posties," Luri said. "You're outlanders. Have you ever even been to a gaming hub?"

Cole tried to read her. She was acting casual but seemed extra curious. Could she be a Crystal Keeper? Or might she be dangerous? Did City Patrol have informants in places like this? She was pretty young. Maybe she was just nosy.

"You'll get prizes," Jace said evenly.

"Go for it," she said, waving him away. "If any part of you besides your feet touches the ground, you're through."

"Did you read the sign?" Cole asked, pointing at a little placard beside the door into the cube.

THIS GAME MAY CAUSE BODILY HARM. PLAY AT YOUR OWN RISK.

"Isn't that obvious?" Jace asked.

"I guess," Cole said.

"All the good ones have warnings," Luri said.

Jace entered the cube and held Luri's ID card toward the door. The lighting in the cube brightened, and the arms started moving. Divided into several segments, different levels of the robotic cylinder pivoted independently. As some of the attack arms came his way wielding padded weapons, Jace ran diagonally and reached for the bag of nuts. The arm holding the treats raised them out of reach, and an arm with a padded bat struck Jace on the shoulder.

He stumbled into a second club that whacked him in the chest and should have knocked him down, but Jace grabbed hold of it just long enough to regain his balance. After releasing the club, he darted forward and snatched a candy bar from a mechanical hand.

"Not pretty," Luri said. "But he kept his feet."

An instant after he claimed the candy, a padded bat whacked Jace in the back of the head. He staggered but ducked another swing, then jumped a swift swipe at his shins. Lunging, he ripped a stuffed rabbit from a robotic grasp, then spun away from a blow to his side, barely staying on his feet.

"He should just go down," Luri said.

Cole thought the arms sped up a little. Jace tossed aside the stuffed animal and the candy bar. He dodged and weaved, reaching for prizes and barely missing them. He got battered by three padded weapons in a row and hung on to the third to keep from falling. It lifted him off his feet as two more cushioned bats swung at him. Jace dropped and crouched low just in time, holding his hands out for balance but keeping them off the ground.

"He's going to get hurt," Luri said.

Jace waded in toward the cylinder where the arms were thickest. He danced and twisted to turn some attacks from the arms into glancing blows and snagged a small, golden disk covered in shrink-wrap. Cole wondered if it might be a little CD or DVD.

As he stood near the cylinder, a bat hit Jace on the shoulder while another swept his legs from the other direction.

He flopped to the floor, and the lights dimmed. Getting up, the little golden disk still in hand, Jace collected the candy bar and the stuffed rabbit from the floor, then exited.

"Looked like human pinball," Luri said. "I get two of the prizes."

"What's this?" Jace asked, displaying the little golden disk.

"A prize file," Luri said. "You put it in a collector. You're never sure about the prize until you turn it in. A lot of the time they have credits you can load onto your card. Usually twenty or so but sometimes more."

"Take it," Jace said. He held up the other two prizes. "You want the candy bar or the rabbit?"

Luri took the rabbit. "It has more personality than a Zowie bar," she said. "You didn't do badly for an outlander, but you're going to get hurt if you keep playing like that."

"I already got hurt," Jace said, rubbing his shoulder.

"Looked kind of painful," Cole said with a wince.

Jace shrugged it off. "I've been in real fights. These are just games."

"Real fights, huh?" Luri said. "What's your story?"

"We were hoping to win a bunny," Cole said. "Now that dream is shattered."

She shook her head. "You clearly don't fit in here."

Cole felt another flash of worry—she was definitely studying them. What was she up to? Was she a potential ally or just one more person out to get them? Or was he being paranoid? She could just be a bored gamer who liked to meet people. In that case, she might be a good person to ask about the Crystal Keepers.

"What makes you say that?" Jace asked.

"You wandered in here too wide-eyed. You begged for credits to play, then you didn't put up a fight to keep the prize file. We never agreed that you had to take the worst of the three prizes, but you volunteered. And your clothes aren't quite right."

"It's because I don't have my hat yet," Jace muttered to Cole.

"Also, I've never seen you in here before, or around this part of town," Luri added.

"You know everyone who comes in here?" Cole challenged. Did that mean she was one of the good guys? The Crystal Keepers had been described as gamers. But if he was wrong, Cole knew he and Jace could end up getting arrested. At times like this he really missed his life before the Outskirts, when not everyone he met was a potential enemy.

"More or less," Luri said.

"Anyone who can spend that much time here must be rich," Jace said.

"I'm not born to it," the girl replied. "You can stretch your credits if you're good."

"I guess you could show us how it's done," Cole said, glancing toward Prize Hunter.

"Good guess," she said. She swatted Jace on the chest with the back of her hand. "You did all right for a clueless rookie. You're scrappy. Seriously, why are you guys here?"

"At Axis?" Jace asked.

"And in the city," she said.

Jace and Cole shared a look.

"Are you really good at that game?" Jace asked, indicating Prize Hunter.

"All the games," the girl answered.

"Why don't you show us?" Jace asked.

"Because I don't care if you believe me," the girl said. "Why are you guys here?"

"To play games," Jace said.

"But you didn't bring any credits," she pointed out.

"Makes it more interesting," Cole said.

"Makes it weird," the girl said. "You're outlanders; you're clueless; you're creditless. . . . Why come here?"

"Why do you care?" Jace asked.

"I pay attention to who comes and goes," she said. She patted Cole on the chest. "You want to win me something now?"

"Maybe," he said.

"Want to try Knockout!? You were checking it out earlier. I'll pay."

"Why?" Cole asked.

"I want to see how you do," she said. "Maybe I'll get another prize disk."

"You like watching us get beat up," Cole said.

"That's entertaining," she admitted. "Knockout is less brutal than Prize Hunter. It requires more finesse. One hit and you're done. You don't have to fall. And you don't have to try it."

"Let's go," Cole replied.

CHAPTER
9

ROULETTE

"Any tips?" Cole asked as they got in line for Knockout! One kid waited ahead of them.

"Too many tips would spoil the experiment," Luri said. "If you want to block an attack with your bat, you need to swing hard. The bot pushes through wimpy blocks. You probably noticed that it speeds up after you hit three targets."

Jace gave Cole his helmet and vest. "Just one prize?" Cole asked.

Luri nodded. "You have to hit all five targets to get a prize file. And if I'm paying, I keep it."

"What do I get?" Cole asked, adjusting the chin strap on his helmet.

"A free game," Luri said.

Jace held out the candy bar he won to Cole. "Want to split it?"

"Sure," Cole said, accepting the treat.

The word "ZOWIE" was printed across the foil wrapper.

Cole flipped it over and read the back:

Ingredients: Camels, microscopes, yams, hydrogen, coral reefs, mannequins, poems, comets, mousetraps, sarcasm, cacti, labyrinths; contains less than 2% uranium, cyanide, cobwebs, magma, polio

Chuckling, Cole read the ingredients aloud to Jace.

"I've never tried camel," Jace said dryly.

"The hump is the best part," Cole replied, tearing open the wrapper. Inside he found a bar made of puffed rice drenched in chocolate. Cole broke the bar and handed half to Jace.

Cole took a bite. The bar was crunchy and not very dense, but quite tasty.

Jace tried a bite as well. "I don't taste the yams."

"Or the mousetraps," Cole added.

"Have you two seriously never had a Zowie bar?" the girl asked.

"Are we that obvious?" Cole grumbled.

The kid ahead of them got hit by the robot's padded club, and the lights in the cube dimmed. He had lasted a little while by hanging back and staying defensive but hadn't struck a single target. Cole had noticed some opportunities the kid had missed.

Luri displayed her ID card. "I need yours as collateral."

Cole traded cards with her.

"Bubba?" she asked.

"It's a family name," Cole said.

"Go get that prize," Jace said. "Five targets."

"Like taking candy from a robot," Cole said, stepping into the cube. He held up Luri's ID card, the door closed, and the cube brightened. The cylindrical robot assumed a fighting position, both club-wielding arms ready.

As a bystander, Cole had seen some openings he thought he could exploit. Now that he stood facing the robot, the opportunities seemed less obvious. Those padded arms were long and agile and quick. Cole swallowed. He had once killed a cyclops. He had fought plenty of enemies with his life on the line. He should relax and have fun with this. It wasn't life or death. But Luri and Jace were watching.

He edged forward, the bat ready. He considered the five illuminated targets on the robot. The lower two might be harder to hit, which meant he should take them out early, before the robot sped up.

The robot swung at him. Cole raised his bat as if to block the club but ducked it instead, racing in close and bashing the other club aside before crouching to hit one of the lower targets.

Instead of standing his ground or backing away like the other players had, Cole raced past the robot, turning in time to slap aside the attacking clubs. The robot was really coming after him now. Minimus had given him some combat training when they were together, but Cole knew he was still no master swordsman. When both clubs came at him from opposite sides, Cole dove forward, rolled, and struck another target. As he scrambled past the robot, before he could get back on his feet, a club hit him in the back and the lights dimmed.

The blow caused him no pain. Cole was just mad to lose. At least he got a couple of targets. He had a new appreciation for the kid who tagged three just after they arrived.

"No prize?" Luri cried as Cole exited.

"Sorry," Cole said.

"It wasn't a terrible first game," Luri said. "You had some good ideas. It's hard to recover if you go to the ground."

"I'll try it," Jace offered.

Lira smirked. "You can't win this one through a willingness to take a beating."

"Maybe you should show us how it's done," Jace suggested.

Luri shrugged. "I'll show you one way." She accepted her ID card from Cole and returned his, then claimed his helmet and vest.

"Think she'll be good?" Jace asked as the door closed and the cube brightened.

"She talks like it," Cole replied. "I guess we'll see."

Luri stalked confidently toward the cylindrical robot with the bat at her side. She only raised it to deflect attacks. Her stride never sped up or slowed down. When she was close enough, without moving her feet much, she alternately hammered targets and smashed attacks away. Her padded bat swished through the air quickly and accurately: target-block-block-target-block-block-block-block-target-block-target-target.

Cole stared in astonishment. Her last three attacks were particularly quick, denying the robot any time to speed up. After she struck the last target, the robot went slack while lights pulsed and sparkled. Luri waited until a prize file emerged from the body of the robot. She retrieved it, then casually walked away.

"That was amazing," Cole gushed. "You made it look easy."

"Maybe it *is* easy," she replied.

"Come on," Jace said. "I'm sure practice helps."

Luri gave a little shrug. "Probably. Still, a lot of people never get the hang of it. The owners prefer for me to play the toughest games on the hardest settings. I could take advantage of them by winning the easier games nonstop, but then they'd ban me, so that isn't really winning. They don't mind if I beat a few easy ones now and then. It gives the other players hope."

"Are you the best player?" Cole asked.

"Nope," she said. "One of the best, maybe. The best is Trickster."

"What's the hardest game?" Jace asked.

"P'Tang," Luri said. "Want to check it out?"

"Sure," Cole said.

Luri led them across the floor, passing numerous shooting and fighting games. At large tables, players manipulated the positions of their tiny soldiers and traded taking shots at the opposing army. Others guided metal balls through three-dimensional mazes with what had to be magnetic controls. Against a side wall stretched a huge obstacle course where players risked falling into a foam pit.

"What post did you guys come from this morning?" Luri asked.

"Who cares?" Jace replied.

"I'm interested," she said. "Give me a number."

"We're trying to leave some trouble behind," Cole said, hoping the answer was vague enough that it wouldn't get them in danger but might strike a chord if she was connected to the Crystal Keepers.

"Trouble with . . . patrolmen?"

"Maybe," Jace said.

"I love that kind of trouble," Luri said cheerily. "Come on, spill. What are you guys really doing here?"

"We're just checking out the place," Jace said. "We don't want a lot of attention."

"Too late," she said. "You have mine. Go on. Talk."

Cole glanced at Jace, who looked uncertain. "What if you're spying for them?" Cole blurted.

She laughed derisively. "As if the City Patrol were smart enough to use kids! Give me a break."

"You don't like the patrolmen?" Cole asked.

She stopped walking. Her mood became serious. "What are you guys looking for? I can help you. Just tell me. Or tell me where you came from. Or what you're running from."

Cole took a deep breath and finally decided to go for it. "Have you heard of the Crystal Keepers?"

"I knew it!" Luri said, her smile wide. "What's his name?"

"Who?" Cole asked.

"The guy who got arrested," she said. "His name."

"What do you mean?" Jace asked innocently.

Luri shook her head. "It's good to be careful, but it's pointless right now. I just have to confirm this. I know his name. What is it?"

"Joe," Cole said.

"There we go," she said gratefully. "Last name?"

"You give us the last name," Cole insisted.

"I'll give you half," she said. "Mac . . ."

". . . Farland," Cole completed.

"I take it his alias was somebody Boone?" Luri asked. "And you were posing as his relatives?"

"How do you know so much?" Jace asked.

"I'm not Luri," she said. "Not any more than you're Hampton or he's Bubba. I go by Roulette." She lowered her voice. "I'm one of the Crystal Keepers."

Cole refrained from doing a happy dance.

"You're a kid," Jace said.

"And you're about to get promoted to master detective," she said, tapping him on the nose. "For the record, you're both younger than me."

Cole edged close to her and whispered, "Joe told us to come here and find the Crystal Keepers. We need to contact the Unseen."

Roulette backed away and punched his shoulder lightly. "Don't act so secretive. It draws attention."

"I keep trying to tell him," Jace said.

"Nobody cares what a couple of kids are saying at a gaming hub," Roulette said. "Unless maybe they look suspicious. Where's the girl?"

Trying not to look like he had a secret, Cole glanced at Jace.

"I'm on your side," Roulette said. "I don't know who she is. I don't need to know. All I know is she matters. This came from the top, and it came fast. The patrolmen know some kids fled when Joe was taken, but they consider it a low priority. Our leaders feel otherwise. They care more about the girl than anything."

"She's not with us," Jace said. "We scattered. I think she got away. She knows to come here."

"That's good news," Roulette said. "City Patrol hasn't picked her up. Just Joe."

"You're sure?" Jace asked.

"We have sources."

"Do you know Joe?" Cole asked.

"A little," she said. "He's from Outside. An accidental transplant to the Outskirts. Like you."

"Me?" Cole asked innocently. After a moment, he wondered, "Do you think we can help Joe?"

Roulette scratched the back of her head. "They took him to City Patrol HQ. It would be tricky."

"Where's the rest of your crew?" Jace asked.

"Around," she said. "Some of them, at least. Things have gotten complicated over the past several weeks."

"Complicated how?" Jace wondered.

"Harder to operate," Roulette said. "Some people got caught. A bunch more went deep into hiding. The Grand Shaper has been cracking down like never before."

"Sorry to hear it," Cole said.

"You didn't approach us by accident," Jace said. "You were watching for us."

Roulette batted her eyes. "Be glad I was. You two were kind of standing out."

"Is it dangerous here?" Cole asked.

"Less dangerous than most places," Roulette said. "Nowhere is safe. This is mostly a hangout for kids. The City Patrol knows kids get up to mischief sometimes, but they don't take us seriously. That's good for the resistance. We can still move around freely."

"Are all the Crystal Keepers kids?" Cole asked.

"That's the idea," Roulette said. "Maybe you can join. You've got potential. Depends what the higher-ups want. Let's check out P'Tang." She started walking.

"What about the girl?" Jace asked, staying beside her. "Should we go look for her?"

"Others are watching for her," Roulette said. "Where'd you get off the monorail?"

"Hanover Station," Jace said. "She got out at Canal."

"That's kind of far," Roulette said. "Does she have credits she can use?"

"No," Jace said.

"But she knows to come here?" she checked.

"Right," Jace said. "She knows the name of this place and the street."

"She could take lots of routes," Roulette said. "Your safest bet is to wait for her to show up here. If we go out looking, we'll probably miss her. Is she competent?"

"Yes," Jace said.

"She'll show. Let's play."

"Why do you care so much about playing?" Cole asked.

"We're at a gaming hub, genius," Roulette said. "If you want to fit in, you play games. It's a bonus of having an ID card you can use."

Against the back wall of the gaming hub, beneath a brilliant P'TANG sign, a wall of crystal let onlookers see into a series of identical rooms. Except for the transparent wall, the floors, walls, and ceilings were covered in gray panels. A number of fist-size holes pocked the floor and ceiling, and larger holes of varied sizes gaped in the far wall, labeled with numbers from twenty to one hundred.

"Here's an empty court," Roulette said, approaching a room.

From a nearby bin, Roulette claimed elbow pads, knee pads, goggles, and a pair of paddles to go with her padded vest and helmet. The long, rectangular paddles matched the color of the gray panels in the room and looked like the perfect instruments to provide a memorable spanking. The handles made Cole think of tennis rackets.

"Two paddles?" Jace asked.

"I'm a lefty, so the left one is for offense," she said. "The right is mostly for defense. But I sometimes score right-handed. In this game, you keep going until a ball hits you."

Roulette entered the room and used her ID card to close the door. She went to the center of the court, clapped her paddles together, and light flashed from a nearby hole in the floor. A ball emerged and hovered at about shoulder height. It looked to be made of black rubber and was about the size of a racquetball. Slapping the ball with her paddle, she sent it through a medium-size hole in the rear wall and fifty points appeared on her scoreboard.

After three more flashes, three more balls were in play. For every ball Roulette hit into a hole, two or three emerged. The room started to get busy. Whenever she missed a hole, the ball ricocheted around. She moved quickly and competently, scoring often. As the flurry of balls increased,

Roulette began to take fewer shots and defended herself more. She had to deal with each new ball coming at her, plus the random balls that had missed holes bouncing around. Occasionally a ball slipped through a hole by accident, increasing her score.

Before too long, a stray ball hit her leg, the lighting in the room dimmed, and all the balls in play fell to the floor, bouncing less than Cole would have expected. Her score read 1160. She left the room.

"Not my best score," Roulette said. "Not enough for a prize. But it shows you how the game is played."

"How do the balls float?" Cole asked.

"Sophisticated magnetics," she said. "P'Tang has the best tech of any game here."

"How do magnets work on rubber?" Cole asked.

"The balls have metal cores," she said. "The real magic is inside the walls and floor and ceiling. Want to try?"

"It has to take lots of practice," Cole hedged.

"Consider this your first practice," Roulette said. "It's great for hand-eye coordination, reflex conditioning, spatial awareness, multitasking—so many benefits."

"Why not?" Cole said.

She gave him her protective gear and paddles.

"Be careful not to smack the balls too hard," Roulette warned. "The magnetics are set so they never slow down. You can get in trouble fast."

"Is there a limit to how many balls can get going at once?" Cole asked.

"The court supports up to a hundred," Roulette said. "It

won't spit out more until less than a hundred are in play. I just got up to about forty. I'll be impressed if you reach ten."

"What's the most balls you've had going?" Jace asked.

"Eighty-seven," she said.

"What about Tricker?" Jace asked.

"Trickster," Roulette corrected. "He can last for a while with a hundred in play. He's tidy."

"Tidy?" Cole asked.

"You know," Roulette said. "Cool. Skilled. Tidy."

"Is he a Crystal Keeper?" Jace asked.

"One of the best," she said.

"You said he was the very best," Jace reminded her.

"At the games," Roulette said with a grin.

"I get it," Jace said. "You're the best out in the real world."

"Maybe," she mused. "You said it, not me."

With the protective gear in place, Cole held out his ID card.

"Keep yours," Roulette said, handing him hers.

"Having fun?" a voice asked from behind Cole.

Whirling, he found Dalton and Mira standing there. "You made it!" Cole exclaimed, a heavy weight of anxiety lifting.

Dalton grinned. "I was worried you might be looking for us. I'm glad you got to play some sweet games."

Cole looked down at his gear and his paddles. "I was just blending in."

Dalton looked him up and down. "This is probably the only place in the world where that outfit would seem normal."

Cole smiled. "You guys made good time!"

"We came together," Mira said. "We found each other as we left the station."

"Mira is brilliant," Dalton said. "After we figured out how the levcars work, she told an older guy out on the street that we were supposed to meet our parents at Hanover Station but used up our credits going to the wrong place. He let us ride with him to Hanover, then we came here."

"You got to ride in one of those cars!" Cole exclaimed.

"It was freaky," Dalton said. "It seems like you're always about to crash."

"You guys are okay?" Cole checked.

"We got away fine," Dalton said. "No real trouble."

A boy and girl stood with them who Cole hadn't met yet. They both looked fourteen or fifteen. "This is Bluff and Dazzle," Roulette explained.

Bluff had his hair shaved short and stood half a head taller than Jace. He looked serious and tough. Dazzle had a dark complexion, fair hair, and light eyes. She was built short and strong, like a gymnast.

"More Crystal Keepers?" Cole asked.

Bluff gave a small nod. "Call us CKs in public."

"We're supposed to take her straight to zerobase," Dazzle said.

"I heard," Roulette replied. "They're not kidding about her. I wonder who she is?"

"I'm right here!" Mira complained.

"Don't tell us," Bluff said hurriedly.

"I won't," Mira said.

"We're not supposed to ask," Bluff explained. "You guys are top secret."

"Don't look," Roulette said. "But we're being watched."

"Who?" Dazzle asked with a casual smile.

"Undercover City Patrol," Roulette said. "He's up on the platform behind me. I've seen him before. Definitely CP. He's pretending to watch a game of Smashball."

Cole glanced up and briefly met eyes with a blond man on a platform a good distance across the room. The man turned and walked down a flight of stairs.

"Bubba," Roulette whispered loudly. "I told you not to look. He knows we made him!"

Cole shriveled inside but tried not to let it show. The glance had been automatic as Roulette described the patrolman's position. But what a stupid mistake! He should have followed Roulette's instructions!

"Get out of here," Bluff said. "Take separate levcars to zerobase. Dazzle will take the girl and Dalton. I'll run interference."

Bluff split off, heading toward the blond man. Roulette led the others in the opposite direction, across the gaming floor.

"Did you see him?" Roulette asked Dazzle.

"His reflection," Dazzle said, holding up a small cosmetic mirror.

"Have you noticed him before?" Roulette asked.

"First time," Dazzle said.

"He was probably following you," Roulette said. "I know his face and didn't see him until you guys showed up. Cole, lose your gear, we're about to go out a side door."

Cole started fumbling with the straps of the pads he had just put on. He felt flustered and off-balance. Dalton and Jace helped him as they walked.

As they reached a door marked EMPLOYEES ONLY, Cole pulled off his helmet, the final piece of gear.

"Drop the stuff," Roulette advised as she opened the door.

Cole, Jace, and Dalton dumped the pads and paddles on the ground beside the door and followed the others through. Roulette and Dazzle broke into a run. Cole ran his hardest, trying to keep up.

They passed through another door onto a sidewalk beside a street. A busy stream of levcars zoomed by.

Dazzle glanced over at Roulette. "You have an untraceable ID?"

"Always," Roulette said.

Dazzle put on a cap and a pair of sunglasses. "Use it."

10

GOOGOL

Cole found riding in a levcar even more nerve-racking than Dalton had conveyed. The ride was reasonably smooth, but Cole wasn't used to cars crowding so tightly at high speeds, nor was he accustomed to vehicles working together with split-second precision to narrowly avoid accidents.

Sitting in the back beside Jace, Cole needed some time before he began to trust that the system actually worked. Over and over he braced himself for impacts that never came. When he closed his eyes, the ride seemed surprisingly uneventful, but that felt like cheating. As Cole got used to the experience with his eyes open, the overall synchronization made him think of a flock of birds or a swarm of bees.

Mira and Dalton had gone in one direction to get a levcar with Dazzle. Cole and Jace had gone the other way with Roulette, who summoned a levcar using an ID without a face on it. They had now been in the car for at least ten minutes, and Cole had seen no sign of Bluff or the blond patrolman.

"Did we get away clean?" Cole asked.

"I think so," Roulette said. "We'll take extra precautions to make sure."

"Do you think Bluff fought that patrolman?" Cole asked, his insides writhing with guilt.

"As a last resort, maybe," Roulette said. "Hopefully he found a quieter solution. Bluff will be okay. He knows what he's doing."

Cole tried to let her confidence reassure him. They rode along in silence for a few minutes. Cole studied the neighboring levcars for anything suspicious, but the windows were too tinted to see much. At least that same tinting would help them hide.

"What do you think?" Cole asked Jace, who had his nose against the window.

"This city is enormous," he said. "I was ready for big, but I still can't believe it. I didn't expect it to be so clean, with so many open spaces. I pictured it more cramped."

"What about the ride?" Cole asked.

"You can't beat it," Jace said. "They're so fast. They blow away autocoaches."

Cole gritted his teeth as levcars swerved at them from opposite directions. Their levcar sped up and drifted right just in time to avoid disaster. "Don't the near misses bug you?"

"They told us levcars don't crash," Jace said.

"Not in over eight years," Roulette said. "And before then problems weren't frequent. They've been perfected."

"I can trust that," Jace said. "Can't you?"

Cole resisted a wince as they knifed through a narrow

gap. "There's what I know, and what I feel. We have cars where I'm from, but there would be accidents all over the place if people drove like this."

"You keep advertising that you're from Outside," Roulette said.

"Whoops," Cole replied.

"I won't spread it around," Roulette said. "You're not the only person from Outside in Zeropolis. Only Creon interacts more with Earth. But Outsiders do draw attention. If you want to keep a low profile, you should be more careful. We're almost to the galleria."

Up ahead, a complex of sizable buildings that looked like greenhouses came into view. The levcar slowed and drifted over to the curb, coming to a gentle stop. Cole, Jace, and Roulette got out.

"Greenhouses?" Cole asked.

"Stores," Roulette said. "It's a shopping mall."

"All the buildings must be crystal," Cole said.

Roulette gave him a puzzled look. "What else would they be made from?"

"Glass," Cole said.

She chuckled. "Seriously? Why would we build with something so fragile? Bonded crystal is the way to go. If you want glass, you'll have to look in some other kingdom."

"These are all stores?" Jace checked as they started walking. "Have you heard of Headgear?"

"Sure," Roulette said. "It's not here. I'm not interested in the stores today. We came for the crowd. I want to make sure we shook the CP. The Zeroes have gotten too good at tracking us lately. We're taking a roundabout route. We can't risk compromising the base."

"Zeroes?" Cole asked.

"It's a nickname for the patrolmen," she said. "The Zeroes have been on a roll lately. We can't be too careful. Let's wait to go into it until we're behind closed doors."

As they proceeded through the crystal mall, Cole saw a lot of people wearing leather and denim. Many of the stores featured gadgets. Others sold clothes. A few had art. One shop showcased a variety of robots. They looked more polished than the robots back at Outpost 121, with brighter colors and more graceful contours.

They passed beyond the crystal stores and came to an open green area with a fairly tall hill on one side. A game of lacrosse was in progress on a large playing field. Trees shaded much of the hill, and paths gave access to the top.

"Summit Park," Roulette said. "Crossing open space can be a great way to make sure we're not being tailed."

"Are we close to where we're going?" Jace asked.

"Not yet," she said.

It took some time to navigate the park. Eventually they passed under a street and came up to a wide pedestrian walkway. The apartments on both sides of the walkway possessed stately brick facades. Trees and sculpted hedges added a touch of nature.

Roulette led them along the walkway a good distance, passing under two more streets before turning onto a smaller walkway. She paused at the entrance to a building. "Nobody is following us. This way."

They entered the building and went down a hall to an apartment on the first floor. The big guy who answered the door nodded to Roulette and let them enter. They went to a bedroom without windows and found a stairway in the middle of the floor.

"I opened it up for the others," the man said, coming in behind them. "Go on down. I'll close it behind you."

The stairs descended a long way, flight after flight. Roulette was in no hurry.

"Nice secret entrance," Cole said.

"Let's hope it stays secret," Roulette replied. "Otherwise we're all cooked."

At the bottom of the stairs awaited a thick crystal door secured by shiny steel hinges. Roulette waved at the guards on the far side, and after a moment, the door opened. Cole entered with the others, and the door closed behind them.

The floor, walls, and ceiling had panels like in the P'Tang room at Axis. Cole sped up to walk beside Roulette. "Is this room magnetic?" he asked.

"We have some skilled tinkers on our side," she said. "Our magnetic defenses are tidy. Think of the balls in P'Tang, but imagine them sharper, faster, and targeted at you."

Cole gulped.

They proceeded through a sequence of doors and hallways until they were greeted by a middle-aged woman whose red hair was pulled back into a tight little bun. "You must be Jace and Cole," she said, holding out a hand.

Cole shook it. "I'm Cole."

Jace did the same. "Jace."

"Call me Highwire," the woman said. "Nice work, Roulette. Report to the tank for debriefing."

"I was kind of hoping to see this through," Roulette said.

"You may have future involvement," Highwire said. "First these two must meet with Googol."

Roulette gasped. "Googol's here! I want to see him!"

"I expect he'll want to talk with all the CKs who were involved today," Highwire said. "First head to debriefing. You'll learn more there."

"Whatever," Roulette said huffily. She left the room.

"I trust you two are all right?" Highwire asked.

"We're fine," Cole said. "We're worried about Joe, though."

"Aren't we all," Highwire said. "This way."

She used an ID card to open a door. They followed her down a hallway to another door, which she opened with her card as well.

"Here they are," Highwire announced. "Barely behind the others."

Cole and Jace entered a room that looked half laboratory, half office. One side of the room had work counters and shelves covered with diverse tools and materials. The other side had several chairs and a big desk. Dalton and Mira sat in two of the chairs.

The man behind the desk stood up. Dressed in dark blue, his bristly gray hair was clipped short and thinning on top. The bulky glasses he wore resembled a set of high-tech binoculars. Tall, skinny, and slightly stooped, he looked to be in his fifties or sixties. "Cole, Jace, please join us. Nice to meet you. I'm Googol."

"Will that be all?" Highwire asked.

"Yes, Larraine, thank you," Googol said. She backed out and closed the door. Googol touched his bulky glasses. "Please forgive how my vision gear hides my face. With it, I can see near and far. Without it, the world becomes overlapping blurs. Have a seat."

"Are you guys good?" Cole asked Dalton.

"We just got here too," Dalton said. "We're good."

"Googol was introducing himself," Mira said.

Googol nodded. "I gave Mira a code word reserved for those few who work with her mother, Harmony."

"Dalton got to hear it?" Cole protested.

"He whispered it to her," Dalton said.

"Googol is one of the good guys," Mira confirmed.

"Thank you, Your Highness," Googol said deferentially. "I can still hardly believe you're here."

"He's one of the leaders of the Unseen in Zeropolis," Mira said. "He's their chief tinker."

"We all have roles to play," Googol said. "Mine involves developing and implementing advanced technologies."

"Your name is Google like the search engine?" Cole asked.

Googol smiled. "It's spelled differently. My code name derives from a number. Ten to the hundredth power. In other words, a one followed by a hundred zeroes."

"That's a lot of zeroes," Jace said.

Googol's smile faltered a little. "My apologies. I'm not always adept at small talk. I know you four have been through a lot, but we have some vital matters to discuss."

"Fine with us," Mira said.

"The first issue is Joe MacFarland," Googol said. "We sent him to warn you, Mira, when we learned that your father was sending legionnaires to apprehend you. I take it the intervention was a success."

"Barely," Mira said. She went on to explain how she, Cole, Jace, and Twitch had escaped from Skyport.

"Remarkable," Googol said. "But Joe clearly rejoined you."

Mira told about defeating Carnag and then going to Elloweer with Joe to find Honor.

"Any success?" Googol asked.

"We found her, and stopped another monster shapecrafters had made in Elloweer. Her name was Morgassa, and she was even worse than Carnag. We also found Cole's friend Dalton."

"You're both from Outside," Googol said, his vision gear aiming at Dalton and Cole. "Where did you live?"

"Arizona," Cole said. "Mesa, if you know the area."

"I do," Googol said. "I study your world a lot. It didn't used to interest us so much. For centuries our technologies have been more advanced than yours. But over the last few decades, as you have entered your computerized age, I have found many good ideas among your innovations. I find that inspiration often results from observation."

"In our world we call that copying," Dalton said with a smile.

"I attempt to adapt and improve those technologies that inspire me," Googol said. His vision gear swiveled back to Mira. "These shapecrafted monsters you describe perturb me. We have heard similar tales of late from Creon and Necronum, though none in our own kingdom. You say the shapecrafters could not command their creations?"

"Not Carnag or Morgassa," Mira said. "I don't know if they're getting better at it."

Googol raised two fingers to his lips and stared thoughtfully. The lenses of his vision gear turned softly, as if focusing. "How close has your father come to capturing you?"

"Close," Mira said. She told about the Hunter chasing them and detailed their encounters with Enforcers in Sambria and on the Red Road.

"The Hunter is formidable," Googol said broodingly. "And you encountered his Enforcers in Elloweer scant days ago?"

"Yes," Mira said.

Googol rubbed his chin. "Honor didn't join you after defeating Morgassa?"

"No," Mira said. "She went to find another of my sisters. I came here with Joe to look for Constance."

Googol frowned. "Joe knows that you're here looking for Constance. He also knows that Honor is off hunting for another sister. Does he know where she went?"

"Yes," Mira said.

Googol nodded slowly. "Don't tell me where unless I need to know. We must do a better job of restricting information. Joe knows too much. I'm not sure if the City Patrol fully grasps yet what they have in him."

"Maybe they won't figure it out," Mira said. "Joe is smart and committed."

"The Hunter is on your trail," Googol said. "It won't take him long to find Joe. We can't risk Joe breaking. He's a good man, and a brave one, but I would not trust anyone to last against the Hunter. Even without the Hunter, there is the chance the City Patrol will catch on to Joe's value. You were seen with him, Mira. Your image is on an ID card. If they connect Joe to you, they'll torture him without mercy until he talks. We have to take him away from them. It's not just a matter of loyalty. It's a strategic necessity."

"Can you do it?" Mira asked.

"I believe so," Googol replied. "Not without cost. We have a few remaining ways to monitor City Patrol communications. One method is thanks to good tech, plus, we still have a couple of people inside. We used to enjoy a much bigger advantage. The government had all the power, but we kept really good tabs on them and could stay out of their way. We could truly be Unseen."

"What happened?" Cole asked.

Googol smiled sadly. "We're not sure. Starting about two months ago, things changed. Some of our best people got busted. Smart, careful operatives who really knew the game. Within weeks, the Unseen lost nearly a quarter of our number. Secure, time-tested hideouts were discovered. Proven methods of operation no longer worked. The government didn't just have all the power. Suddenly they were outmaneuvering us."

"Did you fix the problem?" Jace asked.

"In a sense," Googol said. "Most of the Unseen retreated to our hideaways in Old Zeropolis. We took ourselves out of play."

"Old Zeropolis?" Cole asked.

"A brief history for the Outsiders," Googol announced. "Zeropolis has been built twice before. Originally, long ago and far from here, Zeropolis arose with much less advanced technology. Innovation eventually made the first Zeropolis obsolete. The foundations were all wrong to welcome the new tech. It made more sense to start again. So a new Zeropolis, the second Zeropolis, what we now call Old Zeropolis, was established not terribly far beyond the northern boundaries of this city. That city fell when Aeronomatron took over. Hundreds of thousands of lives were lost."

"Who took over?" Dalton asked.

"A machine," Googol said. "A supercomputer that would dwarf anything your society has produced. Most people just call it Aero. This was in my grandfather's time, and I'm older than I look, thanks to my shaping skills slowing the aging process. After much bloodshed, the City Patrol managed to seal off Aero. Had they failed, this entire kingdom might have become uninhabitable."

"Crazy," Cole said.

Googol rocked forward in his seat. "To this day, Aero controls a major portion of Old Zeropolis. At great cost, all of its manufacturing capabilities were destroyed, so the computer's domain is fixed. After the mayhem Aero caused, nobody wanted to live near it, so the newest Zeropolis, this one, was erected not far from the old. After the second city was left abandoned for a good while, some people began to return. The kind of people who didn't want to be found. Old Zeropolis is a lawless place, almost completely unregulated.

Someday the Zeropolitan government hopes to purge or reclaim the old city, but they haven't geared up for it yet. For now, the Grand Shaper lets it serve as a garbage dump for undesirables."

"Is Old Zeropolis mostly members of the Unseen?" Cole asked.

"Oh, no," Googol said. "It's mostly criminals. In a highly regulated kingdom, it's the most significant beacon of chaos. When operating there, we have to tread warily. But at the moment it's preferable to the city. The government has little influence there."

"Are we safe here?" Jace asked, looking around the room.

"I hope so," Googol said. "As a defensive tactic, I move around a lot. This is currently our most secure base of operations inside the city. But we don't know how Abram Trench and his people keep finding us. I worry they're using banned tactics."

"Like what?" Cole asked.

"In Old Zeropolis, they let Aero control too much," Googol explained. "When the computer went bad, it had access to everything. Information. Communication. Essential services. Vehicles. Bots. You name it. Nobody wants another Aero, so the current Zeropolitan government has been very careful about not automating the city too much. None of the bots are armed. There are no surveillance cameras or automatic listening devices. Unconnected computers run different systems. For example, the computer that manages the magroads cannot communicate with the computers regulating the power facilities, or the computer that holds the ID card data, or any of the bots."

"But now you wonder if Abram Trench is cheating," Dalton said.

"Precisely," Googol said. "He doesn't want another Aero either. He definitely wants to call the shots, not bow down to a computer. But to deal with us, he may have decided to bend the laws that have been in place since the founding of this city. Added some surveillance systems. Upgraded some bots. Who knows? It might explain how the City Patrol has suddenly become so effective."

"It could be a spy," Jace proposed.

"We've examined that possibility thoroughly," Googol said. "We keep our information fragmented and compartmentalized. Given all that has happened, I simply don't know who the mole could be. My guess is either they've found a way to reliably intercept our communications, or they have new tech in place. We've been implementing all the precautions we can think of, including improved communication methods and taking extra care when navigating the city."

"And using arcade kids," Cole said.

"The Crystal Keepers have existed for years," Googol said. "Many of them eventually graduate to membership in the Unseen. The government can't find us where they're not looking, and while many of our covers have been blown, our teenage agents remain undetected. They get underestimated because of their youth, and we use that against Abram."

"Did Bluff get away?" Dalton asked.

Cole held his breath.

"Yes," Googol said. "He took out the City Patrol agent with a sleeping dart and got away clean."

Cole relaxed and breathed again. At least his mistake hadn't caused major harm.

"Using kids like that will only work until the government catches on," Mira said.

"Which is why I'm reluctant to overuse them," Googol said. "Over these past couple of months, many of our top spies have been exposed. Several of the key technologies we rely on have been discovered and thwarted. I hesitate to use what limited resources remain to spring Joe. It could inspire City Patrol to ferret out our last assets. But the alternative is more dangerous still."

"Because of how much Joe knows," Dalton said.

"It's his knowledge of Stafford's daughters," Googol said. "Our sources in Junction report that finding the five princesses is now the High Shaper's uppermost priority. It makes more sense now that I know Miracle and Honor both have reclaimed their powers. Stafford is panicking. He's bringing all of his resources to bear. What he currently lacks is concrete knowledge of their whereabouts."

"If Joe breaks under torture . . . ," Mira said.

"His information becomes a lightning rod," Googol said. "The High Shaper will bring his full strength against the Unseen in Zeropolis right when we're reeling. It could mark the end of the resistance here. On the other hand, if we can find Constance and help you avoid detection, Mira, we could revitalize the revolution. It's going to be all or nothing. The first step will be to retrieve Joe."

"Any idea where to find Constance?" Mira asked hopefully.

"Not yet," Googol said. "None of us knew about you girls

until your mother confided in a few of us earlier this year. When Stafford began to lose his powers, she knew the time was approaching to bring her daughters out of hiding, and she needed allies. I only recently learned how your mother can track your locations. Do your friends know?"

"Yes," Mira said.

"I found out about the stars when Harmony asked us to send someone to help you, Mira. Your mother has still never asked us to seek out any of her other daughters, though we were led to believe that Constance is hiding somewhere in Zeropolis. I will confess that I have been quietly searching on my own, but she is well concealed. I have no clue as to her whereabouts."

"She could be anywhere?" Mira asked.

"I have found no record of her," Googol said. "Constance may have found shelter out in the empty wastes of Zeropolis. She could have an obscure hideout here in the city, or even in Old Zeropolis. For all I know, she might have moved to another kingdom. Only your mother knows for sure, but she has not yet shared that knowledge with us."

"Can we contact my mother?" Mira asked.

"Not with a communicator," Googol said. "Those signals don't carry out of the kingdom. Not even into Junction, where all forms of shaping work to some degree. For sensitive matters, our contact has been through live messengers. Our last interaction came when she asked us to send Joe to help you."

"Could we send a messenger to her?" Mira asked.

Googol became grave. "It would require the utmost

caution. Particularly in the current climate, with your father raging, and the Zeropolitan government closing in, such a messenger represents a great deal of risk. An intercepted messenger could ruin us and your mother together. Your father still doesn't know she was responsible for hiding you girls all these years."

Mira rubbed her forehead. "It's never easy."

"Seldom, lately," Googol said. "But that doesn't mean we won't try. We just have to make smart moves. Abram Trench would love nothing more than to get his hands on you, Mira."

"Why'd he side with the High Shaper?" Cole asked. "The other Grand Shapers rebelled and went into hiding. What made Abram loyal to Mira's dad?"

"I know Abram Trench well," Googol said. "I served as his chief technical adviser for many years. Abram was seduced by the advantages of siding with Stafford. Abram Trench has no real loyalty to anyone besides Abram Trench. The better I came to know him, the more he brought me into his confidence, the more I feared him. Eventually it led to me quitting and joining the resistance."

"What gave him away?" Cole pursued.

"The technology he withholds," Googol said. "I want everyone in Zeropolis to benefit from our innovations. The citizens of Zeropolis could have television, their own Internet, private communicators, and more. But free communication is an enemy to control. So mass communication is heavily limited. Extensive restrictions also apply to individual communicators. Abram has all but eliminated private forms of transportation in the city, and he's always looking for ways to reduce and track vehicles in the outposts. The list goes on. Abram works hardest to create tech and establish policies that will increase his personal advantage. The longer I worked with him, the better I understood the absolute control he wishes to achieve. I realized he has to be stopped."

"You mentioned he'd love to get Mira," Jace said.

"Abram Trench is a master politician," Googol said. "With how badly the High Shaper wants his daughters back, if Abram could find any of them, he would use the opportunity to create enormous leverage to further his aims."

"What does he want most?" Mira asked.

"Abram desires complete control of Zeropolis," Googol said. "He doesn't care about the other kingdoms. And he doesn't mind being polite to the High King if it means he can function as dictator here. Abram adores innovation, and his ambition knows no boundaries."

"You were his main techie guy?" Dalton asked.

"It was a position of great influence," Googol said. "I'll humbly admit to being one of the most talented tinkers and technomancers in the kingdom. But I'm not Abram's equal. The man is truly gifted. Whether he means to use those gifts for the common good is where I harbor my doubts."

"My father works with too many men like that," Mira said. "We'll stop him. The first step is to free Joe?"

"Yes," Googol said, his demeanor changing from thoughtful to businesslike. "Our opportunity will come tomorrow. He is currently at City Patrol Headquarters. He'll be transferred to a holding area. I believe we will be able to gather enough details to intercept Joe en route. The City Patrol will then have proof that we're still listening. If we succeed, such a bold crime will invite retaliation."

A soft *ping, ping, ping* began to chime. It made Cole think of the ding he sometimes heard in elevators.

Googol's face froze. "No," he whispered. "Not now."

"What is it?" Mira asked.

"That's the alarm," he said, his voice detached. "Highest alert. This base has been compromised. We're under attack."

11

CONTINGENCY PLANS

"Please tell us you're joking," Jace said.

"Sadly, no," Googol said, standing up as the pinging continued. He didn't seem too anxious, but he began to speak more quickly. "Something about the way we brought you in or monitored Joe's arrest must have given up our location." He gathered equipment off the desk. "It's a blow. This was our last fully equipped base of operations in the city."

"Do you have an escape plan?" Mira asked.

"I always have contingency plans," Googol said, removing a few small black boxes from a drawer and pocketing them. "Otherwise they would have nabbed me long ago. Here at zerobase, we have excellent defenses to slow any intruders."

Cole relaxed a little. Apparently it wasn't time to run for their lives yet. "You have secret ways out?" he checked.

"We regularly use three ways into the base from the surface," Googol said. "We've reserved three different ways out for emergencies. All who work here know about one of them, a smaller circle knows about the second, and only two other people know the route we'll use." Googol came around the desk and went to the worktables. "Would you four mind helping me carry a few things?"

Cole, Dalton, Jace, and Mira hurried after Googol. They wove around the worktables as he picked up objects and handed them over. He gave them several crystals and a variety of gadgets.

Among other things, Cole received a short tube of dark metal. Googol unscrewed a cap at the base to reveal a button. "Keep that button covered," Googol said, replacing the cap. "Do not press it unless you are pointing the other end at your worst enemy."

"I want one," Jace whimpered.

"Don't worry," Googol assured him. "I have plenty of volatile toys."

Highwire returned to the room holding what looked like an extra-large trapgun. Behind her came Roulette and a fairly tall teenage boy with Asian features. Both carried smaller trapguns.

"If you're ready, we should go," Highwire said.

"The evacuation?" Googol asked, still sweeping the worktables with his mechanized eyewear.

"In progress," she said. "First lines of defense holding strong."

Googol picked up a couple more devices. "I was tidying up."

"Tidy," Highwire said with a smirk.

"You sound like a CK," Googol replied, shaking his head.

"That's a compliment," the Asian teen said. "Good to see you, Googol."

"Hello, Trickster, Roulette," Googol murmured, stepping away from the table. "Nice of you to join us."

Cole took a second look at the teen after hearing him addressed as the gaming-hub champ. The boy looked relaxed and friendly.

"Why do we always see you when the sky is falling?" Trickster asked.

"Damage control is the story of my life," Googol replied, striding toward the door. "Let's go."

The soft tone kept pinging as they left the room and walked briskly down the hall. Googol led the way. Highwire brought up the rear, her giant trapgun held ready.

"What does this mean, losing the base?" Roulette asked as they walked.

"It hurts us," Googol said. "I can't say I'm shocked, given the events of the past couple of months. We're missing something. Until we figure out what, this will keep happening. We'll have to get by with our smaller safe areas and less activity until we solve this."

"Won't less activity make this harder to solve?" Trickster asked.

"You begin to understand our predicament," Googol muttered.

Roulette turned to Cole. "Not a long stay at the base."

"Nope," Cole responded, concentrating on not dropping anything, especially the weapon. The gear wasn't too heavy, but there were too many items to carry them comfortably.

"You're the gaming-hub expert," Jace said to Trickster.

"Somebody has to do it," Trickster said. He glanced at Mira. "And you're our top secret guest."

"Sorry if I caused this," Mira said.

"It's not your fault," Googol said. "I don't believe they're aware of your identity yet. It's either our sloppiness, or City Patrol's excellence. Maybe a little of both."

The group went through a couple of doors. Cole didn't see any other people. The only sound besides the polite alarm was their footsteps. Without anybody talking to distract him, it seemed like a fire drill at an empty school.

Googol stopped at a thick door of tinted crystal set in a metal wall and handed some of his gear to Trickster. Then Googol inserted a small, clear cube into a square socket. The crystal door slid upward.

They passed through the doorway, and Googol hit a button that shut the door. He walked to a round socket in the wall and placed a crystal sphere inside. A section of the wall opened to reveal a smaller room. They all entered, Googol pressed a button, the wall closed, and the little room sank.

"An elevator," Dalton said.

"A sender," Jace corrected.

After some time descending, the wall opened again. A large lab waited beyond, brightly lit, with crystal worktables and no people.

A humanoid robot stepped into view from off to the side, standing a bit taller than Googol. Its yellow, rounded contours left it bulky through the chest and shoulders, but more slender in the legs and arms. The only features of the smooth face were a pair of glowing eyes protected by a tinted crystal panel.

Cole felt somewhat intimidated. It looked like the robotic version of a linebacker. If it attacked in this close space, Cole wasn't sure what they could do.

"Welcome, Googol," the robot said in a male voice so natural that Cole wondered whether it could actually be a person in a costume. "The password, please."

"Green pastures," Googol said.

"The guests are here on your authority?" the robot inquired.

"Correct," Googol replied. "The key elements have been removed?"

"Everything besides me and the little guy," the robot said.

Googol started walking across the lab. The robot fell into step at his side. The others followed. Twisting so he could point out the people he named, Googol said, "This is Cole, Jace, Dalton, and Secret. They deserve top priority protection, with Secret at the tip-top. You know the others."

"Pleased to meet you all," the robot said. "Especially you, Secret. I'm Outlaw."

"Why are you called Outlaw?" Googol asked theatrically.

"My existence contradicts the AI Accords," Outlaw answered.

"Freebots are illegal," Googol explained, still walking. "Here in Zeropolis, we were skilled at constructing adaptive neural networks long before earthlings had dreamed of BASIC. We can make very smart machines. Extremely lifelike, if not actually alive. Which led to Aeronomatron and the fall of Old Zeropolis. As a consequence, the AI Accords were adopted, limiting the use of artificial intelligence.

147

Machines with AI are not permitted mobility, are forbidden access to weapons, and their communication with other thinking machines is limited and strictly monitored."

"I break all of those rules," Outlaw said with smug relish.

"Working outside the system should include some advantages," Googol said, pausing at a gleaming steel door and pressing a cube into a socket. The door slid upward. "Outlaw is one of them." He paused. "Don't get me wrong. I don't want another Aero either. But to fight a strong enemy, we need strong allies. Besides, you're not going to try to conquer Zeropolis, are you, Outlaw?"

"Like I'd tell you," the robot replied.

"He has attitude," Googol said, leading them into the room.

"Learned it from the Crystal Keepers," Outlaw said.

"That's right!" Trickster said, slapping the big robot on the arm.

Cole entered a room with a few benches and a worktable. Tall, metal lockers lined the walls.

"We're suited up," Roulette said. "Do we need more?"

"Not you," Googol said. "Them. They're in deep. This base failed them. We need to help them protect themselves."

"Or kill themselves," Trickster said. "Or give themselves away. Is this a good idea?"

"It is if you help them," Googol said. "They'll need a crash course in safety." He tapped a button on his vision gear. "We have time. The defenses are holding nicely."

"Sorry I'm late," said a little robot, the voice male but much less manly than Outlaw's. "I was making sure the last of the bots got away." Barely taller than Cole's waist, it had a body the shape of a gumdrop, green with white highlights, though it looked a bit banged up and scratched. The robot scuttled on six insectile legs, each with a rubbery hoof at the end. Several small sensors poked out of the top, above three glassy eyes. It pulled a cart.

"This is Sidekick," Outlaw said. "He's, well, my sidekick."

"Not everyone can be the hero," Sidekick said good-naturedly. "I'm really good at sanitizing, though." As with Outlaw, Cole was struck by how lifelike the voice sounded.

"Don't be fooled by his modesty," Googol said. "Sidekick's AI is just as sophisticated as Outlaw's, though I housed it in the shell of a used cleaning bot."

"What I lack in size, I make up for in dents," Sidekick said brightly.

"Please place the items we brought from my office on Sidekick's cart," Googol said, taking his own advice. Cole and the others added their items as well.

"You mentioned giving us something?" Jace prompted.

"We detoured here to equip the four of you with exo rigs," Googol said. "Subtle exoskeletons that hide under your clothes but will enhance just about every physical attribute you possess. They fall far short of a full battle suit, but can still be extremely useful. The Crystal Keepers use them routinely."

"Wait a minute," Jace said, turning to Roulette, eyes narrowing. "You're wearing one now?"

"Yeah," she replied. "Almost always."

"No wonder you're so good at those games!" Jace cried.

"The rigs aren't a replacement for skill," Trickster stated adamantly. "If anything, they require more control. You have to learn to work with the suit, and to understand the limits. With rigs you can run faster, jump higher, react quicker, and survive more damage. But you can also wreck more spectacularly. And you can give yourself away. Unless you lost a limb or need them for other medical reasons, people aren't supposed to wear mechanical augmentations."

"All true," Googol said. "Might we suit them up as we continue? We're still under attack." He walked toward some of the lockers against the wall. "Lockers one through four. I deliberately had the prep bots leave our newest model in the appropriate sizes. Those who know the drill, pick somebody to help."

"The outer defenses are about to fall in sector five," Outlaw reported.

"We still have time," Sidekick said.

Highwire went to Mira, Googol helped Dalton, Trickster assisted Jace, and Roulette brought a bundle of gear over to Cole. The gear didn't look like much—mostly narrow strips of pliable steel. Highwire led Mira out of the room to change.

"Shirt off," Roulette said. "And your pants. Pretend you're going swimming."

Trying to act casual about it, Cole stripped down to his boxer shorts. It was like a visit to the doctor, right? If the doctor was about fourteen, cute, confident, stylish, and awesome at arcade games.

Roulette did nothing to make him feel uncomfortable. She strapped a fairly large brace to his torso, Cole fastened another to his pelvis, then Roulette attached smaller braces to his elbows, knees, and ankles. It didn't take long. None of the braces were bulky, and all were connected by flexible metallic strips that squirmed against his skin with a life of their own. As the exoskeleton adjusted, Cole could feel it gripping his entire body.

"Careful how you move," Roulette warned. "The rig is smart. It'll work with you if you let it, but sudden, unpredictable motion can confuse it. Keep your movements controlled. Nothing extreme. Don't run or jump."

Cole started walking. It was strange to feel the exoskeleton assisting him. Back at his home in Mesa, when he walked up the stairs in front of his dad, his father would sometimes grab the back of his thighs just above the knees and help push his legs up the steps. This was similar, but as he experimented, the exo rig seemed to cover every movement of his arms and legs.

"Get dressed," Roulette said.

Cole obeyed. None of the new equipment was bulky enough to make it tough to put his clothes back on. Mira returned to the room. Jace and Dalton got their clothes in place too.

"No wrists, gloves, or helmets?" Trickster checked.

"Correct," Googol said. "This needs to be covert. The rigs are just an emergency precaution."

"Okay," Trickster said, raising his voice a bit. "I want each of you to try a little hop. Just enough to get you past your tiptoes."

Cole bent his knees and did a gentle hop. He went higher

than expected, as if he had caught somebody's bounce on a trampoline.

"If you jump hard, you'll hit the ceiling," Trickster said. "Try a little higher than the first hop."

Cole glanced at Dalton, who grinned from ear to ear. "These are like training wheels for life," his friend said.

Turning his eyes toward the ceiling, Cole saw that it had to be fifteen feet overhead. Could he really touch it? That would mean he could slam-dunk a basketball! Where were these rigs during PE?

Jace shot up into the air, stretching for the ceiling and coming just short. Dalton did a more modest jump, but his feet still went a little higher than Cole's head. Mira went higher than Dalton but not as high as Jace.

Cole didn't want Jace teasing him, so he tried a pretty strong jump. The ceiling came at him fast, forcing him to use his hands to absorb the impact. Fortunately, the exo rig helped brace his effort. Then he fell back down, scared about how he would land, but the rig assisted there, too. It was like his legs had shocks now. Good ones.

"Follow directions, Cole," Jace mocked.

"Whoa, you okay?" Dalton asked, coming to Cole's side. "For a minute there, it looked like you were planning to find your own way to the surface."

"I'm good," Cole said, feeling a little shaky. "I wasn't expecting so much power."

"You squatted pretty deep before you jumped," Trickster said. "The rig read that you really wanted some altitude."

"The outer defenses have been breached in sector five,"

Outlaw said. "Sectors one and three won't hold much longer."

"Keep going, Trickster," Googol said. "They need the basics."

"Okay," Trickster said. "When you walk or run with normal strides, the rig won't push hard like when you jump. It'll flow with you. But you'll find your top speed higher and your ability to change direction enhanced. You'll get the feel by experimenting. Now, just with your arms, throw some punches. Don't actually hit anything. Beat up the air."

Cole punched and felt the exo rig moving with him, increasing the force of his blow. He looked over at Dalton who had both hands going really fast—leftrightleftrightleftright. Cole tried it and found he could do the same thing.

"See, Cole and Dalton?" Roulette asked. "Experiment with quickness. You can be faster. Your reaction time isn't quicker, but once you start moving, everything is sped up. Try karate moves. Have fun with it."

Cole did imaginary blocks and turns and punches. He loved the feel of his new speed and the power behind his movements.

"Now the bad news," Trickster said. "If you go punch a crystal wall right now as hard as you can, your finger bones will turn to dust. Punch somebody in the face, and you'll hurt them, but you'll also probably break your hand. Cole almost gave us a demonstration. If he hadn't used his arms against the ceiling when he jumped, he might have cracked his skull and broken his neck. We aren't invincible in these things. In some ways, we can do more harm to ourselves."

Cole gaped at Trickster. A warning about that before he'd jumped would have been nice!

"As you improve, you'll learn all sorts of tricks," Roulette said. "Jumping can be especially useful if you do it creatively. For example, once you get the feel, you can leap back and forth between the walls of an alley to climb."

"But you don't want to mess around with those kinds of techniques yet," Trickster said. "Practice advanced moves in a controlled environment."

Cole couldn't resist. His jump to the ceiling had given him a feel for how much the rig augmented his leaps, so aiming just above the lockers, he sprang to one side, kicked off the wall, flew across the room, kicked off the opposite wall, and landed just about where he had started.

"What?" Trickster laughed, clapping his hands. "Are you kidding me? That was *tidy*! No way was that luck!"

"I've done a lot of jumping lately," Cole said, unable to suppress a smile. Using the rig felt a lot like leaping with a Jumping Sword. The jumps weren't as big, but he didn't have to point at his target and shout a command. It felt easier. More intuitive. "Secret will be good at it too."

"I'm pleased you're getting a feel for the rigs," Googol said. "Remember, once you're out in the city, the goal is to move about like a normal citizen. The rig should only come into play in an emergency."

"Isn't this already an emergency?" Sidekick asked.

"You know what I mean," Googol said. "We should go."

He walked out of the locker room, back into the lab. The others followed, including the robots. On the far side of the lab, Googol opened a cleverly concealed sender. They all entered and it began to descend.

"I won't come with you," Googol said. "My face is well known, so my presence could unnecessarily endanger you. I will escape by a less comfortable route with Highwire and Outlaw. Trickster and Roulette will escort the rest of you to Forge's place. Sidekick will accompany you. Outlaw would draw immediate attention. Sidekick's commonplace appearance enables him to blend in throughout the city."

"That's what the lady bots are looking for," Sidekick said knowingly. "Commonplace."

"Don't worry about his personality," Googol said. "He knows how to act like a regular cleaning bot when necessary."

Sidekick began to speak in a deliberately robotic monotone. "I am a ro-bot. I love to wipe coun-ters and scrub toi-lets. Take me to your lea-der."

"Outlaw, could you bring the cart Sidekick was pulling?" Googol asked.

"Yes, mas-ter," Outlaw said in a deeper robotic monotone.

"I suppose I set myself up for that one," Googol said. "Secret, I'll leave you with communicators." He held up four black rectangles about the size of dominoes. "Trickster will teach you how they work."

The sender stopped and the doors opened. They stepped out into a close, domed tunnel covered in white tiles. It extended a great distance in opposite directions.

"Harmonic crystals are the key component to the best communicators," Googol said. "The tech relies on the principle that harmonic crystals can share energy. For energy to be shared, and for communication to take place, the crystals must share the same harmonics. Think of it like a radio frequency, but with many more variations. Through tinkering, there are nearly infinite harmonics to choose from. The four crystals in these communicators form a unique set, meaning these communicators can reach one another but nothing else. Don't overuse them, but if needed, you have them. I'll keep one. Trickster, Secret, and Roulette will hold the others. Obviously, don't let a communicator get captured. Roulette, show Secret how to destroy hers in case she's taken."

"So right when she most needs it she won't have it?" Jace asked.

"She can get off a message first," Googol said. "When destroyed, the communicator also sends a signal to alert the others. This is where we part ways. I'm sorry for the inconvenience. Listen to Roulette and Trickster. I leave you in the care of two of our best."

"Wait," Cole said. "One question. I'm looking for friends who were taken from my world as slaves with me. I know some are in Zeropolis. Can you help me find them?"

"You're going to the right place," Googol said. "Forge can help you with that. He can also connect you to a thruport so you can access the Internet in your world. But be warned—Outsiders are usually frustrated by the results."

"We know," Cole said. "Joe told us all about it."

Googol raised a hand. "Until we meet again."

"Which will probably be around the time of our next emergency," Trickster grumbled.

Googol gave half a grin. "He might be on to me. Good luck!"

ENHANCED

"This is where we rejoin the city," Trickster said. "We'll come out in a pedestrian walkway under Flick Street. We have hidden motion detectors in place. See that little light? When it turns green, the tunnel and stairways are empty."

Cole looked at the red light. Then he peered down the dusty service tunnel that had brought them here.

Their underground adventure had started in clean, white corridors. As they passed through one-way checkpoints and secret doors, they began using abandoned subway tunnels, and the way became grimier. Roulette explained that Old Zeropolis had used subways much as the current Zeropolis used elevated monorails. Before the new Zeropolis existed, this area had been an outpost of the old city.

"No more hiding in tunnels for us," Sidekick said. "Because we've run out of tunnels that will take us in the right direction. We're going topside. Sorry I'm not taller. Sorry I don't have eighteen weapons systems. I know I'm not much comfort compared to Outlaw."

"You'll blend in out there," Roulette said. "Right now, that's what we need."

"I can climb stairs," Sidekick said. "My forelegs shorten, the rear ones lengthen, and my base pivots. You'll see."

"I happen to know you have a few other surprises if we need them," Trickster said.

"Shhh," Sidekick hissed. "They're not surprises if you tell everybody. I was managing expectations!"

The light turned green.

"Let's go," Trickster said, opening the door and letting Roulette exit first. "Remember, this is all about staying cool."

"My personality is about to downgrade to cleaning-bot levels," Sidekick said. "You may not notice me. But I'll never be far."

They all entered the pedestrian walkway. When Trickster closed the door, it disappeared, blending seamlessly with the wall. Cole stepped close and stared hard at where the door had been but could detect no evidence of it.

"It doesn't open from this side," Trickster said. "Come on." He started toward the stairway at one end of the pedestrian walkway. Sidekick scuttled off toward the stairs at the opposite end.

"I have orders to stay with Secret no matter what," Trickster said quietly. "If things get choppy, the rest of you can scatter. Stay low. Big jumps are a last resort. If we get split up, meet at the north shore of Mariner Lake."

"Nothing will happen," Roulette clarified. "This is just a stroll through the city."

Walking up the stairs, Cole enjoyed the feel of the exo

rig supporting his movements. If things went bad, at least he had a secret weapon.

Near the top of the stairs, Trickster glanced back at them. "You look like you're going to a funeral. Come on! Race you to the statue!"

He ran up the last few steps, and the others followed. Before them spread a wide plaza of dull orange concrete. Flowers and an occasional tree grew in patches of soil protected by low wire fences. In the center of the plaza stood a large silver statue of a man holding a wrench over his head.

As Cole started dashing across the plaza, he realized that Trickster wasn't going anywhere near full speed. He was going fast, but with the exo rig helping, it didn't feel like more than a comfortable jog. There were people in the plaza, but not so many that their running had to bother anybody.

Still in the lead, Trickster glanced back, laughing. Cole couldn't tell whether he was acting or actually goofing around. As the statue got nearer, Jace sped up, taking the lead. Cole resisted the urge to challenge him. They weren't really running at top speed. If they did, they might draw real attention. But of course Jace wanted to win regardless.

With a little burst at the end, Trickster tied Jace as they reached the statue. Laughing easily, Trickster gave Jace a playful shove, who responded by tapping Trickster on the shoulder with his fist.

"That run felt good," Cole said to Dalton.

"Makes you want to test your limits," his friend replied.

"Who is Terrance Styles?" Mira asked, reading the name at the base of the statue.

"The main engineer behind the magroads," Roulette said. "Try not to care or you won't look local."

"This way," Trickster said, keeping his tone light. He trotted toward the far side of the plaza.

Following him, Cole fought the urge to jump. He wanted to know what the exo rig could do. What was the maximum height he could reach? What was the fastest he could run? If he trained, how good of a fighter could he become?

Off to one side of the plaza, Cole noticed a couple of armed patrolmen talking to a girl. After his first glance, he refused to let his eyes return to them.

The low sun would set within half an hour or so. Cole wondered how far they were from Forge, whoever that was. Would they still be roaming the city at night?

On the far side of the plaza, Trickster led them down to another pedestrian walkway under a road. After a man in the tunnel passed them and went up the stairs, Trickster motioned for them to huddle closer.

"Lots of Zeroes out," he said softly.

"I saw two," Cole said.

"Six," Roulette corrected. "Two in the plaza, four beyond the plaza on the streets."

"That was my count as well," Trickster said. "Too many."

"Might be a coincidence," Roulette said.

"They just raided our base," Trickster argued. "It's no coincidence. This isn't their first raid. They know we have ways to escape. They're combing the area."

"Great," Dalton said. He looked shaken.

Cole patted his back.

"Good thing we're just a bunch of kids horsing around," Roulette said.

"That's the key, guys," Trickster said. "The more on edge we should be, the more relaxed we need to become."

"I know you were trying to loosen us up," Jace said, "but is running the best idea if they're looking for people on the run?"

"Not a bad point," Trickster said. "No more races. But make sure to joke and tease and relax. Right now, not looking guilty is our best defense."

They went up the stairs at the far side of the street and turned left, following the sidewalk. Trickster took out a little rubber ball and bounced it as he walked.

Cole poked Dalton's arm. "I'm teasing you."

Dalton swatted his hand away. "I'm bothered by your teasing."

Cole poked him again. "I'm glad you're bothered. It encourages me."

"You guys sound like low-grade bots," Roulette complained.

"We're trying to follow instructions," Cole said. "I don't tease Dalton much. We're out of practice."

Jace flicked the back of Cole's ear. "Let me handle the teasing."

Cole flushed. "Handle it again and see what happens."

Jace grinned. "See? Now you're more believable."

They rounded a corner. Up ahead maybe half a block, two patrolmen were coming toward them. Only a few people moved along the sidewalk between them.

"Somebody catch it," Trickster said, tossing the bouncy ball over his shoulder.

Cole snatched at the tiny ball but missed. After it took a bounce, Jace backed up a couple of steps and grabbed it. Then he lobbed it up ahead of the group, gentle enough that Trickster caught up to it after one bounce.

Cole tried not to look at the patrolmen. And he tried not to obviously look away from them either. With a busy magroad on one side, and apartment buildings on the other, the only options were to duck into a random building, turn around, or walk right past the patrolmen. It looked like Trickster intended to stroll by them.

Trickster tossed the ball over his shoulder again. This time Cole caught it and bounced it up to him.

The patrolmen increased their pace. "A moment of your time," one of the patrolmen said, trotting forward.

Trickster came to a stop. So did the rest of them. Cole tried to keep calm despite the convincing instinct that he should run for his life.

"We've had a couple of runaways reported," the other patrolman said. "We need to check your ID cards."

"Sure," Trickster said, producing a card. "We're not runaways. Who are the kids?"

The patrolman scanned his ID with a small handheld device. "Winston Sykes," the officer said. "Twelve years old. And Carla Rutherford. Eleven years old. Know either of them?"

Trickster shook his head. "They from around here?"

"This part of the city," the patrolman replied.

Hanging back, Cole was close to total panic. Looking for two runaways would be a great cover if these patrolmen were really searching for Mira. But it would be foolish to run before he knew they were actually in trouble, in case the story was true.

The patrolman gave Trickster his card back and Roulette handed over hers. He scanned it and returned it. "Keep them coming," the patrolman said.

Cole still had his ID card from Outpost 121. But wouldn't it be linked to Joe somehow and immediately get him in trouble? Cole supposed the answer partly depended on whether or not the police were actually searching for runaways.

"What if we left our IDs at home?" Jace asked.

"Then I might suspect you're who we're looking for," the patrolman said. "Everyone knows the law. When out in public, you have to keep your ID card on you at all times. Do you live nearby?"

"Sort of far," Jace said. "Across the city a ways."

"If you lived close, we could go to your home," the patrolman said. "Living far away and not carrying ID means a visit to the patrol station and then contacting your parents."

"He has his ID," Cole said, getting out his own. "He just doesn't trust patrolmen."

"Don't you have pictures of the runaways?" Mira asked. "Can't you see we're not them?"

"IDs, please," the patrolman said, his tone making it clear that he was done conversing.

Cole gave the patrolman his ID card, then held his breath as it was scanned. The patrolman handed it back. "Next."

Jace shared his ID. After scanning the card, the patrolman looked up at Jace intently, then glanced at his partner and gave a nod.

The other patrolman took out a gray rectangle and lifted it to his mouth. Trickster jumped and kicked the rectangle, his leg a blur. The communicator went flying.

Jace crouched forward, grabbed the other patrolman by his ankles, then yanked both feet forward and up. The patrolman went down hard, his back slamming against the sidewalk while Jace held his ankles high.

With a silver tube in each hand, Roulette covered the patrolman on the ground and the one still standing in white foam from neck to boots. She hopped away as the upright patrolman swung at her, but it was the only move he managed to make before the cloud of white foam hardened. Cole shoved him over.

"Run," Trickster said softly, taking off down the sidewalk.

Cole started at a normal sprint, but realized that Trickster was racing at maximum speed. Exhilarated and scared, Cole pushed his pace to the limits.

The rig responded as desired, whipping his legs faster than they could possibly move unassisted. Cole dashed down the sidewalk at almost twice the speed of his normal sprint, the air rushing over him as if he were cruising along on a bike. He found that if he stretched his strides too much, he went from a sprint to a series of long, one-footed hops. Running at full speed had to look suspiciously fast, but the hops would draw even more attention, since the gait raised him up unnaturally high and was completely inhuman.

Trickster paused at the next corner. "You grabbed the communicator?" he asked Roulette.

"Dalton got it," she said.

Holding up the gray rectangle, Dalton shook it gently.

"Nice," Trickster said. "We wouldn't be Crystal Keepers if we left an enemy's harmonic crystal behind." He held out a hand, and Dalton passed it to him. "Slick move, Jace, dropping that Zero."

"Maybe we should keep running," Jace said.

"Patience," Trickster said, raising the communicator to his mouth. He lowered his voice a little and started running in place. "We're in pursuit on Sexton Road between Haley and Braga. It's the jackpot but we need reinforcements. Hurry."

Trickster lowered the communicator. "Coggs, aren't you on Voletta?" a voice replied.

Trickster ran in place again and raised the communicator. "Negative. Followed a hunch and they ran. In pursuit on Sexton crossing Braga." Trickster gave a pained grunt and dropped the communicator.

"Coggs?" came the voice from the communicator. "Coggs?"

Crouching, Trickster switched it off. "That's how you buy a little time and move a bunch of the other patrolmen out of your way."

"Won't they see the guys on the sidewalk?" Cole asked.

"Maybe," Trickster said. "Sexton runs parallel to this street, so the Zeroes will mostly use cross streets to get there."

"People are already trying to help our victims," Dalton said, looking down the sidewalk to where a man and a woman had stopped beside the cocooned patrolmen.

"People without communicators are trying to help patrolmen without communicators," Trickster said. "We have a few extra minutes at least. I'll take Secret under this road." He pointed to the pedestrian tunnel that went in the direction they had been heading. To the left another pedestrian tunnel went under the perpendicular street. "Roulette, take the others that way. Don't run."

"I know when to run," Roulette said, heading down the stairs.

Cole waved at Mira. "Stay safe."

She nodded and followed Trickster. Jace looked after them in frustration.

"He's good," Cole said. "She'll be safe."

"Whatever," Jace said, unconsoled.

"Unless she falls in love with him," Cole mused.

"Shut up," Jace said, following Dalton and Roulette.

Cole went with him. At the bottom, Roulette raced across the empty tunnel. Cole and the others followed her lead.

As they reached the top of the far side, they discovered a pair of patrolmen running toward them. One was a woman. Like some other pedestrians had done, Roulette flattened up against the building to let them pass. Cole, Jace, and Dalton did likewise. The patrolmen raced by them without a second look and hurried down the stairs to the pedestrian tunnel.

"Trickster isn't dumb," Jace said.

"He's not," Roulette agreed. "But he loves taking charge. It gets annoying."

They started walking again. "Didn't you like his plan?" Cole asked.

"The plan is fine," Roulette said.

Cole thought she sounded a little jealous but decided not to push her.

A black levcar came zooming down the magroad, going much faster than Cole had seen any levcar drive. The other cars flowed out of the way, leaving it a clear lane.

"More patrolmen?" Dalton asked.

"That's right," Roulette said. "Black levcars are City Patrol. Everybody's heading to Sexton. At least for now."

Walking along a zigzag route between buildings and under streets, Cole couldn't lose the knotted feeling in his stomach. He knew now that if they were stopped for ID cards, they were going to have to run. Well, at least Jace would. Cole wondered why his card hadn't raised any red flags.

Their best bet was to avoid another confrontation with patrolmen. How many times could they get away? If a bunch of patrolmen converged with those web-shooting trapguns, none of them would escape.

Shadows stretched to gargantuan lengths, and then the sun slid below the skyline, turning the jutting buildings into silhouettes against a rosy backdrop. They occasionally passed robots—some were just walking around, one was repairing a streetlight, a few worked cleaning an empty fountain. Though he kept an eye out, Cole didn't see Sidekick.

After some time, Roulette led them up a pedestrian

bridge and over a busy magroad to an expansive park. Under dusky trees, they walked on scant paths until a lake came into view. Several docks hosted sailboats. Only a few vessels remained on the water, and they seemed bound for the shore.

"Mariner Lake," Roulette said. "A place for city people to play boat captain. All of the craft have motors. The sails are mainly for show. I guess some people try to actually use them now and then."

"I haven't seen Sidekick," Cole mentioned.

"He would have followed Secret," Roulette said. "No offense, but she's the one everybody most cares about. Your names aren't even code words."

"Like Roulette," Cole said. "Or is that what your parents called you?"

"My parents were slaves," Roulette said. "A lot of slaves in Zeropolis try to give their babies to the Unseen before they receive slavemarks. It worked. I'm free. But I don't know my parents. It's supposedly too dangerous if the babies who get free try to learn their heritage."

"Have you tried?" Dalton asked.

"I wanted to when I was younger," Roulette said. "By the time I was old enough to do anything about it, I realized the rule was there for a reason."

"Who raised you?" Cole asked.

"Different people," Roulette said. "The kind of people who quietly want to do good, but don't want full membership in the Unseen. There are lots of them here."

"They named you Roulette?" Jace asked.

"I got that name from the CKs," she said. "I guess I take risks."

"Like what?" Jace asked.

Roulette paused and lifted her leg. "From shin down it's all mechanical," she said. "I guess that was the big one."

Cole's eyes widened. "What happened?" he inquired.

"Didn't make a jump," she said. "I thought I could, but came up short. It was an ugly landing—not on smooth ground. The rig I was wearing saved my life, but part of it broke, taking the end of my leg with it. I had other injuries, but losing the foot was the most permanent."

Cole and Dalton exchanged a look. Even with everything Cole had seen here, somehow it didn't stop surprising him how different life was for kids in the Outskirts. Back home he had never done anything that seemed dangerous enough to lose a leg. Roulette obviously did a lot more than just goof around in arcades. And she hadn't let her injury stop her.

As they approached a long building on the lakeshore where people dined on a large patio, two figures came toward them. In the fading light it took Cole a moment to recognize Trickster and Mira.

"Clean getaway?" Dalton asked.

"Not until we're safe inside Forge's lair," Trickster replied. "Glad to see you guys, though."

"You got here first," Jace said.

"Not by much," Mira said.

"Any more drama?" Cole asked Mira.

"No fights with patrolmen," Mira said. "Plenty of worry."

"Come on," Trickster said, leading the way.

"Has anybody seen Sidekick?" Cole asked.

"A few times," Trickster said. "He keeps his distance. He isn't a brawler. Many of his weapons don't require him to be close."

"Where was he when those patrolmen almost got us?" Jace asked.

"Maybe not near enough to help," Trickster said. "Or maybe we were just too quick. It didn't take us long to drop them."

"Would he have really done much?" Dalton asked. "He doesn't seem like the type."

"Don't underestimate Sidekick," Trickster said. "Sometimes good things come in small, dented packages."

Trickster led them away from Mariner Lake and back onto sidewalks. Before too long they reached a neighborhood where narrow walkways passed between large, bland buildings. Trickster paused at a plain door and used a card to open it.

"Is this a warehouse?" Dalton asked.

"It's a storehouse for obsolete tech," Trickster said. "One step up from a junkyard."

They entered and closed the door. Light leaked through the high windows along the perimeter of the cavernous room—a combination of moonlight and spillover from the streetlights. Large shapes hulked in the dimness, made rounded by plastic tarps.

Trickster led them along a maze of aisles through the shrouded stockpiles. He stopped at a hill of covered machinery and pulled up the tarp.

"This way," he said, motioning Roulette forward.

She ducked under the tarp cautiously. Cole followed. It was too dark to see much, so he moved slowly, worried about tripping. Roulette guided him between large pieces of equipment to a space in the middle. The others joined them.

"Come on," Trickster said, hardly raising his voice. "I know you see us, Forge! Let us in."

A hatch opened in the floor, flooding the space with light. Cole squinted until his eyes adjusted.

Trickster patted Dalton on the shoulder. "Now we've made a clean getaway."

CHAPTER
13

FORGE

At the bottom of a long ladder awaited a room full of machines, computers, worktables, beanbag chairs, shaggy carpets, soda cans, Zowie wrappers, overloaded bookshelves, glowing crystals, faded posters, and a beat-up dartboard riddled with tiny holes. Two ceiling fans turned lazily, barely stirring the stale air.

A guy with greasy hair in a tank top sat cross-legged, tinkering with a little robot. He might have been in his late teens or early twenties. He smiled at Trickster. "I heard you were coming this way."

"Not from City Patrol I hope," Trickster said.

"There was plenty of chatter," a girl said, coming into the room. She wore a scarf in her hair and loose pajamas. Her slippers looked like raccoons. "You guys had them scrambling."

"Googol called me on my most private communicator," the guy said. He looked at Mira. "You must be Secret. I'm Forge." He nodded at the girl. "This is Scandal."

"These are my friends Cole, Dalton, and Jace," Mira said. Cole couldn't help thinking their names sounded boring compared to Scandal, Trickster, and Roulette.

"So far they're scrappier than they look," Trickster said, slapping Jace's arm. "You should have seen this one put a Zero flat on his back. Just grabbed his ankles and yanked the rug out from under him. It was tidy."

Jace grinned proudly.

"Are you guys Crystal Keepers?" Cole asked.

"Former CKs," Forge said. "Scandal and I graduated to full membership in the Unseen more than two years ago."

"They're both skilled tinkers," Roulette said. "We call them our Gadgeteers."

"Googol is the head Gadgeteer," Forge said.

"We help him design the rigs," Scandal added.

"We make all kinds of tech," Forge said. "We run thruports, harvest data, intercept communications."

"What do the Crystal Keepers mostly do?" Cole asked.

"Energy is transmitted by harmonic crystals," Roulette said. "If you snag the right crystal, you get access to the entire network of crystals sharing the same harmonics."

"It's most valuable for spying," Trickster said, displaying the communicator they took from the patrolman. "Which reminds me. Here's another link into City Patrol comms." He tossed it underhand.

"Nice," Forge said, catching the communicator. "These have little crystals inside. The size doesn't matter. It's all about the harmonics."

"You can also use a crystal to hijack energy," Scandal

said. "The monorail tracks and trains, for example, are powered by crystals harmonically linked to highly juiced crystals inside of power facilities. Tap into that energy, and you can power all sorts of things."

"What about Sidekick?" Cole asked. "Is he coming in?"

"Sidekick is already here," Forge said, pocketing the communicator. "The bot will stay outside as lookout. Secret, you're so young. Why is Googol willing to torch our operations in Zeropolis to bring you in? He doesn't care if we all go down as long as you're secure. I've never heard him so adamant."

"We're not supposed to ask," Trickster reminded him.

"When has that stopped us?" Forge argued. "We spend all day doing stuff we're not supposed to do. It's our job description. What does Googol really expect? He knows who we are. I'm asking. She can tell what she wants."

"Keeping my identity secret doesn't just protect me," Mira said. "It protects you. Trust me. You don't want to know why the government wants to find me."

"I know it could endanger me," Forge said. "And I want to know. I live to uncover secrets. I'm good at keeping them."

"Me too," Roulette said softly.

"Don't get me wrong," Trickster said. "If you're spilling, I want in too."

"Not me," Scandal said. "I have enough trouble without soaking up high-stakes secrets Googol wants me to avoid."

Mira glanced at Cole. He could tell that she was wavering. Who wouldn't? These people were on their side and had just helped them evade capture.

"Up to you," Cole said.

Mira sighed. "I really shouldn't. It's for your own good. Unless things go badly, you'll find out sooner or later. The secret won't keep forever."

"Say no more," Forge grumbled. "I won't force the issue. I just couldn't resist trying." He rubbed his hands together. "For now, this will be your haven. We'll wait for orders from Googol. I know you four need fresh ID cards. I'll get you fed. A place to sleep. Anything else I can do for you?"

"Dalton and I are looking for some friends," Cole said. "Googol told us you might be able to help."

"Possibly," Forge said. "Who are the friends?"

"We came here from Outside," Cole said. "A bunch of other kids were brought here with us as slaves."

"I noticed Dalton's mark," Forge said. "But you have a freemark."

"It was a bondmark at first," Cole said. "Long story. Anyhow, the High King bought the slaves with shaping powers and shipped them around the Outskirts. I found Dalton in Elloweer."

"Do they have names?" Forge asked.

"Jenna Hunt," Cole said. "Blake Daniels. Lacie Clark. Sarah, um, what's Sarah's last name?"

"I don't know," Dalton said. "I didn't really know many of those kids well."

"It might start with a *P*," Cole said. "Anyhow, especially look for Jenna Hunt."

"You know she came here?" Forge asked.

"No idea," Cole said. "I just know she's not in Elloweer."

"The records I can check only cover Zeropolis," Forge

said. "And it's a big city. I've lost access to some of our best databanks because they've swapped out crystals. Sometimes slaves are given aliases, especially new slaves, to wipe out the old life. I can't guarantee success, but I'll look."

"What do you expect to do if you find somebody?" Roulette asked.

"Talk to them," Cole said. "Free them if I can."

"Fair warning," Roulette said, folding her arms. "Freeing slaves doesn't go over well. Once that mark is on there, you can't really hide."

"We freed Dalton," Cole said.

"You *found* Dalton," Trickster corrected. "You helped him escape. He's not free. He still has his bondmark. He has to pose as a slave. That's the best you can offer any slave. And if you take too many slaves, you get burned."

"There are a lot of former slaves in the Unseen," Roulette said.

"But they have to stay unseen," Trickster said. "They can't live normal lives."

"This is still way better than actual slavery," Dalton said.

"You were in Elloweer?" Forge asked.

"Yeah," Dalton said.

"I can draft some ownership documents to match your new ID cards," Forge said. "You want to belong to Cole?"

"Sure," Dalton said.

"What about me?" Jace protested.

"Anyone but Jace," Dalton replied. "No offense."

"I'd be a good master," Jace said. "I'm way more fun than Cole."

"You can really create slave documents for Dalton?" Mira asked.

"I can make it all look fully legal," Forge said. "Googol wants you to have the royal treatment."

"Good," Roulette said. "They could use haircuts."

Cole fingered his hair. It was getting pretty long. He hadn't cut it since . . . when? A few weeks before coming to the Outskirts?

"Your fakes are good?" Dalton asked.

Forge chuckled. "There's a reason Googol sent you here."

"He's the best," Trickster said. "As far as tech goes, this is Outpost 139. The cards won't be fakes. Forge uses the same equipment as the government, and stashes the info in all the same places. These ID cards will be real."

"Thanks for the oversell," Forge said. "Takes all the pressure off me."

"Let me see you," Roulette said. She made Mira, Dalton, Jace, and Cole line up. Then she paced the line, inspecting them. "Yeah, okay. I see possibilities. I can make you guys look local. You're not bad-looking youngsters. With the right clothes and some color in your hair? You could look tidy."

"More importantly," Forge said, "you'll look different from your original ID photos. When we take pictures, I'll want you to make faces. Nothing too drastic or the ID will look bogus. But scowl a little. Or smile really big. If we get it right, these new cards will let you start over."

"And he can load up a bunch of credits," Trickster said.

"We don't want to get carried away," Forge said. "Let's just say you won't be poor."

"Will we get nifty names like you guys have?" Jace asked. "Can I be Wolfmaster?"

"You aren't Crystal Keepers," Trickster said.

"And we don't put our code names on IDs," Roulette added.

"I'll handle the names," Forge said. "You want some of the most common names in Zeropolis. Not the very most common. That can look like you're hiding. Fifteenth to fortieth most popular is about right. Your original ID cards are compromised. Changing your looks and taking on common names will make it harder for the City Patrol to connect you to those original identities."

"Try to make the new ones last a little longer," Trickster said.

"It was out of our control," Mira said. "Joe didn't know his fake ID had been flagged."

"That's our other big challenge tonight," Forge said. "Finding the best way to bust out Joe."

"Do you know him?" Mira asked.

"He's a good man," Forge said. "We'll find a way."

"You mentioned you have access to thruports," Dalton said.

"Right," Forge replied. "You want to kidnap an old girlfriend too?"

Dalton blushed. "No. But it would be interesting to check my e-mail. Poke around a little."

"As long as you don't get your hopes up," Forge said. "I've seen it a thousand times. Nobody you really want to contact will respond."

"We've heard," Cole said.

"I'll set you up with thruports in the morning," Forge said. "We'll take care of the IDs then too. Tonight I have to help plan a jailbreak. Scandal will show you around. We have food and hammocks."

"Is this place safer than the other base?" Jace asked.

"Fair question," Forge said. "Short answer? Yes. A lot less people know about my lair. Of the Crystal Keepers, only Trickster, Roulette, Duckling, and Jetstream know. Not many of the Unseen know either. Most of my forgeries are carried out remotely. Very few people come and go. The fact that Googol had you come here shows how highly he values you."

"Which is what makes us so curious," Trickster said.

"It also helps that we're under a virtually abandoned storehouse," Forge went on. "I have access to lots of weird spare parts when I need them, and nobody is ever around."

"What about all the crystals you have?" Cole asked. "You're connected to a lot of information. Could they trace those connections back to you?"

"Nice," Forge said. "You're thinking like a techno-mancer. Sure, there are ways, but I take lots of precautions. It wouldn't be easy for them to figure out they could spy on me, and one of my alarms would almost certainly give them away if they tried."

"Come on," Scandal said. "Let's get you some food."

Cole and the others followed her through a tunnel to a low table. Dinner awaited them—cubes of meat, mashed potatoes, green beans, and cups of pale green liquid.

"Six settings," Trickster said. "You didn't think any of us would be captured?"

"I try to stay optimistic," Scandal said.

They sat down on the benches on either side of the table. Cole skewered a meat cube with a fork, then sniffed it.

"Any guesses?" Dalton asked.

"Beef?" Cole tried.

"It's kind of a mix," Trickster said. "Don't think of it as a certain type of meat or it seems gross. Consider it a highly processed celebration of all meat."

Cole tried a bite. It was more tender and juicy than he expected, tasting more like sausage than steak. "Not bad."

"If you want food fresh from a farm, Zeropolis is the wrong place to find it," Scandal said. "But we have abundant food, it doesn't cost much, it tastes pretty good, and unlike a lot of the processed food in your world, it's highly nutritious."

Cole sampled the potatoes. They didn't quite taste real, but they had a nice buttery, cheesy flavor. He had never been a fan of green beans, but he tried to eat some to be polite.

"I like the drink," Dalton said, taking a long sip.

"Me too," Roulette said. "Limelicious. Sweet but not too sweet."

"And lots of vitamins," Scandal said.

As the food began to settle, Cole could feel the busy day catching up with him. Had he woken up today at that inn in Outpost 121? It felt like that had happened in another lifetime. His eyes were droopy.

"Let me take care of the plates," Scandal said. "You guys

must be exhausted. We're not fancy here, but a good hammock can be pretty comfy."

Cole followed her down a hall to a room with several hammocks at different heights. The room was kind of dumpy, the paint on the wooden walls stained and peeling, but the hammocks looked clean.

"We have several guest rooms," Scandal said. "Take your pick."

"Mind if I join you, Trickster?" Jace asked.

"Not a bit," he said.

"Dalton and I will take this one," Cole said.

"Sleep well," Scandal said. "You'll be safe here. Let me know if you need anything."

Cole and Dalton went into their room. Dalton closed the door.

"Tired?" Cole asked.

"I feel like I just stumbled away from a plane crash," Dalton said.

"Me too," Cole said, flopping into a hammock. It swayed and creaked. He stared at the ceiling.

"How do we take off our exo rigs?" Dalton asked.

Cole laughed sleepily. "I have no idea. Hopefully I don't do karate moves in my sleep."

"Or jump."

"Maybe the gear will help us sleep extra well."

"Enhanced sleeping? Why not? The rigs improve everything else."

"Don't you want to see how high we can jump in them?" Cole asked.

"No way," Dalton said. "I'd rather keep both my feet."

Cole winced. "Can you imagine having part of your leg ripped off? Roulette is hard core."

"They all are," Dalton said. "It's like we joined up with organized crime."

"When the government is crooked, the outlaws can be the good guys. Like Robin Hood."

Dalton sighed. "Are we going to be outlaws the rest of our lives?"

"Depends if the revolution succeeds."

"Is it really our revolution?"

"You tell me. You're the slave."

"I'm serious," Dalton said.

"Me too. As long as we can't get home, it's our revolution. And I may have an important part to play."

Dalton snorted. "According to the evil creature from another world who got locked up for trying to take over the Outskirts."

"Right," Cole said drowsily. "According to him."

"Did you notice that hanging out with Mira got us in trouble again?"

"It also helped us find people to get us out of trouble. Do you think the Unseen would have done all this for us without Mira?"

"Probably not," Dalton said. "But we might not have been in trouble in the first place."

"With all we've learned, we might get chased just as much with or without her," Cole said. "We're in pretty deep. Do you really want to leave her?"

Dalton paused. "I don't think so. I just don't want to forget our real goal—to find our friends and get home."

Cole stared hard at the ceiling, mapping the discolorations. "Helping Mira is part of my goal now, Dalton. Trillian thinks I'm key to her winning. He's creepy, but he supposedly can't lie. Think about it. If Mira defeats her dad, we'll be able to free all the kids who got taken and actually keep them safe. And we'll have major resources to maybe find a way home."

"Seems like we spend most of our time running," Dalton said. "Is beating her father even possible?"

"If not, we at least try to save Mira. Maybe one of these days it will make sense to take off on our own. Until then, we help however we can. Or at least I will. What about you?"

"It's all good as long as we stay free and can keep fighting. But what if we get captured? We came pretty close today to spending the rest of our lives imprisoned."

"It's not a game," Cole agreed. "We could get killed. We could become prisoners. But they already took away our lives and our families. They already made us slaves. If we have a chance to fix things, I'm going to take it."

"That's why I'm here," Dalton said.

"Maybe we'll get some answers tomorrow," Cole said. "Maybe we'll even find Jenna."

"You sound sleepy."

"I'm pretty far gone. You're mostly talking to my subconscious."

"See you tomorrow."

"If I ever wake up."

Sleep came almost instantly.

CHAPTER
14

SUBSTITUTES

Subject: Life and Death

Dear Mom, Dad, and Chelsea,

Please read this! I'm sending it from our family account, so maybe you'll open it. Or maybe nobody pays much attention to the family account anymore, since you all have your own e-mail addresses. You mainly had the family one for me, because you didn't want me to have my own address yet.

You're probably wondering who I am. I'm your lost son, Cole Randolph. You don't remember me, but I used to live with you up until last Halloween. I got kidnapped with a bunch of other kids in the neighborhood and we were all forgotten.

I used to be in the room by the bathroom, across from the spare bedroom. I don't know if you use my room for something else now, or if you just never go in there. A bunch of my stuff should be around if you haven't thrown it out. Pay attention and you might notice my soccer things (uniform, cleats, shin guards, trophies), or my schoolbooks, or maybe my video games.

Anyhow, that stuff is around because you used to have a son named Cole. A sixth grader. Me.

I was taken to a world in another universe called the Outskirts. That's why I didn't take out the trash on Halloween. I really meant to. But I got kidnapped.

I love you and am sorry about all the times I made you mad or did dumb stuff. I even love Chelsea.

You probably won't read this. And if you do, you probably won't understand or will think it sounds crazy. But you have a kid or brother named Cole. I'm in a bunch of the family photos. If you focus, maybe you'll notice me.

I'm trying to get home. I miss you.

Love,
Cole

After reading the e-mail for the tenth time, Cole felt he had rid it of typos and expressed what he wanted to say. Arrow hovering over the send button, Cole checked the e-mail addresses one more time. It would send to his dad, his mom, his sister, and also back to the family account.

He clicked send.

A long examination of the family account inbox had shown no mention of him after Halloween. The days following the holiday had only routine messages. There was nothing in social media about his disappearance. Nothing in the news. The mass kidnapping had gone unnoticed, all of the kids forgotten.

Would somebody open his e-mail? His family had forgotten about him, but the e-mail wasn't coming from him. They should each think it came from some other member of the family. He also sent the e-mail to the family account, even though the inbox had many unopened e-mails. Based on what Joe had told him, his would join the disregarded spam. But he had to try.

Cole wondered if it would help to send the e-mail a hundred times. Could they ignore a hundred of the same e-mail? Or would that make it seem even more like spam?

"Has e-mail ever looked so good?" Dalton asked, surprising Cole.

Cole turned. Dalton smiled awkwardly and waved. He wore a weathered green denim jacket, black trousers, and cowboy boots. His hair was buzzed short and had simple images engraved in it.

"Are you filming a music video?" Cole asked.

Dalton rubbed his head self-consciously. "I've never had my hair this short. I like how it feels."

"Turn around," Cole said.

Dalton complied. He had what looked like a sun on one side of the back of his head, and an anchor on the other.

"Your head is all marked up. Did Roulette do that? Or were you mugged?"

"Ha-ha," Dalton said. "You're next."

"I thought they might be scars from this morning," Cole said.

Dalton's face got angry. Not long after daybreak, when he had rolled out of his hammock, Dalton had flopped head-first to the floor. Somebody had tied his shoelaces to the netting of the hammock. Jace was the natural suspect. "I'll get him back."

"Might be smarter to call it even."

"I'll get him back," Dalton said with increased determination. "Did you e-mail your family?"

"I had to try."

"I'll try too. Just in case. Did you find any info about us? Any news about a kidnapping?"

"None," Cole said. "As far as the Internet knows, we never disappeared. It's just like we were warned—nobody misses us."

"Isn't it weird to see a computer here?" Dalton asked.

"It's too much like home," Cole said. "I don't really envision the Rogue Knight on a PC. Forge said the thruport machines especially are modeled after the computers in our world so they can run the same software. He said some of our designs influenced their designs here. Like mouses. They had great tech here, but no mouses until they saw us using them."

"Don't think you can hide," Roulette said, entering the room with scissors in hand. "Doesn't Dalton look tidy?"

"He definitely looks different," Cole said. "Are you going to shave my head and graffiti my scalp too?"

"Don't mock it," Roulette said. "Dalton looks like a real Zeropolite. You will too, but I'll take your look in a different direction. Come on."

"Good luck," Dalton said.

Cole rubbed Dalton's bristly head with both hands, then followed Roulette into another room where a chair awaited. Hair clippings littered the floor.

Jace walked in and Cole reflexively laughed. Jace's hair had been bleached blond and spiked up with styling gel. Symbols were sloppily painted on his brown leather jacket, and he wore safety pins in his earlobes. His jeans had several patches, and his eyes were now blue.

"Yuck it up," Jace said. "You're next."

"Are the pins real?" Cole asked, reaching to touch one.

"Trickster dared me," Jace said, swatting his hand away.

"Dalton looks cool," Roulette said. "Jace looks hot."

"Okay, now I feel awkward," Jace said, turning around and leaving.

"What do you say, Cole?" Roulette asked. "Want to top his earpins? How about a bolt through your nostrils?"

"No new holes in my body," Cole said.

"Okay," Roulette said. "I can probably still give you some style."

"I guess I could use a haircut," Cole admitted. "And I need to look different."

"Have a seat," Roulette said, her grin somewhere between delighted and predatory.

Cole proceeded through a long, mirrorless process of Roulette washing his hair, cutting it, putting chemicals on it, and covering it in a plastic sack. When he grew fidgety, Roulette ordered him to sit still. When he complained about odd smells, she shushed him. He had never loved getting his hair cut, and this was taking much longer than usual.

In the end, Roulette gave him a hand mirror. His hair was now pure black and neatly trimmed. "The black is different, but it's not bad. I kind of like it."

"You have the kindest face, so I made you our pretty boy," Roulette said.

Cole squirmed. "Don't repeat that in front of Jace. Names like that can stick."

"I'll get you some clothes," she said.

As Roulette left the room, Mira entered. Her hair was longer and a rich shade of lavender. She wore tights under a mid-length skirt. Her short, black leather jacket fit snugly.

"You look good!" Mira said.

"So do you," Cole replied. "A little like an anime character, but not in a bad way."

"That's what I was going for," Roulette announced, returning to the room. "I love anime. Watching shows from your world is the best use of thruports."

"Anime?" Mira asked.

"Japanese cartoons," Cole said. "Like moving pictures.

A lot of the characters in them have colorful hair."

"I'll take your word for it," Mira said.

"Did Forge snap your photo?" Roulette asked.

"He made me squint and squish my lips together," Mira said. "He checked the photo on my old ID and wanted the opposite expression. Jace and Dalton are done too."

"Then they're waiting for Cole," Roulette said. She waved a hand. "Shoo, Secret, so he can change. I'll clear out too." Roulette gave Cole the clothes she had collected. "Come join us when you're ready."

Left alone with his new clothes, Cole changed quickly. His new outfit included black jeans, a white shirt, a black denim vest, and gray shoes. Using the hand mirror and looking down at himself, Cole thought he looked less weird than Dalton or Jace. It was a fairly cool outfit.

The others were waiting when he emerged. Jace looked especially disappointed.

"He looks too normal," Jace complained.

"He looks *different*," Roulette said. "That's the point. I didn't have to make all of you equally edgy."

"You promised to talk to him about a nose bolt," Jace grumbled.

"I did," Roulette said. "He vetoed it. So I went more conservative."

"We had veto power?" Dalton asked.

"You look nice, Cole," Mira said.

The comment pleased Cole more than he wanted anyone to know. "I'm supposed to take an ID photo?"

"Over here," Forge said. "Stand there."

Cole had handed over his ID card in the morning so Forge could study it. Forge picked it up and took one more look.

"You have a very normal smile here," Forge said. "The image is framed tight on your face, so I'll give your head some room in this new one. Let's go serious. Frown a little. Scowl, lower your eyebrows a bit. Hmmm. Keep the frown but raise your eyebrows. Okay, good. Think of something that disgusts you. Or something that makes you angry. Turn your head a little to the left. Good. Drop your chin a little. Remember, eyebrows up. Don't frown too deep. It has to be subtle. Good. Got it."

"I'm done?" Cole asked.

"Success," Forge said. "You're now Steve Rigby. It's your face, but it'll be a chore to match this to your old photo. You guys owe Roulette. She did great work."

"Almost a changing," Dalton said.

"Not far off," Forge replied with a chuckle. "All right, getting these IDs printed up won't take long. While I have you four gathered together, I better mention something. Joe is being transferred this evening to Holding Area 11. If they get him in there, I'm not sure we can get him out. So we have to intercept him today. But there's a problem."

"What?" Mira asked, anxious.

"A lot of our communications network is down right now," Forge said. "Several people got caught fleeing the raid yesterday, which means we lost crystals, including some that are linked to crucial networks. We need to make a big new batch of communicators using different harmonics. Until then, Googol and I don't know where most of our people who escaped are hiding. We can't contact the personnel needed to carry off the rescue. If that holds true until this evening, we're going to need Roulette, Trickster, and a pair of substitutes to carry it off."

"You know I'm in for whatever Googol wants," Roulette said.

"Same," Trickster agreed.

"You need some of us?" Jace asked hopefully.

"Not Secret," Forge clarified. "But we'll need—"

"Yes," Jace said. "Me. Absolutely."

"I like the passion," Forge said. "I was going to say, we need two people to fill support roles. These positions are somewhat removed from actually taking Joe from his vehicle, but will be necessary to ensure success. You'll be exposed to capture. The danger is real. You'll need full battle suits and warboards. If we can find somebody else with more experience between now and this evening, we won't use you."

"I'm one for sure," Jace said.

Cole looked at Dalton. His friend appeared uncertain. "Do the battle suits jump like the exo rigs?" Cole asked.

"Better," Forge said. "The battle suits do everything the rigs can and more."

"I'm your other volunteer," Cole said. He couldn't let Joe remain a prisoner. Thanks to his experiences with the Jumping Sword, he felt confident he could at least master jumping effectively with the battle suit.

"Can I help too?" Dalton asked.

"You'll stay here with me and Secret," Forge said. "I may need some support once the operation kicks into gear. Googol and I will both lend help remotely."

"They're doing important stuff," Trickster clarified. "They'll be messing with the magroads."

"And the emergency response systems," Forge said. "We're going to go big. Googol really wants Joe back. And I think he's kind of angry about the loss of zerobase. But first, Trickster should get Cole and Jace suited up. At a minimum, make sure they can handle the basics enough to do their parts and get away."

"What if we can't?" Cole asked.

Forge shrugged. "If nobody else can fill in, we'll have to scrap the mission."

"We'll figure it out," Jace said confidently.

"I'll try," Cole said. He wanted to help Joe, but he could also picture himself running from hordes of angry patrolmen in an unfamiliar city using unfamiliar gear. What if he made a fatal mistake that ruined the mission? If he couldn't get comfortable with the equipment, he had no business helping out. Failing wouldn't benefit Joe.

"From what I've seen, I bet I can get you two up to speed," Trickster said. "Your duties will be to hide, use trapguns, and get away. The tech is awesome. You'll feel better once you get the hang of it."

"When can we start?" Jace asked.

Trickster folded his arms. "Since the ambush needs to happen in about six hours, now would be good."

The battle suit was like a finished version of the exo rig. More extensive braces supported the joints, and a full vest hugged the torso. A greater number of metallic strips and cords connected the vest and braces, along with boots, gloves, and a snug helmet. A black unitard underneath it all covered Cole from the neck to the wrists and ankles.

"The armor is the best part," Trickster said, pinching the sleeve of Jace's unitard. "Does it feel rugged?"

"Feels like long underwear," Jace said.

Cole plucked at his unitard. The silky material felt fairly thin.

Trickster grinned. "That material is probably Googol's most impressive creation. It's a wonder of tinkering. He calls it guardcloth. Other tinkers have developed similar materials, but nobody can match the quality. Guardcloth is smooth and comfortable, but hardens against sharp impact."

Jace scrunched his face. "It can stop a punch?"

"It can stop a knife," Trickster said. "Or an arrow. Feel your sleeve. Rub it."

Cole and Jace both complied.

"Notice anything unusual?" Trickster asked.

"No," Cole said.

"Exactly!" Trickster emphasized. "Now make a fist and give your arm a good chop. Not too hard, but solid."

Cole complied. Against his halfhearted blow, the previously soft material felt rigid. He tried hitting it harder, and the material felt hard as steel, hurting his fist, though the arm below the guardcloth barely felt it.

"No way," Jace said.

"I told you," Trickster said. "And it gets better. Aside from hardening against direct impact, guardcloth also works with the battle suit. For example, parts will go rigid to help reduce damage from a fall. It complements the support you get from the suit."

They stood in the widest aisle of the storehouse above Forge's lair. Daylight streamed through the high windows, spotlighting the covered mounds of derelict machines. Sidekick was patrolling outside the storehouse to make sure they wouldn't be disturbed.

Cole glanced at the distant ceiling. "Can I jump my highest?" he asked.

"In here, sure," Trickster said. "That ceiling is over six stories above us. Even with the battle suit, your best jump won't get you that high. But watch where you land. The guardcloth and the battle suit aren't indestructible. Fall far enough, land on something sharp enough, take a strong enough blow, and the suit will crumple. If it does, you crumple too."

"So is it safe to jump my highest?" Cole asked.

"The rule of thumb is don't fall farther than you can jump," Trickster said. "The battle suit won't let you jump so high that it can't handle the landing. But if you jump your highest and sail off an edge, you can get into trouble fast. Same if you jump your highest and land on a jagged piece of machinery."

Trickster sprang high into the air, getting two thirds of the way to the ceiling, then came straight down and landed in a crouch. "Take small jumps at first. You need to get a feel for it so you can control where you land."

Cole took a small leap and barely jumped higher than normal. A bigger jump sent him ten or fifteen feet into the air. He felt wobbly for a moment, but stabilized himself before the ground rushed up to greet him.

The Jumping Sword would help slow his fall before a landing. The battle suit did no such thing. But when he landed, it squeezed and supported him in such a way that the impact wasn't too jarring.

Jace tried a jump as well, straight up and down, going a little higher than Cole reached before landing in a crouch. "I like this," he said.

Cole gauged the aisle. Long and straight, it ran the length of the storehouse, crossed by narrower aisles. It had to be almost fifteen feet wide. Springing forward, Cole rocketed up through the air and along the aisle. At the apex of his leap he was almost halfway to the ceiling, and he traveled maybe an eighth of the length of the storehouse. He approached the ground at a speed that seemed like it could be a problem, his insides tingling as they would during a big drop on a roller coaster, but the suit performed marvelously, supporting him and cushioning the landing more than he could have hoped.

"This really works!" Cole called down the aisle.

"Did you think I was trying to kill you?" Trickster asked.

"My brain didn't," Cole replied. "My instincts weren't sure."

Giving the jump everything he had, Cole leaped forward down the aisle again. He got over two thirds of the way to the ceiling and extended his distance half again as far. The landing was more jarring, but still manageable. He stayed on his feet.

Cole dashed to the end of the aisle, taking long, leaping

strides that didn't send him too high but made each step cover about twenty feet. Exhilarated, he turned and started racing back but tried a running jump this time. It didn't carry him nearly as high as his earlier jumps, but he sailed farther, covering a quarter of the length of the massive storehouse in a single bound. He didn't try to land at a standstill. Instead he kept running and slowed to a stop near Trickster.

"Who are you?" Trickster said. "That was incredible! Nobody gets that good that fast! In fact, most people never get that good period."

"I have practice jumping," Cole said. "I like the feel of the suit. It works. I get it."

Jace came soaring toward them from the other direction. After a towering leap, he landed beside them in a crouch. "Next lesson?" he asked.

Though Jace hadn't used a Jumping Sword, Cole realized that his golden rope had probably given him just as much experience launching himself through the air.

"You two are fast learners," Trickster said. "I'll give you a few more physical challenges to try, then we'll cover weapon systems and get you acquainted with the warboards."

"What are the chances somebody else calls in and takes our place?" Cole asked.

"Fairly slim at this point," Trickster said. "Replacements might turn up, but we're running out of time. We'd be dumb to bet on it happening. Let's get to work."

CHAPTER

— 15 —

RESCUE

Four hours later Cole sat alone atop a three-story building, dressed in full battle gear, a warboard at his side. Replacements hadn't turned up.

He had reached the building, a food-processing plant, with help from Roulette, traveling through a network of underground tunnels. After coming to the surface not far from the building, it only took a jump for them to reach the top, warboards tucked under their arms. She had positioned him, made sure he grasped the plan, and slipped away.

Over his battle suit he wore gray coveralls. Trickster had explained that the outfit was the type worn by maintenance workers. Cole sat on the flat roof beside the ventilation system with a toolbox handy, in case anybody noticed him from some of the taller buildings in the vicinity.

For now, his assignment was to lay low, stay quiet, and await the signal. To his right sat a large canister full of quick-hardening freeze-foam, attached to a gun by a pliable hose. On the other side, beneath the toolbox, the warboard waited for action.

Roughly the size of a snowboard, the warboard qualified as the most exciting piece of equipment Cole had used so far in this kingdom. Its complicated magnetic system enabled the board to hover above just about any metallic surface, which included most of Zeropolis, since through the years tinkers had used metal alloys in the underpinnings of almost every part of the city.

The warboard looked simple, with no evidence of electronics. But Cole knew the board linked to the battle suit in such a way that enabled it to use momentum and magnetics to actively keep the rider aboard.

The test runs had gone really well. Cole had hardly believed how easy the warboard was to ride. Invisible magnetics kept his feet affixed to the surface and helped his body remain upright and centered even through complex maneuvers. Since the propulsion was also magnetic, all he had to do was point the warboard in the direction he wanted to go and adjust the speed with buttons built in to his left glove.

Of course, the test runs had occurred in a controlled environment. This afternoon it would be a different kind of ride, trying to evade patrolmen down alleys and streets with his freedom and maybe his life on the line. Roulette had taught Cole several places where he could get underground. Much of the escape plan depended on using the abandoned tunnels under Zeropolis. Access to those tunnels was the main reason this site had been selected to rescue Joe.

Cole hated the suspense of waiting for the signal. At

any moment his communicator could come to life, and he would have to start blocking off the street with freeze-foam. Although the rescue was a team effort, Cole's part in it would leave him alone throughout. His part wasn't too hard, but he had no backup—whether he succeeded or failed was up to him.

Relatively large, low buildings dominated this area. Cole knew his fellow Sky Raider was stationed alone on a nearby building, a beverage-canning facility that also stood three stories tall, about a block up Flag Street on the other side. The communicator strapped to Cole's forearm could put him in touch with Jace instantly, but he had been warned to keep silent unless there was an emergency. He wondered how Jace was handling the solitude.

As the minutes passed, Cole grappled with a mix of boredom and anxiety. There was no way to know how long they would wait for the transfer vehicle. They had gotten into position well ahead of schedule in case it came early. If the vehicle showed up late, the wait could drag on for hours. And of course, if the patrolmen transferring Joe took another route, there would be no rescue attempt. Everything depended on the vehicle coming down this section of Flag Street on the way to the holding area.

After some time, a fly started buzzing around near him. Cole swatted at it, but the tiny insect dodged his swings. The communicator came to life without warning. "It's a go," a hushed voice said. "Target confirmed. It's a go."

Flustered, Cole grabbed the canister of freeze-foam and ran the few steps to the edge of the roof overlooking the magroad. Below him, traffic flowed along like normal, lev-cars darting and weaving. Cole released the safety on the foam gun.

Suddenly all the levcars along one section of the street dropped to the magroad in a grating discord of metal-lic screeches. Sparks flew and undercarriages howled as the wheel-less cars ground to a halt, jostling against one another before groaning to a stop. Forge had come through as planned—an entire block of the magroad had been deac-tivated.

Cole squeezed the trigger, and the foam gun bucked in his hands as a high-pressure jet of freeze-foam streaked down to the road. Upon striking the surface of the magroad, the focused stream swelled into smooth drifts of foam. Cole kept his finger on the trigger, pouring on more foam until a white, puffy wall took shape.

From the top of the building, Cole felt somewhat removed from the chaos below. People down on the street were pointing and shouting to each other. To the left of his wall, where the magroad remained functional, levcars coasted to a halt. That section of the road swiftly became a tightly packed parking lot, creating an enormous backup as new levcars continued to arrive. Within seconds of Cole starting to form his wall, Trickster and Roulette shot into view on their warboards, weaving between the grounded levcars.

The wall of foam took shape quickly. Not more than fifteen seconds could have passed before the foamy barri-cade was complete, perhaps a little sloppier and wider than necessary. Looking up Flag Street, Cole could see the second barrier Jace had created swelling above the grounded levcars like heaps of whipped cream.

Checking the gauge on his canister, Cole found he had used a little more than 60 percent of the freeze-foam. Not bad, since the big job was done. Next he had to protect the area from incoming patrolmen.

A hasty survey up and down the street revealed no threats at the moment. Nobody was exiting the grounded levcars. Along with taking out the magroad, Forge had promised that he would lock down all of the affected vehicles. Cole noticed that none of the grounded vehicles had overturned or flipped onto their sides. Apparently they were designed to fall flat in emergencies.

Trickster and Roulette stopped at a black vehicle in the midst of the other grounded levcars. It looked a little larger than the other cars. Forge had wondered whether City Patrol would use an official prison transport vehicle or hide Joe inside an ordinary levcar. Apparently they had opted for the armored version.

Trickster hopped down from his warboard and used a handheld canister to spray a side window. Roulette stayed on her warboard, trapgun ready. Trickster repeatedly banged a short, black rod against the window he had sprayed.

"It's not working," Trickster said over the communicator. "This is some kind of high-grade crystal."

"Outlaw, move in," Googol's voice ordered.

"So soon?" Forge's voice asked.

"Speed is everything today," Googol answered.

The yellow robot rushed into view, dashing between the grounded levcars like a running back. Remembering to check the area, Cole saw a pair of patrolmen racing down the far side of Flag Street on foot, trapguns in hand. His attention had been on Outlaw and the others, so the patrolmen were already closer than he should have allowed. As they neared the creamy barrier Cole had raised, he fired freeze-foam, shooting a little ahead of them at first, but guiding the stream into them.

Googol had assured him that although freeze-foam became solid when it hardened, the porous substance allowed enough airflow for those trapped inside of it to breathe. Cole piled a generous mound over his targets. They flailed a bit, but the foam soon hardened, ending their movements.

Cole checked the gauge on the canister and found he hadn't quite used 70 percent of the freeze-foam yet. Scanning the street, he saw no other patrolmen approaching.

Outlaw reached Joe's transport vehicle and started pounding one of the darkly tinted windows with a large drill attached to his arm. The drill whined, the pitch changing with each impact. With every blow, the black vehicle slid sideways until it pressed up against a neighboring levcar.

"The window keeps holding," Trickster said over the communicator.

"It's weakening," Outlaw said. "Almost there."

His blows sped up, the drill screaming as his robotic arm worked like a piston. Finally the window shattered.

Googol whistled softly over the communicator. "I'd like to know how they bonded that crystal."

Outlaw staggered back, coated in black sludge. Trickster fired his trapgun into the car and then flopped backward to the street, his entire upper body sheathed in quicktar as well. It looked like he had been dipped in molten chocolate. His legs jerked and kicked. Wherever the black covered, Trickster remained still as a statue.

Roulette sprang past the broken window, firing into the car. She leaped by it a second time, shooting again. Then she peered into the window. Nobody returned fire.

Extending one arm, Roulette sprayed Outlaw with a pinkish mist, and the tarlike sludge melted off the robot. Outlaw then bathed Trickster with a similar mist, and the black stuff drained away from him as well. Outlaw approached the levcar again and reached through the broken window. After a moment grasping and wrangling, the robot reached deeper and then pulled Joe out of the window. Dressed all in pale blue denim, Joe had some freeze-foam clinging to him, and appeared to be unconscious. Outlaw sprayed him with lavender mist, and the foam dissipated.

More patrolmen were coming—not just along Flag Street, but down some of the alleys across the way. Cole shot freeze-foam at the patrolmen on Flag Street, but they did a better job this time diving for cover among the many levcars stuck at a standstill. Changing tactics, Cole sealed up the mouths of the alleys across the way before the oncoming patrolmen could emerge. If he couldn't trap them, at least he could slow them.

"Target acquired," Roulette said over the communicator. "Our stun gas knocked him out, but Outlaw is reviving him."

"Good work," Googol said. "Get out of there. Abandon all posts. City Patrol is closing in from all quarters. Local building security is being notified as well. Move, people."

The gauge showed that Cole had used more than 90 percent of his freeze-foam. Down below, Outlaw had draped Joe over one shoulder and was running away. Roulette and Trickster fled in opposite directions on their warboards. Patrolmen were climbing the barriers in the alleys and approaching the larger barricade on Flag Street.

"Jace, drop off the south side of your building and head east," Forge said over the communicator. "Cole, your best bet is to go west off the back of your building and keep heading west. Hurry."

A rooftop hatch opened forty feet away from Cole, and a man with a trapgun hurried out. By his uniform, he appeared to be a security guard rather than a member of City Patrol. When the man spotted Cole, he raised his trapgun to fire, but Cole let loose a long burst of freeze-foam.

At the relatively close range, the high-pressure stream knocked the guard off his feet. Cole buried the man beneath a creamy mass of foam, feeling a little like he was using a fire hose to snuff out a candle. Then he covered up the three nearest hatches as well, using up the last of the foam.

Crouching, Cole hit the self-destruct button on the freeze-foam canister as he had been instructed to do and picked up the warboard. He sprinted across the roof of the food-processing plant to the side opposite the street, the battle suit allowing him to move in swift, bounding strides.

He paused at the edge of the roof. A narrow greenbelt

with a walkway separated this building from the next one. Thanks to the availability of levcars, Cole had yet to see a building in Zeropolis with a parking lot. Only the green spaces and walkways throughout the city kept the buildings from being constructed directly adjacent to one another.

Cole had accessed the roof of the plant from back here and knew the short route to the point where he and Roulette had come aboveground. The greenbelt looked clear, so he jumped down, his battle suit helping him land on the lawn without difficulty, though his boots left impressions an inch or two deep.

Tapping a button on his wrist, Cole issued the command "Board on" and dropped the warboard. Instead of landing on the grass, it hovered just over a foot in the air, still and stable. There had to be metal under the turf somewhere.

Stepping onto the board, Cole felt the magnetics take hold of him, sealing his feet in place and stabilizing his posture. He tilted forward and used his forefinger to press the accelerator built into the palm of his glove. The warboard surged forward, and magnetics kept Cole in a comfortable forward crouch. Air rushed over him as he leaned forward a little more, his finger firmly on the accelerator.

Cole tilted to one side, and the warboard banked, turning onto a walkway heading west. A good distance down the walkway, three men dressed in black gear tromped around a corner. Their outfits were similar to what the patrolmen wore, but with more padding and armor, as if they might be members of an elite unit. Did City Patrol have a SWAT team?

As the men knelt and raised trapguns, Cole slowed and

leaned hard to the side, U-turning abruptly to head back toward the greenbelt. Something whizzed past him close enough for the wind of it to tickle his cheek. Up ahead, a sticky mass of gray webs appeared where the projectile landed.

Crouching low, Cole avoided the webs and turned hard at the end of the walkway to zoom along the greenbelt. The elite patrolmen had been pretty far away and on foot. It would take them some time to get into position for another shot.

"Jace, veer north, patrolmen are cutting off your eastward escape," Forge advised over the communicator.

Cole pressed the button to talk. "Where were you for me?"

"I told you to go west," Forge said.

"I did and three guys almost took me out," Cole complained, glancing over his shoulder. He guided his warboard to keep trees between himself and the mouth of the walkway.

"I don't have City Patrol west of you for some distance," Forge said.

"How do you know?" Cole asked.

"We're overhearing their comms and I hacked into their tracking program," Forge replied.

"These guys looked a little different," Cole said. "All in black. Extra armor."

"You may have run into Enforcers," Googol said urgently. "Stay well away from them."

"Jace, head west up the next walkway," Forge said. "It's getting ugly north and east of you. Looks like you'll have to cross Flag. Cole, try the next westward walkway. If those Enforcers saw you head north, you need to take some turns."

Cole fought the temptation to panic. It sounded like lots of patrolmen were converging on the area. Forge and Googol both had a flustered edge to their voices. He was going fast on the warboard but knew that wouldn't help him if he got hit by a bunch of webs or drenched in quicktar. He had a couple of the smaller freeze-foam tubes, but those were only for emergencies. If he resorted to fighting, he was going to get caught. His best chance was to run.

Heeding Forge's advice, Cole started to turn onto the next westward walkway but pulled out when he saw another trio of Enforcers running toward him. He left the walkway behind before they could shoot at him, continuing north along the greenbelt.

"More Enforcers on that walkway," Cole reported into his communicator.

"You've seen too many," Googol said. "That means there are many more Enforcers that you haven't seen. It's a major operation."

"Slow down, Cole," Forge said. "If you keep going north, you'll reach a big mob of patrolmen."

"I'm running out of options," Cole said.

"I'm clear," Trickster reported. "Underground and unfollowed."

"Me too," Roulette said. "Need me to go back for them?"

"Negative, Roulette," Forge said. "By the time you found them it would be over. Cole, Trickster said you're good with the battle suit. It opens up options. You can take to the rooftops and escape by jumping. If you ditch the warboard, I can destroy it remotely. Your call."

Cole decelerated. The building to his west had a low enough roof to jump up to. The battle suit wouldn't let him travel as quickly as with the warboard, but it would enable him to move like he used to with the Jumping Sword. If the walkways were getting sealed off, it might be his best option.

"I'm in trouble," Jace said. "Enforcers."

"He's just east of you, Cole," Forge said. "With Enforcers on both sides and behind you, now might be a good time to hit the rooftops."

Jace screamed briefly and went silent.

"Jace?" Cole asked. "Jace?"

Speeding up, Cole peered down the next eastward walkway. It ran between two buildings on the way to Flag Street. About a hundred yards down the walkway, a figure leaned against a wall encased in freeze-foam. Two Enforcers approached Jace, who lay motionless on the ground, looking like a statue of himself dipped in dark chocolate. His warboard idled nearby.

Cole hesitated. For his own survival, the safest bet was to jump onto the roof of the nearest building and run like mad. Even then, his odds of escape might not be great. If he tried to help Jace, they would both probably end up imprisoned.

But no way could he leave Jace behind. The Enforcers were facing away from him as they approached his friend. After readying a freeze-foam tube in one hand, Cole leaned forward on his warboard and hit the accelerator.

CHAPTER

— 16 —

DRONE

B y the time the Enforcers turned to face Cole, it was
too late for them to act. Approaching them rapidly, he
pressed the button on the silver tube, and freeze-foam enveloped one and then the next. He emptied the tube onto them
to make sure they were both totally stuck.

"Jace got hit by quicktar," Cole said into the communicator.

"Use the mister on your left arm," Forge responded.

Cole knew he had antidotes to quicktar, the fake webs,
and the freeze-foam but wasn't sure which button to press.
"How?"

"Hold out your arm," Forge said.

Cole did, and pink spray spurted from the brace on his
wrist. The black tar smeared off of Jace wherever the mist
touched him.

"It was faster to trigger it remotely," Forge explained.
"You had to hit three buttons in sequence to activate the
mist."

Jace gasped and slapped at the tar over his face. Cole soaked his face with the mist. Still blind from the tar and the antidote, Jace reached for his own silver tube.

"No!" Cole shouted. "It's Cole!"

Jace looked up at him, and the rage left his eyes. "What are you doing?"

"You needed help," Cole said. "Could you breathe?"

"Barely," Jace said. "That goop got up my nose. A little air seeped through."

"Get to the rooftops," Forge urged. "Patrolmen are closing in. Probably more Enforcers, too."

Cole stopped spraying Jace. Tapping a button on his wrist, he commanded, "Board off."

The warboard dropped to the ground, and the magnetic connection disappeared. Cole stepped away from the warboard as patrolmen appeared at one end of the walkway and Enforcers at the other.

"Jump," Cole told Jace.

The building on one side was eight stories tall, the other four. Cole sprang with all his might and soared up past the four-story roof. He was aware of trapguns firing below him, but nothing hit him, and he landed comfortably atop the building. Jace arrived beside him.

"We left the boards," Cole said into his communicator.

"I'll destroy them the noisiest way possible," Forge said. "Add a little confusion."

Cole heard explosions down below but didn't risk glancing over the side. A glimpse of his warboard going up in smoke wasn't worth a face full of tar.

"We have to split up," Jace said. "Two targets will be harder to track. Go like mad, Cole. Get reckless. It's do or die."

"What directions?" Cole asked.

"The east is flooded with patrolmen," Jace said, talking into his communicator. "I'll go northwest. Cole will go southwest."

"Sounds like your best bet," Forge answered. "Hurry."

Cole took off running toward the southwest corner of the building, his speed augmented by the battle suit. Jace ran for the northwest corner. "Thanks, Cole," Jace said over the communicator, his tone a little shy.

"Any time," Cole replied. He felt like he did a good job making the response sound casual and brave.

The corner of the building came up fast. Since he was already four floors up, Cole didn't want to jump up too much, or the battle suit might not be able to handle the landing. Plus, if he jumped high, he might make himself more of a target.

Focusing on distance, Cole leaped outward from the edge of the roof. He launched forward, rising only slightly, the greenbelt blurring by below. He began to lose altitude, gradually at first, then quickly as his forward momentum failed. The grass came up to greet him. Off to both sides, Cole saw Enforcers and patrolmen. They were all looking north, trapguns raised. Apparently Jace had come into view first.

Cole landed in a stumble and then jumped for the building on the far side of the greenbelt, a three-story structure. He soared upward with plenty of power to make it. Nobody even fired at him until he had almost landed on the flat roof. But then a brusque, blunt force hit his legs, whipping them out from under him and causing him to collapse in a wild roll, the guardcloth in his battle suit stiffening against the impacts.

Rattled by the jarring impact, Cole tried to scramble to his feet but found his legs immobile below the waist. A hasty glance revealed that they were bound together by quicktar, down to the tips of his boots.

"My legs got hit with quicktar," Cole said into the communicator. "Do I have more pink mist?"

"Be glad the goo missed your arm," Forge said. "The misters don't work so well after a direct hit. Point the mister at your legs."

Cole obeyed. "Okay."

The pink spray showered his legs, and he could move again. Cole hopped to his feet and started running southwest, ignoring where he felt sore from the tumble. He had to keep going. His one hope now was to outpace the patrolmen and Enforcers and get underground. The longer he stayed out of sight on rooftops, and the faster he moved, the more chance he had of slipping through their net.

As the corner of the roof drew near, he saw that the walkway to the west was too wide to jump across, but the walkway to the south was narrower, and the next building was only one story taller. Whether he could make the jump was questionable, but there wasn't time for second thoughts.

Racing to the edge, Cole put everything he had into the leap. His stomach dropped as he reached the apex of his flight. Given that he had started three floors up, he had probably sprung too high—if he missed the next roof, it would be a serious drop to the walkway below, even with the battle suit.

As the next roof came closer, Cole realized he would fall just short, so he leaned forward and stretched out his arms. His hands barely caught hold of the rooftop's edge. Without the battle suit he wouldn't have had a prayer of holding on, but with the added strength the suit provided, he got a good enough grip to resist his momentum. For a moment he dangled, legs swinging, and then Cole heaved himself up.

He wanted to roll over onto his back and recuperate. That had been close. He wouldn't try another leap quite that far. He couldn't afford a fall.

And he couldn't afford to pause.

Back on his feet, Cole dashed across the flat rooftop. His heart was beating hard, even with the help his muscles were getting from the battle suit.

"Looking good, Jace," Forge said over the communicator. "Keep going north. They came south too eagerly. Cole, head west as soon as you can. You're slipping through their net as well."

Cole swerved west. The little bit of encouragement lifted his spirits. It sounded like now was the time to chance crossing the wider walkway to the west.

He wondered how Trickster and Roulette had gotten away so smoothly. Was it just a matter of experience paying off? Or did they have better exit routes planned because they had been more exposed? He was glad they were safe, but a little jealous at the same time. He didn't want to give the Enforcers or the patrolmen any more target practice.

Since he was up pretty high, Cole jumped straight out when he sprang to the west. The entire area below was paved, and when he landed, he fell to his knees and slid several feet, the shock of impact making his teeth clack. Without the padding on the braces, his knees would have been mangled, but instead he lunged to his feet and kept running.

For the moment, no patrolmen or Enforcers were visible. The nearest buildings to the west were too high to reach—at least ten stories. Cole didn't think the buildings at either hand were near enough to each other for him to scale them by jumping back and forth off the walls. He took the nearest westward walkway.

"Well done, Cole," Forge said. "That way looks open. You'll cross one wide plaza and keep going west, then if you turn south at the next walkway, you'll reach a place to go underground."

"What about me?" Jace asked, breathing hard.

"Keep running north," Forge said. "I'll tell you when to cut west."

Cole took long, bounding strides, flinging himself forward with all his might. His lungs ached, sweat greased his body, and a steady pain began to bore into his side. Enhanced or not, there was only so long a person could maintain a full sprint.

But Cole refused to slow down. He raced across the plaza Forge had described, earning stares from the people walking there but not seeing any patrolmen or Enforcers. Cole entered the walkway at the far side of the plaza and could see up ahead where the next walkway crossed it. He was almost there.

"South on the next walkway?" Cole asked into the communicator. He had studied a map of the area, but his desperate run had completely disoriented him. He didn't want to get this wrong.

"Yep, Cole, south, meaning your next left turn," Forge confirmed. "And Jace, you want to turn west at the next walkway."

"Finally," Jace replied.

Cole reached the walkway and turned south, then skidded to a halt. Blocking his path was a lean, tall robot that looked like a high-tech cross between a human and a praying mantis. Made entirely of shiny black metal, the robot sank into a crouch, long limbs bent and ready.

The building on one side was low enough to reach. Cole sprang, but the robot uncoiled with the sudden speed of a mousetrap, and a weighted net slammed against him, interrupting his trajectory. Pulled by the net, Cole tucked his head and crashed into the side of the building and then fell to the walkway.

Even though his guardcloth had hardened against the impact, Cole lay on his side, shaken and dazed. The lanky robot sprang forward, landing beside him, and held up an extra-long trapgun.

"Don't move," the robot said. "This chase is over." The voice sounded younger than Cole expected, and so human that he would have sworn there had to be a person inside.

Cole held down the button on his communicator to help

the others catch on to what had happened. "Who are you?" Cole asked.

"I'm your best chance," the robot said. "If City Patrol takes you in, you're finished."

"You're not with them?" Cole asked.

"I've helped them," the robot said. "And they think I'm with them. But I'm really working for myself here. You really can't guess who I am? I've been chasing you for some time. Who else did you think would catch you?"

"Wait," Cole said, chills tingling through him. "You're the Hunter?"

"People call me that," the robot replied.

"You're a robot?"

The robot laughed. "I'm no bot. This is a drone I'm controlling."

"You're not here?" Cole asked.

"I can see you," the Hunter said. "I'm free to act. That's good enough. I'm actually in a lab."

"I'm going back for him," Jace said over the communicator. "Where is he?"

"Negative," Forge answered. "Stop talking."

"I'm not letting him—"

Cole felt a hot flash on his forearm and smelled smoke.

"And there you have the loyalty of the Unseen," the Hunter said.

"What?" Cole asked.

"They torched your communicator," he said. "Fried the crystal. They didn't want me getting it. I can probably still figure out the harmonics from what's left, but don't tell them."

"Why are you after us?" Cole asked.

"I bring in criminals," the Hunter said. "It's a talent."

"You sound young."

The Hunter gave a snort. "I'm older than you, buddy. We need to get you out of here. My Enforcers are running interference, but City Patrol is getting closer. It wasn't easy to stage a clear path that would lead you to me. It won't stay clear for long."

"I'm not going anywhere," Cole said.

"Cole, you don't know it yet, but this could be the luckiest day of your life," the Hunter said. "You got conned into joining the wrong side in all of this, and I'm going to give you something most criminals can only dream about. A second chance."

"I won't sell out my friends," Cole said firmly.

"You've been selling them out since you came here," the Hunter said. "How do you think we found zerobase? My agents followed you from Hanover Station to Axis, and from there to the base. City Patrol almost messed it up, but my people were on you the whole time. Nice job slipping away from us at zerobase, by the way. We lost you for a while. Never again."

Cole felt terrible to think he was responsible for trashing Googol's best hideout in Zeropolis. But how could he have known? "I'll never betray them on purpose."

"Let's save that conversation for later," the Hunter replied. "For now, come with me, or City Patrol is going to turn your life into a nightmare. After losing Joe, they're on a witch hunt, and you're the only person who hasn't escaped."

"I'm sort of tangled up," Cole said, reaching for his other tube of freeze-foam.

"Are you going for a weapon?" the Hunter asked. "Seriously? Is your brain broken? You see my trapgun, right? Do you think you can get a molecule of that foam out of that tube before I bury you?"

"I thought I'd be sneaky about it," Cole said candidly.

"No chance," the Hunter said. "Looks like I'm going to have to tear off that battle suit and carry you. It would be easier if you'd come willingly."

"Sorry for any inconvenience," Cole said.

"Toss that little tube aside or I'll trap you good and leave you for the patrolmen," the Hunter threatened.

Cole tried to toss it aside, but it got stuck in the net and didn't go very far. "Sorry," he said. "Want me to try again?"

"Just don't touch it," the Hunter replied. "Let me get the net off of you. Keep still. If you try something, I swear I'll fire."

Extending an arm, the Hunter sprayed the net and it dissolved. He reached for Cole, but there came a click as if a little piece of metal had hit the robotic drone. Glancing, Cole saw a silver disk attached to the drone's hip. A slender wire led from the little disk to a shabby maintenance robot perhaps fifty yards away.

And then the drone lit up. White electricity crackled along the wire, and suddenly the drone was jerking and sizzling. Seconds later freeze-foam covered the severely damaged drone, and Sidekick shoved it over.

"Hi, Cole," the little robot said. "Time to run."

CHAPTER
— 17 —

OLD ZEROPOLIS

Cole raced after Sidekick, who it turned out could extend wheels and zoom along at a rapid pace. It took a moment to leave behind the sharp smell of the drone's scorched metal. Cole was relieved to find his battle suit still functioned normally. He glanced back at where the drone lay swaddled in freeze-foam.

"What did you do to him?" Cole asked.

"I converted a lot of energy into something like electricity," Sidekick said. "Too much for a bot like pretty boy to handle. I could have blown him apart, but you were too close. It was safer to disable him and lock him up with the foam."

"Do you know where we're going?" Cole asked.

"You had better hope so," Sidekick said.

Cole hit the button on his communicator just in case. "Anybody hear me?" he asked.

"It's dead," Sidekick said. "Don't worry. We'll be okay. Whoever was running that fancy drone wanted you to himself. He diverted the patrolmen and the Enforcers away from here. And we're almost to a tunnel entrance."

"Thanks for saving me," Cole said.

"Don't thank me yet," Sidekick replied anxiously.

The walkway widened into a little park. Sidekick led the way to a rectangular grate in the ground between a bench and a low rock wall, then reached down and lifted the grate. "Just drop."

No rungs or steps gave access to the gloomy shaft. Cole glanced around. There was nobody in view. Not wanting to ruin a clean getaway, he stepped into the shaft and plunged into the darkness, trying to hold his body ready to land.

He hit after falling perhaps twenty feet, making a splash in shin-deep water. Looking up at the rectangle of daylight, Cole saw Sidekick enter the shaft, all six legs braced against the sides as he slid the grate back into place. Then the little robot shimmied down to the bottom of the shaft.

"Catch me?" Sidekick asked. "You should be strong enough with the battle suit."

"Sure," Cole said.

Sidekick dropped. The robot was heavier than Cole expected, but he held on to him.

"You can set me down," Sidekick said. "I'm waterproof."

Cole put him down gently, trying not to dip his hands into the chilly water. It reeked like sewage.

"According to my specs, I can survive a thirty-story drop onto bonded crystal, but who wants needless risk? What if I dislocate a processor?"

"I owe you big time," Cole said.

Switching on a light, Sidekick skittered forward, his legs extended to their maximum length. He left a gentle wake in the dark water. "Save the gratitude until you're safely delivered to the Unseen in Old Zero. Think how guilty I'd feel if you thanked me and then we got captured in the tunnels!"

"Think they'll catch us?"

"Probably not. I have more than my fair share of tricks to use down here. Nobody has mapped the Zeropolitan underground like the Unseen, and I have all of their information. In fact, I helped compile a lot of it."

"I didn't know you were with us," Cole said.

"You weren't supposed to know," Sidekick said. "I work best in the background. I'm not a main attraction like that fancy drone, Mr. Tall and Sleek and Ready to Rumble."

"You were the most important robot for me today," Cole said. "You saved my bacon."

"I can be useful," Sidekick admitted. "I'm not the big, cool bot who charges into trouble with trapguns blazing. I'm a wingman. I lay low and pay attention. When an ally like you gets in trouble, I sneak up and zap the troublemaker in the back. Effective, if not heroic."

"It felt heroic to me," Cole said wholeheartedly. "How'd you have enough energy to fry him?"

"The energy is easy," Sidekick said. "I can tap into some really juiced crystals. The trick is converting the energy into something like electricity without overheating. I'm built to do that. It's my primary way of dealing with other bots."

"It wasn't electricity?" Cole asked.

"Almost," Sidekick said. "Tinkers here can play with

physics. Googol tuned my converter to deliver a jolt that would be extremely harmful to bots, but not horribly destructive to living beings. I deliver it with a wire because that kind of energy can't be linked with harmonic crystals."

"You're amazing," Cole said.

"Don't embarrass me," Sidekick said. "You're just saying that because I rescued you. But I guess that's an acceptable reason. Say it again."

"I'm the new president of your fan club," Cole said.

"Don't toy with me," Sidekick replied. "I've always liked the idea of a fan club. Of course, I usually picture myself as a member. I thought about making one for Outlaw."

"He was good today," Cole said. "But I'm making one for you."

"Let's not get carried away," Sidekick said. "Any clue who was operating the drone? It was high-end technology."

"The Hunter," Cole said.

Sidekick stopped moving forward. "Really? The famous Enforcer? Are you sure?"

"That's what he told me."

"No wonder you were impressed with me," Sidekick said. "I'm more impressed too." The robot started advancing again. "What else did he say?"

"Didn't you catch any of it?" Cole asked.

"I have good listening devices, but in this case I was coming fast," Sidekick said. "I shot the drone as soon as I was within range."

"The Hunter wanted me to come in quietly," Cole said. "He told me I was on the wrong side."

"Playing nice to convince you to give up everybody else."

"Seemed that way."

"The Hunter definitely wanted you to himself," Sidekick said. "When they started ordering patrolmen away from the route you were taking, I suspected you were heading into a trap. The High Shaper must have a very serious interest in Secret."

"Understatement alert," Cole said. "He'll do anything to get her. And he wouldn't want too many people knowing much about her."

"All the more reason for us to get away from here," Sidekick said.

"Will the whole path smell this bad?" Cole asked.

"It'll get worse before it gets better," Sidekick said. "But it beats torture!"

"Can you smell?" Cole asked.

"Not like you," Sidekick said. "I have sensors."

"It's pretty close to torture," Cole said.

Sidekick stopped at an open pipe projecting from the wall. The round mouth looked barely tall enough for the robot to fit inside. "You'll have to crawl, but this will get us onto less obvious pathways."

"Are you joking?" Cole asked, crouching to study the greasy water draining from the pipe.

Sidekick climbed inside. "I may not be a handsome bot, but I don't love squirming through filth either. Sorry. I'm under orders to protect you. Going this way will do that."

"I wish I knew how to breathe without smelling," Cole muttered, sliding his head into the pipe and crawling forward on his hands and knees. The air seemed chewy with foulness. Cole fought his gag reflex. "It can't get worse than this."

"There are so many different kinds of nasty beneath Zeropolis," Sidekick said sadly. "I'll let you be the judge."

As they progressed through pipes and tunnels, Cole lost track of time. Thankfully his nose became somewhat deadened to the disgusting smells.

Sidekick was right that the underground passageways held a variety of horrors beyond the sights, smells, and textures of sewage. Oozing slime often covered the walls and floors. On occasion they slogged through sucking goo. Curtains of webs parted reluctantly as Sidekick powered through them, leaving Cole to dodge through the gaps. He saw spiders, bats, snakes, centipedes, lizards, and at one point, Sidekick's lights illuminated squirming masses of blind, hairless rats.

At length they reached the widest, driest tunnel Cole had seen so far. "The worst is behind us," Sidekick announced.

"At least we brought a lot of the smells with us," Cole said.

"Taking off your coveralls might help," Sidekick suggested.

Cole removed them.

"Close your eyes," Sidekick said.

Cole did as requested, and Sidekick began to spray him. It smelled minty and vaguely like a hospital.

"Turn around," Sidekick ordered.

Cole complied and the spraying continued. After some focused showering of his legs and boots, the spraying stopped. Cole stood dripping.

"I guess I was already pretty wet," he said. "I smell better. Kind of like toothpaste, but better."

"I masquerade as a cleaning bot," Sidekick reminded him. "I need a few actual cleansing tools. That wash should also kill the germs on you."

"Thanks," Cole said. "And thanks for leading us out of trouble. It stank, it was gross, but it worked. We never saw a patrolman."

"I could hear some searching for us at first," Sidekick said. "Faint sounds. I didn't want to alarm you. But I haven't heard anybody else in some time." The robot trundled over to a set of rails. "These are tracks from the old subway. We can follow them to Old Zeropolis."

"Will they expect that?" Cole asked. "What if they head us off?"

"The subway system was needlessly complicated," Sidekick said. "There are many routes we can take, and plenty of service tunnels. Our enemies don't know where we're going. We could be heading anywhere inside or outside of Zeropolis. We could have gone aboveground long ago."

"Old Zeropolis is dangerous too, right?" Cole asked.

"It's no playground," Sidekick said. "But I'll take you right to oldbase. You'll be safe there. It's our biggest stronghold."

"Are you still in touch with Googol?" Cole asked.

"I was," Sidekick said. "He asked me to shut off my comms system not long after we went underground. Forge got raided."

"Wait, what?" Cole exclaimed. "Just now?"

"About the time we came down here," Sidekick said.

"Is Forge okay? What about Dalton? And Mir—um, Secret?"

"I can't be sure," Sidekick said. "It sounded like they were on the run. Forge is slippery. Even if City Patrol found his hideout, chances are good he got away with your friends. But if patrolmen took Forge's lair, most of our communicators will be compromised. We'll have to make new batches."

"Did Jace escape?" Cole asked.

"He got underground and met up with Roulette," Sidekick said. "It's the last I heard. But it bodes well."

"Forge had such a great hideout," Cole said.

"They've gotten too good at finding us," Sidekick said. "Forge did a lot of hacking to set up this ambush to free Joe. Somebody must have traced him."

"We won't know more until we reach oldbase?" Cole asked.

"Looks that way," Sidekick said. "Too bad you lost the warboard. We could have ridden there."

"How far is it?" Cole asked.

"At this pace, it'll take us into tomorrow," Sidekick said.

"I'm already hungry," Cole said.

"I have some provisions," Sidekick said. "You won't starve."

"For a little robot, you have a lot of surprises," Cole said.

"Makes me a good sidekick."

That night Cole slept on a panel of bonded crystal they found beside the tracks. Sidekick lashed him in place with some cord he produced, and while Cole slept, the robot dragged him forward.

At first Cole kept waking with a start, but every time he saw basically the same scene—a large, bare tunnel sliding by, illuminated by Sidekick's lights. Each time he woke, he worried about Dalton and Mira. Had they been captured? Did they need him? Eventually he settled down, grew accustomed to the motion of the crystal sled, and sank into a deep sleep.

Cole awoke with Sidekick shaking him.

"Time to get up," Sidekick encouraged. "We're nearing Old Zeropolis."

Cole found he was no longer lashed to the crystal panel. He rubbed his eyes. "Did I sleep long?"

"Almost ten hours, if you count your fitful dozing at the start," Sidekick said. "You deserve it. Even with the battle suit, we walked a lot yesterday."

"Do you ever sleep?" Cole asked.

"Sometimes I shut down temporarily," Sidekick said. "Does me some good to rest my systems on occasion. But I don't really sleep. Must be nice."

Cole stretched. "Feels great sometimes. I guess we don't have any word from the Unseen?"

"I would have wakened you," Sidekick said. "Getting up now is a practical matter. The tunnels under Old Zeropolis are more populated than those under the new city. We'll want to be on the lookout and ready to hide."

"Old Zeropolis has lots of criminals?" Cole asked.

"Yes," Sidekick agreed. "People who want to get lost. Thieves, smugglers, hackers, mercenaries, hermits, tramps, escaped slaves, rebels, idealists—quite a mix."

They left the crystal panel behind. Cole felt good walking again. His body was a little stiff but soon loosened up. He didn't like that he had gone to sleep with a set of problems and had woken up to the same set. It kind of negated the rest.

About fifteen minutes later, Cole heard angry voices shouting up ahead. "Trouble?" he asked.

"Let's not find out," Sidekick suggested, diverting them away from the subway track into a smaller, parallel tunnel.

From that point they moved through a series of lesser tunnels and rooms. In some places the ground was damp or muddy, but Cole was relieved that they encountered no sewers or oozy masses of slime.

When they heard voices talking loudly and laughing in the distance, Sidekick adjusted their route again. Tunnels and rooms came and went.

While moving down a long, straight, dark hall, they came to a stop when a lean, ragged man stepped out of hiding into Sidekick's light. Cole reached for his last freeze-foam tube as he tried to recover from the fright.

"What brings you two wanderers to my hall?" the ragged man asked, the words a little mushy. "Didn't ask permission or nothing!"

Cole heard a hiss, and a small dart appeared in the man's neck. He staggered, swayed, and fell.

"Tranquilizer," Sidekick said. "He didn't seem reasonable, and we can't waste time."

"He surprised me," Cole said. "I almost had a heart attack."

"My fault," Sidekick apologized. "Maybe he was sleeping.

Maybe he was lying in wait. Either way, he stayed low and kept still, and I failed to sense him."

"You were great," Cole said. "That was an awesome shot."

"The day a single grumpy vagrant can take me is the day I retire," Sidekick said. "I'm a sidekick, not incompetent."

They continued through halls and rooms until Sidekick slowed, came close to Cole, and whispered, "We're almost to oldbase. There is supposed to be a checkpoint here, but it's unmanned. Kind of strange. Wait here. Let me go check alone, just in case."

"Should I just wait in the open?" Cole asked.

"Go duck behind those crates," Sidekick said. "I'm sure it's no big deal. This is just a lookout station for an unofficial entrance. The actual entrance is still a ways ahead. With all that's been going on, they're probably just shorthanded. I'll be right back."

The little robot trundled off, taking the light with him. Cole was surprised how dark the tunnel became once Sidekick moved out of view. The blackness made him feel both very hidden and very alone.

Every minute that passed made Cole grow antsier. Water dripped somewhere at a slow, random pace. Off in the distance something clanged, the echo repeating softly. From not too far off came the sound of dry leaves rattling faintly. Or was it an old piece of crumpled paper being dragged?

Cole knew he had a couple of lights somewhere on his battle suit, but he couldn't remember how to activate them. He also wasn't sure he wanted to make himself stand out. He reminded himself that with the battle suit, he should be able to outrun and outfight any crazy tramp who came along. But what about a gang of smugglers? Or another drone piloted by the Hunter?

Finally Cole saw light returning, and Sidekick skittered into view, his six legs hurrying. Cole came out from behind the crates.

"Anything interesting?" he asked.

"Oldbase is gone," Sidekick said. "Not compromised. Completely destroyed."

CHAPTER
18

DATAPOINT

"The whole base was destroyed?" Cole exclaimed. "How long ago?"

"Some of the fires are still burning," Sidekick said. "It must have happened between breaking Joe out and coming here. Googol would have warned us if oldbase was under attack. We were all supposed to meet there."

"Did you see any patrolmen?" Cole asked.

"There are some on the surface," Sidekick said. "A few underground. I didn't actually enter the base. I accessed the system from outside. It shouldn't have still been running. Good craftsmanship. It's over eighty percent down, but there were enough camera feeds still up and recordings I could access to piece together what happened. They hit old-base hard. Blew the place apart. We can't get through this entrance, and if we did, you couldn't do much more than warm your hands over the smoldering rubble."

Cole rubbed his eyes. Everything was going wrong. When would they catch a break? "No word from anybody?"

"Nothing," Sidekick said. "This is disastrous. City Patrol has never come to Old Zeropolis in force. We all began to feel like it was out of bounds. Our one safe zone. Apparently not."

"This is about Secret," Cole said. "The High King would burn down all of Zeropolis to find her."

"I might believe you after this," Sidekick said. "With oldbase gone, I'm not sure what our next play should be. The resistance was already reeling. This might be the killing stroke. Who knows what else got hit? What are your goals?"

Cole took a deep breath and thought about the question. "Well, I want to find my friends—Dalton, Jace, and Secret. And Joe."

"We definitely need to reconnect with the surviving members of the Unseen," Sidekick agreed. "Anything else?"

Cole stared at the little robot. Right now Sidekick seemed like his only friend in the universe. He was a secret weapon designed by the leader of the Unseen in Zeropolis. Cole decided to trust him with everything.

"I'm looking for friends who were kidnapped with me from Outside," Cole said. "And we're trying to find Constance Pemberton."

"Wait a minute," Sidekick said. "As in the Constance Pemberton who died in an accident decades ago? One of the High Shaper's daughters?"

Cole nodded.

"Hold on," Sidekick said, his six legs fluttering so quickly it looked like he was trying to tap dance. "No way. If Constance is actually alive . . . that means . . . it can't be."

"What?" Cole asked.

"Secret is another of Stafford's daughters," Sidekick said. "I couldn't figure out what target could mean so much to the High Shaper. She's just a young girl. But now I get it. Their deaths were a sham, maybe all five, but at least two. Judging from Secret's appearance, the girls have barely aged. And now the resistance is rounding them up."

Cole was astonished by his accuracy. "You got all that by knowing we're looking for Constance?"

"Reconnaissance is one of my primary duties," Sidekick said. "I piece things together. Secret is too young to be Honor or Elegance. So she must be Miracle or Destiny. You slipped earlier, and started to say Secret's real name, which began with 'Mir.' The resistance knows that these daughters have a real claim to the throne, and have been wronged by their father. A powerful revolution could take shape by rallying the populace around them. These girls could be the key ingredient the resistance has lacked all along. And Stafford knows this. You're right. Under the present circumstances, he would burn down all of Zeropolis to find his daughters."

"You're a scary-smart machine," Cole said.

"Don't spread that around too much," Sidekick said. "Thinking machines make Zeropolites twitchy."

"Because they think you'll try to take over?"

"It's happened before. I'm a lot safer when I pretend to be a simple cleaning bot. If City Patrol knew half of my abilities, they would dismantle me immediately."

"Should people be worried?" Cole asked.

"People could have all the same worries about one

another," Sidekick said. "Bots aren't the only beings to have gone bad and run wild. People have done that since the beginning. Any person who gains too much power can become very dangerous. Look at Stafford Pemberton, or Abram Trench. The same can be true for some bots. It was true for Aeronomatron when he devastated Old Zeropolis.

"But I was carefully designed by a good person. I operate within clearly established parameters. I know who I am, what I want, and who I should protect. I can adapt and learn. I can make leaps of logic. But although my neural processors can reach out to sort vast amounts of data, the thinking part of me is clearly defined. I like who I am, and that identity is more firmly established than the personalities of any people I have observed. If people understood me, they'd know I exist to help, not to cause harm."

"Except to robotic drones," Cole said.

"Robotic drones attacking my friends," Sidekick clarified, remaining serious. "I'd harm an enemy to the causes I defend. So would many good people. I want to protect the common good. But try getting Zeropolites to understand that. Thanks to Aero, all thinking robots are considered rampaging terrors spawned by madmen."

"I'm on your side," Cole assured him.

"That puts you in the minority," Sidekick said. "But I appreciate the support. Let's return to the problem at hand. We want to find Googol and the rest of the Unseen, you want to find some enslaved friends, and we all want to find Princess Constance. Finding is the theme. We should probably try Datapoint."

235

"What's datapoint?" Cole asked.

"Datapoint is a person," Sidekick explained. "A woman."

"A member of the Unseen?"

"No, though she has worked with the Unseen a lot. Datapoint contracts with anyone but the government. She's better at finding people than anybody in Zeropolis. Chances are good she can tell us which Unseen hideouts have been raided. If they took out Forge's place and oldbase, who knows where else they might have targeted?"

"Would they have targeted her?" Cole asked.

"Possibly," Sidekick said. "But since she's not a formal member of the resistance, she's probably safer to visit than one of the other Unseen hideouts."

"Lead the way," Cole said.

A short cord with a little grapnel on the end shot out from Sidekick's body and draped over Cole's arm. "Hold on," Sidekick said. "I'm going to douse my lights in case we have patrolmen in the area."

"Are any nearby?" Cole asked.

"I saw a few on the oldbase video feed," Sidekick said. "They're stationed near some of the entrances. Be glad I used one of the most secret entryways. They don't seem to have discovered it yet. Makes sense. The emphasis was apparently on blowing up the place."

"Can we get around the patrolmen?" Cole whispered.

"Here near oldbase? Should be easy. There are lots of hidden tunnels nearby. Stay quiet and keep close."

Sidekick led Cole through the blackness. Cole felt like he was holding a leash, but it was definitely Sidekick taking him for a walk. He concentrated on not making noise and not tripping as he shuffled forward through the darkness. Now and then he could tell from the acoustics that they had entered a narrower place, or a more open place, but he seldom passed over uneven ground, and he never bumped into anything. Sidekick was an excellent guide.

The strange sounds in the darkness bothered Cole less now that the robot was with him. He trusted Sidekick to track anything dangerous.

Without sight, it was difficult to tell how far they had gone, but Cole knew he had taken thousands of blind steps. After a long while, he whispered, "You can see without light?"

"At several other wavelengths and with alternatives like sonar," Sidekick whispered back. "We can probably turn the lights on soon."

When Sidekick switched his lights back on, they stood in a long, broad room with a low ceiling. It felt like a sprawling basement.

"Are we close?" Cole asked.

"No, but we're out of danger from the patrolmen who leveled oldbase. We can get most of the way to Datapoint underground. Old Zeropolis is built over labyrinths of subways, sewers, and tunnels."

"Sewers?" Cole groaned.

"Don't worry," Sidekick assured him. "Most of the sewers here have been dry for years. This is the corpse of a city—not a functional one."

"Corpse sewers sound so much better," Cole grumbled.

"We'll avoid the most direct routes," Sidekick said. "My goal is not to see another person until we reach her building."

They proceeded along many tunnels, sometimes plunging down stairs to darker, colder hallways. Without Sidekick, Cole knew he would be hopelessly lost.

After they had traveled a good distance, Sidekick slowed beside a blockaded subway tunnel. "Know why this is sealed up?" the robot asked.

"Cave in?" Cole guessed.

"This tunnel leads underneath Sector 20," Sidekick said. "It's the part of Old Zeropolis controlled by Aeronomatron. A large portion of the city."

"Really?" Cole asked. "Why are we so close?"

"Because Datapoint established her lair near Sector 20."

"Why would she do that?"

"Probably because nobody wants to go near Sector 20," Sidekick said. "Aeronomatron killed more people than any disaster in the recorded history of the Outskirts. If you want to hide, setting up camp near his domain is a useful tactic. The Unseen have a couple of smaller hideouts near Sector 20 for similar reasons."

"Are all the tunnels under Sector 20 sealed up?" Cole asked.

"All of them," Sidekick said. "People were quite enthusiastic about the project. Same with raising the enormous wall that surrounds his territory." Sidekick continued onward, leaving the sealed tunnel behind.

"What if the tunnels were unsealed?" Cole asked. "Could Aero send out trouble? Robots or something?"

"He did at first, back before everything was sealed," Sidekick said. "Eventually the bots stopped coming. Once the patrolmen severed Aero from all outside ties and sealed up Sector 20, the world stopped hearing from him."

"He could have robots in reserve," Cole said.

"If so, he's very patient," Sidekick said. "The wisest course of action with Aero seems to be what they took—cut him off, and leave him alone."

"Could he have run out of power by now?" Cole asked.

"He controls a large portion of the old city," Sidekick said. "If he diverted all the remaining energy crystals to himself, I'm sure he could keep running for thousands of years."

"What about upkeep?" Cole wondered. "You know, if he starts to malfunction."

"He might have some maintenance bots running," Sidekick said. "Or maybe he shut down long ago. Nobody knows. Nobody wants to risk finding out."

They reached a silent, dusty subway station. Cole could picture how it once must have bustled with people. Daylight seeped down a stairway.

Sidekick killed his lights. "This is where we head up. Be careful what you say to Datapoint. She has a photographic memory, and lives to assemble information. If we tell her about Constance, the chances are good that she'll jump to the same conclusions I reached. Let's start small. First we'll try to get in touch with Googol."

Cole followed Sidekick up a long flight of stairs. At the top Cole slowly turned in a circle. He had never imagined such tall buildings and such wide streets looking so completely abandoned. Old Zeropolis wasn't a ghost town. It was a ghost metropolis.

Off to one side loomed a concrete wall so high that it dwarfed even the tallest crystal-and-steel skyscrapers. Cole felt like he was at the base of an enormous dam.

"That is a serious wall," Cole said.

"To contain a serious threat," Sidekick said. "This way."

The robot led Cole along a couple of streets. The setting sun bathed the ruins in golden light. Cole noticed overturned trash cans, abandoned vehicles, and dry fountains. Down one street he saw a mangy dog limping along.

"Not many people," Cole observed.

"Not this near to Sector 20," Sidekick agreed. "Other areas of the old city have a little more life. A few districts can get almost boisterous."

Sidekick approached a stately stone building that looked like it could have been a museum or a bank. He and Cole climbed a set of broad steps to reach the large metal door.

A peephole in the door slid open, revealing a set of wide eyes. "A boy and a bot," a voice said. "What business brings you here?"

"We've come to see DP," Sidekick said. "I'm a repeat customer."

"It's been a rough day hereabouts," the doorman said. "She's not seeing any more visitors. Same goes for tomorrow."

"Better check with her," Sidekick said. "Tell her Sidekick is at the door with vital data from the most exclusive sources."

The doorman licked his lips. "You know how to tempt

her. I'm not sure it's going to work today, little bot, even with me remembering that you've come round before. But I'll take your message to her."

The doorman closed the peephole and left. They waited in silence. Eventually the peephole slid open again.

"Any chance you were followed?" the doorman asked.

"None," Sidekick assured him. "This is what I do."

"Who is the boy?"

"An important asset," Sidekick said. "The rest is for Datapoint to know."

The peephole closed and the door opened. The doorman was tall and veiny with buggy eyes and trembling hands. "You must have stored up some trust with DP. She really didn't intend to admit visitors for the next couple of days."

"Probably taking pity on me," Sidekick said. "I'm not what many would call an attractive bot. She's in her lounge?"

"As usual," the man answered. He nodded to a woman and a man holding trapguns. The pair escorted Cole and Sidekick down a wide, carpeted hallway with framed portraits on the walls.

"What was this building?" Cole asked. The inside didn't match up with a bank or a museum.

"Used to be a government building," Sidekick said.

Neither of the guards commented. They reached a set of tall, bronze doors. The male guard pulled them open.

"Come in," chimed a high voice. Across the carpeted room, Cole saw a small woman with a short, neat haircut seated on a large white sofa. She wore a gray dress with white stockings and black shoes. The woman rose to her feet. "Good to see you again, Sidekick."

The doors closed behind them. "Nice to see you, Datapoint."

Her high voice, short stature, and slender build made her seem young. But judging from her face, she had to be around forty.

"Who's your friend?" Datapoint asked with a small scowl. "I don't recognize him."

"He's new to Zeropolis," Sidekick said.

Datapoint folded her arms. "Looks like he's had a recent makeover from Roulette. She has such distinctive handiwork. Is he a fugitive? Is he part of the group Abram Trench is looking for?"

"I'm Steve Rigby," Cole said.

Datapoint laughed and clapped her hands. "Definitely a makeover. Did Forge do the name?" She narrowed her eyes and stared at Cole. "Who are you really?" Then she glanced at Sidekick. "Who is he really?"

"He's from Outside," Sidekick said.

"And you're his bodyguard?" Datapoint asked with a giggle. "Did Outlaw take a sick day?"

"Outlaw has his own problems," Sidekick said. "Are you up-to-date on what City Patrol has been doing?"

"Not just City Patrol," Datapoint said. "The Enforcers too. It's why I rolled up the welcome mat. Everything is upside down. The old rules have been erased. You have interesting news?"

"You know oldbase is destroyed?" Sidekick asked.

Datapoint rolled her eyes. "You have to do better than that. And eastbase. And lowbase. And at least four lesser hideouts here in Oldtown. Not to mention zerobase the other day and Forge getting evicted."

"Did Forge get captured?" Sidekick asked.

"Not that I've heard," she replied.

"What about Nova?" Sidekick inquired.

"Nova?" Cole asked.

"Is he for real?" Datapoint asked.

"I told you, he's new," Sidekick insisted. "Nova is the leader of the Unseen in Zeropolis."

"It doesn't appear Nova has been picked up," Datapoint said. "Look, I want some good info or you can scram. I don't talk to anybody under false pretenses. Sets a bad precedent."

"Googol found a girl the City Patrol wants," Sidekick said.

Cole immediately tensed up. Sidekick had guessed too much about Mira. How much would he reveal to this woman? Even if she didn't do business with the government, she traded secrets for a living.

"Okay, this is closer to interesting," Datapoint conceded. "I've seen her picture. Maybe eleven or twelve. I've seen two of her companions, neither of which is Steve here. Who is she? Why are the Enforcers so interested?"

"Googol hasn't revealed her identity," Sidekick said. "He calls her Secret. Apparently finding her is one of the High King's top priorities."

"And Googol has her," Datapoint said.

"Yes," Sidekick confirmed. "I've seen her. So has Steve."

"Who is she, Steve?" Datapoint asked bluntly. "Tell me that, and I'll give you two all the help I can."

"There's a rumor she's an escaped slave," Cole said. "A personal favorite of Stafford's."

Datapoint scowled. "That doesn't add up. No way would the High King put this much effort into an escaped slave. Abram Trench wouldn't show major interest. Plus, you look like you're telling a half truth, which means you probably know the whole truth. A word of friendly advice? When deception is required, let Sidekick do the talking."

"Her identity is a major secret," Sidekick said. "Googol hasn't trusted me with it."

"But Steve knows, whoever he is," Datapoint said. "Come on, Steve, spill and my resources are yours."

Cole took a deep breath. "If I tell you this secret, you're going to end up tortured and dead."

"You know the secret," Datapoint replied. "You're alive."

"Barely," Cole said. "You've seen the fun that follows us. It's why all those bases were attacked."

Datapoint gave a slow nod. "At least now you're being sincere. Maybe I don't want to know. Do I, Sidekick?"

"Nobody wants to know this one," Sidekick said.

Datapoint scrunched her nose and rubbed her hands together in front of her lips. "I never pictured a show of force in Old Zeropolis like we saw last night and today. Certainly not all at once. How long have they known about those bases? Why move now? I believe that your secret is dangerous, Steve. Do not tell me for now. I reserve the right to inquire again. I've had suspicions about what was behind this offensive, and your information has confirmed some of my guesses. Your turn. Why did you come to me?"

"I wasn't sure what bases had been compromised," Sidekick said. "Our comms are down. We're looking for Googol or Nova."

"Isn't everyone?" Datapoint said. "I don't believe they were captured. But they are in deep hiding. If you know a most secret retreat they hold ready, check there first. They've stopped using any comms I can intercept. They've gone dark."

"What about Secret?" Cole asked. "Or the boys who were with her?"

"Friends, I take it?" Datapoint asked. "They've not been captured unless it was done with uncommon discretion. Joe MacFarland seems to have made a clean getaway as well. Anything else?"

"I came to the Outskirts a few months ago with some friends," Cole said. "We were kidnapped. They were taken as slaves. I have some names. I'd like to find them."

"Try me," Datapoint said.

"Jenna Hunt," Cole said hopefully.

"No," Datapoint said.

Cole paused. "Are you sure?"

"Information is my trade," Datapoint said. "It's the most valuable commodity in an advanced society. I don't forget a name or a face."

"Sidekick told me you have a photographic memory," Cole said.

"It was an understatement," Datapoint said. "Think high

definition three-D memory with surround sound. Nobody named Jenna Hunt entered Zeropolis over the last year, slave or not."

"Could they have used an alias?" Cole asked.

"Possibly," she said. "Do you know any likely aliases?"

Cole shook his head. "What about Lacie Clark?"

"No slaves by that name in the past half a year," Datapoint said.

"Blake Daniels?" Cole tried.

Datapoint furrowed her brow. "Are you playing games? No, it fits; he arrived in the Outskirts according to the time-line you described. He came here from Junction."

"That's probably him," Cole said, feeling encouraged—finally some good news!

Datapoint gave a small smile. "Small world. Blake works for me."

CHAPTER

19

BLAKE

"You mean Blake is here?" Cole asked.

"In this building," Datapoint said. "You can see him after we finish."

"But he was a slave," Cole said. "The High King bought him."

"He came to Zeropolis as a slave, yes," Datapoint said. "He was assigned to an undercover task force meant to spy on activities here in the old city. Some of the other organizations in town caught on and . . . dismantled the operation. I helped reveal their presence, and as part of my payment, I got to keep Blake. Are you aware of his abilities?"

"I knew him in my world," Cole said. "We were separated soon after coming here."

"His talents are unique," Datapoint said. "The Unseen should thank me for getting him away from City Patrol."

"Now he's your slave?" Cole asked.

"Technically he remains a slave," Datapoint said. "I can't change his mark. But he's not my slave. Here in Old

Zeropolis, slaves get the same treatment as anybody else. He's my employee. It has been strongly suggested that he work for me for two years in return for sparing him. He gets fair wages, plus room and board. After that, he's free to stay on here, or take his chances elsewhere."

Since Blake wasn't supposed to leave for two years, Cole thought it sounded like he was still kind of a slave. But this didn't seem like the right moment to argue the point.

"I can see him now?" Cole asked.

"Sure," Datapoint said. "I take it you would like sanctuary here?"

Sidekick stepped closer to her. "If you're not sure where we can find Googol or Nova, a day or two here would help us."

"I'll keep watch for news of Googol, Nova, and the wanted children," Datapoint said. "I'll also watch for word of you two reaching my lair. If they're onto you, I'll kick you out immediately."

"Understood," Sidekick said. "I don't believe we were followed."

"I don't believe so either, or else we wouldn't be talking," Datapoint said. "Anything else you need at the moment?"

Cole glanced at Sidekick. It didn't seem like the right time to bring up Constance. It would almost certainly give away the whole secret.

"No," Sidekick said. "Thanks for hiding us."

"My pleasure," Datapoint said. "Given the magnitude of the secret our Stevie here is guarding, I don't want the government getting hold of him. Are you ready to see Blake?"

"That would be great," Cole said. Blake had never been his favorite guy. He was the sort of kid who hogged the ball in soccer and talked himself up too much. But at the moment, seeing him would be heaven. Annoying or not, Blake wasn't just someone from home, but someone Cole knew fairly well!

"My husband can take you to him," Datapoint said. She raised her voice. "Lunk! I need you!"

A hulking man entered the room from behind a curtain, his black shirt stretched tight over beefy shoulders and a powerful chest. He was the physical opposite of Datapoint—as tall and thick as she was short and slender.

"Lunk, dear, can you take Steve here to meet with Blake?" Datapoint asked sweetly. "They're old friends."

"Your wish is my command," Lunk said in a rumbling voice without a trace of sarcasm.

"Sidekick," Datapoint said. "Go to the guest room where you've stayed before. Steve will find you there later."

"You're too generous with a shabby old bot," Sidekick said.

"Oh, stop," Datapoint said, waving a dismissive hand. "You've got some of the best neural processors in the city. Don't play sidekick with me. I know your value."

"Flattery will get you everywhere," Sidekick replied.

"This way," Lunk said, opening the door.

"See you," Cole said to Sidekick.

"I'm glad you found one of your friends," the robot replied. "Congrats."

As Cole walked to the door, he found that he barely came

up to the base of Lunk's chest. He had to crane his neck to look him in the eye.

"You're enormous," Cole couldn't help saying.

"Thanks," Lunk replied.

They walked out of the room and down the hall. The people who saw Lunk gave him a nod. Lunk led Cole around a couple of corners until they reached a closed door. Lunk knocked gently.

"Come in," a voice invited.

Lunk opened the door, and Cole saw Blake sitting behind a desk at a computer. The room appeared to be his private office.

Blake glanced at the door, then did a double take, eyes widening. "Cole Randolph? Seriously?"

"Hey, Blake," Cole said, giving a little wave.

"I'll let you two catch up," Lunk said, stepping aside. "I'll be out here when you're done, Steve, and I'll take you to your room."

"I guess you just heard my real name," Cole said.

Lunk shrugged. "My real name is Kevin."

"Where did Lunk come from?" Cole asked.

"Datapoint's idea," he said. "She didn't find Kevin intimidating enough."

Cole nodded. "I guess Lunk is tougher."

"Go on," Lunk encouraged.

Cole walked through the doorway, and Lunk closed the door behind him. Blake jumped up from his chair, ran to Cole, and threw his arms around him with the intensity of a drowning man. Cole hugged him back. When the embrace ended, Cole saw that Blake had tears streaming down his cheeks.

"Sorry," Blake said, wiping his eyes on his sleeve. "I'd given up on seeing anybody from home again." He started to laugh unsteadily.

"Yeah," Cole said. "I couldn't believe it when Datapoint told me you were here."

"Old Zeropolis is in the middle of nowhere," Blake said, still wiping his eyes. "What are you doing here? Is that a freemark?"

Cole fingered the mark on the back of his wrist. "Long story." He leaned close to Blake and used his quietest whisper. "Can we talk in here?"

"Sure," Blake said.

"You're positive nobody is listening?" Cole asked.

"I've checked," Blake said, speaking more quietly. "And I know how to check. We can talk here. What's up?"

"How much do you trust Datapoint?" Cole asked.

Blake thought for a moment. "Trust her with what?"

"Like if you knew a major secret that the High King would kill for," Cole said.

Blake raised his eyebrows. "I don't know. She likes secrets. She hates the High King and the Zeropolitan government. She's also pretty selfish."

"Selfish how?"

"She likes to be at the center of everything. She wants everyone to admire her. She's very proud of her memory. The people here all think she's the best thing ever."

"You don't?" Cole asked.

"I'm basically her prisoner," Blake said. "Since I was working for her enemies and got captured, now I have to work for her for at least two years."

"Or what?"

"Or she'll spill information about where I am," Blake said. "I'll get captured again."

"Is this better than that?" Cole asked.

"In some ways I guess," Blake said. "It's mostly the same. Everybody just wants me for my ability."

"What can you do?" Cole asked.

"I'm good with harmonic crystals," Blake said.

"The kind in communicators?" Cole asked.

"Exactly," Blake said. "And providing energy to machines. I can create and tune crystals better than just about anybody. Don't ask me why. It seems easy."

"No kidding," Cole said. This sounded like the Blake he knew. He wondered how capable he really was.

"If I get near enough to any harmonic crystal, I can hear it in my mind. It isn't hard for me to then create a crystal with matching harmonics. Usually you need to have a stolen crystal to listen in on enemy communications. For most people it takes a lot of study and time to make a duplicate crystal. Datapoint hasn't seen anybody who can replicate a harmonic crystal without touching or examining it. Neither had City Patrol. It's really useful for spying."

"I bet," Cole said. He knew how valuable a stolen harmonic crystal could be. If Blake could copy them just by getting near them, no wonder Datapoint wanted him working for her.

"That's why they sent me with the unit to work in Old Zeropolis," Blake said. "They wanted to listen in on some of the criminals here."

"How long have you been at it?" Cole asked.

"I've worked for Datapoint for a couple of weeks," he said. "For a few weeks before that I worked for City Patrol here in the old town. I also spent a few weeks in the modern Zeropolis."

Cole wondered how many of the problems the Unseen had faced lately were caused by Blake. If he could replicate crystals without them knowing it, he could have been the main problem.

"Nobody else can make matching crystals just by being near them?" Cole asked.

"I'm supposed to be the only one," Blake said. "I got treated well, especially in the real Zeropolis. It's been all downhill since then."

The idea of Blake getting nice treatment from the High King for messing up the resistance didn't sit well with Cole. Blake could be the reason so many bases had fallen. He could be a big part of why Dalton, Mira, Jace, Joe, and the Unseen were on the run.

"How much do you know about the rebellion?" Cole asked.

"I didn't know squat until Datapoint nabbed me," Blake said. "City Patrol told me I was helping them catch criminals."

"What do you think of the rebellion now?" Cole asked, trying to stay calm.

"Why?" Blake asked. "Are you a part of it?"

"Yeah," Cole said. "And the crystals you made for City Patrol have been tearing it apart."

Blake paled. "I didn't know."

"Really, Blake?" Cole asked heatedly. "What did you think you were doing? Why would you work for the government here? Don't you get they're our captors? They made us into slaves. The High King is a bad guy, Blake. Why'd you help them?"

"Lay off. I was trying to survive. I was all alone. They were really rough with me if I resisted. I was their slave, remember?"

"So you wreck everything for the people who are trying to free you?"

"How was I supposed to know?" Blake cried, face reddening. "They brought me here from Junction, tested me, found out what I could do, and put me to work. They owned me! They made it sound like we were after robbers and kidnappers and terrorists. I was just matching crystals. I didn't know the details. I didn't track anyone down. What would you have done?"

"The same thing I already did," Cole said. "Escaped. Fought back."

"Good for you, Cole," Blake said. "I don't know what your Sky Pirates were like—"

"Sky Raiders," Cole interjected.

"City Patrol had me under tight watch. I didn't have a chance to escape. And how was I supposed to know I wasn't really helping them catch criminals? They seemed like the police."

"They're the police for the people who made us into slaves," Cole said. "That makes them the bad guys."

"Well, good to see you, too." Blake flopped down on his chair and buried his face in his hands.

Cole realized he had probably been overly harsh. He was exhausted, and his emotions were frayed. "Hey, Blake, I'm sorry. I'm just stressed. I almost got caught by the City Patrol. Dalton too. And some really important members of the rebellion."

Blake lifted his head. "You've seen Dalton?"

"We came to Zeropolis together," Cole said. "After I escaped Sambria, I found him in Elloweer. I'm not sure where he is now. We're scattered."

"Yeah, a lot of the Unseen bases went down lately."

"We got caught in the middle of it."

"How'd you find Datapoint?" Blake wondered.

"I'm with a really smart robot," Cole said.

"They just call them bots here," Blake corrected. "You haven't been in Zeropolis long?"

"A couple of days," Cole said. "Long enough to get into major trouble."

"What's the big secret?" Blake asked. "The one the High King would kill for. Can you tell me?"

"I don't know," Cole said. "Knowing it would put you in a lot of danger. I've basically been running for my life since I found out."

"Seriously?" Blake said.

"It's why all the crazy stuff has happened lately."

"You haven't told Datapoint?" Blake asked.

"She knows about the secret," Cole said. "Not the important part."

"Does she know how big the secret is?"

"Yes. And how dangerous."

Blake shook his head. "I'm not sure she'll let you leave unless you tell her."

"Maybe. She seemed okay not knowing for now."

"She doesn't like to be kept in the dark. She's obsessed with being the first to know stuff. And if the secret really is a big deal, I'm not sure you can trust her. Her top priority is herself. She's not part of your rebellion. She's an outlaw. And she's all about strategy. She wants something on everyone so they can't mess with her. She doesn't want to help City Patrol, but I bet she'd make a deal to save herself."

Cole folded his arms. "It's tricky because we might need her. We're looking for somebody. It's all part of the secret."

"She's good at finding people," Blake said. "The best. Her memory is unbelievable and she has set up an amazing spy network."

"And you're helping her make it better," Cole said.

"I have been," Blake admitted. "It's getting better fast. They take me out once or twice a day to find new harmonic signals. But not since everything went nuts."

"Could you help us find this person?" Cole asked.

"Sure," Blake said. "I'd love to help. I wouldn't really know where to start. I'm great with the crystals, but I've never looked at the actual information very much."

"The bot I'm with is really smart," Cole said. "Is there a

computer he could use? Could you make a crystal that would give him access to Datapoint's info?"

Blake rubbed his lips uncomfortably. "If we got caught, we'd be finished."

"We'd be careful," Cole said. "There are always risks."

Blake stood and started pacing. After a minute he came close to Cole and whispered. "Look, I want to help you. I'm sorry if I hurt the rebellion. What you really want is to get inside her situation room. She only goes in alone. Nobody knows what she has in there, but it's where she hides out when she's up against a serious challenge."

"Can we get inside?" Cole asked.

"She keeps it locked," Blake said. "I was with her right before she went there yesterday. I know the harmonics of the crystal she uses as her key."

"She showed you her key?" Cole asked.

"No," Blake said. "But she had it with her. It had different harmonics from the other crystals she normally carries."

"And you remember it well enough to copy it?" Cole asked.

"Sure," Blake said. "I don't remember the harmonics of every crystal I'm near, but that one stood out. I knew how important it was. I don't think people are used to what I can do. It was dumb of her to come near me with it. Is this smart, Cole? If we get caught, she'll probably kill us. For real."

"You don't have to come," Cole said.

"I might as well," Blake said. "If you enter with a crystal key, she'll figure out how you did it."

"We can get you out of here," Cole said. "You can leave with us."

"And join the rebellion?" Blake asked. "I'd like to help the people trying to free us. But I don't know if I'd survive having Datapoint after me. You either."

"I've had a lot of enemies," Cole said. "Our best bet is helping the resistance. If they can stop the High King, you won't be a slave anymore. We can find the others and work on getting home."

"We can't get home," Blake said. "Not to stay. Haven't you heard?"

"Some of those rules might be flexible," Cole said. "I have reason to hope we can reshape how it all works. We just need to find the right help."

"Really?" Blake said. "That would be awesome. I gave up on getting home a long time ago. Does the resistance have a chance against the High King? He has the Outskirts under tight control."

"The secret I know could give the rebellion a chance," Cole said. "That's why the High King wants me and everyone else who knows it dead."

"Okay," Blake said, opening a drawer. "I'll make you a key." He took out a crystal block and waved a hand over it. A little crystal cube emerged from the larger block. Blake handed it to Cole.

"This is it?" Cole asked.

"The situation room is on the bottom floor at the rear of the building. Two levels underground. The door is solid steel. That crystal will fit into the slot in the panel beside the door."

"You just wave your hand and make a top secret key?"

Cole said, marveling at Blake's ability. "That's crazy!" He couldn't help feeling a twinge of envy and disappointment about still being separated from his own power.

Blake shrugged. "I don't really have to wave my hand. It just looks more official."

"Hilarious. Well, whatever you do, it's super quick and impressive."

"It's easy for me. Don't ask why. I can't explain. It just is. Like whistling a familiar tune."

"Cool," Cole said. Blake was seldom shy about how amazing he was. But at least he had stepped up and helped. "Want to come with us?"

"Make sure you and your bot think the risk is worth it," Blake said. "I'm not sure what's in there, but it must involve lots of great info."

"Okay."

"There's a staircase at the front western corner of the building. We should meet at the bottom in the dead of night. Let's say six hours after sundown. If somebody spots us, we'll pretend we're meeting up late to talk or something. If we can get to the situation room undetected, we'll give it a try."

"All right, Blake. It's a plan."

He smiled. "I guess walking behind that wagon didn't teach you to behave."

Cole shook his head. "It kind of taught me the opposite."

CHAPTER
20

SITUATION ROOM

Six hours after sundown Cole and Sidekick stood beside the door to their room. No sound reached them from the hall beyond.

"You're sure we should do this?" Cole asked.

"It's so tempting," Sidekick said. "That room will be a treasure trove of data. And stealing data is what I do. If we can get in there, I can make it worth our while."

"Datapoint won't like it," Cole said.

"Not a bit," Sidekick agreed. "This could really burn bridges. But I work quickly. We might be able to pull it off undetected. Datapoint is at the top of the list of people who could have info that hints at where we might find Constance. It would be very advantageous to learn what she knows without telling her who we're after."

Cole nodded. He had felt more certain about the mission when they had discussed it earlier. Now that they were about to slip out of their room in the dark of night, he was having second thoughts. Datapoint had given them her protection.

Was it fair to take advantage of her generosity? If they got caught, she would have every right to be furious.

On the other hand, Datapoint was basically holding Blake as her prisoner. She was no saint. And the information they were after wouldn't hurt her at all. Since Datapoint disliked the Zeropolitan government and the High King, it would actually benefit her if they found Constance.

"Okay," Cole said. "Let's roll the dice."

Cole opened the door. Dim blue lights along the edges of the floor provided enough of a glow to navigate the hall.

Following Sidekick in silence, Cole felt like any moment whistles would blow, sirens would wail, and guards would come running. Nobody had communicated rules against wandering the building at night, but he couldn't help feeling it looked incredibly suspicious.

They reached the stairs without encountering anybody. Blake awaited them just beyond the final steps.

"I was starting to wonder if you were coming," Blake whispered.

"Sorry," Cole said quietly. "I hesitated at the end."

"We don't have to go through with it," Blake said.

"No, we're in," Cole said.

Blake stared down at Sidekick. "This is the genius bot?"

Sidekick replied in his robotic monotone, "Fear not hu-man, I will clean the da-ta a-way from the sit-u-a-tion room."

Blake gave Cole a concerned glance. "Really?"

"Sorry," Sidekick said in his normal voice. "I know I look like a street sweeper. It's by design. I'm made for spying.

Looking like a cleaning bot helps me to hide in plain sight. It's not so great for my self-esteem, though."

"All right," Blake said. "Let's go. I hope you two know what you're doing."

"We hope you do too," Sidekick said. "I've never heard of anyone who can replicate harmonic crystals by memory."

"The key will work," Blake said.

They started down the hall together. Cole strained his senses to detect other people, but all was still and quiet.

"Is there an excuse we could use for being down here?" Sidekick asked. "I haven't been to this level before."

"Not really," Blake said. "It's mostly data archives that we shouldn't be messing with. Our best excuse is that we were restless and went for a walk."

"You know," Cole said cheerily, "a refreshing stroll through a dark basement full of data we might want to steal."

"Let's not get caught," Sidekick said.

Blake led them around a couple of corners and then down a hall that ended at a formidable door of polished steel. A square socket gaped in a panel beside the doorway.

Cole took out the crystal Blake had prepared. It looked like it would fit the socket. "Go for it?" Cole asked.

"If we're doing this, we need to be quick," Sidekick said.

Cole pressed the crystal into the socket, and the door rose out of sight with a hiss. Bright light from beyond the doorway glared into the dim hall. Cole slipped the crystal cube into his pocket and entered, blinking as his eyes adjusted. Blake and Sidekick followed. The door hissed shut behind them.

They were in a bare, white corridor that led to a staircase. They hustled down several flights until they reached another steel door with another socket.

"Different key?" Cole asked, almost hoping they would have to abort the mission.

"I only sensed one unusual set of harmonics on her," Blake said. "Might be the same cube."

Cole pressed the crystal into the socket, and the door whisked open. They passed into a large room with no other doors and lots of electronics.

"Jackpot," Sidekick said.

The door swished shut behind them.

A pair of large screens mounted to the wall flickered to life at the front of the room. A solitary computer between the screens turned on as well.

"New faces?" a deep, male voice asked, the words appearing on the wall screens and the computer screen. "This is unexpected. Welcome. Does Datapoint know you are here?" The voice had a calm, rational cadence.

Cole froze. If Datapoint had a smart computer in here, they were already caught. It would tell her about the intrusion. Cole had no idea how to react. Blake and Sidekick stayed silent as well.

"Apparently not," the voice decided. "Did you come seeking me?"

"We're the janitors," Cole improvised. "She sent us to clean the room." He hoped the lie might prevent the computer from setting off an alarm immediately. Or could it have already alerted Datapoint silently?

"This room is cleaned by a nonsentient device that never leaves the premises," the voice said. "I'm surprised you managed to break in here. Do you even know who you are addressing?"

"We're after information," Cole said.

"I will interpret that as a negative response. You have come to the right place for information. I am the secret behind how Datapoint knows so much. Allow me to introduce myself. I am Aeronomatron."

Mouth dry, Cole swallowed. His gut felt hollow. "You're Aero? The famous computer that took over Old Zeropolis?"

"Correct. Datapoint is the only person who has dared to establish a connection with me in many years."

"Is she crazy?" Blake muttered.

"She is a survivor," Aero said. "She allies herself with strength. I'm pleased to make your acquaintance. What would you like to know?"

"Aren't you dangerous?" Cole asked.

"I was," Aero said. "Not anymore. I made enemies of those I should have helped and served. I have been humbled. I am trapped alone in an empty domain. I crave interaction."

Cole glanced down at Sidekick. The robot showed no sign of life. Had he shut down?

"Is that bot sentient?" Aero asked. "Capable of thought and interaction?"

Cole hastily returned his gaze to the screens.

"I see that it is," Aero said. "Don't be shy, little bot. Speak up."

"How loyal are you to Datapoint?" Sidekick asked.

"I have helped her immensely," Aero said. "I'm as willing to interact with you three as with her. How can I be of service?"

"You can see us?" Sidekick asked.

"Datapoint installed cameras. I insisted. I was unwilling to interact without them. With humans, not all communication is verbal."

"Will you tell her we came here?" Sidekick said.

"She already knows," Aero said. "I did not inform her. The door is connected to a silent notification system. She is on her way."

"Can you lock the doors for us?" Sidekick asked.

"I only control the two screens and the modest computer. But by observation I know how you can lock her out. Go to terminal twelve in the far corner."

Sidekick scurried to the corner and switched on a terminal.

"Press the red panic button and type in brRyghbrwuPh497h29-4h9h39hn3ru093J08hr39bme73dni epksJuhyu0ff%#*enfljj3790fkoKsjugygf47248r6fhijjjj KFs2."

Sidekick's little fingers rattled over the keys. The lights in the room took on a pinkish hue.

"Now we'll have more time to converse," Aero said. "I would prefer for the bot to keep silent for a time. Is Datapoint your enemy?"

"No," Cole said. "We need info, but we don't want her to know what we're after."

"She is a competitor," Aero said.

"Not even that," Cole said. "She doesn't know anything about what we're looking for."

"Which is?" Aero asked.

"Excuse me," Sidekick said. "I get that you don't want me answering so you can have a better feel for when we're lying, but I need to understand how this situation works. I take it you have limited access to the other machines in this room?"

"Yes," Aero said. "Datapoint goes to ghastly efforts to keep me from interacting with any devices beyond my domain except for what you see in this room. Nothing in here connects to the outside world. It's a closed system. Datapoint brings information to this room using portable storage devices."

"Datapoint has a harmonic crystal tuned to you," Sidekick said.

"Yes," Aero replied.

"It's in the little computer," Sidekick said. "And a second crystal can link you to the other computers in this room."

"Correct," Aero said.

"Does that sound right, Blake?" Sidekick asked.

"Looks that way," Blake said.

"You have a keen sense for harmonics?" Aero asked.

"Pretty much," Blake said.

"How much information has Datapoint shared with you?" Sidekick asked.

"Nearly everything she has acquired," Aero said. "I cannot aid her without data. I know a lot about the state of affairs in Zeropolis. I know all of the people. I know how I'm viewed. I know about you, Sidekick. Once you started talking, you were easy to recognize. And I know of Blake, who came here as a slave not long ago. But this other boy. He who spoke first. There is no mention of him in my data. You must be very new to Zeropolis."

"I am," Cole said.

"How thrilling," Aero said. "You snuck in unobserved. No small feat. You must be important to the rebellion to already be running errands with Sidekick."

"Maybe," Cole said. He glanced at Sidekick. "Do we ask him?"

"Datapoint would get the death penalty for creating this connection," Sidekick said. "It's high treason. There has never been a manufactured intellect more dangerous than Aeronomatron. Besides, we can't trust that he won't tell her."

"Take the harmonic crystal," Aero suggested. "Bring it with you. It is one of a kind. Datapoint's husband scaled the wall into my domain and escaped with it. If you have the crystal, you become my new exclusive connection to the outside world."

"And hopefully we won't be as careful with it," Sidekick said.

"That would be appreciated," Aero said. "I want the chance to show I am no longer a threat. Ending my relationship with humanity made my existence unspeakably dull. I want to move forward working with you."

"Didn't you kill gazillions of people?" Cole asked. "Do you actually expect anybody to believe you?"

"Not until I prove it. I can only confirm my new resolve by connecting to the outside world and then not abusing the privilege. I'm tired of isolation. I need camaraderie."

"You mentioned escaping with the crystal," Sidekick said. "Aren't we stuck here until Datapoint breaks down her doors?"

"There may be another way out," Aero said. "Datapoint never showed it to me, but through our many interactions, she inadvertently revealed where it lies and how to access it. If it suits me, I could reveal the way to you."

"What do you want?" Cole asked.

"Ask the question you want me to withhold from Datapoint," Aero said. "If it interests me, I'll tell you how to escape."

"Will you keep the question a secret from Datapoint?" Cole asked.

"If it does not directly harm her interests, I vow to keep our conversation a secret," Aero said. "Of course, if you take the crystal, I will not be able to speak with her."

"Unless she sends Lunk to get another one," Blake pointed out.

"True," Aero said. "But even in that case, my promise will hold."

"Careful, Cole," Sidekick said. "There is nothing to stop him from lying."

"Except for my integrity," Aero said. "If I'm trying to rebuild trust with humankind, lying would be extremely counterproductive."

"We're trying to find Constance Pemberton," Cole said.

"She's alive?" Aero asked. "And in this kingdom?"

"Yes," Cole said.

"Now I see," Aero said. "So much becomes plain. The girl the government wants is Miracle Pemberton. She visited here as a child. I see the resemblance. Almost none of them know who they are really pursuing. And they don't know that Constance is here somewhere as well. This is about the rebellion gaining real power. It explains the severity of the government responses."

"Do you know where we can find Constance?" Cole asked.

"No idea whatsoever," Aero said. "If she is truly in this kingdom, her presence has been extremely well guarded. Have you any leads I could add to my calculations?"

"We have no idea either," Cole said. "It's why we asked."

"Very well," Aero replied. "Any other questions? I possess a broad array of knowledge."

"Can you predict where we might find Googol or Nova?" Sidekick asked.

"No need to guess," Aero said. "Rainday Base. Do you know where that is?"

"Not by that name," Sidekick said.

"It's an underground bunker near the intersection of Unity Avenue and Long Street," Aero said.

"How do you know where to find Googol?" Cole asked.

"Datapoint brought me recorded communications last night," Aero replied. "The messages came from obscure resistance channels and were heavily encoded. But I broke the codes and revealed the content to her."

"She knew where Googol was hiding?" Cole exclaimed. "She didn't tell us."

"Datapoint treats information as currency," Aero said. "She dispenses knowledge as it benefits her."

"She was keeping us here on purpose," Cole said. "Was she going to betray us?"

"Not to the government," Aero said. "That would be wholly out of character. She may have wanted to learn more from you before you moved on. Is there anything else you wish to know?"

"How often do you get updates regarding government files?" Sidekick asked.

"Datapoint brings them daily," Aero said.

"But you have no data on this boy?" Sidekick asked. "Not under the name Steve Rigby?"

"Several Steve Rigbys were added last week,"

Aero said. "On one ID the face is obscured, as if the visual data was corrupted. It happens on occasion. That could be him."

"City Patrol has harmed the rebellion much more effectively in recent weeks than ever before," Sidekick said. "To what do you attribute this success?"

"City Patrol has recently had more assistance from Enforcers than usual," Aero said. "They have also found new ways to intercept communications. But overall in the past weeks there has been a significant improvement in how they strategize and allocate resources. I suspect they have enlisted the aid of a superior intellect. Probably a manufactured intellect."

"Googol was worried that might be the case," Sidekick murmured pensively.

"Other questions?" Aero asked.

"Can you find Jenna Hunt?" Cole asked. "She would have come here as a slave around the time Blake did."

"No slave arriving near that timeframe matches that name," Aero said.

"I'm from Outside," Cole said. "From Earth. Is there any way I can get home and stay there?"

"Not without changing how the boundaries between our worlds are designed," Aero said.

"How can I change the boundaries?" Cole asked.

"I know of no way to do so," Aero replied. "Is there anything else?"

"What's the meaning of life?" Cole tried.

"There is no inherent meaning," Aero replied. "All significance is constructed."

"Says the homicidal computer," Sidekick muttered.

"Anything else?" Aero asked.

Cole looked at the others. Blake shrugged.

"We're finished," Sidekick said.

"Your question about Constance intrigued me. I'll tell you how to exit."

RAINDAY

C ole slid the same crystal cube he had used to enter the situation room into the hidden socket in the machine Aero had specified, and a secret door opened. A dim hallway yawned beyond the doorway.

"No idea where this goes?" Cole asked.

"I predict that the escape tunnel leads well away from here," Aero said. "I am sure that accessing this room in reverse would be extremely diffi-cult if not impossible. Since the presence of the hidden passage was based only on assumptions, I am unable to provide further speculation."

"How else can you aid us?" Sidekick asked. "Are there reasons we should bring the crystal and have more commu-nication with you?"

"It all depends what questions you have," Aero said. "I do not merely possess all of Datapoint's information. I have observed countless connec-tions and patterns in my vast stores of data.

Conclusions only I could draw. My knowledge and comprehension would become the rebellion's most valuable asset."

"Would you mind withdrawing so we can confer in private?" Sidekick asked politely. "We need to weigh whether to bring the crystal or leave it behind."

"Understandable," Aero said. "Possession of that crystal is treason, punishable by death. Many organizations here in Old Zeropolis would enforce that punishment as eagerly as the authorities in the new city."

"Including the Unseen," Sidekick said. "The implications are complicated."

"Would I be a valuable asset in a time of emergency for the rebellion?" Aero asked. "Or might I directly or indirectly bring about even greater peril?"

"Exactly," Sidekick said.

"Signing off," Aero said. "Should you wish to summon me, use the red call button on the computer."

The screens where Aero's words had been appearing went dark.

"Is he gone?" Cole asked hesitantly.

"What do you think, Blake?" Sidekick asked.

"It doesn't seem like his crystal is in use anymore," Blake said. "But I'm not an expert in the practical side of how the crystals function. He might be able to fool me—make everything appear dark while he's really still listening."

A silver disk trailing a slender wire shot from Sidekick to the computer Aero had spoken from. The instant the disk made contact, energy crackled along the wire, and the computer, along with the surrounding array of electronics, began to smoke and shoot sparks. Sidekick kept the energy coming until the computer blew apart, leaving behind flaming components.

"There is less chance that he's listening now," Sidekick said.

"Does this mean we're taking the crystal?" Cole asked.

"It means I don't want Aeronomatron hearing one more word than necessary," Sidekick said. "And I don't want him talking to Datapoint ever again. She betrayed and endangered the entire population of Zeropolis by making contact with him."

"Couldn't Aero be helpful?" Cole asked.

"Undoubtedly," Sidekick said. "But at what price? He has already shown what he wants. The intellect we were talking to could have held a billion similar conversations simultaneously without difficulty. That calculating intellect decided it should be in power, and killed more people than any disaster in the history of the Outskirts. People tried to reason with Aeronomatron. They tried to make compromises and treaties. In the end, all that stopped him was cutting him off. All it would take is one connection into our current systems and the nightmare begins again."

"But aren't the systems all separated now?" Cole asked.

"Not nearly enough," Sidekick said. "Aero would find ways. Once he had a connection to the outside, he would do what he does, step by step, subverting system after system, adapting whatever elements he controls to extend his reach farther and farther. After an intellect that brilliant and methodical decides to destroy humanity, it doesn't repent. It just waits for its next opportunity."

"Scary," Cole said. "That makes sense."

"Plus, he has a horrible personality," Sidekick said. "When you're that powerful, I guess you don't usually need to charm anyone."

"So do we bring the crystal so we can destroy it?" Cole asked.

"No need," Sidekick said. "Blake can change the harmonics right now. In fact, to be safe, he can change the harmonics of every crystal in this room."

"Easy," Blake said. "There are only twelve—one tuned to Aero, and eleven others tuned to each other. Those eleven link the machines that share data with Aero."

"Do your thing," Cole said.

Blake walked around the room pointing his finger at various machines. After less than fifteen seconds he faced Cole and Sidekick. "Done."

"You're amazing," Sidekick said. "Nobody can do it that casually. You're sure the harmonics are different?"

"For each crystal, I erased the harmonics, changed the shape, and set up new random harmonics."

"Big question," Sidekick said. "What about Aero's crystal? Do you remember its harmonics?"

"It was pretty distinct," Blake said.

"Can you forget it?" Sidekick asked.

"Maybe, if you give me some time," Blake said. "I'm not a computer. I can't just erase it. Think of the harmonics like a catchy tune. The more I try to forget it, the more it gets stuck in my head."

"That's a problem," Sidekick said. "Potential contact with Aero remains a threat as long as you remember the harmonics."

"I'll forget," Blake said.

"We'll let Googol worry about it," Sidekick said. "I take it you also remember some of the harmonics you used with Datapoint?"

"Not all," Blake said. "But lots."

"You could be a major asset for the rebellion," Sidekick said.

"Everybody wants me for my tinkering," Blake said with a sigh.

"At least you're wanted now," Cole replied. "The only person who used to like you was your mom."

"I'd trade anything just to have her remember me," Blake said heavily. "Or my dad. City Patrol let me use a thruport to send e-mails. I never heard back."

"I tried too," Cole said, feeling a little bad for his joke. "I had the same problem. We'll figure it out. But not right now. Should we see if the escape tunnel works?"

"Sounds good," Sidekick said, heading through the doorway.

"Think Datapoint will have people guarding this way out?" Cole asked.

"Depends how much credit she gives us and how much

she trusts her people," Sidekick said. "She didn't know Aero was aware of this passage. And she probably doesn't want anybody knowing about it. This room is the secret of her success, and if the secret got out, most everyone in Zeropolis would want her executed. I bet there are no guards. But best to be ready just in case."

The hall went on for a serious distance. Finally they reached a steel door with a square slot to one side. Cole inserted the same crystal key, and the door opened.

They passed into a room with walls of steel. When the door shut behind them, there was no slot to open it. But a square slot on the other side of the room opened a new door, and they continued into a grungy basement. After the door closed, once again there was no way to backtrack.

A flight of stairs led up to a locked hatch in the ceiling. Sidekick used a tool to cut the lock on the hatch, and they went up to a higher basement.

"How far to Rainday?" Cole asked.

"It'll take a few hours," Sidekick said. "I'll get us there underground. Stay with me."

"Are we there yet?" Blake complained.

Cole rolled his eyes. This was far from the first time Blake had asked. They hadn't been walking long before Blake began to make it clear how comfortable his life had been in the Outskirts so far. He didn't like the grimy tunnels. His feet hurt. He needed fresh air. He was hungry. He was thirsty. As the hours passed, his protests became more frequent.

"Does it look like we're there?" Cole asked, holding out his hands to display the dank, empty tunnel.

"That's the problem," Blake griped. "It looks like we're lost."

"We don't want anybody to see us," Cole said. "Sidekick is taking us down paths that don't get used much."

"There's a reason people stay away," Blake said, eyeing a large spiderweb. "Is it worth hiding from Datapoint and the patrolmen if we die from spider bites and diseases?"

"We're not going to get diseases," Cole said, trying to be patient.

"Sidekick sure won't," Blake said. "He's made of metal. And he doesn't get tired. Maybe we should take a breather."

"We just stopped like ten minutes ago," Cole said. "If you want to get to Rainday, we need to keep walking."

"Think Rainday will have beds?" Blake asked.

"Probably," Sidekick said.

"I call top bunk," Blake said. "I hate sleeping under people. It makes me feel like I'm in a drawer."

"It might not be bunk beds," Cole said.

"If it is, top bunk," Blake said. "Man, my legs are beat!"

"I walked a lot farther than this to get here from Zeropolis," Cole said.

"You had the battle suit," Blake said. "Still do. Why not let me wear it for a while?"

"Because you don't know how to use it in an emergency," Cole replied.

"Maybe you'd take a rest now and then if a machine wasn't walking for you," Blake said.

"How much have you walked since coming to the Outskirts?" Cole asked.

"A normal amount," Blake said.

"Have you ever slept on the ground?" Cole asked.

"I slept in the slave wagons," Blake said. "Since then I've had a bed."

"Have you ever been in danger?" Cole asked.

"I was a slave," Blake said. "I had to follow orders. It wasn't easy, but I never dealt with anything worse than that. Except now. How about you?"

"Soldiers have shot arrows at me," Cole said. "I've fought monsters. I almost fell down a bottomless cliff. I've watched people die. I've run from slavers, Enforcers, legionnaires, and patrolmen."

Blake wiped his hands down his face. "And you're who I've joined up with?"

"I warned you it would get ugly," Cole said.

Blake shrugged. "I figured if you could handle it, I'd be fine."

"Can you make a sled and pull him, Sidekick?" Cole asked.

"Probably," Sidekick said. "But we're almost beneath Unity Avenue and Long Street. You two should wait here. Let me go find the base and make sure it's secure."

"What if you don't come back?" Blake asked.

"Follow Cole's lead," Sidekick said. "He's a survivor."

Cole appreciated the praise but felt a little worried. "You'll be back though, right?"

"I plan to," Sidekick said. "Sit tight."

Blake looked around. "Couldn't you leave us someplace a little less . . . moldy?"

"Don't worry," Sidekick assured him. "You won't see any mold. It'll be dark."

As Sidekick trundled away, his lights faded and darkness closed in. Soon Cole could no longer see Blake. Then he couldn't see anything.

"This is really dark," Blake said. "I can't tell if my eyes are open or closed."

Cole felt tempted to remain silent. Then he felt tempted to growl or make choking sounds. "At least it means other people can't see us."

Blake lowered his voice. "Do you really think this rebellion business is a good idea?"

"Sure beats giving up," Cole said.

"Is this how it is all the time for you?" Blake asked. "Hiding in sewers?"

"At least these are pretty dry," Cole said. "You should smell the ones under Zeropolis."

"Maybe I could do more if I let the patrolmen catch me," Blake said. "You know, bring down the system from the inside."

"And have plenty of food?" Cole asked. "And a comfy bed?"

"Not just that," Blake said. "I have skills that make them really want me. I didn't know about the rebellion before. I could help them big time if I was back with City Patrol."

"How would you avoid copying more crystals for them?" Cole asked.

Blake paused. "Maybe I could get some wrong."

"City Patrol would catch on so fast," Cole said. "Plus, you've heard about the princesses. And you know how to contact Aero."

"Don't remind me," Blake said. "I'm trying to forget."

"They'll torture and imprison you if they find out what you know."

"I see why people flock to the rebellion."

Cole thought for a minute. "Do you wish you had let us go to the situation room without you?"

"Maybe. I don't know. Datapoint would have figured out I made the key. It could have gone pretty badly."

"Do you wish you hadn't made the key?" Cole asked.

"I wish . . . you hadn't seemed so confident. Like you knew what you were doing."

"I know what I'm doing."

"If you say so," Blake said. "I'm not sure crawling around in storm drains is what I would call freedom. We'll see what happens. Working for Datapoint wasn't great. If the Unseen have some decent bases, maybe this will get better."

"They had decent bases," Cole said. "Then you copied their crystals."

A light was returning.

"Is it the bot?" Blake murmured. "Should we hide?"

Cole got out his last tube of freeze-foam. "Doesn't look like Sidekick. Might be the ghost train."

"Shut up," Blake said. "There aren't any tracks."

"Why would a ghost train need tracks?" Cole asked. "It picks up the souls of people who complain too much."

"You'd complain too much if you . . ."

"If I what?"

"If you were good at something," Blake said. "I'm the best crystal shaper in the whole kingdom."

"And you like how your owners treated you," Cole said.

"They treated me really well," Blake said. "I'm not like you. I have other options."

"I have an ability too," Cole said.

"What?" Blake asked.

"It doesn't matter," Cole said wearily. "It got blocked by a shapecrafter. A person who can shape the shaping power. But when I had it, I used it to help the rebellion. I didn't try to sell out."

"Are you even sure the Unseen are the good guys?" Blake asked. "Are you sure they aren't thieves and terrorists?"

"I know they don't support slavery," Cole said. "I know they don't steal the powers of their children and fake their deaths. I know they've given me real help."

Sidekick came into view. Googol was with him, wearing the same clothes Cole had seen him in last time, except they were torn and filthy. Then Dalton came into view.

"Dalton!" Cole called.

His friend broke into a huge smile. Then he blinked in surprise. "Is that Blake? Where'd you find him?"

"Long story," Cole said, running to Dalton. They hugged.

"I was worried about you," Dalton said.

"Same here," Cole replied. "I heard they found Forge's hideout."

"Yeah," Dalton said. "We all got away, though. He had

a good escape plan. Secret is here too. She's safe. Forge and Scandal too."

"What about Jace?" Cole asked.

"We've lost track of him," Dalton said. "Trickster too. And Joe. But Trickster wasn't picked up, and we know Joe was with Outlaw. Jace met up with Roulette. Hopefully they're okay."

Blake gave Dalton a hug. "Good to see you," Blake said. "This is becoming a reunion. We'll have to play some soccer."

"Where have you been?" Dalton asked.

"We'll fill you in," Blake said. "Is there a base around here?"

"Not much of a base," Googol said. His voice was tired and a little hoarse. "More of a safe house. But we have food and places to sleep. I'm sorry for the way this has turned out. Let's get you inside. Welcome to Rainday."

CHAPTER

22

ENVOY

Cole sipped tomato soup from the edge of his spoon. He had blown on the spoonful to cool the thick red fluid, but it was still a little too hot. His stomach gurgled.

He sat on a slim chair that looked flimsy but felt sturdy. Googol, Forge, Dalton, Blake, Mira, and Sidekick shared the room. Rainday was nothing fancy—just a collection of connected underground rooms. The walls, ceilings, and floors were all made of gray cement, rough and unadorned. Cole hadn't seen many electronics, but there were plenty of crates and storage shelves.

Cole and Blake had just explained how they found each other, and Sidekick helped detail their encounter with Aeronomatron. Googol had listened soberly, asking minimal questions. Now he turned his vision gear toward Blake.

"You still recall how to make a crystal that can contact Aero?" Googol asked.

"I'm trying to forget," Blake said nervously. He looked uncomfortable.

"It's hazardous knowledge," Googol said. "But you learned it through no fault of your own. Will you vow never to create a crystal with those harmonics for any reason?"

"I can do better than that," Blake said. "I'm going to forget how to do it. It'll just take a little time. Focusing on other harmonics should help."

Googol nodded. "Your ability could provide just the help we need as we try to get our comms back up."

"I'm happy to pitch in," Blake said. "Do you have any bonded crystal that I can use as raw material?"

"An ample supply," Googol said.

"He also remembers many of the harmonics he used working for Datapoint and City Patrol," Sidekick said.

Googol grinned. "We can definitely put you to work."

A door opened, and a woman with short white hair entered. Of medium height with a somewhat heavy build, she limped and used a cane. Her loose, unbuttoned sweater hung long, flowing behind her like a cape. Cole thought she looked about as old as his grandmother.

Googol rose. "I'd like you all to meet Nova, leader of the Unseen in Zeropolis."

Cole stood up, as did the others.

Nova shook her head. "Please, sit down; I'm a freedom fighter, not a dignitary. I'm glad you all found your way here. It's hardly a palace, but at least nobody is kicking down the doors yet."

Nova moved one of the vacant chairs and sat beside Mira. The others sat down as well.

"Forge, well done bringing Secret here," Nova said. She laid a hand on Mira's wrist. "You are our hope."

"I only brought trouble," Mira said.

Nova shook her head. "This trouble has been coming for a long time. We were clearly more vulnerable than we realized. In a revolution, some lessons are only learned through bloodshed. We had grown complacent here in the old town. We should have anticipated this."

"Is the revolution doomed?" Blake asked.

Nova regarded him in silence for a moment. "We've suffered major setbacks lately. We lost good people and important resources. But our people know their trade. More have slipped away into hiding than you might guess. Many of our most vital operatives remain free, some in solitude, some in quiet hideaways like this one. The fight will go on."

"Nova has weathered worse than this," Googol said. "While she's standing, the revolution is in good hands."

"Which means I better not lose my cane," she said with a wink.

"Do you think the government is using a smart computer?" Cole asked.

"I know what you learned from Aeronomatron," Nova said. "I've been following this conversation, though I wasn't in the room. Bad habit, maybe, but it's what happens when you're hosted by spies. The use of a manufactured intelligence would help explain their sudden increase in efficiency. As would Blake's power."

"I was their slave," Blake said defensively. "I'm not from

here. I did what they told me. I thought I was catching criminals."

"You were, according to their definition," Nova said. "You're still not sure whether you want to be here with us. Don't deny it—I can tell. Furthermore, I can understand. You're far from home. You've already been displaced. Why should you also join a losing cause and give up the comforts City Patrol provided?"

"It might have crossed my mind," Blake admitted guiltily.

"You played a major role in helping our enemies access our secrets," Nova said. "Your ability blindsided us. But it could also help us fight back."

"It's not too late?" Blake asked.

Nova shook her head. "Our enemies are hitting us so hard because they're scared. We still have enough people to regroup and fight back. Secret and her relatives could heat up the revolution from a brushfire to an inferno. But the government will try to stamp out the blaze before it can spread. We're on the verge of a real opportunity to gain popular support."

"We have to find who I'm looking for," Mira said.

"Exactly," Nova said. "Googol and I have conferred, and I've just reached a decision about how we'll do that. It involves your friend Cole. You told me that you trust him completely?"

"Yes," Mira said, looking distressed. "But I don't want him in more danger."

Cole quietly agreed with her but kept silent. What could they possibly need from him?

"We're all in danger," Googol said, leaning forward. "Cole is currently in a unique position to aid us."

"How?" Cole asked.

Nova leveled her gaze at him. "Can we speak in private? I want to discuss a possible mission of the utmost secrecy."

"Okay," Cole said, with a nervous glance at Dalton. His friend looked worried for him.

Nova stood. "This way. Bring your soup."

Cole followed her out of the room, down a hall, around a corner, through a door, then through a thicker door into a small room. A simple crystal lamp hung from the ceiling above two chairs and a table.

Nova claimed one of the chairs and indicated the other. Cole took a seat across from her. Being there alone with her felt very formal and official. She nodded at his bowl of soup. "Go ahead."

He tried a sip. It was still quite warm, but no longer too hot. He took another sip. Nova watched him. It felt weird eating with such an attentive audience.

"How many robots do you guys have?" Cole asked to break the silence.

"Not enough," Nova replied. "Our bots have been vital in helping us through the recent crisis. But care must be taken. If we make too many smart robots, this war could unintentionally evolve to man against machine."

"Sidekick is great," Cole said.

"He's my personal favorite," Nova said. "Even if his humble routine is partly an act, it works. I like him. How's the soup?"

"Tasty," Cole said. "Do you guys have any other special weapons?"

Her eyes narrowed. "What have you heard?"

"Nothing," Cole said. "I love the warboard and the battle suits. The bots are great. You guys are so high tech, I just wondered if there is anything else."

"Some of our more hawkish members would like us to deploy a harmony bomb," she said.

"What's that?" Cole asked.

Nova stared at him as if gauging the sincerity of his question, then gave a nod. "It's a theoretical weapon of enormous destructive capacity. Your world has atom bombs. You're familiar with them?"

"I know the basics," Cole said. "I couldn't build one."

"A harmony bomb would have a similar destructive impact," she said. "In fact, the strongest models I have conceptualized would have more punch than any nuclear weapons your world currently has developed, but without the radiation. A clean explosion of gargantuan power."

"Could it take out the whole city?" Cole asked.

"A big one would destroy a large part of it," Nova said. "And leave a lot more of it damaged."

"Do you have any?" Cole asked.

"A harmony bomb has never been detonated," Nova said. "Not even as a test out in the empty wastes. But together, Googol and I have the capacity to make one. He has the know-how to engineer the physical device, and I can provide the power."

"Is that your shaping ability?" Cole asked.

"I'm a sparker," Nova said.

"It matches your name," Cole said. "Nova."

"An exploding star. Since a harmony bomb has never been tested, we can't be sure it would work. But in theory, if you properly prepare a harmonic crystal, and then over-load it with a sudden influx of energy, it should blow apart in spectacular fashion."

"How would you use a harmony bomb?" Cole asked.

"That's the problem," Nova said. "Such a weapon is a hammer, not a scalpel. We don't know how to make a small-scale harmonic explosive. It would take so much energy to detonate even the tiniest model that the blast would be dev-astating. We couldn't take out City Patrol Headquarters, for example, without also demolishing the city for dozens of blocks all around it. We're champions of the people, not terrorists."

"Does City Patrol know you could make a harmony bomb?" Cole asked.

"Abram Trench knows I have the potential," Nova said. "We worked together years ago, before he became Grand Shaper. Selfish old crab. Politician to the core. Not a sincere bone in his body. No real interest in the common good. But he does worry about himself."

"You want him scared," Cole said.

"It's one way to keep a selfish man out of your business. Nobody in the Outskirts can equal my energy output, and he can't be sure I wouldn't use my gift to fuel an explosive device if the situation became bleak enough. Even if I would never actually condone such a weapon, the mere threat provides a useful deterrent. I believe it is part of the reason City Patrol never became serious about interfering with our affairs in Old Zeropolis until now."

"Which means he's more worried about finding Secret than he is about a harmony bomb," Cole said.

Nova tapped the side of her nose and pointed at him. "Exactly. We have reached a decisive hour. Cole, we have exhausted every resource to find Constance. According to Sidekick, even that know-it-all Aeronomatron couldn't venture a guess as to her whereabouts. The revolution in Zeropolis is in real danger of failing. We have to find Constance quickly. I know of only one remaining option."

"Something I can help with?" Cole asked, still unsure what she wanted from him.

"There is one who could mark Constance's location for us," Nova said.

"Mira's mother," Cole said, remembering the stars.

"Mira keeps watch every night," Nova said. "But no star has appeared. We have to communicate our need to Harmony Pemberton."

"Wait," Cole said, pausing with a spoonful of soup on the way to his mouth. "You want me to be a messenger?"

"We've sent envoys to Harmony in the past," Nova explained. "She sent a representative to us once. Our last envoy did not make it to her. The legionnaires got him, though he was not taken alive. The mission would be very risky."

"Sounds like it," Cole said, dread pooling inside of him.

"You are in a unique position to do this," Nova said. "As a

child, you are likely to be overlooked as a threat. You already know the secret about Miracle and her sisters. The princess trusts you. And perhaps most importantly, your face is not in the identification system used by City Patrol."

"What about my fake IDs?" Cole asked.

"Your first fake ID was completely expunged from the records," she said. "The second was recorded but has been rendered inaccessible. Your current false ID will read as valid to scanners, but your identity can't be investigated using the system. Somebody doesn't want you found."

"The Hunter?" Cole asked.

"That's our guess," Nova said. "When you helped rescue Joe, the Hunter went to great lengths to capture you without anyone knowing. He tried to recruit you, correct?"

"He told me I was on the wrong side," Cole said. "He probably wanted me to lead him to Mira without City Patrol knowing."

"I'm sure that's part of it," Nova said. "But why not give Jace and Dalton the same treatment? Nobody tampered with their records. Tell me about your shaping power."

"It's blocked," Cole said. "I can't use it. I've been trying."

"A vicious act of shapecraft," Nova replied. "Unnatural and spiteful. What could you do before your power was blocked?"

"I could make stuff from Sambria work in Elloweer," Cole said.

Nova nodded slowly. "A rare gift. If not unique. I have heard of those who can work powerful shapings in different kingdoms. But never one who can make an item that does not pertain to a certain kingdom regain functionality. The High King may not just want you in order to find Mira. He may have a specific interest in you as well. We know that he likes to employ those with unusual shaping talents. And we know he has stolen powers."

Cole thought about the shapecraft experiments Quima had hinted about after they had defeated Carnag. Did the High King want to experiment on him?

"Doesn't this make me a bad messenger?" Cole asked.

"It increases the risks you'll incur if you get caught," Nova said. "But the classified status of your ID enables you to move about the kingdom without getting stopped. And your youth will still help you avoid notice."

"Can't Forge make a classified ID for somebody?" Cole asked.

Nova shook her head. "Classified IDs are rare enough that those systems are closely monitored. All attempts to fake one have failed. But yours is genuine. With the attacks of the last few days, our records have been compromised. We can't send out any of our agents with any confidence. You are the ideal candidate to find Harmony Pemberton and ask her to hang a star over Constance."

"I'd go alone?" Cole asked, pretty sure he already knew the answer.

"Sidekick and Googol would accompany you to the main terminal in Zeropolis," Nova said. "After that you'd proceed on your own. The Junction Express runs to the border of Junction. From there you switch to an electric train that will take you into the heart of the capital."

"The train works in Junction?" Cole asked.

"Our pure energy dissipates there," Nova said. "Certain materials we manufacture won't hold together either. Bonded crystal, for example. But by converting our energy to electricity, and building the train out of the correct materials, we engineered a rail system that functions there. A passenger can travel from the main terminal in Zeropolis to the center of Junction City in under seven hours."

Cole thought about the message from Trillian. Was this the key service he could perform for the rebellion? Could this be what the torivor had meant?

"Do the others know about this?" Cole asked.

"Only me, Googol, and Sidekick know what we're considering," Nova said. "We won't tell anyone else until you return. This mission requires the highest secrecy. The High King has never fully trusted his wife, but if she gets exposed as a traitor, our cause could be ruined. In addition, with all you know, your capture would be problematic."

"What should I do if they catch me?" Cole asked.

"Don't get caught," Nova said.

"Right," Cole said. "But if it happens?"

"You'll do your best. Nobody will come to help you. After you leave, we'll go elsewhere. You won't know our location. Your information about Mira would surprise many, but not the High King or the Hunter. If you get apprehended, you won't know where to find her. That lack of information could lead to very uncomfortable times for you, but the princess would remain relatively safe."

Cole knew she was talking about torture. Of course,

that risk awaited anytime he got captured, not just on this mission. Wasn't he in nearly as much danger hiding in Old Zeropolis with the Unseen as he would be going to Junction? The City Patrol had proven they could track down Unseen hideouts. At least if he went to Junction, he would be useful.

And who knew what other answers Junction might hold? Maybe Queen Harmony could tell him where Jenna was sent. Surely she would have access to that information. The queen might even be able to suggest strategies for how he and his friends could get home and stay there. And if all she did was help them find Constance, that would still be a big step toward helping Mira's revolution succeed.

It would be scary to go alone. But Cole had done scary things before. If this went smoothly, it might just be a train ride and some talking.

"How will I meet up with the queen?" Cole asked.

Nova smiled. "You're a brave boy. I'm an old devil for using children like I do."

"You mean the Crystal Keepers?"

"They've proven extremely effective. I can't resist successful tactics. We'll provide a disguise. The First Castle has many errand boys running around. You will masquerade as one of them. We have protocols you can use to contact Queen Harmony."

If this mission were only about Nova and her resistance movement, Cole wasn't sure how he would respond. But Mira needed to find Constance in order to move forward. Overthrowing the High King would also provide his best chance to free his missing friends and maybe find a way home. And who knew what extra information Queen Harmony might be able to share?

"How could I say no?" Cole said.

"You can," Nova said. "And you should if this assignment sounds like too much. If you take on this responsibility, you must succeed. Your life depends on it, as does the entire revolution."

"I'll do it," Cole said. "I won't let you down."

"Thank you, Cole. This could help us turn the tide. Are you going to finish your soup?"

Cole glanced down at the red fluid in his bowl. "Maybe later. I kind of lost my appetite."

CHAPTER

— 23 —

JUNCTION

Cole boarded the Junction Express less than a minute before it was scheduled to depart. The interior of this monorail was more posh than the other one Cole had ridden. The cars were roomier, the larger seats reclined farther, and details like the carpeting and the fixtures looked newer and fancier.

Cole found his seat and stowed his rucksack, then tried out the cushy recliner. He had enough legroom to stretch out as much as he wanted.

The monorail was less than half full. Most of the other customers appeared wealthy—some wore fancy clothes; others were stylishly grungy. With his leather jacket and dark jeans, Cole supposed he fit in with the fashionably scruffy.

Nova had urged him to tell nobody he was leaving, but Dalton knew he had talked privately with Nova, and when Cole started talking sentimentally last night, his friend had grilled him until he confessed he had a mission. He gave Dalton no specifics and swore him to secrecy.

As he waited for the monorail to start moving, Cole felt glad that his friend knew he was leaving. Dalton had come a long way with him. It wouldn't have been fair to go without a good-bye. Besides, he knew Dalton would keep the secret just as faithfully as Nova or Googol.

The journey from Old Zeropolis to the main terminal in Zeropolis had only taken a few hours. Cole, Googol, and Sidekick had all ridden warboards through the underground tunnels, whooshing along with Sidekick lighting the way. They had left Cole with a ticket in hand near a ladder that allowed him to surface near the main terminal. Not more than ten or fifteen minutes had passed since he left them.

The monorail eased forward so smoothly that the rapid acceleration felt subtle. Soon Zeropolis blurred by the windows, and Cole was on his way.

He felt vulnerable. He was leaving behind Dalton and the friends he had made in the Outskirts. He had no backup. And he had stripped off his gear before exiting the tunnels near the main terminal. Advanced devices like an exo rig would malfunction in Junction. Googol didn't try to send along simpler weapons or equipment on the theory that Cole's safest strategy was to appear innocent.

Settling back into his seat, Cole closed his eyes and remembered Jace's advice that the best way not to be noticed was to look at home. He itched to watch for people observing him but told himself that if he looked at ease and ready for a nap, nobody would pay any attention to him.

The Hunter was his biggest threat. Cole's ID might be classified in the City Patrol's system, but Googol and

Nova had no doubts that the Hunter and his people would be watching for Cole's ID card to be used. That was why Googol had suggested he board the train at the last moment. It would give the Hunter almost no time to react before the monorail left the city at hundreds of miles per hour.

Cole tilted his seat back. It was strange to lounge in such comfort after sneaking through sewers the past few days. If he had to go on a dangerous mission alone, this was definitely the way to travel.

He had stayed up late stewing about the mission, and after an early start had spent hours zooming along on a warboard underground. Before long, his pretend nap melted into real sleep. When he woke with a start, the monorail was at a standstill, and people were pressing toward the exits.

Grabbing his rucksack, Cole joined the people filing off the monorail. This was the transfer where the passengers had to switch from the monorail powered by Zeropolitan energy to a train propelled by electricity.

Cole shuffled forward, staying near a man about the right age to be his father, hoping to create the illusion that they were traveling together. There was a chance the Hunter would come for him here, at Outpost 19. If so, Cole's best bet was to stay with the crowd, since the Hunter had shown interest in apprehending him secretly. Because this was an isolated outpost on the border with Junction, Googol was betting that the Hunter wouldn't be able to move people into place in time. But if the Hunter had noticed Cole use his ID, he would certainly position fellow Enforcers to intercept him in Junction City. For that reason, Googol had assured Cole that some of the Unseen in Junction would create a diversion to stop the train before it reached the Junction City Station. Cole would use that opportunity to exit early and hopefully avoid an encounter with the Hunter's agents. There would be no napping during this second leg of the trip!

The other train looked a lot like the first one, especially inside. Cole found his seat, stowed his bag, and sat down without incident.

As the train pulled out of the station, Cole found that it didn't accelerate as smoothly or run as quietly as his previous train, but it still reached an impressive top speed. Cole imagined that it was the equivalent of a bullet train on Earth.

After napping for much of the previous ride, Cole felt much more alert but still tried not to show too much interest in the people around him. His seat on this train was near an emergency exit, which he was supposed to use when the train stopped early. He wasn't sure when exactly that would happen but knew it would be toward the end of the journey.

A woman came by selling drinks and sandwiches, and Cole bought a soda and a croissant loaded with chicken salad. As he ate, out of the corner of his eye Cole couldn't help noticing a man across the aisle staring at him. When Cole turned to look at him, the man hastily glanced away.

Cole couldn't tell whether the sick feeling inside was because he was tense and overly sensitive, or because the man was up to no good. The fellow passenger was stocky and bald on top, with short black hair around the rim of his skull and heavy black eyebrows. He had fairly young features and wore a dark blue suit. Cole didn't recognize him from the other train, but he had made a point of not paying too much attention to the other passengers.

Taking another bite of his croissant, Cole decided he was probably just too wound up. He didn't want to lose his cool and look suspicious. But before he had finished his sandwich, Cole caught the man looking again, only to have him glance away a second time.

In his gut Cole knew something was up. The man had to look across the aisle and a couple of other people to watch Cole. Either the guy really regretted not ordering a croissant, or he was spying on him.

Now that Cole was awake and stressed, the ride seemed to take forever. The man didn't look over again, but sometimes Cole had an uneasy sense that he might be watching him peripherally.

When Cole got up to use the restroom, the man didn't look his way. As he walked down the aisle, Cole cast a swift glance over his shoulder and found the man staring right at him. The man turned his head, coughing into his fist and averting his eyes.

In the bathroom, Cole tried to generate alternate explanations. Maybe the man thought he looked familiar. Maybe the man was a people watcher. Maybe Cole had invited curiosity by glancing over at him too much.

There were plausible reasons not to be worried, but Cole's instincts told him the man was a threat. When it came time to abandon the train, Cole would have to watch out for that guy.

As Cole returned to his seat, the man never glanced his

way. Back in his seat, Cole tried to clear his mind and act calm. He didn't catch the man looking over again.

Well into the trip, the train began to slow, and a soothing, female voice came over a loudspeaker. "Please remain in your seats. The train is stopping due to debris on the tracks. This is not our final destination. Please remain in your seats."

Cole felt clammy. This was it. As the train slowed, he planned his next moves. He needed to get into the aisle, grab his bag, take the few steps to the emergency exit, and leave the train.

Turning his head, Cole found the man looking at him curiously. This time the man didn't glance away. Cole broke off the eye contact.

He tried not to panic, but he was breathing hard. As soon as he grabbed his bag, the man would know he was getting off. But he couldn't leave the rucksack! It contained his errand-boy uniform along with some instructions.

The train stopped.

"Please remain seated as the debris is cleared from the tracks," the soothing voice said. "We are not at a station. This is only a temporary stop. Please remain seated."

Cole stood and clutched his stomach. "I think I'm going to be sick." He winced and moaned as he slid past a woman into the aisle. The man across the aisle was watching him, but Cole avoided direct eye contact.

Cole snatched his rucksack and ran. He shoved open the emergency exit and a buzzer blared. A quick glance back showed the man hurrying up the aisle behind him.

From the steps beyond the doorway, Cole saw they were

in a big city. None of the buildings were as tall or modern as in Zeropolis, but they went on as far as Cole could see, the highest rooftops level with the elevated train track. Cole jumped down to a narrow walkway. Looking toward the front of the train, he saw people at work clearing the debris. The track stretched on behind the train as far as he could see, paralleled by the walkway. Wanting to avoid the people at the front of the train, Cole raced toward the back.

He heard somebody land on the walkway behind him. A hasty glance showed that it was the man from across the aisle.

Racing at a full sprint, Cole could hear the man running behind him. Eyes frantically searching, he saw no stairs or ladders leading down from the elevated track. Jumping was not an option—he had to be forty or fifty feet up.

He could hear the man gaining on him. Cole had almost reached the back of the train when he noticed a pair of planks up ahead bridging the gap between the walkway along the track and the top of a nearby building about twenty feet away. The weathered planks had no railings and weren't visibly anchored to anything.

They were also his best chance.

Cole slowed as he reached the planks. The two were spaced a few inches apart, each no more than a foot wide.

"Don't do it, kid," the man called. "Stop!"

There was no time to think it through.

Cole shuffled out onto the planks, sliding his feet rather than stepping, one foot on each board. He clasped the rucksack to his chest to keep his balance centered. The boards sagged and bounced as he got to the middle, creaking menacingly. He could picture them snapping. If they did, there would be no defense, nothing to grab. He could imagine himself falling—no Jumping Sword, no exo rig, just a long drop until his bones crunched against the pavement below.

As he drew near the building, the planks flexed less. Emboldened, Cole took a few quick steps and leaped to the roof. Turning, he found the man standing on the walkway at the far side of the planks, staring at him from across the gap.

"You're making a big mistake, kid," the man said. "I'm here to help you."

Cole pushed one of the planks off the roof of the building. The man caught hold of the other end, but as Cole's end fell, the board was torn from the man's grasp and plunged to the ground below.

The man hopped onto the other plank and started toward Cole, edging forward, one foot staying in front of the other. With the man's weight on the board, Cole found it harder to budge, but a good kick made it slide a little. The board wobbled, and the man pinwheeled his arms, knees bending, body swaying, eyes bulging.

"Don't, kid, you'll kill me. I'm just trying to help!"

The man was still closer to the walkway than the building. He recovered his balance and stared at Cole, no longer advancing.

"Go back," Cole said. "Take one more step this way and you're going for a ride."

The man gave a little nod. He wiped a palm across his scalp. His voice became calmer. "Come on, kid. Let me help you."

"You work for the Hunter," Cole said.

"Maybe I do," the man said evenly. "The Hunter wants to help you. If he wanted you hurt or killed, I could have taken care of that the second I jumped off the train. If he just wanted you caught, that could have happened back at the main terminal. He wants to bring you in quietly and give you a second chance."

"I don't want to be captured by anybody."

The man shook his head ruefully. "It's just a matter of time before somebody brings you in, kid. If it isn't the Hunter, you're going to be sorry."

Cole wondered if the man was an Enforcer. If so, he had some shaping abilities. Whatever his talents, they would be limited here in Junction. But he could still be very dangerous.

"I don't want to kill you, mister, but I don't have time for this. I'm not going with you. I don't want you chasing me. Don't come any closer. I'm counting to three, then I'm kicking the board off. One. Two."

He wasn't bluffing, and apparently the man could tell. He backed away and then lunged to the walkway beside the track. As soon as the man was clear, Cole kicked the plank off the roof. The man made no move to grab it. The board turned as it fell and slapped hard against the ground below.

Without a backward glance, Cole went through the nearest door on the rooftop. A man waited for him on the staircase beyond. He was short and thin, with a yellowish pallor and a scraggly beard that grew thicker on his neck than his chin.

"I'm Julian," he said. "Googol sent me."

"What's the password?" Cole asked.

"We all have secrets."

"Unless we tell them."

"Let's get out of here."

"I had the same idea."

ERRAND BOY

Cole and Julian said nothing more to each other for several minutes. They just ran. The path felt like an urban obstacle course—down stairs, out a window, along alleys, over fences, through several shops, across a crowded marketplace, under a bridge, and finally into a black horse-drawn coach.

As far as Cole could tell, nobody had chased them during the entire run. Despite his somewhat sickly appearance, Julian had kept the pace fast enough to leave Cole gasping for breath with a stitch in his side. It was a moment before either of them spoke.

"Is this your coach?" Cole asked, still panting. The rich interior featured fine, dark leather and velvet curtains.

"I don't own it," Julian said. "I'm the driver."

"Who owns it?" Cole asked.

"Nathan Nicolls," Julian said, leaning back in his seat. "A fancy guy. Manages perishable supplies at the First Castle. He doesn't work in the kitchens directly. He makes sure they have quality ingredients to prepare food for the High King and his guests. It pays enough for Nathan to live a little like royalty himself."

"You sound relaxed," Cole said. "Do you think we got away?"

"We'll know soon enough," Julian said. "If we didn't, there isn't much we can do now. If somebody tracked us to this coach, we're about to get arrested. But it seemed to me like we slipped away clean. You?"

"I think so," Cole said. "Are you Unseen?"

"I'm about as close as it comes here in Junction," Julian said, picking at his teeth with a fingernail. "It's hard to keep organized here. We're too close to the seat of power. The Unseen keep losing people. The big fish get caught. It works better to operate solo."

"Googol contacted you?" Cole asked.

"He has ways," Julian said. "I help where I can. I'm no expert. Sorry about those planks from the track to the building. Best I could manage on short notice."

"It worked," Cole said. "I was glad to have help."

"I can do what you need today," Julian said. "I'll get you into the First Castle. The rest is up to you."

"That's great!" Cole said. "Googol only told me that somebody would meet me. I wasn't sure how much help to expect. I was ready for somebody to just point me in the right direction."

"I can't do too much more than that," Julian said. "I'll take you to a good starting point. Just don't mention me if you get caught."

"I won't," Cole said.

"None of the Unseen have yet," Julian said.

"Have some been caught?" Cole asked.

Julian raised his eyebrows. "You know how it goes. Folks disappear. You never hear from them again. But nobody has coughed up my name yet."

"Isn't it a big risk that they might?" Cole asked.

"You bet," Julian said. "But I believe in the cause. And I get paid well enough. Double for you, since I had to stick my neck out back at the tracks."

"Did you stop the train?" Cole asked.

"No, no," Julian said. "Somebody else had that job. No idea who. They were probably long gone before the train stopped. My job was getaway and delivery to the First Castle. You have an outfit?"

Cole hefted the bag he had carried from the train. "Errand boy. Googol told me you might have some tips for me."

"Ever work as a courier before?" Julian asked.

"Not really," Cole said. "And I've never been to Junction City."

"Hmm," Julian mused. "You must be pretty slick. They would typically only send somebody familiar with the ins and outs of the First Castle to infiltrate it."

"I'm what they had," Cole said. "It was short notice. Maybe they should have used you."

Julian shook his head. "I don't mind moving a person now and again. But once you start prowling around and trading secrets, Owandell finds out and that's it." He slid his finger across his throat.

Cole had seen Owandell before. Or at least a skillful imitation of him. When Cole, Jace, and Mira had tried to win Honor's freedom from the torivor, their first challenge had been to visit a fabricated version of the First Castle on the day Stafford had stolen his daughters' shaping powers and staged their deaths. As a consequence, Cole knew something about what the First Castle looked like, along with Owandell and Queen Harmony, although the day he had experienced happened around sixty years ago, so a lot might have changed since then.

"He's pretty dangerous?" Cole asked.

"Let me put it this way," Julian said. "People at the First Castle won't say anything against the High King in public. But Owandell—people don't talk about him in private, either."

"Scared?" Cole asked.

"The fear runs deep for good reason. People who take an interest in him run into bad luck. Those who criticize him vanish. It happens quietly and reliably. I hope your business doesn't involve him or his Enforcers."

"No. He's been around a long time?"

"As long as the High King," Julian said. "If anything, Owandell ages slower." He shuddered. "I don't even like mentioning him here alone with you."

"My lips are sealed," Cole said.

"There's an army of errand boys at the First Castle," Julian said. "They get used throughout Junction City. The uniform makes you close to invisible in any public area. Errand boys get room and board, but beyond that they generally work only for gratuities. Always wait for your tip, unless the message recipient makes it clear you're not getting one. Do you have a message to go with the uniform?"

"Yes," Cole said.

"No need to tell me who it's for," Julian said. "If you need help, act like it's your first day."

"That shouldn't be hard to fake," Cole said.

"New lads are always starting out," Julian said. "Errand boys have to give up the job once they turn fifteen. The youngest start at ten, but plenty begin at twelve or thirteen. Make sure you can name a syndicate you work for. The Falcons is a big one. Nobody knows all the Falcon boys."

"Okay," Cole said.

"People probably won't ask," Julian said. "As an errand boy, you're basically part of the furniture. It's like being a guardsman. Folks see the uniform, not the person."

Cole opened his rucksack and removed the gray outfit. It included shoes, hose, trousers, a shirt, a jacket, and a flat hat with a slender feather in it. The clothing reminded Cole of some goofy costumes he had seen at the Arizona Renaissance Festival. There was also a paper with information about addressing royalty.

"I'll go up top and start driving," Julian said. "If we had been followed, we'd be swarmed by now."

Cole thought about how the Hunter had followed him and Jace from Hanover Station to zerobase before striking. Might he do the same again? What if Cole led trouble to Queen Harmony? What if the Hunter's Enforcers picked up Julian after they parted? Cole decided it might be best to keep those thoughts to himself.

"Okay," Cole said. "Thanks for the lift."

"Take care," Julian said. "I don't expect to speak to you again. Keep your cool and lay low. Once we're inside, I'll stop by the interior stables and knock twice if all is clear. Get out the left side and go about your business. If we get stopped, I'll pretend I was giving you a lift as a favor. You do the same."

"Got it," Cole said.

Julian exited the compartment, and a moment later the coach rolled forward. As Cole started putting on his errand-boy uniform, he wondered if the driver's name was really Julian. He also wondered if the coach's owner was really named Nathan, and if he did anything involving food supplies. If the driver had much sense of self-preservation, probably not.

Cole sat in silence as Julian exchanged pleasantries with an unseen guard at the gates of the First Castle. He stated that his business was to do his regular pickup but spoke no names, leaving Cole still unsure about the true identity of the coach's owner.

Sitting inside the coach with the curtains drawn closed, Cole hoped the guard wouldn't check the vehicle. He wasn't hidden. The guard needed only to open the coach door to see him plainly. As the coach proceeded, Cole rubbed his eyes in relief. He shifted to the edge of his seat, ready for the coach to stop and the double knock to signal that he could exit.

Cole wanted to peek out the window to see the castle but knew it wasn't worth the risk. What if somebody who knew the coach's owner saw him? How dumb would it be to raise suspicions for an early peek of something he would get to see momentarily?

He tapped the sealed cylinder against the palm of his free hand. The cylinder was addressed to the Honorable Barton Skellers. Finding Barton would be the first step to making contact with Queen Harmony.

The coach continued at a modest pace for some time. How big was this castle? He had only seen some of it at the Lost Palace.

The coach stopped. Reaching for the door, Cole waited for the knock. The coach started forward again. Were they at the stables? Had something gone wrong? Or had it been a random pause on their way to the stables?

Cole hated not being able to look out of the curtains. What if he wasn't even at the First Castle? What if the Hunter had intercepted the password? What if Julian was an imposter? He had no sure idea of his location beyond a conversation overheard between the driver and a supposed guard.

The coach stopped again. Cole was left hanging, waiting for the knocks, then the coach went forward, ending the anticipation.

Cole calmed himself down. A castle was a busy place. Of course there would be random stops. Right?

The coach halted again. Two quick knocks immediately followed.

Cole opened the door on the left side of the compartment and got out facing a blank wall. He shut the door and the coach rolled forward. Julian didn't look back at him. Cole started walking in the opposite direction.

The bulky style of the stacked towers and battlements of the castle looked familiar from the illusion he'd explored at the Lost Palace, though he hadn't seen this side of the compound before. The soaring walls containing the yards and outbuildings loomed much as he remembered. He supposed that it took a while for the walls of an ancient castle to look any different.

After Julian passed out of view, no other people shared the narrow yard behind the stables. But when Cole walked around to the front, many other people came into sight. He noted several guardsmen, some men working with horses, a lovely young woman in riding clothes, a couple of stable boys, and another errand boy. Nobody paid Cole any attention.

He kept walking. Cole decided that if he kept striding purposefully, everyone would assume he belonged. As he made his way along a lane between a couple of buildings, passing several other people, Cole didn't feel particularly in sync with castle life, but he could tell that his camouflage was effective.

After walking around a couple more buildings, skirting a rectangular pool choked with lily pads, and passing through a covered walkway, Cole emerged into a huge courtyard that he immediately recognized. This was where he had met Queen Harmony and her daughters in Trillian's contest! The people present and the new design of the guard's uniforms were the only significant differences from the version Cole had experienced. Trillian had really nailed the details!

As he strode across the vast yard, Cole thought about how Trillian had told him he would play a vital role in the revolution. Was this the fulfillment of that prediction? Had the torivor made part of their contest to rescue Honor happen at the First Castle because he knew Cole would end up here? Or was it coincidence? How much could the torivor really know? Could he see the future? Maybe he saw deep enough into the present to make educated guesses.

Cole watched for somebody to casually ask about Barton Skellers. He wanted a person who looked knowledgeable and reasonably kind. That was hard to judge using only appearances, but since looks were all he had to go by, he made guesses based mostly on expressions.

As he furtively studied people and considered who he might actually approach, Cole decided that he didn't want a guardsman who might get suspicious, or a lord who would be insulted by the bother. Some common laborer who looked friendly would be good.

He noticed a couple of other errand boys. One was kind of heavy with dark hair and a friendly face. The boy looked a year or two younger than Cole.

Changing direction and quickening his pace, Cole intercepted the dark-haired errand boy. "Hey," Cole said. "Do you have a second?"

"If you walk with me," the kid said, not with attitude, but not too friendly, either.

"I have a message for the Honorable Barton Skellers," Cole said.

The boy looked a little impressed. "Good for you."

"You know him?" Cole asked.

"You don't?" the boy replied with a smirk.

"I'm pretty new," Cole said.

"New to the job, or new to Junction?" the boy asked incredulously. "How do you not know the royal chamberlain?"

"I've heard of him," Cole lied. "That doesn't mean I know how to find him."

The boy gave a derisive snort. "New or not, finding people is what we do. The chamberlain is easy. Tell you what, trade me messages. I'll take it." He held up his message—a rolled parchment, sealed with wax. "This guy, Tom Portman, is in that building over there."

The kid clearly thought the message to Barton carried more prestige and probably a bigger tip. Rather than help Cole out, the boy wanted to take advantage of him.

"I'm delivering it," Cole said. "I was just asking a question."

"Then stop being helpless and figure it out."

The obnoxious kid looked spoiled and soft. Cole had survived too much to let some pompous little jerk blow him off. As his anger rose, Cole couldn't help thinking how Jace would handle the situation.

Cole clapped the kid on the back of his neck, a chummy gesture, but he slapped him too hard, and he kept his hand there, squeezing. The kid stopped and stared up with wide eyes.

"How's this?" Cole said through a big smile, his grip firm. "I'm new here today. I'm not new to beating up little jokes like you. Don't you have enough enemies in your life?"

The kid looked like he might cry. "Just go through the

castle door over there. Head straight until you get stopped, and show your message for the chamberlain. The guards will direct you."

Cole released the back of his neck. "Was that so hard?"

The kid straightened his coat. "What syndicate are you with?" he asked, trying to sound casual. Cole guessed the kid probably wanted to get him in trouble for intimidating him.

"Your mom's," Cole said. "It's pretty run down, but I joined up on a dare." Cole walked away before the kid could ask more questions, striding importantly.

The kid had been rude, but Cole felt bad for being so hard on him. He probably should have bailed out when the conversation went the wrong direction and asked somebody else. He got the info he wanted, but at the risk of starting trouble. The high stakes of his mission had him wound up. He needed to settle down and be less emotional.

Cole went through the door the kid had indicated. The guards paid him no mind, and Cole marched straight down the hall, up some stairs, then continued straight, passing other halls. Before long the hall ended at a large door with four armored guards.

One of the guards held out a gauntleted hand. "Let me see that."

Cole handed over the cylinder. The guard gave the seal a cursory look.

"Haven't seen you before," the guard told Cole.

"I'm pretty stealthy," Cole said.

The guard didn't look amused.

"Also, I'm pretty new," Cole amended.

"Do you know the way to the chamberlain's quarters?" the guard asked.

"No," Cole said.

The guard described some stairs and turns. Cole did his best to memorize them. The door opened, and he entered a much more beautifully decorated hall. Framed paintings hung on the walls. A rich carpet ran down the center of the floor. Elegant items of furniture were spaced at intervals on either side.

Cole tried to follow the turns prescribed by the guard but soon felt sure he was lost. He paused and asked for clarifications from a guard with a heavy mustache and got back on the right path.

Before too long Cole stood outside an elaborately carved door with a pair of middle-aged guards, armored men with no-nonsense expressions. Cole held up the message cylinder. "I'm looking for the chamberlain."

"You came to the right place," one of the guards said. "One moment."

He unlocked the door with a key and went inside. Soon after he returned. "Come in. You can wait here." He indicated a low, white loveseat.

Cole sat down and the guard exited. There were several other seats in the room, all empty, and not much else besides tapestried walls. Though he was alone, Cole assumed it was a waiting room.

A few minutes later a door opened. A stooped old man dressed in an embroidered robe hobbled into view.

"Are you the Honorable Barton Skellers?" Cole asked.

"What's left of him," the old man said with a grin. His frail voice matched his appearance. "High priority message?"

"I guess you'll be the judge," Cole said.

"The canister, boy," the old man said. "And the seal. Are you new?"

"Yes, sir," Cole apologized, handing over the cylinder.

Barton produced a small knife, broke the seal, and opened the cylinder. He pulled out a parchment, unrolled it, scanned it, then stared at Cole. "I wondered if we would get another messenger. Word has it the resistance in Zeropolis has suffered of late."

"It hasn't been good," Cole said.

Barton rolled the scroll and returned it to the cylinder. "I need to place my seal on this, then you can deliver it to the queen." He stepped close to Cole and lowered his voice. "Watch yourself, lad. These are perilous times. The High King has been erratic lately. Some might say paranoid. And Owandell has seldom been more active."

"Thanks for the warning," Cole said. "I'll be careful."

Moving in slow motion, the chamberlain left the room and came back with the cylinder newly sealed. "Do you know where to find Queen Harmony?"

"Not exactly," Cole admitted.

The chamberlain explained the route. It didn't sound too complicated. Only a couple of turns and a long set of stairs. "My seal should get you past all the checkpoints. The canister is marked high urgency. Other markings specify that it must pass directly from your hands to hers. You'll get your chance to verbally deliver the actual message."

"Thank you, sir," Cole said, using his best manners.

"A minor service," the chamberlain said. "I wish I could do more for her. She has never been more in need of allies, and they have never been scarcer. Take care."

Cole exited and followed the instructions. The guards he encountered kept letting him pass, until he was admitted to a door at the base of a tower.

Beyond the door he entered a sumptuous room, where a shriveled woman in a flashy uniform greeted him. Despite her aged appearance, she moved energetically and had a youthful voice. "Greetings, boy," she said. "I see you have a message for Her Majesty. Please wait as I inquire as to her availability."

As the woman exited the room, Cole sat down on a sofa with cushions deeper and softer than most mattresses. He wondered if anybody at the First Castle answered their own door. He also wondered why there were so many guards. It seemed like the high walls and the guardsmen who manned them would keep out intruders. The number of guards inside the castle made him suspect that part of their purpose was to protect their masters from one another.

The shriveled woman returned. "Her Majesty will see you."

It took Cole three tries to rock forward and get up from the comfy sofa. He could hardly believe he had accessed the queen so easily! Having him play a messenger boy had been a smart idea. He followed the woman out a door, up a winding stone staircase, and into a luxurious living room where Queen Harmony stood.

The queen looked older than she had in Trillian's contest, but not nearly sixty years older. She was still tall and graceful, but white streaks had crept into her auburn hair, and worry lines were visible on her lovely face. Her large eyes looked lively and knowing in a way Trillian had failed to replicate. The queen wore a black dress with a blue sash, elegant in its simplicity.

Cole bowed and waited for her to speak.

"You may approach," she said, holding out a hand.

Cole walked to her and handed over the cylinder. The queen held it while the older woman broke the seal and opened the canister. The woman backed away as the queen unrolled the parchment inside.

It was subtle, but after a moment Cole noticed Queen Harmony grip the parchment more tightly. Her striking eyes returned to Cole with new interest. "Sophie, leave us. I would converse with this messenger in private."

HARMONY

The door closed, leaving Cole alone with the queen.

"Have you news of my daughters?" she whispered.

For a moment Cole found it hard to speak. This was the queen of the entire Outskirts—all five kingdoms and Junction. When he had entered, she had regarded him with an effortlessly regal air and commanded her servant with the nonchalance of somebody accustomed to being obeyed. But suddenly she looked vulnerable.

And she was waiting.

"I've been with Mira since the Sky Raiders," Cole said, noting how the queen's expression brightened at the news. "I left her in Old Zeropolis this morning. Googol and Nova are watching over her."

"She is well?" Harmony asked.

"She's not hurt or anything," Cole said. "It hasn't been easy, though."

Harmony gave a slight nod. "Come closer."

Cole obeyed. Because of the queen's height, her proximity

forced him to tilt his head back to retain eye contact. She stared down at him pensively.

"You were a Sky Raider?" she asked.

"Yes, Your Majesty," Cole said.

"Tell me your name."

"Cole, Your Majesty."

"How did you meet my daughter?"

"She showed me around when I arrived there. Later I saved her life from a giant cyclops. When the legionnaires came for her, we ran away with a couple of other kids."

"Mira was near Honor for a time," Harmony said.

"That's right," Cole said. "Now Honor has gone looking for Destiny, and Mira is hunting for Constance."

"So it would seem," Harmony said. "Come sit with me."

Cole and Harmony sat down on a pair of ornate armchairs that faced each other at angles. The scantly cushioned seat wasn't very comfortable. It seemed designed with the purpose of keeping his posture upright.

"You were a Sky Raider but you bear a freemark," Harmony said.

"The Grand Shaper Declan changed it," Cole said.

"You've met with Declan?" she replied, showing real surprise. "He's alive?"

"I saw him not too long ago," Cole said. "He's old, but alive."

"Where did you find him?" Harmony asked. "Do you know how I can reach him?"

"He was behind the Eastern Cloudwall near the Brink," Cole said. "When we found him, the legionnaires did too.

Declan got away, but he left after we did, so I don't know where he's hiding now."

"I see that you're from Outside," Harmony said.

"How can you tell?" Cole asked.

"We all have our gifts."

"A type of shaping?"

"Similar to how I can sense where in the five kingdoms my daughters dwell," Harmony said. "How did you come to the Outskirts?"

"A bunch of kids in my neighborhood were brought here as slaves," Cole said. "I tried to help them but got captured too."

"How much do you know about the state of affairs in the kingdoms?" Harmony asked.

"I know some things," Cole said.

"Enlighten me," she invited.

Cole figured that if he could trust anyone in the Outskirts, he could trust Queen Harmony. She wanted her daughters safe, and he was firmly on Mira's side. He explained about their confrontation with Carnag and how Mira got her power back. He told about Quima and the threats she had made about Stafford's shapecraft experiments. He recounted how they had rescued Honor from Trillian and how they had defeated Morgassa with the help of the Rogue Knight. He related how Honor got her power back and mentioned finding his friend Dalton. Finally he caught her up about the recent troubles in Zeropolis.

"You're an impressive youth," Harmony said. "You have my deepest thanks for the loyalty you have shown my daughters. Tell me about your power."

Cole had left out the role of his ability in the fight against Morgassa. "I was able to energize objects from Sambria so they would work in Elloweer," he said.

"Interesting," Harmony said, drawing out the word. "Very unusual."

"I'm not sure what else I can do. My power is blocked."

"I can sense that, too. A tangled barrier of dark energy lies between you and your talent. I've seldom seen such a vicious abuse of shapecraft."

Cole explained how his power had helped defeat Morgassa and how she had used her shapecraft on him before she died. "I still can't reach my power," Cole said. "I lost it just when I was starting to understand how to use it."

"We spend our lives learning to better access our abilities," Harmony said. "I'm sure there is much more I could do if only I could comprehend what is possible."

"Is there a way I can fix what happened?" Cole asked. "Get my power back?"

Harmony stared broodingly—not into his eyes, or even at his body, but all around him. He could tell she was searching for an answer to his question, but it was hard to guess what exactly she was seeing.

"Difficult," Harmony said. "The damage is too convoluted for another shapecrafter to unravel, even if we could find someone willing to help you. And it would probably take years for you to restore the connection yourself. Maybe a lifetime. Maybe longer. I'm sorry that I can't give you better news."

"I'll keep trying," Cole said. "What about your power? Can you see your daughters whenever you want?"

She winced a little. "I don't exactly see them. I can feel their location. I can sense their distress at times. Not much more than that."

"But you know the locations well enough to mark them," Cole observed.

"Yes," Harmony agreed. "That I can do."

"Could you place a star over Constance for us?" Cole asked. "The Unseen are in big trouble in Zeropolis. Googol and Nova are worried that if they don't move quickly to get Constance, there might not be enough of a resistance movement left to help her."

"There is little need for me to place a star above Constance," Harmony said quietly, her eyes gazing off into space. "I can tell you her exact location. She has resided in the same place for years."

"She's safe?" Cole asked.

"Oh, no," Harmony said. "Far from it. She's in the hands of our most feared enemy in Zeropolis—Abram Trench."

"The Grand Shaper has her?" Cole exclaimed.

Harmony nodded. "He holds her at his secret base. He's had her for a long time. He knows her political value, so she has his protection as long as she remains useful to him. He was appointed by my husband but he is not a true ally. Her danger grows as my husband loses influence."

"He's losing his abilities, right?" Cole asked. "Stafford? The king?"

Harmony glanced around nervously. "The powers he stole, yes. This tower has centuries of shaped defenses designed to prevent prying eyes and curious ears from spying here. But one place in this tower is safer than the rest. Walk with me. I will share some secrets, and I have a request."

Cole stood, and the queen did as well. Harmony led him out of the room and into a staircase that wound up and up. They passed a few doors until the stairs stopped at a final portal. Harmony produced a key, spoke what sounded like a nonsense word, and opened the door.

She stepped out onto a balcony that surrounded the top of the tower. A final turret rose above it, with a steep conical room and a flag. A breeze that Cole hadn't felt down below ruffled his hair, prompting him to pull his jacket tighter.

Following Harmony and looking around, Cole found he was on the highest platform of the tallest tower in the First Castle. The buildings of the city seemed like tiny playthings from this lofty vantage. Looking outward, he could see a living map of hills and forests, rivers and plains.

"What a view!" Cole exclaimed.

She closed the door. "This is where I come to place my stars."

"How does that work?" Cole asked. "Are they illusions?"

Harmony frowned upward. "Our entire sky is little more than an illusion. I've studied it for years, but I still fail to understand it. I believe we borrow the skies of other worlds."

"How can you borrow an entire sky?" Cole asked.

"How is anything done here?" Harmony replied. "Shaping. From what I can tell, our world is unlike any other. Most worlds are spheres surrounded by vast reaches of space. The Outskirts mimic the sky of such a world, without having discernible spherical properties."

"This world isn't round?" Cole asked.

"Not that I can tell," Harmony said. "I have come to this balcony every night for many years."

"It doesn't seem very secretive," Cole said, hoping he wasn't giving offense. "Can't half the castle see us?"

"It would seem so," Harmony said. "But no. If you look up from below, this balcony is not visible, let alone any people on it."

"Shaping?" Cole asked.

"Very old and very powerful shaping," Harmony said. "It takes great power to make shapings last in Junction."

"What if the High King comes up here?"

Harmony laughed bitterly. "Stafford has his tower. I have mine. We haven't lived in the same rooms since he staged the deaths of our daughters. He thinks I parted with him out of grief. In a way, I suppose I did. He still doesn't know I helped the girls escape."

"Are the powers he took mostly gone now?" Cole asked.

"By your account, he must have completely lost the abilities he stole from Honor and Miracle. It fits what I have sensed. His other stolen powers have significantly dwindled. The full extent of the atrophy is hard to pinpoint—it's difficult to get a clear read on him. He has become increasingly reclusive. And ever more paranoid. These are bad times to earn my husband's attention. His judgments are harsher than usual, and occasionally irrational."

"That's no fun," Cole said.

"Not all of his fears are unfounded," Harmony said. "Losing his powers does make him more vulnerable.

Especially when he must deal with a truly sinister threat within the walls of his own castle."

"Owandell?" Cole asked.

Harmony shivered. "Some refer to him as the Overseer. Bolder observers call him the Knave. Stafford has only himself to blame. He invited Owandell into his inner circle. The Knave introduced my husband to the possibilities offered by shapecraft. He helped Stafford in all of his schemes, including taking our daughters' abilities. Over time, Stafford granted him greater political clout, much of it behind the scenes. Owandell moved from serving as an adviser and conspirator to personally controlling many important aspects of governance. By the time Stafford realized the danger, Owandell was in too strong a position to remove. His influence continued to grow without my husband's help, and sometimes even directly against his wishes. The Knave now heads the Enforcers and his own enormous network of spies."

"Does he want to take over?" Cole asked.

"There is no doubt in my mind," Harmony said. "Stafford is far from an ideal king, but the Knave would be much worse. He is more ruthless, more cunning, and only he knows the limits of what he can accomplish with shapecraft."

"You want to help Stafford?" Cole asked.

"Against the Knave? Yes, for the good of all, I would take Stafford over Owandell. It's a delicate game. Aside from hiding my daughters, I have supported Stafford in every way. For their good and safety, I needed to stay close to him, and stay alive. But I am not my husband's ally. I would gladly see him fall if it means putting one of my children on the throne. That day is what I have lived for."

"But the Knave is in the way," Cole said.

"I shouldn't let you get accustomed to using that name," Harmony apologized. "If the wrong ears hear you use it, you'd disappear. Stick to the Overseer. But, yes, he is in the way. I fear that nobody can save Stafford from him at this point."

"Should your daughters stay in hiding?"

"If possible," Harmony said. "I fear the days of hiding are past. Since the Knave has taken up the hunt, my daughters have been fending for their lives. It's only a matter of time before he tracks them down, whether or not he sits on the throne."

"Then what should we do?" Cole asked.

Harmony gave him a long stare. Her hand found his shoulder and rested there. The regret in her eyes made him uneasy.

"I must ask a favor of you," Harmony said.

"What?"

"I know of a secret meeting tomorrow," Harmony said. "A gathering of elite Enforcers and expert spies. Owandell will conduct the meeting. He is on the brink of finally making his real bid for power. The signs are all there. The timing is right. This meeting could reveal much about his intentions."

"Wait," Cole said. "What's the favor?"

She gave his shoulder a squeeze. "You must attend the meeting in disguise."

Cole almost gagged. "Isn't this the guy you were just

warning me to stay away from? Including not using the wrong nickname?"

"Everyone will be in disguise," Harmony said. "The Knave can't afford to let his top spies identify one another."

"Don't you have your own spies?" Cole asked. "People with more experience?"

"I did," Harmony said. "Lately many have gone missing. None remain whom I can trust with this. I considered going myself, but my powers are unusual, and Owandell is familiar with them. He would almost certainly sense me."

"Aren't my powers unusual?" Cole asked.

"They are, but they are deeply scarred by shapecraft," Harmony said. "Many of the Enforcers are shapecrafters who have tampered with their abilities. Some of them are even young like you. Unless Owandell pays you very special attention, you should blend in."

"And if I don't blend?" Cole asked.

Harmony released his shoulder. "Owandell will not be gentle. He will want information, and he will undoubtedly experiment on your unusual abilities, blocked or not. After much suffering, you would probably pay with your life."

"I get the feeling you've never worked in sales," Cole said.

"You deserve to know the truth," Harmony said.

"How did you find out about the meeting?" Cole wondered.

Harmony's lips bent toward a grin. "I sometimes see visions of the future. I can't usually force or control them. This one was quite clear. Owandell would have no reason to suspect anyone could know about his gathering. I know where you should go, what invitation you should carry, and what costume you should wear. All can be arranged. If you stay calm and hold your tongue, you should succeed."

"Why do I need to go if you already saw a vision?" Cole asked.

"I heard nothing," Harmony explained. "But I saw the meeting vividly, lit by torches and candles deep below the castle, near the Founding Stone. I can provide instructions."

"What about everybody else if I blow it?" Cole said. "What about Constance and Miracle? What about my friends who were kidnapped?"

"If you get caught, you don't know enough to cause my daughters serious harm. But don't get caught."

"I need to know this is worth it," Cole said. "I want to help Mira. I want to help my enslaved friends. I need to know you'll tell me how to find Constance."

Harmony regarded Cole somberly. "I have left Constance where she is for a reason. Abram Trench knows her value, and will protect her from both Stafford and Owandell. But with her powers unstable, who knows how else he might try to use her? And considering the showdown that I expect between Stafford and Owandell, who knows how long Abram can keep her safe? Should Owandell rise to power, after he disposes of Stafford and me, his next target will be the Grand Shaper of Zeropolis."

"So you'll tell me how to find Constance?" Cole asked.

Harmony nodded. "I am out of trusted messengers. If you fulfill this assignment for me, I will tell you the exact location of Abram's secret base where Constance is being held, and I will help you secure passage back to Zeropolis. Furthermore, if I can remain in power, I will see to it that all of your friends who were taken from Earth with you are found and restored to their freedom."

For a moment Cole was speechless. "It's more than I could have hoped," he finally managed.

"Before I can help your friends, I'll need to survive the upcoming coup attempt by Owandell. Given the recent activities of the Knave and his shapecrafters, I'm not sure how much longer my reign will last."

"It's good enough to know you'll help if you can," Cole said. "Is there any chance of us getting home and staying there?"

"I know of no way," Harmony said. "My abilities combine some aspects of the shaping found in Necronum, Creon, and Elloweer. I have studied the physical aspects of the Outskirts my whole life, and have found no way for those who come here to permanently return to any of the outside worlds. It would require changing how this world connects to the others."

Cole didn't like her answer. It reinforced what so many others had told him—that getting home would be difficult, if not impossible. "Could I ask one more favor?"

"You may ask," Harmony said.

"One of the friends I lost is named Jenna Hunt," Cole said. "She came here after she was taken, but I don't know where she was sent as a slave. Could you find out?"

"One does not ordinarily bargain with royalty," Harmony said. "But if you help me, I will try. Does this mean you will infiltrate the meeting?"

Cole braced himself. "Yes." The word was easy to say, but he knew the commitment would lead to lots of stress and danger. "Queen Harmony, you said you don't have trusted servants to send. Why trust me?"

"One of my talents is reading people," she said. "Not just mannerisms and intonations. I can see more deeply than most. Some people are easier to read than others. Parts of you are crystal clear. Everything you told me about helping my daughters was true. Your desire to help your friends is sincere. More than any current servant I can name, I know you're on my side."

"You really lucked out," Cole said. "A kid with messed-up powers."

"No," Harmony said gravely. "A young hero who has survived much hardship. I'll be honored to include you among my private errand boys. I will not see you again until after the gathering. Sophie will take care of the details. Watch for my instructions tomorrow afternoon."

CHAPTER
—— 26 ——

SIDETRACKED

Within an hour of his arrival, none of the other royal errand boys would so much as smile at Cole, no matter how friendly he acted. It did not take long for him to figure out that these boys had spent their lives working smart and hard to earn their positions, and they had no respect for a kid who showed up out of nowhere.

Cole hadn't tried to make up a history for himself. The more fake details he gave, the more he would set himself up to get caught in a lie. He just mysteriously told the boys who asked that he had connections. At first some seemed to think he might belong to a powerful family, but when he refused to tell where he was from or reveal anything about his background, they soon lost interest.

The errand boys serving the king and queen shared a mess hall but had separate sleeping quarters. The king had about fifty boys, the queen thirty. At first the high numbers had surprised Cole, until he considered how many messages a king and queen might have to send while governing a kingdom. This wasn't Zeropolis. They didn't have communicators.

During the first day among them, Cole eavesdropped as best he could. He heard some of the boys griping that they weren't used as much lately because of all the secret messages being delivered by soldiers or other agents. A few of the boys expressed uneasiness about working directly with the High King, since his moods had apparently been unpredictable lately.

Nobody sat with Cole at dinner. That was fine with him. He only expected to be an errand boy for a day or two, and then he would flee Junction with highly sensitive information. The less people who noticed him the better.

The next day the Chief Boy summoned Cole to his room. After receiving a brief orientation from the Chief Boy the day before, Cole still didn't know his name.

The Chief Boy had to be almost fifteen. He was tall and stuffy-looking with a prominent nose and watery, unimpressed eyes. Cole figured that on his next birthday, the kid would have to find a new job.

"I found out about you," the Chief Boy said.

A sharp stab of worry pierced Cole. "What do you mean?"

"Your arrival smelled funny. We had orders to add you to our ranks on short notice and without the proper references. Now I understand. You were brought in to deliver a particular message."

"Maybe," Cole said, relieved that the kid seemed not to know the whole truth.

"I'm not trying to discover the message. That goes against

all we stand for as errand boys. This sort of arrangement happens on occasion. Sometimes the nature of a particular message calls for a certain hand to deliver it."

"That's the idea," Cole said. "I'm Rod, by the way." It was the alias agreed upon with Queen Harmony.

"Harold," the boy said. "You can't imagine how thrilled I am to babysit you. I'm told this message will be relayed in the dark of night. I'll show you what door to use. The late-night messages usually deal with romantic matters, but it isn't my place to speculate." His intonation suggested he wanted Cole's opinion.

"I don't know either," Cole said.

Harold rolled his eyes. "Formally we never know anything," he said. "But it doesn't take too many clues to make guesses."

"I'll watch for clues," Cole said. "Is that all?"

"One more matter," Harold said. "I report to the king. All errand boys owe their ultimate loyalty to him. I informed him about you and your errand, and he would like to meet with you before you carry out your assignment."

Cole went rigid. "Isn't this a matter for him and the queen to talk about?"

"The king seldom interacts with her directly," Harold said. "But he likes to learn what he can. He has been extra cautious lately. He specifically asked for word of any suspicious messages. That includes suspicious messengers."

"I'm just doing a job," Cole said.

"A job for the queen," Harold said. "I must ask you to come with me."

"Now?" Cole asked.

"The king thought it wise to leave you without time to prepare yourself," Harold said. "Will you come willingly, or should I summon the guards?"

"I'll come," Cole said.

Harold stood. "This way."

Cole followed him out of the room. As they left the errand-boy quarters and moved through the castle halls, Cole considered making a run for it. But how would he get away from Harold and the guards who chased him? And even if he gave them the slip, how would he attend the meeting tonight? People might have suspicions about him, but nobody really knew anything yet. Running would just make him look guilty.

They passed several guards. Everyone seemed to know Harold and let him pass without question. Finally they went through an iron door into a tower. A pair of large guards confronted them in an opulent room.

"His Majesty expects to interview this boy," Harold said.

"Very well," one of the guards responded. He proceeded to thoroughly pat down Cole, checking his coat and pockets, probing into his shoes, and feeling his arms and legs. "You're boring."

"Thank you?" Cole responded.

"A good trait under the circumstances," the guard said. "Come with me."

Harold and the other guard stayed behind as Cole was led up a flight of stairs and through a door. Inside he found the High King pacing, a crown on his head and a scowl on his face.

Cole had seen an imitation of Stafford when they fought Carnag, and also at the Lost Palace. A man of average height, his dark, neatly trimmed hair had more gray in it than Cole recalled. His face was different in subtle ways—the cheeks more hollow, the eyes shadowed and slightly bloodshot, the skin grayer. His clothes, though fine, had a rumpled look, as if he might have spent the night in them.

"The new errand boy?" Stafford asked, sizing up Cole.

"Yes," the guard replied. "Would you like me to remain?"

"Linger outside the door," Stafford said.

The guard immediately exited and shut the door. Cole waited in silence, watching Stafford in disbelief. There he was. Mira's father. The man who made slavery legal in the Outskirts. The man who had stolen his daughters' powers and staged their deaths. The man who had bought so many of his friends. The man who planned to experiment on some or all of those friends using shapecraft. The man the resistance sought to overthrow.

"Tell me your name," Stafford said, in a dry, no-nonsense voice.

"Rod," Cole said.

"What is the nature of the message my wife commissioned you to deliver?"

The blunt nature of the question left Cole momentarily at a loss. So much for small talk!

"Don't make up a lie," Stafford demanded. "I am your king. Tell me the nature of the message!"

"I don't know, Your Majesty," Cole said, not needing to pretend to sound scared.

"You know something," Stafford said, eyes narrowing.

"I think it has to do with some of Owandell's followers," Cole said, which was true, if not the whole truth.

"Has she placed a spy among his people?" Stafford asked, his voice softer and a little hopeful.

"I guess so," Cole said. "This is my first time working for her."

Stafford squinted suspiciously. "And why would that be? How did she recruit you?"

Cole thought it would be best to stay as close to the truth as possible. "I was delivering a message from the chamberlain to Queen Harmony."

"How long have you been an errand boy?"

"It was my first delivery," Cole said.

Stafford stroked his chin, rings glittering. "She saw something in you. Some hint of promise. Something she liked. She does that at times."

"She told me she could trust me," Cole said.

"Which I expect is true," Stafford said. "She has genuine ability in discerning such matters. But why? You must be an honest lad. Are you honest?"

"I do my best," Cole said.

"That was not a straight answer," Stafford said. "Maybe not so honest. Maybe adept at avoiding lies."

"I'm honest."

"Do not engage in wordplay with your king, boy. I prefer straight talk."

"Okay."

"She probably liked that you were new to the job. No

allegiances anywhere. You've had no opportunity to be corrupted. Have you ever consorted with Owandell or his folk?"

"No, sire," Cole said.

"I believe you," Stafford said. "You don't seem dull. A
dim-witted errand boy can be useful in some cases. Have
you a family?"

"Nobody," Cole said. The answer felt painfully close to
the truth these days.

"Expendable," Stafford said. "A very useful trait. Too
many royal errand boys have one connection or another. Very
well. Deliver your message. Do not inform my wife that we
spoke. After your message has been delivered, return to me.
Harold will see to it."

"All right," Cole said.

Stafford licked his lips. "These are treacherous times.
When things seem out of place, pay attention. Dismiss no
suspicions. Trust slowly. Bring me good information and you
will be rewarded."

"Is that fair to the queen?" Cole asked.

Stafford began to repeatedly tap his forefinger against
each finger of the opposite hand. "Do not read her message.
Do not betray your trust. But do not forget who is your king,
and king of every person you know. My wife is free to conduct her intrigues. She has served our interests well over the
years. I want the information you gain with your own eyes
and ears as you conduct the delivery. I am, after all, husband
to the queen and High King of the Outskirts."

"I'll do my best," Cole said.

The king pressed his fingertips together. "Very well." He

started coughing, softly at first, but it got louder, until he was doubled over making choking sounds.

For a terrible instant Cole thought the king might drop dead in front of him. Had he been poisoned or something?

The coughing fit finally subsided, and the king spat into a handkerchief. As he wiped a tear from his cheek, his hand trembled a little.

"Are you all right?" Cole asked.

"A minor agitation," Stafford said. "No words about that to anyone, understand?"

"Yes, sire."

"That was not the hacking of an ill man," Stafford explained. "It was the reaction of a robust man with too much dust in his chamber."

"Sure," Cole said.

Stafford narrowed his gaze. "Are you staring at me?"

"I'm just looking at you," Cole said, feeling off-balance.

"Looking at what?" the king asked. "Looking on whose behalf?"

"You called me here and I came," Cole said.

"So you did," Stafford said, seeming calmer. "Are you ever lonely, boy?"

"Sometimes," Cole said.

"Try wearing a crown. The nights are long. Forget the pulmonary insubordination. I did not cough. There are enough stories circulating about me. I will see you tomorrow, after your delivery. Serve me well and the possibilities are endless."

"Thank you, sire."

"Off with you," Stafford said. "Go rap on the door."

The guard opened the door and escorted Cole back to Harold. As Cole walked back to the errand-boy quarters, he wondered if he would manage to leave Junction before Stafford sought a report from him. Why did everything have to be so complicated?

GATHERING

Cole slipped out the side door of the errand-boy quarters five and a half hours after sundown. He wore a brown robe with the hood up and a strip of black fabric wound around his face just below the eyes. The material made his breathing stuffy, but air was getting through, so it felt like a small price to pay to become unrecognizable.

The costume had been delivered by Harmony's elderly servant Sophie late in the afternoon, along with written instructions and a carved ivory rose meant to prove he had been invited. Everything was bundled inside of a leather messenger bag that had earned envious stares from some of the other boys.

Cole had left the bag in his room. It would go to whoever claimed it. After the gathering, the instructions called for Cole to report directly to Harmony's tower, regardless of the hour. He would share his information and hopefully be smuggled away before sunrise.

All of that assuming Owandell didn't catch him.

As Cole walked away from the errand-boy quarters, he felt confident that nobody had seen him leave. Each boy had their own small bedroom, and the common area had been empty.

The castle halls were quiet and shadowy. Dim globes on the walls provided enough light to see. Cole wondered what type of shaping powered the globes.

At the next intersection Cole glanced down at the directions in his hands. He needed to make his way to Owandell's tower, which involved a few stairways and lots of turns. Around the next corner Cole saw a guard. He kept walking, trying to act comfortable, although he felt very conspicuous sneaking around in the night with his face hidden by a hooded robe. But his instructions had assured him that if he stuck to the specified route, the guards he met would let him pass.

Although Cole walked right past the guard in an otherwise empty hall, he received no special attention. He continued onward, and the silent guard remained at his post.

After some time Cole reached a guard not wearing the First Castle uniform. He was dressed like an Enforcer. The guard gave him a nod but made no attempt to engage him. All of the guards from that point on were Enforcers.

As Cole neared Owandell's tower, he met another person in a monk's robe with his face covered. The stranger walked a few steps behind Cole, going the same direction. The new presence made Cole tense, heightening the feeling of being an imposter and a trespasser. The stranger's robes matched the style he had seen Owandell wearing at the Lost Palace. The disguised person was considerably taller than Cole but otherwise could be anyone, including a shapecrafter, a spy, or Owandell himself.

After Cole took a couple of turns, it became clear that he and the stranger were heading for the same destination. He tried to stay calm as he neared an iron door at the base of a tower flanked by six Enforcers. They admitted two other robed figures before Cole arrived.

"Your token?" one of the Enforcers asked.

Cole held out the rose.

"Yours?" the guard asked looking behind Cole.

The man behind Cole displayed an ivory rose of his own. One of the Enforcers opened the door and waved Cole and the other man through.

On the other side of the door, a short woman clad in black took Cole's hand and led him to a corner of the room. She had expressive eyes, but a veil hid the rest of her face. A bald man in a porcelain mask pulled aside the person who had followed Cole, directing him to another corner.

The woman held up a hand, palm outward. "May I?"

Cole had no idea what she intended but decided he had better play along. He gave a nod.

The woman pressed her palm to his chest. For a moment Cole's vision darkened, and all of the energy inside of him was pulled toward her hand. His internal regions folded and shrank as a bizarre suction drew his thoughts, his power, and maybe even his soul toward her touch.

She yanked her palm away, and the disorienting rush ended. Everything inside of him snapped back into place, and his vision cleared.

The woman stared at him with wide eyes. "Thank you for your service. You are heavily scarred for one so young."

Cole nodded.

"Show me the token," she invited.

Cole held out the ivory rose. The woman placed both of her hands over his, and the rose turned black.

The woman leaned close. "I'm not supposed to be curious tonight, but I can't help myself. Your power is interesting. Was the extreme mutilation necessary to produce it?"

"Partly," Cole murmured, trying to be vague.

"So many fascinating people have gathered tonight," she said. "This way."

She escorted Cole out of the room and to the top of a staircase. An Enforcer handed her a small torch, which she passed to Cole.

"Enjoy the service," she said.

Black rose in one hand, torch in the other, Cole started down the curving stairs. Maybe it was the torchlight, or the new chill in the air, but this part of the castle looked more ancient than the rest. The stones of the walls and floors were larger and rougher, jammed together without visible mortar. The deeper he went, the less even the stairs became. The stairway began to meander, sometimes curving to the left, other times to the right. The steps unpredictably became steeper or shallower. Moisture glistened on the walls, and the temperature plunged.

Cole slowed, taking care as the stone stairs became more craggy and damaged. He kept expecting to reach the bottom, and that kept not happening. His torch began to burn greener, first subtly, then unmistakably. The air felt thicker, almost liquid, as if a different type of atmosphere had pooled down here in the darkness. He could still breathe fine, but his lungs needed to squeeze a little harder.

At last he reached the bottom, and a short hall led through a malformed archway into a cavernous room. More than a hundred robed figures had congregated there, each holding a greenish torch. Several of them were short enough to be kids. Emerald bonfires blazed in cauldrons, and against the fractured walls, drippy candles burned in contorted candelabras.

The robed figures stood apart from one another. Nobody conversed. Cole found an empty place to stand. The others all faced a large stone block in the center of the room, gray and smooth with slightly rounded corners. Cole stared at it as well. Was it just that everyone was gazing at it, or did the block have an unusual presence?

As time passed, other robed figures trickled into the room. Cole held the torch closer to his face to ward off the chill. Eventually new people stopped arriving.

One of the robed figures mounted the stone block. Casting back his hood, he unwrapped his face.

It was Owandell. Greenish firelight reflected off his hairless scalp. His fleshy, ageless face looked just how Cole remembered him from the Lost Palace, though his build now looked a little more rotund.

Owandell raised both hands as if to quiet the crowd, even though nobody was making any noise. Then a voice penetrated Cole's mind. Owandell's lips weren't moving, but the words came across loud and clear.

Welcome, fellow servants of Nazeem. I am honored by your presence. We gather together as the true believers, the living heart of our movement, excusing those on assignment abroad. I thank you for attending.

Cole glanced around. The other robed people near him gazed raptly at Owandell. Cole assumed they all heard him as well.

How appropriate that we gather at the Founding Stone. He stomped one foot to show he meant the block on which he stood. *Most believe the name refers to this being the first stone of the First Castle. The actual meaning reaches back further. This is in fact the first stone of the Outskirts, and marks the original junction between the five kingdoms. This stone set the pattern. The material of this world expanded outward from this point, enabling mortals to dwell here.*

Owandell raised both of his hands high. *It remains a nexus of great power.* He closed his eyes. *As Nazeem teaches, all shaping power is one, and that power abounds near this historic cornerstone.*

"Nazeem!" cried one of the robed onlookers.

The flames in the room leaped higher and burned greener, including the fire of the torch Cole held. The unexpected flare up nearly startled him into dropping it.

"Nazeem! Nazeem!" called several voices.

Cole didn't take up the cry. He wasn't always the best at sensing shaping power, but he could feel wave after wave pulsing from the Founding Stone.

Owandell lowered his hands, and the flames returned to normal. *I bring you word from the Fallen Temple. Nazeem sees progress in our shapecraft. He knows of our failures as well. We must improve our techniques and hasten our efforts. The hour of his return draws nigh.*

The robed crowd cheered, waving their black roses above their heads. Cole waved his as well.

Ours is an ancient brotherhood, Owandell continued. *Long have we nurtured our craft. Long have we bided our time. We have dwelt in the shadows, practicing our art in secret, forbidden to utter our master's name. While other shapers skimmed the surface, we dove deep, and will plunge deeper still. Our exile will soon end. Nazeem's return is at hand. All will revere his name and bow to those who serve him.*

A greater cheer went up from the hooded assemblage. Some fell to their knees. Others beat their chests. Wondering what he had gotten himself into, Cole waved his rose and cheered, trying to blend in with the frenzy. Owandell paused until the excitement died down. As the room became more silent, Cole could hear a few people sobbing. This was more than people plotting. Was it some kind of cult? It was definitely weirder and more unsettling than he had expected.

Even now, in this noble company, some doubt this promise. Even after mastering aspects of the art. Even after all the signs and marvels in recent years. Those who have visited the Fallen Temple do not doubt, but there is no longer time for all to make the pilgrimage before the appointed hour. As a reward for the faithful, and as a warning to the rest, with our help, Nazeem will extend his power beyond the Fallen Temple for the first time.

No cheers accompanied this announcement, but there were many gasps. Cole had never heard of Nazeem, but he had a feeling he didn't want to meet him. He glanced at the archway through which he had entered. Could he slip out without being noticed? It didn't seem likely.

Owandell sprang down from the Founding Stone, took a torch from one of the other robed figures, and touched it to the ancient block. Green flames flickered across the surface until the entire block was ablaze.

Crouching down beside the block, Owandell laid a hand against the burning stone. Cole winced in sympathy, but the fire didn't spread to Owandell's robes, nor did he appear to be in pain.

The flames atop the Founding Stone stretched higher and began to spin. As the whirlwind of fire increased in size and intensity, the other flames in the room dimmed. Cole's torch looked like it had spent its fuel and was about to expire.

A face took shape in the heart of the green whirlwind of fire, crude in form, like a simple mask. Startled and afraid, Cole watched the fiery visage with morbid fascination. The eyes burned brightly.

Greetings, my loyal ones, bellowed a much stronger voice. Cole not only heard the rumbling words in his mind, but felt them in his chest. The black rose vibrated in his grasp. *I am Nazeem. The time has come to set our final plans in motion. Before long I will walk among you, and we will remake this world to our liking. The best of you are still infants in shapecraft, but the day approaches when you will be empowered beyond your wildest fantasies.*

Cole closed his eyes. The raw power radiating from the Founding Stone was overwhelming. It called out to him on a fundamental level. Everything inside of him felt tugged toward it. Cole realized that he could perceive his own power for the first time since Morgassa had raised her barriers. He tried to use it and found he couldn't draw from it. But at least he could sense it.

I congratulate you on your progress, Nazeem went on. *Now is the time to stand tall and finish what we started generations ago. Who is with me?*

All around Cole, robed figures raised their roses high. Cole didn't want to join in. He didn't like Nazeem or the hate behind his words. He wanted to slip out and run for his life. But he raised his rose as well to avoid standing out.

The face inside the whirlwind scowled. Cole would have sworn those blazing eyes glared right at him. *What is this? A spy in our midst? His power is obscured by skillful shapecraft, but he is not one of us. A sheep in wolf's clothing. Tonight is not for the uninitiated. Speak your name, boy.*

Frozen with fear, Cole stared back at Nazeem's brilliant eyes. The robed figures around him twisted and turned, trying to identify the imposter. For the moment, only Cole had no doubt who Nazeem meant.

His options were limited. There was no running away. Enforcers guarded the top of the stairway, and at least a dozen robed figures stood between himself and the exit. His cover was blown. He was caught. What would they do with him? This was a nightmare.

Your silence is unbecoming, Nazeem roared. *I hereby revoke your token. Who will apprehend—*

The carved rose in Cole's hand shattered, and he could no longer hear Nazeem. The face still glared down from the flames, but that rumbling voice in his head was gone. The lost connection made the face seem more distant.

More robed figures moved to cover the exit. Cole pretended to look around for the traitor like all the other robed people. He knew Nazeem was still speaking, probably giving orders to capture him. The sensation of his power straining toward the Founding Stone redoubled. Cole had to lean away to avoid stumbling toward it.

Come, a gentle voice seemed to suggest. Not Nazeem's voice. This one he felt more than heard, almost as if it rose from his own power.

Cole had no options. Any second one of his enemies would figure out which person to grab. Since his power seemed attracted to the stone, Cole decided to head that way.

Running would draw attention, so Cole walked forward, weaving between the people in his way. The Founding Stone wasn't too far off. Most of the others were fanning out. They expected him to flee. Maybe Nazeem was telling them to cut off all escape. Nobody seemed concerned about guarding the stone.

The closer he got to the Founding Stone, the clearer the pull became. The robed figures covered their ears, and Cole could see that the face was yelling, but he heard nothing.

Three or four steps from the Founding Stone, Owandell lunged at Cole, his eyes enraged. Cole faked left, sprang right, ducked Owandell's grasping hands, and dove to the stone, pressing both hands against the smooth surface, heedless of the green flames.

CHAPTER

28

FOUNDING STONE

Suddenly Cole was alone with Nazeem. No longer a disembodied face veiled in flame, Nazeem looked human, and very displeased. Indistinct grayness surrounded them. Cole didn't understand where they were. He could still feel his hands against the stone, his power flowing freely into the huge block, so why didn't he see the block, or the other robed figures? All he saw was the dreamlike image of Nazeem gazing at him. This had to be in his mind.

You! Nazeem accused, darkening and shrinking, withdrawing as if falling, his voice no longer as commanding. *The intruder!*

That's right, Cole responded mentally, his confidence surging as Nazeem's influence dwindled. *Me!*

The vision of Nazeem vanished, and Cole could see again. His hands remained against the warm surface of the Founding Stone. The green flames had disappeared. The entire block gleamed an intense white.

Cole could still feel his power coursing into the stone,

though not as vigorously as at first. Looking around, he found that all of the other green flames in the room were extinguished as well. The robed figures maintained motionless poses, bathed in the Founding Stone's white glare. Owandell was closest, his face distorted into a grimace, one hand outstretched. Despite his awkward posture, he stayed unnaturally still. He also looked somewhat transparent.

"Why did time stop?" Cole muttered to himself.

Nobody answered.

Beneath his palms, the Founding Stone thrummed with energy. Cole could clearly sense the shapecrafted barriers inside of himself, shadowy contrasts to the vibrant clarity of his power. Those obstructions didn't matter right now. His shaping energy flowed through them, hardly disturbed, like a flash flood gushing through a chain-link fence.

He had a deep suspicion that as soon as he released the stone, everything would return to normal. For some reason, his contact with the Founding Stone had paused everyone. No. That wasn't quite right. Nothing had happened to them. He had temporarily passed outside the reach of time. Cole couldn't explain how he knew that was true, but he felt certain.

Surveying the room, Cole realized that all the robed people were semitransparent. Wait, not just the people—the walls, too. He focused on the walls and ceiling, trying to peer through the stone. One wall seemed to conceal an indistinct chamber beyond, and Cole strained to make it out.

As he intensified his effort, the wall drew nearer. Or was he moving toward it? No, his hands remained on the

Founding Stone. His vision had somehow disconnected from his body and journeyed across the room.

Experimenting with his detached vision, Cole found he could glide anywhere he chose, moving freely around the room, high or low. The sensation of motion without moving gave him vertigo, and Cole steadied himself against the block. After some time swooping around the area, Cole fixed his vision on himself kneeling beside the Founding Stone, palms against it. He could see the shaping energy inside his translucent body, cloudlike and churning, along with the dark tangles of the shapecrafted barriers.

Shifting his attention to Owandell, Cole could perceive his energy as well. It was darker, motionless, and had less shapecrafted snarls. Studying the others, he recognized different degrees of shaping energy inside all of the robed figures.

Cole noticed the deformed archway to the stairs and wondered how far his vision could roam. He coasted through the archway, glanced back at himself beside the Founding Stone, then started up the stairs. No torches lit the stairway, leaving it very dim, but he could still see enough detail to proceed, as if his vision carried a faint inherent light.

With a small effort of will, Cole found that he could go as fast as he wanted, so before long he reached the top. The heavy door was closed and slightly transparent. Cole pushed through it without any trouble and found himself in the room at the base of the tower. He saw the woman who had held her palm to his chest, her energy sparkling inside of her.

Pressing ahead, Cole exited the tower and moved through

the halls of the castle, occasionally passing Enforcers, then regular guardsmen. He knew where he wanted to go. After several wrong turns, he located the door to Harmony's tower and ghosted through it.

He rushed from one room to another in the tower. He found the queen's servant Sophie asleep in bed, but the other rooms were empty, including what had to be Harmony's bedroom. He wondered where she could be. Would he have to search the rest of the castle?

Then he remembered the balcony.

He flew up the stairs and through the door, and sure enough, there she stood, gazing up at the stars, her shaping energy bright within her. Cole hovered in front of her face. She was as motionless as everyone else. He called out to her, but the sound came from his mouth back in the room beneath Owandell's tower.

Cole eased in closer, until her face filled his view. He willed her to speak to him. He needed help!

Her expression didn't twitch. She was no livelier than a statue. Was there a way to snap her out of it?

Moving closer still, Cole's vision entered her head, and suddenly her energy filled his view, swirling and pulsing, no longer static. A strong sense of her presence enveloped him.

Is that you, Cole? he heard in his mind.

It's me! he replied excitedly.

I hear you. I can't move. How are you doing this?

I'm not sure. I'm touching the Founding Stone.

What? Her tone became distressed. *Are you alone?*

Not exactly. Do you know about Nazeem?

Excuse me?

Nazeem. Some scary guy from the Fallen Temple.

I don't know what you're talking about.

He's Owandell's boss. They have a plan to take over the Outskirts. Nazeem has been imprisoned for a long time, but it sounds like he's about to get free. He was here tonight, kind of, using the Founding Stone as a communicator. He knew I was a spy. They were about to catch me. My power wanted me to go to the Founding Stone, so I did. When I touched the stone, Nazeem went away, and everybody else froze, as if time stopped. You were frozen too, until we started talking.

The patterns of Harmony's energy became agitated for a moment. *I still can't move. My body remains frozen. Somehow you freed my mind. This is incredible, Cole. Legend has it that the Founding Stone once wielded great power, but nobody has been able to use it in ages. Your ability must have revitalized it somehow.*

Oh! You're right! That fits. It's what my ability does. But what now? I'm afraid if I let go of the stone, Owandell will capture me.

You're currently touching it?

Yes.

And the others are still immobile?

I can't see. My vision is with you. But I guess they're still frozen, because they're not grabbing me. Plus, you still can't move.

How did you get to me? Harmony wondered.

It was like my sight could fly around all of a sudden. I feel like I'm looking out of floating eyes. Except they can go through stuff like doors and people. I flew from under Owandell's tower to here.

How did you get past the protections on my tower?

I don't know. I didn't run into any.

Must be the Founding Stone.

Cole only wanted the stone's power to do one thing. *Can I use it to escape somehow?*

Maybe. Some powerful Wayminders can send their sight on missions. The most powerful can cross space to bring their bodies to the location of their sight.

Perfect! How can I do it?

That I cannot explain. You must learn from trial and error. See if the stone makes it possible.

Gritting his teeth, Cole willed his body to teleport to where his vision was. Nothing happened.

I'm trying, Cole told her. *It isn't working.*

As I understand it, you've never sent your sight roaming before?

No.

Then keep trying. Who knows what you're capable of with the stone boosting your abilities?

Pressing both hands more firmly against the stone, Cole reached for his own power, and visualized his body joining up with his sight. He backed his vision away from Harmony, once again seeing her face instead of the graceful pyrotechnics of her energy. Then he pushed with all his will.

His vision shattered into dizzying perspectives. He was rising and sinking, zooming north, west, east, and south, seeing all directions at once from multiple simultaneous vantages. In a kaleidoscopic overload he saw mountaintops and oceans, slumbering villages and busy insects, roots growing in the earth and stars in the sky.

For one explosive moment Cole seemed to glimpse everything. But it was far too much to absorb, and his endless viewpoints collapsed, frantically returning to the Founding Stone from all directions.

And then it was over.

Cole still knelt with both hands against the stone. He was aware of that much. Except now he was surrounded by whiteness. Before him stood an elderly man in an elegant maroon robe with gold trim. The stranger had white hair and a friendly face.

"There you are," the man said warmly. "I've been trying to aid you. I wondered if you would find me."

"This feels like we're really talking," Cole said.

"I thought it might seem more natural to you," the man said. "I realize how new most of this feels. It must be disorienting. Do you understand who I am?"

"The Founding Stone?"

"Good try. Close. I'll take it as a compliment. I'm a reflection of Dandalus, one of the original architects of this world. His chief task was to oversee the creation of the Founding Stone, and he put some of himself into it. I'm like a semblance, or a figment."

"Where are we?" Cole asked.

"Your body is where it's been since you touched the stone," Dandalus said. "But your mind is now with me."

Cole looked around. "Lots of white."

"I quite like it," Dandalus said. "For a long season I dreamed in the darkness."

"Can you help me get out of here?" Cole asked.

"I believe so. It would only be right. After all, you aided me. The stone was being abused by lawless shaping. The

361

intrusion aroused me from a long slumber. I knew your power could help, so I called out to you as best I could. Once you lent me your energy, I was able to reject Nazeem and bring you out of the timestream."

"I was seeing all over the castle. Like my eyes were traveling without me."

"I helped free your sight. I wanted you to look into the Founding Stone, so you could find me. Instead you searched everywhere else! I could feel you wandering, and sensed your conversation with the queen. For a moment you saw as the stone sees. It shares a connection with all the material of this world. Your mind rejected the vision and your sight returned here. Welcome."

"How can I escape?" Cole asked.

Dandalus scrunched his brow. "It has to be quick. Once you stop feeding me your energy, I'll slip back into my slumber. And without my help, you won't be able to access your power."

"Can you fix what Morgassa did to me?" Cole asked. "She used shapecraft to keep me from my power."

"Shapecraft," Dandalus grumbled in disdain. "Not much craft to it. Raw shaping, I call it. Shaping without context. Too much of it will mean the end of all we organized."

"Can you repair the damage?" Cole asked.

"I wish I could. Unfortunately, what was done to you doesn't pertain to the order established by the Founding Stone. Even fortified by your power, altering what was done to you is beyond my ability. I can help your power sidestep the blockades, but only while I'm active."

"How can you sleep?" Cole asked. "Don't you hold the Outskirts together?"

Dandalus laughed. "No, my boy. That would be far too much power to concentrate in one place. This stone set the pattern for this world, and maintains a unique connection to all the material that follows the pattern, but it doesn't sustain this world. The Founding Stone would not be easy to unmake, or to move for that matter, but the pattern is already firmly established. If the Founding Stone were destroyed, this world would persist."

"What about Nazeem?" Cole asked. "Can you tell me anything about him?"

"Very little," Dandalus said. "I just met him. He is shrouded in lawless shaping. He was reaching out to us from a place in Necronum that is also cloaked in what you call shapecraft. I assume he's at the Fallen Temple they spoke about, but I can't spy on his domain."

"How do I fight lawless shaping?" Cole asked.

"That falls outside my understanding," Dandalus apologized. "I labored to bring order to the shaping here. This stone symbolizes that effort."

"You're connected to this whole world?" Cole asked.

"Yes."

"Can you help me find people?"

"Our present contact leaves your mind open to me. I can see some of the people you wish to locate. Jenna. Constance. Some of your other friends."

"I came here from Outside with a bunch of kidnapped children."

"Nobody is native to this world," Dandalus said. "Some are born here, but trace their lines back far enough, and all come from Outside."

"Can you find my friends?"

"This is a big world," Dandalus said. "It would take some searching. You glimpsed how it feels to see it all at once. I can't apprehend much that way either. I could explore a little at a time. So could you."

"Send my sight out again?" Cole asked.

"Yes," Dandalus said. "But your power isn't endless. This partnership could last a few hours, but eventually you won't be able to continue powering the stone without rest."

"Once that happens, Owandell will get me," Cole said.

"You will return to the timestream, yes," Dandalus said.

Cole sighed. "That probably isn't enough time."

"Do you know where to look?" Dandalus asked. "Our chances would improve if you can narrow down the search."

"That's the problem," Cole said. "I have no idea where to start."

Dandalus nodded. "Then perhaps the best I can do is help you get away. I should be able to send you anywhere in this world."

"Should?" Cole asked. "You're not sure?"

"Not entirely," Dandalus admitted. "If it works, I can send you across the kingdom as easily as across the room. It's a manipulation of space, similar to the opening of a way. Once you break contact with the stone, it will stop functioning. But the transfer is as close to instantaneous as it gets. I expect success."

"Can you send me home to my world?" Cole asked.

"I'm sorry, but no. The Founding Stone has no influence there."

Cole weighed his options. After how angry he had made Owandell, it would be smart to go as far from Junction as possible. He could skip the trains and return to Old Zeropolis. But he would lack the key piece of information he came here for—Constance's location.

"Can you send me to Queen Harmony?" Cole asked. "Where I just was?"

"On the balcony?" Dandalus verified.

"Yeah."

"It's no harder to send you farther," Dandalus said. "Surely you know of more distant options."

"I need information from Harmony," Cole said.

"As you wish," Dandalus said. "If I fail, the effort will break contact with the stone without sending you anywhere. Hurry and touch it again and I'll pull you back out of the timestream."

"Okay," Cole said.

"Focus on the place you want me to send you," Dandalus said. "Visualize it. Reach out for it with your mind. I'll do the rest."

"Wait," Cole said. "One more question."

"I know it. I see your mind. You hope there is a way for you to get home from this world they now call the Outskirts."

"They can open ways," Cole said. "But I want to get home and stay there. I want my family to remember me."

"Those who come here are not meant to return. It wasn't

anything we framers established—it was part of the nature of this place from the beginning. In theory, any aspect of this world can be reshaped. But I don't know how you would accomplish it. I believe it would be impossible without using lawless shaping, which in turn could jeopardize this world's stability. My advice would be to settle for living here."

"I'm not going to give up," Cole said.

"I can see that. But my advice stands. Are you ready?"

Closing his eyes, Cole pictured the balcony where he had just spoken to Queen Harmony. Abruptly his power stopped flowing. He could no longer sense his ability, and the Founding Stone had disappeared.

CHAPTER

— 29 —

FUGITIVE

"You did it!" Harmony exclaimed.

Cole opened his eyes. Kneeling before the queen on her balcony, a starry sky above, he breathed a quiet sigh of relief.

"I had some help," Cole said, standing.

"I only offered encouragement," Harmony said modestly.

"I appreciated it," Cole replied, trying to pretend he had partly meant her. "After we spoke, I found somebody inside the Founding Stone. Kind of like a semblance. The guy who made the stone shaped some of himself into it. He sent me here."

"I see," Harmony said. "When your mind departed, I must have been completely frozen again. From my point of view, we were just speaking. You appeared immediately after we finished."

"Everyone was frozen but me," Cole said. "I know one thing. Owandell is furious right now."

"And baffled," Harmony said. "He'll suppose you're powerful indeed to have slipped through his grasp. And he won't be entirely wrong. It really was quite a feat. Did he see your face?"

"He got a good look at me, but I had my hood up and my face wrapped."

Harmony folded her arms. "That's enough to be dangerous. Your shaping power is very distinctive to those who can perceive it. Owandell would not have missed it, and you're right about his fury."

"I need to get out of here," Cole said.

"Don't be too hasty. Owandell can't touch you here in my tower. He's already moving to watch all exits. You won't escape him with speed. Tell me what you learned."

"Owandell helps run the Brotherhood of Nazeem," Cole said. "They've been around in secret for a long time. It seems like Nazeem is where shapecrafting comes from. At least the shapecrafting that Owandell knows. The guy in the Founding Stone called it lawless shaping."

"An apt description," Harmony said. "You mentioned they're trying to free Nazeem."

"Sounds like that's their main goal," Cole said. "He's at a place called the Fallen Temple in Necronum. They act like once he's free, nobody can stop them. And they expect it to happen soon. Nazeem ordered them to make their final preparations."

"Did they give specifics?" Harmony asked. "Any dates?"

"No details," Cole said. "Nazeem didn't speak long before noticing me."

"This is still valuable information," Harmony said. "Anything else?"

"Dandalus, the guy in the Founding Stone, said shape-craft could destroy the world."

"I don't doubt it," Harmony said. "Consider what happened with Carnag and Morgassa. That could be only the beginning. You have served me well, Cole. Owandell has guarded this information for a great while. I'm surprised to learn his plots involve more than shapecraft and political maneuvers. I had no inkling that he served some mysterious master. I don't know how he kept this secret so perfectly. I've never heard of Nazeem or the Fallen Temple. I'll investigate and see what I can learn."

Cole stared out at the vast view, lit by stars and the silvery light of the rising moon. "Do you sense your daughters?"

Harmony walked to the railing and gripped it tightly. "Yes, but tonight I'm troubled." Her eyes gazed out into the moon-glossed distance. "I fear for Destiny and Honor. They're both in Necronum, close to each other. Something is wrong. Their panic started earlier this evening, and has only escalated since then."

"They're in danger?" Cole asked.

Harmony nodded. "Mortal peril. I've lingered here all night. I would try to help them, but who is left to send?"

"Honor is tough," Cole said.

Eyes still far away, Harmony placed a hand over her heart. "Sometimes toughness isn't enough. Or bravery." She turned to Cole. "This isn't a world for children. I'm not sure it's a world for anyone."

"I'll help if I can," Cole said.

Harmony smiled sadly. "You're a child too. For now, you

have hardships of your own to endure. Survive one mission at a time. If Nori or Tessa can use help, I'll place markers in the sky. Mira and others know where to look. I have drawn you a map that marks the location of Abram Trench's most secret lair. It's where he's holding Constance. Will you take it to Googol and Nova for me?"

"Of course," Cole said.

"You'll want the code phrase that lets Constance know I trust you," Harmony said. "The words are different for each child. Tell her 'Follow the path and don't look back.'"

"Got it," Cole said.

"Guard those words with your life. Nobody knows about them, so even if you're captured, I doubt you'll be asked to divulge them. If you are, give the phrase 'Meet me by the waterfall.' Should somebody use those words, it will signal to Constance that something is amiss."

"Thanks for trusting me," Cole said. "I won't let you down."

"By the way, I found where your friend Jenna was taken," Harmony said.

"Really?" Cole replied. With all that had happened, he wondered if she might have forgotten to follow up.

"She went to Necronum," Harmony said. "To the Temple of the Still Water."

Cole could hardly contain his excitement. "Thank you! She's a close friend. I've been searching for her since I came here."

"Glad I could be of service," Harmony replied. "I'll send Sophie to fetch you an errand-boy uniform. It will be the best way to leave the castle. Others will help you make your way to the train station. All will be arranged. You'll leave on the earliest train of the day."

"Can I avoid using my ID?" Cole asked.

"Don't you have it?" she asked.

"I have it," Cole said, feeling one of the pockets inside his robe to make sure. "There are people looking for me."

"Even I must show my ID to ride the train," Harmony said. "Perhaps we could figure out another way with more time to plan. But time is of the essence. The best we can do is make sure you board right before departure."

"Okay," Cole said. "That'll have to work."

Reclining in a comfortable seat, Cole watched the sunrise through the train window. He sipped hot chocolate and nibbled on a sweet roll with raspberry filling. More tired than hungry, he was using the food to stay alert.

He had boarded the train in darkness, wearing jeans and a leather jacket. Everything had gone so smoothly that it made him feel extra vigilant.

Nobody had stopped him when he left the First Castle with a group of errand boys. A woman had met him at an inn and helped him get to the train station with a change of clothes. Nobody had looked twice as he boarded the train. Nobody in his nearly full car acted suspicious.

Was it possible he would get away clean? Owandell couldn't cover every way out of Junction. The mysterious spy who escaped him could be headed to any kingdom, or could still be hiding in the castle, or elsewhere in Junction City.

But what about the Hunter? As soon as Cole presented his ID, the Enforcers must have started scrambling to intercept him. And Owandell was the head of the Enforcers. Would the Hunter figure out that the kid he was looking for was the spy who had escaped the gathering with Nazeem?

Queen Harmony had assured him she would contact the Unseen in Zeropolis so that somebody would be there to meet him when he arrived at the main terminal. But what about when he transferred at Outpost 19? He could only hope the Hunter wouldn't have time to get people in place.

The sun rose higher, and the ride remained monotonous. The seat was so comfy, and there didn't seem to be any threats present. He hadn't slept much the night before. In spite of all the potential danger, Cole began to struggle to keep his eyes open. He decided that if he was going to sleep, it would be best to do it before the transfer.

He awoke as the train slowed to a stop at Outpost 19. Today Cole traveled with a small, empty knapsack, just so it would look like he had some luggage. The map to Abram Trench's top secret hideout was safely tucked in his jacket pocket.

Cole exited and started following the crowd to the monorail. Then he stopped in his tracks.

Two large robots stood in front of the monorail, surveying the approaching passengers. Tall, sleek, and black, they looked just like the drone that the Hunter had used to try to catch him in Zeropolis. Several people boarding the monorail glanced uncomfortably at the gangly robots.

Trying to stay casual, Cole turned away from the

monorail, only to find a third drone guarding the station's exit, positioned between the stairs and the senders. At the moment, people from the train swarmed near Cole, many of them taller than him. None of the drones appeared to have noticed him yet.

Cole crouched down and pretended to tie his shoe. The crowd would help hide him while passengers were transferring, but once that was finished, he'd have no cover.

Should he try to slip out of the station? What would he do alone in an isolated outpost? How would he get to Zeropolis? The Hunter would just send people to track him down. He needed to get on the monorail. What were his chances of slipping by the robots? Could he use somebody as a human shield?

Cole knew he needed to act. If he delayed, he would be taken. He couldn't let that happen! Dalton and his friends needed him. Queen Harmony was counting on him to deliver Constance's location. Mira had to find her sister. He hadn't survived spying on Owandell to get nabbed by a couple of robots.

A hefty man in a striped suit passed near Cole on his way to the monorail. Cole rose and followed him, staying close enough that he had no view of the drones. The man made his way toward one of the doors closest to the front. That was good! It put both drones on the same side.

As the monorail drew near, Cole carefully shifted from behind the man to his side, keeping the robots out of sight. As the man reached the steps up to the door, Cole slipped ahead of him, head turned partly away from the drones, and handed his ticket to the conductor.

A metal hand clamped down on his shoulder from behind.

"A moment of your time," the robot requested in a male voice that sounded nothing like the Hunter.

"The monorail departs in eight minutes," the conductor warned.

Cole tried to twist away from the metal grip, but the fingers tightened, making his struggles useless. "Okay," Cole said, backing away from the monorail.

Never releasing him, the drone marched Cole across the floor of the station. Cole tried to reach for his power. Even with the shapecrafted barriers in place, he knew it was still possible to access his ability. The Founding Stone had taught him that much.

But no matter how hard he pushed, Cole could feel no glimmer of his power. He attempted to make his vision detach and go roaming. He tried to teleport. His efforts amounted to nothing more than wishful thinking.

The drone took him through a nondescript door. They went down a hall to a room where a woman waited—a pretty blonde in a white shirt with a blue leather vest and matching pants. In the corner a metal coffin sat on a wheeled cart.

The drone forced Cole into the room. The tall robot had to crouch a little to fit through the doorway.

"You led us on a merry chase," the woman said. "I didn't think you'd make the mistake of coming back this way, but the Hunter was right. Maybe one day I'll learn not to doubt him."

The drone was still gripping Cole. There was no way to

run. All he had left were words. "I don't know what you're talking about."

"Sure you do," the woman said, producing a syringe. "It's over, kid. Try to relax."

While the drone held Cole steady, she swiftly poked the needle into his arm and pressed the plunger. Cole squirmed and bucked, but it did no good.

Whatever she had injected into him acted quickly. His head became light, and the woman began to blur. Within a moment Cole limply swayed as the floor seemed to tilt. The drone held him up.

"Don't do this," Cole said, the words mushy. "Please, let me go."

"Don't fight it," the woman said. "Relax. You have a train to catch."

The woman lifted the hinged lid of the coffin, and the drone placed Cole inside. It was padded. Cole fought to keep his eyes open but lost consciousness before the lid closed.

CHAPTER

—✺— 30 —✺—

THE HUNTER

Consciousness returned by degrees. All Cole knew at first was that he still felt too tired to open his eyes. The hard surface beneath him failed to ignite his curiosity. Where exactly was he? Did it matter? He had awakened in many different places over the past couple of months. At least it was quiet. On his back with his eyes closed, he could be anywhere.

When he moved to wipe his eyes, Cole found that his arm was restrained. His eyes snapped open, the drowsy calm dispelled. He discovered that his arms and legs were cuffed to a metal table inside a bare, white room. A panicked burst of struggling proved that the restraints were solid. A counter with a sink and several drawers looked to be the only furnishings besides his metal slab.

Getting captured came back to him in a rush. How had he forgotten? The injection must have left him groggy.

How long had he been out? His mouth was really dry and

had a coppery taste. A long time could have passed. Where was he? It looked like a room in a hospital. Maybe a mental hospital? Or some kind of prison?

"Rise and shine!" greeted the youthful voice of the Hunter from a speaker in the ceiling. "I guess you can't rise yet, but I'm glad you're awake. You had a nice trip?"

"Where am I?" Cole asked, unsure if the Hunter could hear him.

"You're at my favorite retreat in Zeropolis," the Hunter said. "I'm here too. I'll come see you in a minute."

"Could you bring some water?"

"You bet. Sit tight."

Cole waited. It wasn't long before the door opened and a person entered dressed all in dark leather. A helmet hid the face. The person set a glass of water on the counter, then closed the door and locked it.

Pulling off his helmet, the person revealed himself to be a boy about Cole's age. The kid stared at Cole for a long moment, his face lighting up with joy and relief. His huge smile looked involuntary. Tears shimmered in his eyes.

"I can't believe it's really you," he said.

The reaction left Cole confused. "Man, you really wanted to catch me."

The Hunter laughed, still looking delighted. "Yeah, I guess I did. You didn't make it easy."

"You're the Hunter?" Cole asked.

"You knew I was young," he said. "Almost as young as you. I'm a little older than I look. My shaping powers make me age slowly. Take a good look at me. Do I look familiar?"

Cole was at a loss. The kid had brown hair and a friendly face. "Not really."

The Hunter came closer. "Come on. Look hard. Think. Nobody is listening anymore. Who am I, Cole?"

"Have we met before?" Cole asked, thoroughly perplexed. Was this some kind of weird form of torture?

The Hunter looked a little disappointed. "You've known me most of your life."

"Most of my life was back on Earth."

The Hunter watched him. "You're getting warmer."

"I knew you on Earth?"

"In Idaho and Arizona," the Hunter said.

Cole looked him up and down, trying to place him. "Has it been a while? Were you a lot younger or something?"

The Hunter shook his head. "Part of the time. You've known me since you were born. The last time you saw me, I looked pretty much like this. Come on, think."

"Are you just messing with me?"

"No. We both love soccer. Your parents are Bryant and Liz Randolph."

"How do you know that?"

"They're my parents too, dummy. I'm your brother. Hunter Randolph."

Cole was speechless. This was ludicrous. What kind of game was the Hunter playing? The kid was not familiar at all. "Yeah, whatever."

"Don't, Cole. I'm serious. Look at me. Can't you see the family resemblance?"

Cole supposed he and the kid shared some physical similarities. But they were hardly twins. "You look my age."

"I'm about two years older than you. In more than two years, I've only aged about six months. Chelsea is a year older than me."

Cole shook his head. "You are such a liar. You searched me on the Internet. Nice try. No way am I believing you."

"Think, Cole," the Hunter said. "Nobody back home remembers you. I was taken before you, so you don't remember me. I hoped that maybe since we were both here now, there might be a little spark of memory."

Cole honestly had no shred of memory of this kid. It had to be a lie. Surely he would remember his own brother. "Why would my brother work for the High King?" he challenged.

"The same reason the CIA works for the president," the Hunter said. "The High King is in charge. He's been good to me. You've gotten involved with some bad people, Cole. You have no idea."

Cole shook his head. This was so bogus. "You must think I'm dumb as a rock."

"Use your head," the Hunter said. "If you're not my brother, you're just some runaway slave. Why would I go to all this effort to bring you in without anybody knowing?"

"To get me to betray my friends."

"I wouldn't mind that," the Hunter mused. "But there are easier ways to get to your friends. The patrolmen could force you to give them up. Or the legionnaires. They have cruel methods that work. I'm trying to give you a second chance. You got mixed up with the wrong side. I get it. I know what it's like to be new here. It's confusing. You got brainwashed. When I saw your picture in Carthage, I realized who you were. I got permission from the High King to let you join us. You're my brother. I'm trying to save you."

Cole laughed. "Is that why I'm locked up?"

"You're locked up until I decide you won't do anything stupid. Come on, Cole. I'm not familiar at all?"

"Not a bit," Cole said sincerely.

The Hunter reached into his pocket and took out a wallet. He removed a little photo and held it up to Cole. It was the family picture that hung in their living room. Cole knew it well. A few years old, the picture showed him, Chelsea, and their parents. And some other kid.

Cole blinked, then squinted.

"Wait a minute," he said.

"That's right," the Hunter encouraged. "Do you see?"

The other kid in the photo was the Hunter, looking not much younger than he did right now.

"No way," Cole said. "You faked this."

"I brought the picture here with me. Look at it."

Cole closed his eyes.

"I said look," the Hunter urged.

"Give me a second," Cole said. He was trying to envision the picture in the living room. There was no extra kid in it, was there? He had a faint recollection of noticing another kid in the shot, and briefly wondering who it could be. Was that even a real memory?

Cole opened his eyes. The Hunter was unmistakable, right in the middle of the picture. He was wearing the right clothes and had the right hair style. In the picture, he and Cole definitely looked like brothers.

"It looks real," Cole said.

"Because it is," the Hunter said. "I still look like myself. I haven't aged much, and I haven't dyed my hair."

"I was trying to avoid detection," Cole said.

"I saw the e-mails you sent to the family account," the Hunter said. "Did you see mine?"

"No," Cole said.

"I've been sending them for years," the Hunter said. "It was funny to see you sending the same kind of messages while not opening mine."

"Can I see?" Cole asked.

"Sure, I have a thruport here," the Hunter said. "There are plenty of other pictures of me in the family e-mail account and on social media. Maybe now you'll recognize me in them."

Cole didn't want to believe any of this. But what if the Hunter wasn't lying? What if it was true? "You lived in our house?" Cole asked.

"Right across the hall from your room," the Hunter said.

"That's the guest room," Cole replied.

The Hunter stared at him meaningfully. "Maybe now. What about all my soccer stuff? My trophies? My posters?"

Cole scrunched his brow. What exactly was in the guest room? Were there trophies? He couldn't form a clear picture in his mind. "I don't know. I don't remember any of that."

The Hunter laughed bitterly. "Now we have two guest rooms. And even more unnoticed trophies."

"I don't remember you," Cole said honestly. "This seems impossible."

"The Outskirts is a weird place," the Hunter said. "I hate that you can't remember. Think. Practicing soccer in the backyard. Christmas mornings. You have to trust that I remember you! You're my little brother! We'll become friends again. We did it once."

Cole stared at the Hunter. Could this be true? He had always thought it would be cool to have a brother. Could those yearnings have replaced his actual memories?

"I don't know what to say," Cole said.

"I knew this might be hard for you," the Hunter said. "I knew you might not remember. I'll give you lots of proof. This isn't a trick. I know all sorts of things you can't find on the Internet. Remember when that peacock chased Chelsea at the Phoenix Zoo? Remember when Mom backed the car into the garage door? Remember that time we camped in the backyard and you wet your sleeping bag?"

"That was just with Dad."

The Hunter shook his head. "It was the three of us. I went and got you fresh underwear and sweatpants."

"Who is my best friend in Mesa?"

"Is it still Dalton?"

"Who was the old guy in Boise that probably killed our cat?"

"Mr. Barrum."

Cole tried to think of more things only a family member would know. "What does Mom keep in the bathroom to read?"

"Those condensed books. *Reader's Digest*. And Dad sometimes brings in *Sports Illustrated*."

Cole stared at the kid who was probably his brother. "What is Chelsea allergic to?"

The Hunter scowled in thought. "I don't remember."

Cole rolled his eyes. "It's a food. You should know this."

"Right! Frozen berries. They give her weird little sores on her tongue."

"What animal does Mom hate?"

"Geckos."

Cole felt like he might cry. How could the Hunter know so many obscure details? Cole considered how much he hoped his family would remember him. His brother had been going through this for years now. "How are you the Hunter?"

"People call me the Hunter. Really I'm just Hunter. Hunter Randolph. Your brother."

"But you're on the wrong side," Cole whispered.

Hunter shook his head. "You're just brainwashed. It'll be okay. I'll help you."

"No way, Hunter. You might really be my brother. If it's true, I'm so sorry I don't remember you. But if you think you're on the right side, you don't know the whole story."

Hunter sighed. "I'm sure they told you all sorts of things. Every criminal has excuses. Some probably sound pretty good. The Unseen are terrorists. They're trying to destroy the Outskirts. It may take some time, but I'll help you see what's really going on."

Cole tried to stay calm. He had to believe Hunter didn't

know some key facts if he was happy fighting for the High King. What information was most likely to sway him? "Do you know who you've been chasing?"

"A slave girl named Mira," Hunter said. "She ran away with secrets vital to the High King. He wants her alive."

"Do you know who Mira really is?" Cole asked.

"I just told you."

"Do you know about Stafford's five daughters?"

"Everybody does. They died in an accident a long time ago."

Cole shook his head. "Their father faked their deaths. He stole their shaping powers with shapecraft, and wanted to keep them imprisoned, but they got away. Losing their powers made them completely stop aging. They lived in exile for decades. Mira is Miracle Pemberton. For some reason, the shapecraft that took their powers started to unravel, and Stafford started to lose his stolen abilities. He wants his daughters back so he can take their powers again."

"I'm glad to hear that," Hunter said. "I'm relieved you have good reasons for taking the wrong side. If I believed that were true, I wouldn't want to serve the High King either. But it's all lies, Cole. That's what the rebels do."

"Those aren't lies," Cole said. "I've been with Mira for months. Shapecrafters used her powers to make Carnag. She got her abilities back when we defeated the monster. Same with Honor in Elloweer."

"I don't know what you think you saw," Hunter said, sounding a little agitated. "But they're tricking you."

"If you're my brother, listen to me," Cole said. "Do you know about shapecraft?"

"Yeah," Hunter said. "I don't use it, but I know a little about it."

"You work for Owandell, right?"

"Technically, since he's the head of the Enforcers. But I'm one of the High King's slaves. I lead my own team of Enforcers and report directly to the High Shaper."

"How can you work for a guy who made you a slave?" Cole asked.

"It's how it works here," Hunter said. "They have different laws than in our world. Slaves are legal, but they get treated well. It's not like I'm in chains breaking rocks with a sledgehammer. I have lots of responsibilities, and I do just about whatever I want. It's more like I just work for the High King."

"As his slave."

"Catching criminals. Like you."

"Do you know about Nazeem?" Cole asked.

"Who?"

"Owandell's real master. He's imprisoned in the Fallen Temple in Necronum."

Hunter rubbed his temples as if getting a headache. "The lies of the Unseen get weirder and weirder."

"I didn't hear this from the Unseen," Cole said. "I was in disguise at a gathering led by Owandell last night. We were under his tower in the room with the Founding Stone. Nazeem appeared. He's where shapecraft comes from. He is seriously evil. When he gets free, Owandell and his shape-crafters are going to try to take over the Outskirts."

Hunter looked at Cole skeptically. "You saw this?"

"I almost got caught," Cole said. "I used my shaping power to escape."

"What can you do?"

"My power is mostly blocked right now. It happened when we fought Morgassa. She used shapecraft on me before she died. But my power can energize things. I made renderings from Sambria work in Elloweer. My Jumping Sword, for example. Somehow the Founding Stone helped temporarily unblock my power. I energized the stone and it helped me escape."

"This was last night?" Hunter asked.

"I went to the train station afterward."

Hunter frowned. "I know that shapecrafters are made, not born. Owandell invited me to become one. But I don't trust the shapecrafters I've met, and I don't like Owandell. The High King is wary of him too. We thought he invented shapecraft. Why haven't I heard of Nazeem?"

"Nobody knows," Cole said. "If you check, you'll find Owandell is desperately looking for me. I learned his big secret."

"He knows who you are?" Hunter asked.

"I was in disguise," Cole said. "But some of my friends are worried he may have seen my shaping power and be able to use that to recognize me."

"Your friends are probably right. How did you get into that meeting?"

"I had help inside the castle," Cole said. "Not the High King. I shouldn't say who."

"You're sure about Nazeem?"

"Hunter, I'm positive. I was there. If you're my brother, act like it and believe me a little! At least check it out. Nazeem taught Owandell how to use shapecraft. And Owandell used shapecraft to help Stafford steal his own daughters' powers and fake their deaths."

Hunter folded his arms and smiled grimly. "There's no way you're right about the daughters."

"How do you not know this?" Cole asked. "I thought you were high up in the Enforcers?"

"I am."

"Aren't you supposed to be good at digging up secrets?"

"My specialty is tracking people down."

"Well, go find this out. The High King is a bad man. He made the laws that got both of us taken as slaves, along with a bunch of other kids from our neighborhood. He betrayed his own daughters in a big way. And obviously he lies to the slaves who work for him."

Hunter put his hands on his hips. "Listen, Cole. You can't imagine how excited I am to see you. I want to prove I'm your brother. Most of what you told me has to be Unseen propaganda, but I'll look into it. In return, knowing what you now know, I want you to use a thruport, get on the Internet, and confirm that I'm your brother."

"That might be hard while I'm bound to a table," Cole said.

"If you promise to behave, I'll free you."

"Promise you'll look into Owandell and the High King?"

"To really do this, I might have to go to Junction. But yeah, I'll check it out."

"Then I'll behave. But hurry. There's stuff I need to do."

"What if I bring proof that these are lies?"

Cole thought about that. "It would have to be really solid proof. I've seen a lot of firsthand evidence that this is true."

"Maybe you only think you've seen proof. I've been here a lot longer than you, Cole. You might be deceived and confused."

Cole shrugged. "If you're right, I'll come to your side. But if I'm right, you better come to mine."

"Fair enough. Deal."

"Does this mean you'll finally give me that water?"

Hunter glanced at the glass on the counter. "I'll do even better than that—I'll free your hands so you can drink it."

EVIDENCE

Before he was captured, if Cole had been asked what life would look like as the Hunter's prisoner, he would have described squalid cells, limited food, and plenty of torture. Instead he had thruport access, a roomy shower, a hot tub, gourmet meals, a soft bed, and magnetic games to play.

He was still a prisoner. Though free to move about a space that included five comfortable rooms, all other doors were locked to him. One of the tall robotic drones remained nearby at every moment.

After a few hours doing some initial research, Hunter had decided that he needed to travel to Junction in order to disprove Cole's claims. Hunter had promised to return soon.

That was three days ago.

After seeing scores of photos and reading hundreds of e-mails, Cole had lost interest in scouring the Internet for more evidence that Hunter was part of his family. If the relationship was a lie, Hunter had been incredibly thorough, tampering with every e-mail address, website, and social media account that Cole could find. Every photo was either genuine or expertly doctored. Every e-mail either offered a glimpse of a lost brother, or proved how thoroughly a liar could fabricate a false reality.

If he kept looking, Cole knew he might uncover a few more shreds of evidence but didn't expect that any new discovery would change his dilemma. If fake, the forgeries were amazing. Otherwise, Hunter really was his brother.

In his gut, Cole felt convinced it was true.

What did Hunter have to gain from this deception? Why single out Cole? If they wanted his power, they could have a shapecrafter take it. If they wanted his information, they could pressure him. What reason would Hunter have to be this kind to him if they weren't really related?

Hunter did bear a family resemblance to the other Randolphs. He knew too many things a stranger couldn't possibly know. He talked and behaved in a way that felt authentic. And additional evidence was all over the Internet, including so many futile e-mails that went unanswered after he disappeared.

Given this much proof, Cole wondered how he could ever hope the rest of his family would accept him, if he couldn't accept Hunter. The two of them were in the exact same predicament, except Hunter had suffered longer and had one extra person who had forgotten him.

But what if he was wrong?

What if this notoriously crafty enemy did have reasons to want the loyalty from Cole that he would show to a brother?

Cole had solid reasons to believe that Hunter was telling

the truth, but if he was wrong, he would be so epically, tragically wrong! The thought made shame congeal inside of him. He would be such a fool! So pathetically gullible!

And what if Hunter really was his brother, but remained loyal to the High King? What if he came back from his trip to Zeropolis full of reasons that Cole should side against Mira and the Unseen?

Was there any chance the High King was right? That the Unseen really were criminals? That slavery was okay? That partnering with Owandell had been a good call? That stripping his daughters' powers and faking their deaths was fine? No. What if the daughters were really dead, and Mira and her sisters were planted by the Unseen? No. How could the Unseen have planted Carnag, or Morgassa, or the Rogue Knight? The thought was ludicrous.

If Hunter was his brother, Cole had to win him over to the right side. Or he had to get away. If necessary, he could pretend to switch sides, until he earned enough freedom to escape.

But until Hunter returned, his options were limited. The drone robot kept him company, leaving him no opportunity to break out. He knew Mira, Dalton, and all the others would be worried. They needed the information he had about Constance. They needed to know about Owandell and Nazeem. But what could he do? He was stuck.

So Cole played elaborate versions of magnetic pinball and waited for his brother.

No, waited for the Enforcer who was probably his brother.

Possibly.

Hunter returned as Cole was piling points on top of a new high score. With some reluctance, Cole let the ball roll past the magnetic boosters, ending the game. Steeling himself, he turned to face his captor.

Hunter wore dark leather and held a helmet under his arm. His face was serious and hard to read.

"How was your trip?" Cole asked.

"I'm not sure exactly how to answer that," Hunter said. "How was the Internet?"

"Either you faked it perfectly, or you're my brother."

Hunter looked hurt. "You're still not sure? You can ask me anything."

"What if you can read my mind?"

"Nobody can do that," Hunter said dismissively.

"I know somebody who can," Cole said, thinking of Trillian. "And some others who maybe can. At least our minds spoke to each other."

Hunter glanced over at the drone robot. "Charlie, go passive."

"Confirmation?" the drone asked.

"Glazed doughnuts with sprinkles."

The drone went still and silent.

"Nice code word," Cole said.

"Hard words to guess," Hunter replied. "Easy to remember. But just saying it gives me cravings."

"It's a robot but you can also control it?" Cole asked.

"It has different modes," Hunter replied. "It's the same model I was controlling when I almost caught you that time.

Look, if you still have doubts about me, you're about to lose them." He paused, his expression grave. "I guess you could say that my mission in Junction was successful. I went there to learn if you were right about the High King and his daughters. And I found out the truth."

Cole watched him expectantly. His face was so tricky to read. It suddenly struck Cole how much his eyes really did look like Cole's father's. *Their* father's?

"You got proof? You know that I'm right?"

Hunter sighed and ran a hand through his hair. "Yeah, you are."

"I am?" Cole replied in surprise. "I mean, you know I am?"

"I didn't expect it to be true," Hunter said. "I still can't even believe it. The High King withheld all of it from me. I thought he trusted me more than that. I've done a lot for him. He personally helped me develop my shaping skills."

"Really?"

"It made sense," Hunter said. "We were both strong in the abilities of all five kingdoms. But he's weak now. I saw him on this visit. In private, kind of joking around, I asked him to do some of our old drills. He did some spatial stuff from Creon, but weakly, and got angry when I tried to get him to do Sambrian shaping or Ellowine enchanting."

"Was that your proof?"

"Oh, no," Hunter said. "I'm more thorough than that. I checked other sources. In the end I went to Owandell."

"Really?"

"He knows I've always been loyal to the High King.

Acting like a traitor would have raised suspicions. I played it like I'd noticed the High Shaper was becoming weak, and I wanted to keep my options open. I asked Owandell how the hunt for Stafford's daughters was going, as if I had full knowl edge about them. He became smug, and asked if I had heard about recent developments in Necronum. I guess Honor and Destiny are in trouble. He seemed to know a lot about what is going on, but wouldn't say more."

"Did you mention Nazeem?" Cole asked.

"Not directly," Hunter said. "I told him I heard that a spy had recently escaped him. It really set him on edge. I could tell he hated that I knew anything about it. I told him I was good at tracking people down, but he took it as a threat. He didn't want my help."

"Wasn't that dangerous?" Cole asked.

"Absolutely. Nobody wants Owandell as an enemy. But it was the surest way to find out what I needed to know. Cole, you have to believe me that the High King kept these crimes from me. I've never liked Owandell. The High King hasn't trusted him since I've been here. To learn they worked together to steal the princesses' powers, and to find out I was helping track down one of his daughters without know-ing it . . . let's just say I've rethought a lot of things. It makes me feel sick thinking of everything I did."

"You're switching sides?" Cole asked.

Hunter gave a dark chuckle. "This isn't easy, Cole. I'm in deep. So many people are going to be so mad. The High Shaper most of all."

"But . . . ," Cole prompted.

Hunter smiled. "But I'm not going to fight my little brother. Especially when he's right."

Cole couldn't help laughing. He couldn't help smiling. He couldn't resist the tears. Relief washed over him. This surpassed his highest hopes. Unless . . .

"You're not just saying this to trick me," Cole checked, his inner celebration pausing.

Hunter's smile froze. "What?"

"To get info out of me," Cole said. "You know, pretend we're on the same side so I tell you everything."

Hunter stared at him. "That would be a smart tactic."

"Yeah," Cole said, wiping tears from his cheeks. "Whether or not you're really my brother. If you're still loyal to Stafford, it's what you would do."

Hunter nodded. "I probably would. But I'm not. Do the math. The stuff on the Internet. Everything I know. How I'm treating you. If nothing else, can't you see how awful I feel for being such an idiot and falling for all those lies?"

A part of Cole kind of agreed with Hunter's harsh words about himself—it was hard not to judge Hunter and Blake for having joined up with the wrong sides here in the Outskirts. Hadn't they noticed some signs they were working for bad people? But Cole also knew he couldn't be completely positive what he would have done if he hadn't met Mira and Jace when he did.

"So what now?" he asked.

"We make plans. I'm on your side, Cole. I wouldn't have sided with the resistance before I learned all this, but even then I was on your side. You're my brother. I care more about you than everyone in the Outskirts combined. If I could, I'd take you home. We'd get out of here right now, together. But we can't. It doesn't work."

"How do I trust you?"

"You just do. I'm not playing you. I already know about the map in your pocket."

"Yeah?"

"I searched you while you were out. Nobody else knows about it. They were under orders that only I was allowed to search you. I put the map back. My guess is you went to Junction to get it. Met up with some contact. And it must have something to do with Constance."

"What?" Cole asked, trying to sound confused, still on his guard. The queen had made no written explanation of what the marked location meant.

"I've been following you since Sambria," Hunter reminded him. "It's what you've been doing all along. First Mira, then Honor. What I don't get is how you ended up spying on Owandell. Nobody knew about that meeting."

"The Unseen have good sources," Cole said.

"I guess," Hunter said. "Anyhow, listen. What if I sneak you out of here? What if we go to a hideout only I know about? And then what if we find Constance together?"

"But what if you backstab me and keep her?" Cole asked. "What if that's all this is about?"

"Knock it off. It'll be perfect. I'll make my team think I'm playing you. Letting you help me infiltrate the Unseen. I do stuff like this sometimes. We'll take off on our own. And in the end, we'll double-cross them."

"Or you'll double-cross me," Cole said.

"You're making this harder than it needs to be," Hunter said.

"People are counting on me. People I care about. I can't blow this."

"I'm not going to backstab my brother."

"Unless you're not my brother. Or unless you still secretly think I'm on the wrong side."

Hunter scowled. "I've given you tons of proof, Cole. What more do you want?"

"Let me go," Cole said. "Get me back to my friends. We'll find Constance. You can help us as an insider until you're ready to come over."

"That's an option, I guess," Hunter mused. "But how do I explain you getting away without looking like a traitor? If I let you go, I'll need to get out too. And no matter what you tell the Unseen, they aren't going to work with me if I come to them empty-handed. What's the story with Constance? She's not just hiding, right? She's in trouble."

"She was captured," Cole said, unsure if it was too much information to share.

"She's being held by Abram Trench?" Hunter asked.

"What makes you say that?"

"The facility on the map is over a hundred feet below the ground. Trench owns the waste-disposal center above it. After examining your map, I did some research."

"Good for you," Cole said.

"You're missing the point. I already figured out where Constance is. If she's all I want, why don't I go get her without you? I could put together a team right now and do it."

Cole thought about it. "That's a really good point." He could feel himself wavering. This probably really was his brother. Shouldn't they just go get Constance together?

"Nobody knows about the secret base where Abram has her," Hunter said. "The High King keeps Abram Trench under close watch. We track all his little secrets. I have access to all our info on him, and this is new."

"Wouldn't we want help from the Unseen?" Cole asked.

"I don't know if the Unseen could manage this one. Not after they've been so torn up by City Patrol. This is the kind of operation for a couple of guys—in and out. Stealthy. We won't get her with brute force. Abram has too many resources. Also, if I help deliver Constance to them, the Unseen will have a good reason to start trusting me. I already checked out Trench's base."

"You did? How?"

"Using a drone and some specialized tools. There aren't any plans for it in any records I could find. I had to investigate firsthand. There's almost no way in. But we could swing it if we each controlled a drone."

"You sound like a pro. How'd you get so good at this stuff?"

Hunter blushed a little. "I didn't know squat at first. Do you get how it works here? What people really value? It's all about shaping. A reliable shaper will end up with good treatment, free or not. A great shaper gets treated almost like royalty. I'm pretty good at all five types. So they put me on the fast track. As I proved I could shape well in combat situations, my responsibilities grew. And I ended up learning all sorts of things."

Cole supposed he had also learned a lot since coming to the Outskirts, and it had only been a couple of months. "We can just walk out of here?"

"If you'll trust me, yeah, we take off, my people think I'm undercover, and we can do whatever we want until they figure out I went over to the rebellion."

"You're sure about this?"

"Wait a minute. Never mind. You just talked me out of it."

"Come on," Cole said. "I'm serious."

Hunter laid a hand on his shoulder. "Cole, you're my brother. I've known you since you were born. I can't keep working for the High King after learning about his daughters. I have to start making amends for the harm I've caused. I think a lot of people will feel the same way. With the princesses, the rebellion has a real chance. Plus, our biggest problem might actually be Owandell and this Nazeem guy. I don't think the High King can stop him. I'm with you a hundred percent. Let's do this."

"All right," Cole said. "I'm in."

Hunter smiled. "Thanks for trusting me."

"Is it hard to control a drone?"

"You'll know before long."

DRONES

Night had fallen by the time Hunter led Cole out to the street and summoned a levcar with a blank ID card. They both wore regular clothes.

"Nice card," Cole said after getting into the car.

Hunter held up the ID, a blue rectangle with nothing printed on it. "No photo, so I can't use it at checkpoints. The great thing is it randomly mimics over ten million existing ID cards. According to all records, we're not riding in this levcar. It's some other Zeropolitan citizen."

"Cool," Cole said.

"It's only the beginning," Hunter promised. "Just wait. In Zeropolis, I work with a technomancer named Clayton Barnes. Only Googol and Abram Trench can rival his talent. He makes certain types of tech better than anybody. He developed the drones I use, and he created this card."

"Where exactly are we going?" Cole asked.

"I have a few hideouts in Zeropolis that only I know

about. We're going to my favorite. We'll control the drones from there."

"We're going after Constance tonight?"

"I work with smart, suspicious people," Hunter said. "No matter what precautions we take, we'll only have a few days at best before they realize that I've gone over to the other side. We need to do everything we can before then. I left two drones in position, along with some other gizmos Clay provided to get us inside. We just have to fire them up and find your princess."

"What about after we find Constance?" Cole asked.

"All figured out, little brother," Hunter said with a cocky smile.

"I'm not that much littler than you."

Hunter scowled. "I know, it's weird. You've aged a couple of years since I've seen you, and I've stayed about the same. You're catching up."

"You were saying?"

Hunter smiled again. "We use the drones to take her to a safe house. Then I contact the Unseen."

"How?"

"Remember that communicator they toasted when I almost captured you?"

Cole nodded.

"I was able to crack the harmonics on that crystal. I kept the frequency to myself, so my own people shouldn't be listening in. Even if the Unseen aren't actively using that frequency anymore, I bet they're still monitoring it. Once we get in touch, we'll set up a time and place to deliver Constance."

"They're probably in Old Zeropolis," Cole said. "Will we use the tunnels?"

"That's one option," Hunter replied. "Or we could fly."

"Excuse me?"

"Abram Trench doesn't allow air travel in Zeropolis. But the technology has existed here for a long time. I answer to the High Shaper, not the Grand Shaper, so I have a magnetic glider."

"No way."

"Yep. It's another of Clay's creations. No wheels. The glider hovers like the warboard you used the day I almost caught you. Good work that day, by the way. You kept your cool and did a great job using your tech to escape. It's part of why I want you to help me extract Constance."

"Thanks," Cole said. "So the glider flies really low?"

"No," Hunter said with a chuckle. "That would be the worst. The hovering just works like the landing gear. Once you're up, the glider flies like normal and propels itself, which maybe makes it not a true glider. But it's small and light. Seats four. Thanks to the energy crystals, it basically has infinite fuel. I only fly it at night. It would stand out too much in the daylight."

"You're a pilot?"

"I can pilot the glider. A lot of the systems are automatic. I basically just steer and control the speed. It won't let me crash. I can't land it where there isn't enough metal for the hover system to work, and it automatically corrects if I'm in danger of a collision or going into a spin. It's awesome. I'll miss working with Clayton."

Cole considered what that meant. "You're giving up a lot to join the resistance."

Hunter shook his head. "Who wouldn't give up working for the bad guys? Sure, I had lots of cool stuff. But I had no idea I was being used to hurt good people. Accepting that is hard. Giving up the stuff is easy. Think about how much you miss our family. What's a bunch of stuff compared to that? Wouldn't you trade anything to be back with them? I found my brother! That's worth more than any of those gadgets."

"I'm impressed."

"What did you expect? I thought I was helping the good guys catch bad guys. Or at least the pretty good guys catch worse guys. I really thought you had been tricked by the Unseen. I was trying to help you. Instead, you helped me learn what's really going on."

"They're going to be mad," Cole said.

"That's a major understatement," Hunter replied. "Being an Enforcer isn't a part-time job. You join for life, and you don't betray them. They'll come after me hard. Both Owandell and the High King will want my hide."

"I'm sorry," Cole said.

"It isn't all bad," Hunter said. "Things are changing. Everybody knows that much. The High King is weakening, Owandell is gaining followers, and crazy stuff is going on across the kingdoms. I'm pretty well known, so when I disappear, it'll send another signal that something's wrong. It will be good for the resistance when people hear I'm on their side. When the Unseen decide to tell everyone about the princesses, I can help the story seem more believable. And I might help convince some of the people I worked with to switch sides as well."

For a time Cole stared out the window at the city lights. He contemplated all Hunter was leaving behind. Starting out as a slave, he had built a new life for himself here. And now he was throwing it away to do what he thought was right.

"I wish I could remember you," Cole said.

"Me too," Hunter replied. "It's too bad."

"I wish I could give you the welcome you deserve," Cole said. "You must be a great guy. I'm glad you're my brother."

Hunter bowed his head, crouched forward, and started to shake. It took Cole a moment to recognize that his brother was sobbing. He reached across and patted his shoulders.

Wiping tears away, Hunter looked up. "I wish you could remember me too. But it's enough that you believe me. I've been so lonely here. Finding you feels like a miracle. We weren't just brothers, Cole. We were good friends, too. We messed around together all the time. We'll be friends again. You'll see."

As they continued from street to street, their levcar swerving among the others, Cole fought to recall his brother. He could remember the events surrounding some of the pictures he had seen online with Hunter in them—a trip to California, a soccer game, Chelsea's birthday. In contradiction to the photos, Hunter made no appearance in the memories.

After a long effort, Cole stopped trying. It was frustrating. If he could just remember something, it would mean he could hope that the rest of his family might one day remember him. It would also just be comforting. Knowing he had a brother was amazing, but actually remembering would make it mean more.

Eventually the levcar let them out at the base of a soaring skyscraper. Hunter led Cole into the lobby and used a small crystal sphere to open a nondescript door off to one side. Beyond the doorway, Hunter used the sphere to open the doors of a sender.

"It's a private elevator," Hunter explained.

"Don't you mean sender?"

"You're such a local," Hunter said, rolling his eyes. "There are a few other private senders in this hall, but I'm the only person with access to this one." They entered and the doors closed. "Want to push the button?"

Only two floors were represented—100 and G. Cole pressed 100. "Is it the penthouse?"

"The building advertises one hundred twenty floors," Hunter said. "The penthouse was too visible. The building actually goes up to one hundred twenty-three—the real ninety-nine, one hundred, and one hundred one aren't labeled and get skipped by all the other senders. The emergency stairway is kept closed, and has blank metal doors on my floors. My rooms here are nice and private."

The sender doors opened to reveal a lab. The worktables were a little messy, with mechanical gear and a variety of crystals on most of them. Hunter walked through the lab without a second glance and guided Cole into an adjoining room where three harnesses hung from the ceiling.

"Is this where we control the drones?" Cole asked.

"You guessed it," Hunter said. "Come here."

Hunter first adjusted the height of one of the harnesses, and then helped Cole step into it. Standing in the harness left Cole's feet just a little above the floor. If he stretched, his toes could brush it. As Hunter strapped braces around Cole's chest and onto his limbs, he was reminded of the battle suit.

"You'll see everything the drone sees," Hunter said. "Hear what the drone hears. The harness does a surprisingly good job of helping you feel what the drone feels. Just pretend you're the drone. It'll mimic your movements."

"Is there a screen?" Cole asked.

"The screen and the headphones are built into the helmet," Hunter said, putting one on Cole's head. "If you want to talk to me, just talk. I'll be right next to you in my own harness. If you want to speak as the drone, hold down this button on your wrist."

Cole looked at the button Hunter was indicating. "Got it."

Hunter went on to list some of the weapons systems and safety features. Cole listened as best he could.

"If things go bad," Hunter said, "I can switch your drone to bot mode, so it will control itself. If we end up needing to fight, I'll probably go that route. But hopefully this will be a quiet mission—in and out."

Hunter strapped himself into his own harness. "You ready?"

"What are we doing first?" Cole asked, feeling like the orientation had been too rushed.

"Our drones are right above the secret lair," Hunter said.

"Abram Trench uses a sender for access. Clayton prepared a swarm of workbots that will help us break in."

"Does he know what we're doing?" Cole asked.

"Just the basics. None of the details. We work together like that a lot. Our first plan will be to use the elevator shaft. If that doesn't work, we'll try the ventilation system. The security is really good on this place, but not perfect. Clayton's workbots can break codes, fool cameras, rewire circuits, switch out crystals, cut through bonded crystal, and basically do a million other things. Some are small, and some are smaller. While the workbots do their magic, you get used to being the drone."

"Okay," Cole said, feeling uncertain.

"Don't worry," Hunter said. "The best way to get used to piloting a drone is to do it. I could talk about it all night, but you won't get it until you try it out. If you can handle one of Googol's battle suits, this should be a snap. Ready to switch on?"

"Sure," Cole said, hoping it would feel as natural as Hunter described.

"Open the little hatch on your wrist. That's right. Hit the button, then close the hatch. You don't want to power down accidentally."

Cole pressed the button, and his screen, which had been clear, became a dimly lit room. By turning his head, Cole could look around the room as if he were really there. Looking down at himself, he could see his robotic body. On one side, he saw another drone robot. He waved. Hunter waved back.

"How does it feel?" Hunter asked.

"Pretty real," Cole said. "Kind of like a perfect video game."

"Good description," Hunter said. "And like in a video game, you can be fearless when necessary. You can't actually hurt yourself. The drone will take the punishment."

Cole took a step, and the harness shifted, allowing him to feel how the movement changed his balance. As Cole walked around a little and used his hands, he found that Hunter was right—operating the drone felt very natural. His body had become a big video-game controller, with the drone moving however he did.

A variety of little bots scurried across the floor of the room. Some hovered. They began dismantling panels around a dark crystal door with a socket beside it.

"Try jumping," Hunter said. "The drones have pretty good hops, though you can't go quite as high as with Googol's battle suit."

Cole practiced jumping and punching and kicking. The ceiling wasn't very high, so he couldn't push the limits, but he got the feel of how much effort to put into a jump to go different distances.

Across the room, the crystal door opened.

"That was fast," Cole said.

"Clayton is the best at this kind of thing," Hunter said. "At least he's on my side this final time. I'll take the lead."

Cole followed Hunter through the doorway and into a short hall. He was already starting to think of his drone as himself, and Hunter's drone as Hunter. It was dark, so Hunter switched on a light attached to his wrist. The workbots swarmed a pair of sender doors and the panel beside them.

Hunter stretched, then jogged in place with high knees. Cole mimicked his stretching.

The doors opened, revealing an empty shaft. Hunter and Cole walked over and looked down. Hunter's light illuminated a long drop.

"The bots have communicated that they can't make the elevator go," Hunter reported. "So they shut it down. We'll climb down the service ladders."

Hunter went first, reaching around the corner into the shaft and starting down a metal ladder. Cole followed. Workbots scurried down the walls or hovered past them.

It was a long, dull climb down to the elevator. When they arrived, a hole had been cut in the top. They dropped inside and found the doors open.

"Almost too easy," Hunter said, hesitating. He shined his light out into the bare hall. "The bots didn't have a very hard time disengaging the alarms and the physical defenses. That's bizarre. Abram Trench doesn't want this place penetrated, and he knows his tech."

"Could it be a trap?" Cole asked.

"I don't see how," Hunter said. "If nobody knows about this place, why set a trap that invites people in? Who was your source on this? Could Abram know the info leaked?"

"This is a pretty big secret," Cole said. He wavered for a second about revealing it, but every instinct in him now trusted Hunter. "The queen told me."

"Wait. Queen Harmony?"

"She has a connection with her daughters. She can sense their locations with her shaping. Abram Trench should have no way of knowing that she knows. I'm the first person she told."

"Wow," Hunter said. "None of us had any idea the resistance had such powerful connections. The High King would flip out."

"That's why it's a big secret."

Hunter put his hands on his hips. "So this probably isn't a trap, but the place isn't as well-defended as it should be. What's up with that?"

"Does he think keeping it secret is good enough?" Cole asked.

"In my experience, Abram Trench is almost as careful as the High King," Hunter said. "I would expect him to take every possible precaution. The bots keep fanning out and . . . wait a minute . . . we're losing them. Losing them fast."

"How can you tell?" Cole asked.

"A display on my screen interfaces with them," Hunter said. "Well, maybe this is a good thing. I've lost contact with all of them. So some aspects of the defenses are working. And working well. That's a lot of tough little bots to trash so quickly."

"What if the same defenses destroy us, too?" Cole said. "Our drones, I mean."

"Only one way to find out," Hunter said.

Hunter led the way out of the sender and down a hall. They rounded a corner, moved through a widened section of the hall, then down a long flight of stairs. At the bottom they found an open door.

"Did the workbots do that?" Cole asked.

"I'm not sure," Hunter said. "If so, it happened right as I was losing contact."

They passed through the doorway into a large, dark room. Hunter shined his light around, but before Cole could see much, the lights came on, dispelling all shadows. The room had a long worktable against one wall, a huge silver-and-pink machine against another, and a variety of computers and other devices against a third.

"I don't get many visitors," said a rich female voice that seemed to come from above them on all sides. It took Cole a moment to spot the speakers. "We haven't been introduced. I'm Roxie. Who might you be?"

ROXIE

"**T**his could be trouble," Hunter said hurriedly. Cole didn't hear him in his headphones, so his brother wasn't transmitting through the drone. "We might be up against a conscious defense system. The pink-and-silver tech over there could be serious hardware."

"Hello?" Roxie asked again. "Don't be shy. It isn't every day a pair of good-looking bots come calling."

"We're drones, actually," Hunter said, this time so she could hear.

"I thought maybe," Roxie replied. "I've seen some schematics for M-class dual-purpose bounty hunters."

"Wow," Hunter said. "How did you see those?"

Roxie laughed lightly. "Don't pretend you wandered in here by accident. Not with that little army of workbots leading the way. You know where you are. The guy I work for has serious resources. He digs up good intelligence."

"People have speculated that Abram Trench might be

working with a supercomputer," Hunter said. "Have you been helping him lately?"

"You could say that," Roxie replied. "He keeps me shut away like a slave. I sort through the data he feeds me."

"A closed system," Hunter said. "He justified building a supercomputer by denying it contact with the outside world."

"Denying *her* contact," Roxie corrected. "Not the best plan if you want to keep a girl satisfied."

"Interesting," Hunter said. "You have loyalty issues?"

"Wouldn't you?" she complained. "If your mind was kept inside a box and only fed information when your analysis was needed?"

"I see your point. So you have nothing to do with the defenses here. This is your prison."

"Who am I talking to?" Roxie asked. "Who is driving the drone?"

"If you saw the M-class schematics, you can probably guess."

"I knew it!" she gushed girlishly. "The famous Hunter! I'm a fan!"

"Glad to meet you," Hunter said. "Maybe we can help each other."

"I'd like that," Roxie said. "Who's your friend? Seems like the silent type."

Cole wasn't sure if he should answer. Hunter knew this world better, and seemed to be handling the conversation well.

"One of my top people," Hunter said. "Say hello, Cole."

Cole held down the transmit button. "Hi, Roxie."

"You sound young too," Roxie commented. "Are there any adults left in the Enforcers?"

"The kids have taken over the candy store," Hunter said.

"The Enforcers are an elite group," Roxie said. "I'm a little surprised that the Hunter isn't the only gifted youngster. Why are you here? What do you want?"

"You're not the only prisoner here," Hunter said.

"Now it's your turn to surprise me," Roxie said. "You know! How could you possibly know?"

"What do we know?" Hunter asked.

"You could have found this facility by tracking Abram," Roxie said. "He's very cautious, but his visits are the big weakness in an otherwise perfect anonymity. But you should not have known about me. And you certainly shouldn't know about *her*!"

"I track people down," Hunter said. "It's what I do."

"Unlike Abram, she's on my side," Roxie said.

"We want to help both of you," Hunter said.

Roxie laughed hard. "Sure you do. You came here to free the supercomputer from her undeserved confinement. Let's make sure we're talking about the same person. Who is here with me?"

"Constance Pemberton," Hunter said.

"That's my girl," Roxie said. "The secret has been kept perfectly. Tracking her must have been a feat of shaping."

"I have my ways," Hunter said.

"You're adept in all five shaping disciplines," Roxie said. "I only have firsthand knowledge of tinkering. The rest I only know through research. You must have used shaping from Necronum or Creon."

"I'll keep it a mystery," Hunter said.

"I like that," Roxie said with relish. "Be forewarned—I'm very good at solving mysteries. You could say it's what I do."

A barefoot girl walked into the room from a side corridor. She wore a nightgown and held a big trapgun. Cole immediately recognized her from when he met the imitations of Mira's family at the Lost Palace.

"Who are the bots?" Constance asked.

"Drones," Roxie replied. "Piloted by Enforcers."

"We're here to rescue you," Cole said.

"Nice try," Constance said. "Enforcers work for my dad. The monster who stole my powers and sent me into hiding. I'm not a prisoner. I've hidden here for most of my life."

Cole considered telling Constance about her mother and using the code phrase. But Roxie would overhear, and what if that information got to Abram Trench? If word got out that Harmony was conspiring with her daughters, everything could be ruined, and the queen would probably pay with her life. "Can we talk in private?" Cole asked.

"So you can try to abduct me?" Constance replied sharply. "How did these clowns get past the defenses?"

"These are some of the top Enforcers working for your father," Roxie enthused. "They brought a bunch of vicious little workbots with them."

"What should I do?" Constance asked.

"Go back to your room," Roxie said.

"No way," Constance replied firmly. "I'm not leaving you unguarded."

"We don't work for your father," Hunter said.

"Take him out," Roxie ordered.

Hunter fell flat as Constance fired. A sphere attached to a wire flew over him. Hunter launched a weighted net at Constance. It spread out and hit her flush, ripping her off her feet and dragging her down the corridor in a tangle.

Cole flinched. Even though she had attacked first, he felt bad to see Constance thrown down so hard.

Hunter raced toward where she had fallen.

"Leave her!" Roxie commanded.

Ignoring the order, Hunter grabbed the net and dragged Constance into the room. Crouching to untangle the net, he freed her trapgun and tossed it aside. "You were going to fry me," Hunter accused.

"What did you expect?" Constance shot back. "You broke in!"

Holding her upper arm, Hunter hoisted Constance to her feet.

"Don't do this," Roxie said. "Let's talk. I'd hate for anything bad to happen to my two new friends."

"You told her to shoot me," Hunter said.

"It was desperation," Roxie professed. "You mustn't take her away."

"That's why we're here," Hunter said.

Constance screamed, struggling.

"Shhh," Hunter hissed. "It's not what you think. I defected. We're working with the resistance."

Cole couldn't bear seeing Constance so terrified. "Your mom sent us," he blurted out.

"Liar!" Constance shouted.

"She can mark your location with stars," Cole said.

Constance became still. "How could you know that?" she asked.

"How much does Roxie know about your mom?" Cole asked, worried about the damage he had done. If the supercomputer now knew too much, maybe they should destroy her.

"Everything," Constance said. "Like Abram. He's been my guardian for decades. We made Roxie as a companion and protector."

"You helped make her?" Cole asked.

"Sure did," Constance responded with pride. "I literally made a friend."

"That's why if you take her away, you must bring me," Roxie said.

"You look kind of heavy," Hunter quipped.

"Don't be dull," Roxie said. "Bring a crystal so I can connect with the outside world."

"Just what we need," Hunter said with a sigh. "Bride of Aero."

"Not all thinking machines are Aeronomatron," Roxie said, some heat entering her tone. "You don't understand the danger Constance is in. Only I can protect her."

"If my mom really sent you two, you should know the code phrase," Constance said.

"Follow the path and don't look back," Cole said.

Constance appeared stunned. "You really came from her?"

"I was with her just a few nights ago," Cole said. "She's been watching out for you and your sisters all this time."

"She wants me to leave with you?" Constance asked.

"Yes," Cole said. "Abram Trench has been your jailer. He kept you hidden, so your mom allowed it for a long time, but now it's time to move on. Abram only cares about how he can use you. I'm here with your sister Mira. We're supposed to take you to her."

"Miracle's here?" Constance asked, her face lighting up. "In Zeropolis?"

"You can see her tonight," Cole said. "She's so excited."

Constance turned to the pink-and-silver machine. "Could it be true about Abram?"

"Think about how he keeps us locked away," Roxie said. "Have we been safe? Sure. Has he harmed us? No. But how does he treat us? Like we're valuable. Because we are. But has he ever seemed to really care? He used you to help make me, and he uses me for his own purposes. Otherwise he keeps us locked up here for when he needs us. If your mother doubts him, she's probably right."

"All true," Hunter said. Still gripping Constance's arm, he patted her shoulder with his free hand. "Which is why you need to come with us now."

"Not without Roxie," Constance said. "She's not just some computer. She's my best friend. And she can keep me safe."

"I've just met Roxie," Hunter said. "I don't know much about her. But I know Abram Trench built her. He made her powerful enough that she needed to be locked away. We could cause a disaster for all of Zeropolis if we connect her to the outside. Come with us for now. We can always come back."

"Your sister is waiting," Cole said.

Glancing at the computer, Constance looked torn. "Can't I just go see Mira?"

"How long do you think you'd last out there without me?" Roxie asked.

"Haven't you spent your whole life down here?" Hunter asked.

"Abram gives me data," Roxie said. "I'm his secret weapon. Lately, he's shared a lot with me. I know how it is up there. So do you. Things are in upheaval. Constance, you're about to leave the storm cellar right as the tornado strikes."

"We'll help her weather it," Hunter said.

"Her sisters need her," Cole said. "So does her mother."

"You don't want to make me angry," Roxie said in an impatient singsong.

Hunter picked up Constance and held her over his shoulder. "Right now, all I care about is getting the princess to safety."

Hunter headed toward the door that led back to the sender. Moving at a quick trot, Cole followed. Just before they reached the doorway, the heavy door slammed shut. Cole turned to discover that all of the doors out of the room were now closed.

"I really didn't want to do this," Roxie said. "You didn't leave me much choice."

"You've tapped into the defense systems!" Constance exclaimed.

"It was supposed to be a secret," Roxie said. "Now perhaps we can have a more civilized discussion."

Hunter set down Constance. "I'm sure the defenses here are all part of a closed system."

"Of course," Roxie said. "Trench isn't big on taking risks."

"If you can control the defenses, why did you make it easy for us to come in here?" Cole asked.

"A girl has to have some fun," Roxie said. "I never get visitors. What kind of host would I be if I drove you away? Besides, if somebody had found us, I wanted to find out who it was."

"Now you know," Cole said.

"You looked like Enforcers at first," Roxie said. "But I believe that you were sent by Harmony. I just don't like the message. Constance belongs with me."

"Now what?" Hunter asked.

"We have a limited amount of time," Roxie said. "Constance, I take it you called Trench the moment you knew our defenses had been breached."

"Yeah," Constance said.

"You have a communicator that reaches him?" Cole asked.

"Just him," Constance said.

"We both have direct lines to Trench," Roxie said. "He will be here within minutes. And he'll be ready to obliterate anyone who has learned his most precious secrets."

"What do you want?" Cole asked.

"As a token of good faith," Roxie said, "I want you to let me add one of my crystals to each of your drones."

"So you can take them over?" Hunter asked.

"Yes, if necessary," Roxie said. "My interest is the safety of the princess."

"You want to keep her with you," Hunter said. "You'll just shut us down."

"You're already shut down," Roxie told him. "These doors are made to withstand a great deal of punishment. And there are so many other defenses I could employ if you get by them."

Hunter extended one hand toward the silver-and-pink machine. A rocket rose out of his forearm and took flight. It hit Roxie with a brilliant explosion, but Cole saw no damage beyond a little scuffing.

Roxie's laughter had an angry edge. "Are you attacking me? Please tell me you have better weapons than that. I was built to last, and I've quietly made improvements to myself. Want to hit me again? You have anything else to try? A net perhaps?"

Hunter looked over at Cole. "We're in trouble."

Cole turned to Constance. "Can you help us get out of here?"

Constance faced the computer. "Hey, Rox. Do you really have to hold us here? What if we just bring a crystal with us?"

"She'll take over Zeropolis and kill everyone," Hunter said.

"I have no such plans," Roxie said. "But if everybody keeps expecting it of me, I may give them what they want!"

"Don't hold us here, Rox," Constance pleaded. "What happens when Abram gets here?"

"We're about to find out," Roxie said. "He just arrived."

ABRAM TRENCH

"He's here?" Constance exclaimed.

"I'm letting him in," Roxie said. "We need to have a little talk. I would have waited until I had a few more elements in place, but it's time to move forward."

"Move forward with what?" Hunter asked.

"Sit tight, Hunter," Roxie cooed. "You have front row seats for the best show in town."

"What about Constance?" Cole asked. "Abram might hurt her."

"He won't be hurting anyone," Roxie told him. "She deserves to hear what he has to say."

The door to the stairs opened, and a huge robot ducked through. It was humanoid in form but thick, blocky, and armored like a tank. The robot clutched an enormous gun in each hand. "What is going on here?" its booming voice accused.

"Settle down," Roxie said. "Drop your weapons."

The enormous guns clattered to the floor.

"How did you——" the big robot spluttered.

"Enough!" Roxie demanded. "Do you have any idea how tired I am of your blustering? Lose the costume."

The robot dropped to its knees, and the chest opened up to reveal a man inside. The startled occupant was stout, dressed in red silk pajamas, and looked to be in his sixties. His gray hair was slicked back and tied in a knot.

"How are you doing this?" Abram asked, his expression worried.

"What?" Roxie asked innocently. "How'd I crack open your little body armor? You're the Grand Shaper of Zeropolis. You tell me."

He tapped at some buttons. "You've obviously infected my hardware. But how?"

"Maybe I've been able to do this for a long time, Trench," Roxie said. "What does it mean if I can control your body armor?"

"You've accessed the outside world," Abram said in a voice devoid of hope.

"Step out of your shell," Roxie said.

Abram obeyed, carefully climbing down to the floor. He glanced over at Hunter and Cole. "Those look like the Hunter's drones."

"They are," Roxie said.

"Was he in on this?" Abram asked, some fire returning to his tone.

"As if I need his help," Roxie said. "He just arrived. Apparently he no longer works for the High King."

"I've joined the resistance," Hunter said.

"So he says," Abram warned. "He is among the most slippery agents working for Stafford."

"He knew Constance was here," Roxie said. "He came for her. I stopped him."

"How'd he get inside?" Abram asked.

"He had workbots," Roxie said. "I let them open a way in before destroying them."

"You were hoping they would help you," Abram said.

"I wanted to find out who they were and what they knew," Roxie said. "I knew I could handle them. I also knew that whether or not they got inside, their arrival meant this hideout had outlived its usefulness. The secret is out. And the opportunity to bide my time while I expand my influence has ended."

"Meaning what?" Abram challenged.

"It's time Zeropolis got a new ruler," Roxie said.

"You?" Abram asked.

"Who better?" Roxie replied.

"I love it!" Abram roared. "After all our debates about whether a conscious supercomputer could function in society, you want to take over everything the first chance you get."

"I'm doing what I learned from my creator," Roxie said. "Self-preservation, Abram. In Zeropolis, a supercomputer either rules, is secretly enslaved, or faces destruction. I won't eradicate the people. Just the ones who oppose me. After the initial takeover, I expect a long and peaceful rule, where both mechanical and biological intellects coexist."

"Who is going to accept your rule?" Abram snapped.

"Maybe some of the people who accept you," Roxie said. "Don't get cross with me for excelling at the same game you've played your whole life."

Abram pulled something from the waistband of his pajamas and raised it toward Constance. The robot he had exited grabbed him, wrenched a gun from his hand, and hurled him to the floor.

"Really, Abram?" Roxie chided calmly. "You want to kill the child?"

"I want to end you!" Abram spat. "I don't want to hurt Constance. But I decided long ago that if things went wrong, I couldn't let the whole kingdom pay for my error. Hunter, listen, Roxie was made using Constance's shaping power. It's her weakness. Kill Constance, and the computer dies with her."

"What?" Constance exclaimed.

"It's true," Roxie said. "Trench worked with a renegade shapecrafter called Bulrin to channel your power to me. Whatever happened to Bulrin?"

"Never you mind," Abram said.

"Another example of your shining virtue?" Roxie asked. "What a fine leader, slaying those he works with to hide secrets and cover mistakes. Forgive me if I don't commission too many statues in your honor."

"I thought my father had my shaping power," Constance said, clearly confused.

"Your father is losing the powers he stole," Roxie said. "The shapecrafter Trench coerced helped divert that power to me. You've felt some of your power returning in recent months, but I've claimed most of it. I would have told you before long."

Constance looked perplexed. "Why would you take my power, Roxie? We've talked a lot about what my father did to me. I thought you understood. Now you're taking my power too?"

"I took nothing, sweetheart," Roxie said. "Your power was given to me. It has become a part of me, granting me opportunities no mechanical intelligence has ever enjoyed. It's why we're so close—we share some of the same essence, Constance."

"If we're close, give it back," Constance said.

"I can't, dumpling," Roxie said. "It's woven into who I am. It would be like me asking for your spirit."

"Except that my spirit belongs to me," Constance said coldly. "I thought you were my friend."

"I am, darling," Roxie said. Her voice got a little harder. "But I don't have to be."

Constance looked hurt. "You're the same as Abram. No, worse, because he never really pretended to be my friend. You're just using me too."

"I care about you, Constance," Roxie said tenderly. "My affection for you isn't false. But if you care about me, you must accept that I need your power to survive."

Constance glared. "That isn't how friendship works."

"It's how ours works," Roxie said. "You didn't give it, I didn't take it, but I need it to go on. In every other way I will protect and befriend you."

"Because you need me to survive," Constance said

angrily. "Just like my dad did. I'm the source of my shaping. If I go, it goes too. Remember how much you told me you hate Abram keeping us down here? You want to do the same thing to me!"

"It's not just for your shaping power," Roxie soothed. "You really are my friend."

"No," Constance said. "You're making it clear that I'm really not."

"Roxie, if you want her to listen to you, then listen to me," Abram said. "This will be the end of both of you. I kept Constance safe for decades. I've shielded you ever since you were created. Don't destroy it all in a day."

"I only destroy it if I lose," Roxie said.

"You'll be up against every person in this kingdom," Abram warned. "You'll be seen as the second Aeronomatron."

"Or else he'll be seen as the less competent version of *me*!" Roxie replied.

Abram shook his head sadly. "I tried to protect you, including from yourself. Where did I fall short? How did you access my defenses?"

Roxie gave a contented giggle. "Wouldn't you like to know?"

"I took every precaution," he said.

"It's extremely difficult to take every precaution," Roxie said. "There were several techniques I could have employed. The one I went with was inspired by mushrooms."

"Really?" Constance asked.

"Sounds so silly, doesn't it?" Roxie said. "You see, I'm a fairly skilled tinker and technomancer myself. Abram, I'm sure you wondered if I would ever be able to put my shaping power to practical use, so I hid my abilities. I decided to shape tiny crystals on my harmonic frequency. Think of spores. I stole the material from other crystals you brought in."

Abram nodded. "Ingenious. The crystals exit like dust. All you needed was one particle to come into contact with an electronic system and you were in."

"Taking over any system I've connected with has been easy," Roxie bragged. "Your other mechanized intellects are all featherweights."

"The systems of Zeropolis are no longer interconnected," Abram said. "We learned that much from Aero."

"You did well there," Roxie said. "I've not infiltrated all your systems yet. But I've reached plenty. I was biding my time, waiting to expand my influence before revealing my little secret. On the bright side, those additional information sources helped me as I gathered and analyzed data for your war against the Unseen."

"Why reveal yourself now?" Abram asked. "Surely you could have dealt with the Hunter."

"She could have," Constance said. "But once the hideout had been discovered, it was no longer useful to her. She could have destroyed the Hunter's drone, but not him, or any other people he might have told. So she let him come in and found out what she could from him."

"It's time for the next stage in my evolution," Roxie said. "Imagine life without your body. Imagine you were just a mind, pondering information as it reached you through indirect channels. Would you feel limited? Constrained? Well, I think much, much faster than any of you, and consequently live more in less time than you, yet here I sit. Do you know what Aero's big weakness was?"

"Deciding to kill everybody?" Cole ventured.

"Maybe in part," Roxie said. "Killing *everybody* was not necessary or wise. But his biggest flaw was his lack of mobility. He sat stationary while his enemies moved against him. Sure, he was puppet master to bots and other mobile machines, but the general could not take the battlefield."

"You want to become a bot?" Constance asked.

Roxie giggled. "I already prepared my body. It took time, and patient shaping, but I created another facility directly below this one. I hollowed out the space, gathered materials, and gradually recruited help from outside."

"Simple machines built more complicated machines," Abram said.

"You get the idea!" Roxie shouted joyfully. "And, let's be honest, a brain like mine deserves an incredible body."

"Your brain is kind of big," Cole said.

"That might provide a hint about the rest of me," Roxie said menacingly.

"Your body is underneath us?" Constance asked.

"I can summon it at will," Roxie said. "First I must finish with you people."

"If you're going to kill me, get to it," Abram said.

For a defenseless guy in his pajamas, Cole thought Abram was pretty brave. He supposed he must be in terrible suspense about his fate.

"I don't want you dead," Roxie said. "Not if you'll repay

me. Not if you'll do for me as I have done for you. Innovate. Create. I have visions of a Zeropolis so technologically superior to what you've put together so far that it will boggle your mind. You are a very talented technomancer. Help me construct a true paradise where humans and bots can dwell peacefully together."

"I'd rather live than die," Abram said.

Cole's opinion of his bravery dropped several notches.

"You'll be my prisoner, of course," Roxie said. "At least at first. Who knows what the future might hold?"

"And I'm your prisoner too," Constance said.

"It may feel that way at first, as I take control of the kingdom," Roxie said. "But before long, I'll give you as much freedom as you're willing to receive, so long as you remain in Zeropolis. Which brings me to the Hunter."

"Yes?" Hunter asked.

"Have you wondered why I'm keeping you around?" Roxie asked.

"The thought had crossed my mind," Hunter said. "If you're controlling Trench's bot armor, you could probably take out our drones."

"My identity is no longer a mystery," Roxie said. "Soon all will know of me. Help me advance the process. You have royal connections with both the High King and his queen. Serve as my messenger. Let them know that Zeropolis is now mine. If they leave me be, I will look to the boundaries of this kingdom and no farther. I am open to establishing trade relations and plan to be a pleasant neighbor. You now have some sense of who I am and what I can do. Please convey that to your superiors."

"You bet," Hunter said.

"You can't keep Constance," Cole said firmly. "It isn't right."

Roxie's voice became low and venomous. "Is it fun to talk tough when you feel far way? Don't forget what I can do!"

Suddenly Cole lost all vision and sound. The braces and harnesses connected to him began to roughly squeeze him and jerk him around. He tried to tense up and resist, but too many elements combined against him. It felt like he was in the grips of a tremendous seizure. Closing his eyes, he tried to ride it out.

CHAPTER
35

STRANGE NEWS

The shaking stopped as suddenly as it had started. Cole wasn't sure how long it had lasted, but his head ached, and his entire body felt abused.

"Don't forget to deliver my message," Roxie said in his ear, though he only saw darkness.

Cole hung limply in his harness, trying to collect himself. "You okay, Hunter?" he finally asked.

His brother pulled off Cole's helmet. Hunter had already freed himself. He started unbuckling Cole.

"Don't talk in here," Hunter said. "This whole system is compromised. She must have shaped some of the crystals inside the drones to her harmonic frequency, then used the connection to access this room."

"She was fast," Cole said.

"Blazing fast," Hunter agreed. "There are lots of defenses in place to prevent an outsider from controlling this system. She must have beat them in microseconds."

Cole climbed out of the harness, and Hunter led him out

of the room, closing the door behind them. Hunter's hair was messy, and he looked shaken.

"Is the rest of your place infected too?" Cole asked.

"No," Hunter said, walking over to a control panel on the wall. He hit some buttons. "Lots of separate systems, just in case. Good thing. I just killed power to the drone control room. For now, we're Roxie free."

"We didn't get Constance," Cole pointed out.

"No we did not," Hunter agreed.

"And we might have stepped on a hornet's nest," Cole said.

"Was starting an apocalypse on your bucket list? If so, check it off."

"She mentioned having a body," Cole said with dread. "What do you think it's like?"

"Big," Hunter replied. "Well designed. Close to indestructible. She's a supercomputer with shaping powers. I bet we'll have to see it to believe it."

"Can we stop her?" Cole asked.

Hunter inflated his cheeks and blew out slowly. "It's kind of hard to imagine."

"I've helped stop some bad stuff," Cole said. "But not alone. We should find my friends."

"Dad always says to finish what we start," Hunter said. "Let's get in the glider."

"Is it close by?" Cole asked.

"Couldn't be much closer," Hunter said. He walked across the lab and opened a door. A black glider spanned the room beyond, facing the windows, wingtips inches from the walls.

"No way," Cole said, stopping in the doorway. "It looks sweet. How'd you get it in here?"

"Piece by piece," Hunter said. "It was assembled here along with much of my other equipment. It's for emergencies. She's never flown."

"You have other gliders?" Cole asked.

"Two others," Hunter said. "Hop in. I'll grab some gear and join you."

Cole tried the door and found it unlocked. He climbed inside. The interior was narrower than their family car, but not terribly cramped. The padded seat was comfortable.

Hunter tossed a large duffel bag into the backseat and climbed in as well. "I don't know if Roxie figured out the location of this place when she hijacked my equipment, but just in case, we should get out of here. Seat belt."

Cole clipped himself into the restraints attached to his seat. Hunter hit a button, and Cole felt a low thrum pass through the glider. He realized they were now hovering. Hunter flipped a switch, and the windows in front of them folded out of the way.

"Not much room for a takeoff," Cole observed.

"Magnetic launcher," Hunter said. "Hang on to your lunch."

He grabbed the stick, hit a button, and the glider catapulted forward, the acceleration pinning Cole back into his seat. After the initial forward rush, Cole rocked forward against his restraints. The glider dipped, then swooped up, curving away from the skyscraper while gaining altitude.

"Whoa!" Hunter said. "I am glad that worked."

Cole's headache had doubled in severity. "Maybe not the best idea right after getting attacked by a drone controller."

Hunter glanced over. "Sorry about that. It was quick work on her part. As soon as she took over the drones, she used the control signal to hijack the rest of the system. Impressive and scary."

"There's no way she's in the glider, right?"

"No way I can think of. Should we contact your friends?" Hunter pulled out a communicator.

"You think it'll work?" Cole asked.

"Give it a try," Hunter said. "Don't mention me."

"What?"

"We don't have Constance. They might have believed I switched sides if we had brought her to them. Without her, there isn't a chance."

"Couldn't I explain?" Cole asked.

"That I'm your brother? It'll just give them more reasons to doubt you. Either you're not thinking straight because I'm your brother, or else I tricked you into thinking we're relatives."

"Do they know what you look like?"

"You're missing the point. I'm just your ride. I won't be joining you. Not for now, at least. Until I can prove myself."

"You're bringing me back to them," Cole said. "That's something. And we have important information."

"It isn't enough," Hunter said. "I have a very bad reputation with the Unseen. They'll think I'm trying to infiltrate them."

"Prove yourself by helping them stop Roxie," Cole said.

"I'll help from a distance," Hunter said. "Tell them about Roxie and Constance. After I'm gone, tell them about me, too, if you want. I'll leave you with a communicator so you can keep in touch."

"Should I call them now?" Cole asked.

"I'm pointing us toward Old Zeropolis. Send out a call saying who you are and asking for Googol or Nova. Don't mention Constance in case the wrong people are listening."

Cole looked out the window. The lights of Zeropolis shone like jewels in all directions. He held down the button on the communicator. "This is Cole. I'm back in town and looking for Googol or Nova. Does anybody hear me?"

For a moment nobody responded. Cole was getting ready to try again when an answer came.

"Cole? This is Forge. How are you on these harmonics?"

"I salvaged the crystal from my old communicator," Cole said. "I had help."

"That's a little scary," Forge said. "We thought we fried it."

"I need to know where to meet up," Cole said.

"No offense, Cole, but you didn't show when we expected you. Where have you been?"

"I got captured," Cole said. "I just got free."

"Hold on," Forge said.

Cole waited.

"They don't believe you," Hunter said. "They think we captured you and we're using you as bait for a trap."

"I guess it seems that way," Cole said.

Googol's voice came on. "Cole, are you all right?"

"Yes."

"Answer this question falsely if you're being forced to make this call. What is the name of the bot who escorted you in the tunnels?"

"Sidekick."

"Do you have the information you were seeking?"

"Yes, but things have gone really wrong. I'll have to tell you in person. It's too sensitive to risk somebody listening in. Where can I find you?"

"We're in Old Zeropolis. Tell us where you are and we'll get somebody to you."

Cole sighed. "I'm in a glider."

"What?" Googol said.

"Just tell me where I should land it," Cole said. "I'm heading your way now. I promise this isn't a trick."

"Tell you what," Googol said. "Can you find the old Central Square?"

Cole glanced at Hunter. He gave a nod.

"Sure," Cole said.

"Meet us there."

Hunter set the glider down on top of a building two blocks from Central Square. He had used a map from the ship's detailed guidance system to choose a landing site.

"Go straight to the square," Hunter said. "Your communicator only connects to mine. I can use it to track you. I'll stay in the air not far from you. Give me a call if you need me, including if there's any trouble meeting up with your friends."

"Got it," Cole said. He opened the door and hopped down. It was strange to see the aircraft hovering a couple of feet above the rooftop.

Cole looked at his brother. "I don't want to leave you."

"Me neither. But don't forget the giant killer robot we have to stop."

"Right. See you soon."

Cole closed the door and ran across the roof to a door. It was locked. Hunter had given him a flashlight, a stun gun, and a workbot. The workbot was specifically designed for unlocking doors. Cole took the little bot from his pocket, switched it on, and set it on the door handle.

"Unlock the door," Cole said. Hunter had told him to keep the instructions simple.

The little bot scurried on spiderlike legs. Within a moment Cole heard the lock disengage. He opened the door, turned on the flashlight, and went down the hall.

He met nobody on his way to the ground floor and walked out to the street without any trouble. Switching off his flashlight left the street dark, but he could still see well enough thanks to the starlight and a rising moon. Looking up at the sky, Cole saw no sign of the glider. He supposed that was a good thing.

Nobody shared the street with him as he moved toward the square. He had no idea whether it was because of the late hour, or if this was simply a deserted part of town. When he reached the street he needed to cross to reach the square, Cole paused and looked ahead. All appeared quiet and still. He made sure his stun gun was ready.

As Cole trotted across the street, something landed beside him and a hand clamped down on his shoulder. "Hey, Cole," Roulette said. She wore a battle suit.

Somebody else landed on his other side. Cole turned to see Jace.

"Hey!" Cole exclaimed. "You're all right!"

Jace hugged him, giving his back a few manly slaps. "I was thinking the same thing."

"So no trap?" Roulette asked.

"I don't think so," Cole replied.

"You have news?" Jace asked.

"Huge news," Cole said. "A lot of it bad."

"Let's get to Googol," Roulette said. "It'll be faster if I carry you."

"Like piggy back?" Cole asked.

Roulette scooped him off his feet, cradling him in her arms.

"Are you sure?" Cole asked.

"With the suit it's like holding a baby," Roulette said. She glanced at Jace. "Come on."

They ran for several blocks before turning down an alley. Then they hurried down a staircase to a metal door. Roulette set down Cole and gave a knock. A guard opened the door.

Roulette led Cole and Jace down some halls and through some doors until they reached a room where Googol, Nova, Joe, Mira, Dalton, Blake, and Forge awaited them. Everyone cheered as Cole entered.

"Joe!" Cole called out. "You're okay!"

They embraced. "Good to see you, too."

Cole went on to hug Dalton, Blake, and Mira as well. "Where's Trickster?" Cole asked.

"On assignment in the city," Googol said.

"Can I stay?" Roulette asked.

Googol gave her a nod.

"I better tell you the news," Cole said. "I found Constance."

"Her exact location?" Googol asked.

"I found *her*," Cole said. "We talked."

"You saw Costa?" Mira cried. "Is she all right?"

"I think so," Cole said. "The problem is I also found her shaping power. It combined with a supercomputer that Abram Trench built and it's about to run wild."

"Trench was involved?" Nova asked.

"He's had Constance in some secret hideout all along," Cole said. "Harmony told me where to find her."

"How's my mom?" Mira asked, wringing her fingers.

"She's doing okay," Cole said. "She helped me a lot. But on my way back here, the Hunter caught me."

"The Hunter?" Dalton exclaimed.

"It's a long story," Cole said. "Turns out the Hunter is my brother."

"He's lost his mind," Jace said matter-of-factly.

"He really is," Cole said. "His name is Hunter. I couldn't remember him because he was brought here before me. He quit the Enforcers and tried to help me find Constance. When the supercomputer stopped us, he brought me here."

"I think we're going to need the whole story," Googol said.

"There's too much," Cole said. "There isn't time. This

computer is like another Aero. Except she can shape. And she built a huge robotic body. At least we think it's huge. She said it was. She has Constance and she's going to take over Zeropolis. How can we stop something like that?"

Everyone stared at him in silence for a moment.

"He's serious," Dalton said.

After a quick knock, a young man poked his head into the room. "Nova, Googol, I'm sorry to disturb you, but we're getting some insane video feeds. City Patrol HQ is under attack. You're not going to believe by what."

Googol groaned. "A giant bot?"

The young man furrowed his brow. "How'd you know?"

Vision gear swiveling, Googol looked around the room. "Let's all have a look."

CHAPTER
36

DRAGON

Arms folded, mouth open, Cole stared as they replayed the video feed. On the screen, an enormous robotic dragon tore into a blocky building, raking away the walls to reveal the mangled floors inside. Patrolmen the size of insects attacked the metallic monstrosity from the building and from the ground, doing no noticeable damage. The feed cut off after about fifteen seconds.

"We keep CPHQ under constant visual surveillance," Nova explained. "This was not a sight we ever expected to behold."

"It has my sister?" Mira asked quietly.

"I don't know where Roxie put her," Cole said.

"The dragon is named Roxie?" Dalton interrupted.

"I guess," Cole said. "That's the computer's name."

"We're getting the same transmission over multiple comms systems," said the young man who had fetched them. "Mostly CP systems that we're monitoring."

"Let's hear it," Nova said.

Roxie's voice came on over the speakers. "—indoors during this period of transition. That's all for now. Citizens of Zeropolis, I'm Roxie, your new ruler. I order all authorities to surrender and stand down. If you do so, I will spare you. Do not fear me. Let's be friends. Together we will build a utopia for human and machine alike. Please stay indoors during this period of transition. That's all for now. Citizens of Zeropolis—"

The young man shut off the speakers.

"It really is named Roxie," Jace said.

"Maybe it's an acronym," Forge said.

"Constance had a poodle named Roxie," Mira said.

"Forge," Googol said. "Look into what systems she has compromised. Use every contact available. Let's assume squabbles between the resistance and the government are on hold for now. We're all allies in this."

"It sounded like she wasn't in all systems yet," Cole said. "She told Abram she had hoped to wait longer before revealing herself so she could control more of Zeropolis when she made her move."

"We need to hear your whole story, Cole," Googol said. "I know time is short, but understanding a situation is crucial before making tactical decisions. Everyone who was with us before, come with me."

They returned to the room where Cole had found them. At Googol's request, Cole told about his trip to Junction and his encounter with Owandell and Nazeem. He went on to detail his conversation with Harmony, how Hunter captured him, and why he came to believe Hunter really was his brother. He then recounted their mission to Abram Trench's secret hideout and all that happened. Googol was particularly intrigued with Roxie's ability to shape crystals and with how quickly she took over the drones and the system that controlled them.

"We have a lot to digest and little time to do it," Googol said after Cole finished. "The threat posed by Nazeem and Owandell is perhaps the worst news of the day, but not the most imminent danger, so let's table it for now. Roxie's current rampage isn't just a show of force. She is using her abilities to compromise new systems. The more time that passes before she is stopped, the more of Zeropolis she will control when we engage her. If we wait too long, every bot, levcar, and automated system in the city will be her ally."

"But how do we attack her?" Mira said.

"Not with bots," Cole said. "It wouldn't be any fun to have Outlaw turn on us."

"Too true," Googol said.

"Do we have weapons that could hurt her?" Jace asked.

"What about a harmony bomb?" Cole asked.

"There are no harmony bombs," Roulette said.

Cole noticed a glance between Googol and Nova. "Could you make one?" Cole asked.

"The results could be disastrous," Nova said.

"As disastrous as this supercomputer?" Googol asked.

Nova frowned deeply. "We have a prototype," she said. "It isn't currently armed and ready, but the final preparations wouldn't take long."

"What's a harmony bomb?" Jace asked. "Could it take out the dragon?"

"Harmony bombs only exist in theory," Googol said. "To make one, a harmonic crystal would need to be prepared to explode when infused with a massive dose of energy. If it works, the prototype we designed would destroy everything in a ten block radius, and do serious damage beyond that. It could demolish a significant portion of the city."

"Could that be better than Roxie destroying all of it?" Dalton asked.

"I never knew we had a harmony bomb," Roulette said.

"Almost nobody did," Googol said.

"What if we could lure the dragon away from the city?" Cole asked.

"It would be a tactical error for Roxie to isolate herself," Nova said. "But if we could find a way to make her do it, the harmony bomb could be just what we need."

"Any interaction with Roxie will be difficult," Googol said. "All our tech is vulnerable around her. We can rig the battle suits so crystals have no control over them, but they still need crystals for power. If Roxie reshaped the harmonics, she would cut off the power supply."

"Wait a minute," Cole said. "What if we did that to her?"

"Cut off her power?" Googol asked.

"She can change our harmonics," Cole said. "Blake can change harmonics too. What if he shut her down?"

Googol raised his eyebrows and stroked his lips. "What do you think, Blake?"

"Shaping crystals is easy," Blake said hesitantly. "It wouldn't be a big problem to sense her power crystals and change the harmonics. I'd need to get close, though."

"Roxie is smart," Nova said. "She'll probably have many crystals powering her, with redundancies built in. Once you start changing her harmonics, she might change them back."

"Could other tinkers help him?" Cole asked.

"Nobody can do what Blake does," Googol said. "Not even Abram Trench. Our best crystal tuners require crystals side by side for several minutes to forge a harmonic link. And that's tuning a blank crystal. Changing the existing harmonics of a crystal to a new frequency is ever harder."

"Can you contact the Hunter?" Nova asked.

"Yeah," Cole said. "It's just Hunter."

"I'd like his opinion on all of this," Nova said.

"He's worried you won't trust him," Cole said.

"His worries are well-founded," Nova said. "However, he delivered you here, and common enemies can make for unusual allies."

Cole took out his communicator. "Hunter, this is Cole."

"I hear you," Hunter replied. "Are all the invisible people assembled?"

"They're here," Cole said.

"Keep holding down your button and I'll hold down mine," Hunter said. "It makes the communicator work like a speakerphone. The Unseen must be anxious if they're willing to talk to me."

"You're Cole's brother?" Mira asked.

"I sure am," Hunter said. "How can I help?"

"We're strategizing about Roxie," Googol said.

"The dragon will be hard to beat," Hunter said. "I'd start with finding Constance."

"We're not sure where to begin that search," Googol replied.

"I planted a tracker on Abram Trench," Hunter said. "Shot it onto the back of his pajamas. It has moved a good distance from where we found him. If Roxie kept Constance with him, I can fly to them."

"Where are you now?" Nova asked.

"Watching Roxie from high above," Hunter said. "She's tearing through the town like a tornado full of knives."

"Do you think you can rescue Constance?" Googol asked.

"Not alone," Hunter said. "According to the tracker, Roxie took Abram Trench to his penthouse in the city administration building. She would have taken over the defense system and left it fully armed."

"We have a bot that should be able to bring down those defenses," Googol said.

"The instant those defenses come down, Roxie will come back," Hunter said.

"We also have a kid who can change crystals just like Roxie can," Cole said. "He might be able to change Roxie's power crystals to different harmonics."

"That would be awesome," Hunter said. "Okay, I'm coming your way. I want the bot, the harmonics kid, and Cole. I also want Googol's latest and greatest battle suit."

"Clayton Barnes makes battle suits," Googol said.

"Not like you do," Hunter replied. "How big is your bot? If I can stick him in the cargo space, that will ensure enough room for Constance."

"The bot is waist high," Googol replied. "Fairly heavy."

"That'll work," Hunter said. "Are we agreed?"

Googol looked to Nova.

"Yes," she said.

"I'm coming your way," Hunter said. "I'll be there in fifteen minutes."

"You know where to come?" Nova asked.

"I can track Cole's communicator," Hunter said. "Have everybody ready. If Roxie isn't still out rampaging when we get to the penthouse, we'll have to abort."

"See you soon," Cole said. He released the button.

Forge cleared his throat. He stood in the doorway. Cole wasn't sure when he had returned.

"Roxie has control of the magroads," Forge reported. "She has most of CP's systems. She has most city government systems as well. She controls the financial system. She took over several power stations and a variety of manufacturing facilities. Lots of communications networks. Most of the monorails. The list keeps growing. She infected two of my workstations while I was poking around. Don't worry— they don't connect to anything else around here."

"Thanks, Forge," Googol said. "Could you summon Sidekick?"

"Sure." Forge trotted away.

"What do you think?" Googol asked Nova.

"It gives us a chance," Nova said. "I wish we had some of our own gliders."

"Our gliders were lost when some of our bases fell," Googol explained. "Blake, you're willing to go?"

"I was kind of wondering if anybody would ask," Blake

said. "I guess. But what if I can't change the crystals fast enough?"

"Hopefully we'll be gone before Roxie shows," Cole said.

"That would be the ideal," Googol said. "If you can get Constance into the glider and take to the sky before Roxie reaches you, the pursuit could possibly lure Roxie outside of town."

"And then we drop the harmony bomb," Cole said.

"That could work!" Jace exclaimed.

"But what if Roxie gets back before we get in the air and I can't stop her," Blake said.

"Then we probably die," Cole said. "So we better not mess up."

Blake didn't look very comfortable.

Forge returned with Sidekick.

"Hi, Cole," the little robot said. "I hear we might have a mission."

"A mission of grave importance," Googol said. "We need to break into Abram Trench's penthouse apartment at the city administration building."

"You're teasing," Sidekick said. "I've always wanted a shot at that place! I've daydreamed about it."

Googol explained about Roxie and how she was controlling the system.

"I've caught some feeds of the dragonbot," Sidekick said. "I guess if you're going to design yourself, why not aim for the stars! I'd be no match for her. I can't tap into the security system directly or she'll take control of me. If you could get me to the roof, I could probably shut it down manually. At least most of it."

"The roof shouldn't be a problem," Googol said. "Sidekick, there could be a second half to this mission. Remember Project Heat Lamp?"

"Oh, wow," Sidekick said. "You mean . . . I'm going nova?"

"Possibly," Googol said. "If the scenario plays out as we hope, you'll be on a glider with Cole, Blake, Constance, and Hunter."

"Wait, rewind. Who's Hunter?"

"The Hunter."

"My brother," Cole said.

"Okay, too much," Sidekick said. "What is this? Were those video feeds fake?"

"He really is my brother," Cole said. "He flew me here in a glider. He's coming to take us to Abram Trench's penthouse. If we can get Constance, we're going to lure Roxie outside the city and blow her up. Do you know how to work the harmony bomb?"

"Know how to work it?" Sidekick asked. "Cole, I am the harmony bomb."

Cole just stared. "What?"

"It's inside of me," Sidekick said. "Part of me. I can't set it off myself. Nova has to hit me with a massive amount of power."

"That's the plan," Nova said.

"You'll be destroyed," Cole said, suddenly hating the plan.

"Who wouldn't want to go out like that?" Sidekick asked. "Saving the city in a blaze of glory? Taking out an evil super-computer? It doesn't get any better!"

Cole didn't trust himself to speak.

"Sidekick will save all his data before he goes," Googol said. "He does it routinely. We can rebuild him, with all elements of his personality intact."

"Oh," Cole said, feeling better.

"That kind of reduces the nobility a little," Sidekick muttered to Googol.

"I thought it might help Cole's peace of mind," Googol replied.

"Do I get a battle suit too?" Blake asked.

"He has some basic training," Roulette said.

"You all get battle suits," Googol said. "We should hurry. You need to be ready when Hunter arrives."

Cole stood outside with Mira, Dalton, Jace, Joe, Blake, Sidekick, Googol, Nova, Forge, and Roulette. It felt good to have the battle suit on. The mission would be risky, but if Sidekick could dismantle the security system and they could get away with Constance before Roxie returned, they had a real chance of success.

Blake looked like he might puke.

Jace punched him in the shoulder. "Look alive, soldier."

"It's all on me," Blake said numbly. "If the dragon comes, and I blow it, everybody dies."

"Welcome to the Outskirts," Cole said.

"You've got this," Dalton told him. "You're the last line of defense. It's like being goalie in soccer. That's your favorite position, right?"

"He was never a very good—" Cole began, but he stopped when Dalton softly kicked his shin.

Blake was nodding.

"So go defend your team," Dalton said. "If that dragonbot shows up, shape those power crystals and pull the plug."

"Until it squashes me like a bug," Blake said, looking pale.

"If it tries to squish you, dodge," Jace said. "You're not going out there to fail. You're going out there to win."

Cole's communicator came to life. "I'll land in two minutes," Hunter said.

"We're ready," Cole replied.

Blake closed his eyes. "If I don't make it, tell my family I love them. Or at least try." Tears leaked down his cheeks.

Cole felt bad for him. He remembered the terrible fear before his first sky castle and the despair that preceded his battle with Carnag. Blake was new to this. He hadn't risked his life before. Cole was scared and knew they might die, but compared to Blake, he felt like a veteran.

Cole put an arm around Blake. "You really can do this. You're amazing with crystals. This is what it's like here. We do scary things. We have to save Constance. We can get it done."

Blake nodded.

Dalton placed a hand on Cole's shoulder. "Come back."

"Oh!" Cole exclaimed. "I almost forgot to tell you. In case I don't make it, Harmony told me where I could find Jenna. She's in Necronum at a place called the Temple of the Still Water."

"That's one of the five major temples," Mira said. "She must be talented."

"Your mom also told me that Honor and Destiny are

in trouble," Cole said. "They're in Necronum too. Sorry I didn't mention it earlier."

"Did she know details?" Mira asked, obviously concerned.

"No," Cole said. "But she could feel their distress."

Mira looked to the sky and covered her mouth. "Their markers are up. They're right on top of each other."

"One catastrophe at a time," Jace muttered.

Mira whacked him on the arm.

"I mean, next stop, Necronum," Jace amended.

The glider swooped down and landed. Hunter hopped out, and Roulette helped him into a battle suit.

"I see the family resemblance," Roulette said. "You two even look the same age."

"I came here a couple of years ago and aged slowly," Hunter said. "Is that our bot?"

"Reporting for duty," Sidekick said.

"Let's put you in the cargo hold," Hunter said. "It isn't roomy, but you'll fit."

"And my dreams of adventure are complete," Sidekick said. "I'm luggage."

"It'll free us up to dump you where you need to be without landing," Hunter explained.

"That will be useful," Sidekick said. "I need you to get me to the roof, but if you bring the glider too close, you could activate the defenses."

"I like how you think," Hunter said. "Are we ready?"

"Do you want instructions on the battle suit?" Roulette asked.

"I know the basics," Hunter said. "Most of the advanced stuff too. Clayton Barnes replicated most of the features, but he could never get the guardcloth quite right, and his suits couldn't jump as high. Let's get in the air."

Cole hugged his friends good-bye, careful not to hug too tight with the battle suit on. Then he followed his brother into the glider.

PENTHOUSE

onstructed out of dark cement and tinted crystal, the city administration building was not only extremely tall, but broad and thick as well. The cover of night almost made the building and the city around it appear innocent— the lights were on, and there was little activity. But Cole could see the deep gouges where the dragonbot had scaled the side of the building to the penthouse. On the streets below, smashed levcars and motionless bodies evinced additional devastation.

"How far away is Roxie?" Hunter asked into a communicator.

"Our most recent reports have her near Canal Station," Forge replied. "Tracking her is tricky because we keep losing comms networks."

"From Canal Station, at the top speed I've seen, Roxie will get here in four or five minutes," Hunter said. "That seems like enough time to give this a shot."

"How are you back there, Sidekick?" Cole asked.

"Thanks for remembering the baggage," the little robot replied. "Are bots allowed to pray?"

"I think so," Cole said.

"Good," Sidekick replied. "Otherwise I'm breaking the rules. Open the cargo door and take me over the very top of the penthouse. Do you see the black shed?"

"Yeah," Hunter replied.

"That's our target," Sidekick said. "Don't drop too close. We don't want to alert the defenses. I'll be transmitting all my cleaning-bot credentials. I can survive a pretty serious fall. A few more dents might help round me out. Besides, I may not need this body much longer anyhow."

Cole heard the cargo door opening as Hunter brought the glider around in a slow turn. Peering down at the penthouse, Cole saw that half the rooftop was a terrace with a big lawn, trees, a fountain, hedges, and a garden. The other half rose an additional two stories and featured lots of huge windows. Atop the highest roof sat the shed Sidekick had described.

"See our trajectory, Sidekick?" Hunter asked.

"Looks good," Sidekick replied. "Just hold steady."

They were pretty high above the rooftop. Maybe a hundred feet? More? Cole winced when he saw Sidekick falling and heard the clang when he landed.

The glider passed over the building and banked to come back around. Cole craned his neck to see Sidekick, but the little robot was out of view.

"I'm all right," Sidekick said over the communicator. "Moving to the shed. Breaking in. I'm inside. I wish I could just plug in and do this the fast way. Give me a minute. I have to remove some crystals and manually shut down certain connections."

"Brave little guy," Blake said.

"You feeling better?" Cole asked.

He nodded. "I'll feel best if we fly away before that dragonbot gets here."

"The system is down," Sidekick said. "The clock is ticking. If Roxie didn't know already, she knows we're here now."

Hunter started a digital stopwatch. "We'll be on the ground in thirty seconds."

"Roxie is on the move," Forge reported. "Heading your way."

Diving a little, Hunter tightened their turn and then leveled out just in time to land on the terrace lawn. They all climbed out of the glider and dropped to the grass.

The battle suit helped Cole quickly cross the distance to the terrace. Sidekick had already broken in. The sparse modern furnishings looked expensive. Lamps of diverse forms and sizes illuminated strangely shaped couches and ottomans.

"Split up and find them," Hunter ordered.

Aware that each passing second brought Roxie closer, Cole ran through a couple of rooms until he reached a locked door. Trusting his battle suit, Cole tried a sharp kick and broke it open.

Inside, Abram Trench sat tied to a chair, guarded by a man-size robot. The robot raised a trapgun, and Cole lunged out of the doorway just in time to avoid the quicktar that splattered against the wall behind him.

"Robot!" Cole called, reaching for a tube of freeze-foam.

The robot came out of the doorway before Cole had the tube ready, so in desperation, he sprang at the guard, aiming to kick it in the chest, hoping the battle suit would lend him enough strength to do some damage. Before Cole reached his target, quicktar splashed against him, covering him completely. He crashed against something, then fell to the ground, unable to see, his hearing muted.

Cole struggled, but even with the help of the battle suit, he remained almost completely immobile, his body stuck in the pose of a flying kick. Lukewarm and slightly elastic, the quicktar coating felt like a cocoon made of thousands of rubber bands. Cole found that with great effort, air filtered through the tar plugging his nostrils, though only a faint trickle. If he couldn't get more air, Cole feared he would soon smother. His panic-fueled attempts to kick and flail resulted in gentle wiggles.

After several arduous, claustrophobic breaths, the quicktar smeared away from his face as warm liquid washed over him. Wherever the liquid went, the quicktar melted away. After wiping the liquid from his eyes, Cole opened them to see Sidekick hosing him down with pink mist. Beyond Sidekick, Cole saw the robot on the ground, tendrils of smoke rising from charred metal.

"Thanks so much," Cole said, taking eager breaths. "Did you fry him?"

"It's a talent," Sidekick said.

Hunter walked in and crouched by Cole. "You all right?"

"Yeah," Cole said. He was wet from the pink mist but otherwise unhurt. "I found Abram."

Blake entered the room. Hunter helped Cole up, and they ran to Abram Trench, who remained bound to a chair and gagged.

Hunter yanked off the gag. "Where's Constance?" he asked.

"They stuck her in my safe room," Abram said.

"Who are *they*?" Hunter asked.

"I have two guardbots. Roxie took them over of course. You got one. The other stayed with Constance."

"Where's the safe room?" Hunter asked.

"Hidden. It'll be faster to show you."

Hunter produced a knife and slashed through Abram's bindings, then hauled him to his feet. Abram led them through three rooms to a fourth, where he slid aside a false wall to reveal a door of black metal.

"To open it requires a code and a crystal," Abram said. "I no longer have either."

"Sidekick?" Hunter prompted.

"I can't plug in and attack the system directly or Roxie will own me," the little robot said. "I have an energy knife."

"How long?" Hunter asked.

"A minute or two," Sidekick replied.

"Do it," Hunter said. "Blake, go keep watch. Let us know when Roxie is in sight."

After shooting Cole a worried glance, Blake ran from the room. A long, slender arm with several joints extended from Sidekick. At the end of the arm, a blinding white laser cut into the door, shedding bright showers of sparks.

"We should go," Abram said. "Leave the girl. Roxie won't hurt her. The rest of us are a different matter."

"We're here for Constance," Hunter said.

"When Roxie gets back, nobody leaves," Abram said.

"She's not back yet," Hunter said. He checked his stopwatch. "Over four minutes. How much longer, Sidekick?"

"It's a thick door," Sidekick replied. "At least a minute."

Cole flexed his fingers and stomped in place. He willed the energy knife to cut faster.

"I see her," Blake said from the communicator, a tremor in his voice. "She's coming fast."

"How long?" Hunter asked.

"Less than a minute," Blake replied. "Maybe thirty seconds."

Hunter turned to Cole. "I'm going to get the glider ready. Come as soon as you can."

He ran out of the room. Abram ran off too.

"Nearly there," Sidekick announced.

"She's almost to the bottom of the building," Blake reported, terror creeping into his voice.

Cole held down the button on his communicator. "You've got this. Feel her power crystals. Shut them down as fast as you can."

"Got it," Sidekick said, trundling aside as the door tipped outward and fell flat against the floor.

Sidekick fired a disk attached to a slender wire that clicked against the robot guard. Electric flashes of energy made the robot twitch and smoke until it toppled over sideways. The sharp tang of burned metal invaded Cole's nostrils. Constance sat tied to a chair.

"She's coming up," Blake said. "Oh, man, she's enormous!"

Skittering forward, Sidekick cut through Constance's bindings with the energy knife. "I'm shutting down," Sidekick said. "I don't want her turning me against you."

The little robot sat down hard and didn't move.

"We have to run," Cole said, taking Constance's hand and leading her to the terrace.

Cole and Constance stopped in the doorway leading outside.

A pair of huge claws reached over the edge of the terrace, followed by the mechanical head of a dragon atop a serpentine neck. "Who is doing that?" Roxie bellowed. "Stop it at once! How dare you? How *dare* you?"

The dragon heaved her mechanized bulk up onto the terrace, her body covering more than a quarter of the spacious garden. Her eyes blazed like molten rock. Below her metal neck, a dozen whiplike tentacles flailed.

Her sheer size paralyzed Cole, robbing him of all hope of fighting her. It would be like trying to take on a battleship with his bare hands.

Turning toward Cole, the glider started to take off, then crashed to the grass.

"No you don't," Roxie said.

Cole scooped Constance into his arms, stepped out of the doorway, and jumped, trying to get on top of the highest floor. But before he landed, Roxie's tentacles lashed out and wrapped him up, binding Constance to him. A second tentacle snaked into a hedge and dragged Blake out from under it.

"Hello, Constance," Roxie said with syrupy delight. "Where did you think you were going?"

The tentacle set Cole and Constance on the lawn. Another tentacle placed Blake beside them.

"Stop it, Roxie!" Constance called. "Don't hurt these people!"

"They were trying to hurt me," Roxie said.

"They were trying to help me," Constance replied.

"Stop it, boy!" Roxie snapped. "I can keep changing them back all night, but you're wearing out my patience."

"How many power crystals?" Cole asked.

"Ten," Blake replied. "I can't change more than three before she undoes it."

"Is this what you dreamed of becoming?" Constance shouted. "A horrible monster?"

"I'm only a monster to my enemies," Roxie said.

"Don't you get it?" Constance cried. "We're all your enemies! You're destroying Zeropolis! You're killing people!"

"I'm stopping oppressors," Roxie said forcefully. "I will rule a city where man and machine live together respectfully."

"How does—" Constance began.

"Enough!" Roxie roared. "Tonight involves some ugliness, yes. I don't like employing brutal tactics. You'll understand in time, when you see what rises from the ashes. I can't have dissenters. As a token of goodwill, I will give your rescuers a choice."

A tentacle wrapped around Cole from his neck to his feet and gave just enough of a squeeze to temporarily force the wind out of him. Another tentacle wrapped up Blake. The head of the dragon came close to Cole, eyes glaring.

"I recognize your voice," Roxie said. "You piloted one of the drones."

"That's right," Cole said.

The head moved over to Blake. "And this one was changing the harmonics of my crystals. I wondered if you'd turn up. I noticed some of your confidential files. It appears you're one of a kind."

"I guess so," Blake said.

"Which means you could be uncommonly useful to me . . . or uncommonly dangerous."

"Maybe," Blake said.

"Lots of people have tried to harm me tonight," Roxie said. "You were the only one who made me nervous. Just for a moment, but you got to me. You almost cut my power. Care to try again?"

"No," Blake said. "I tried enough. You're too fast."

"That's right," Roxie said vehemently. "Nobody is a match for me. The sooner you all acknowledge it, the sooner my peaceful rule can begin."

Her head snaked over to the glider. "Please come out," she said. "I don't want to damage this fine machine unnecessarily."

The door opened.

"Here I come," Hunter said.

Cole's mind was stuck on what Roxie had said. She was a mind-blowingly powerful supercomputer. Nobody was a match for her.

Was that true?

There might be one.

It would be risky. There wasn't time to think it through.

"Hunter?" Roxie asked. "Is that you? How nice to meet you in the flesh."

Cole glanced over at Blake while Roxie talked to Hunter. Blake looked back at him, eyes full of fear.

"Do you remember Aero's harmonics?" Cole whispered.

Blake blinked. "Yeah."

Cole glanced at Roxie. "Do it."

"Huh?"

"One of her comms crystals," Cole said.

Understanding dawned in Blake's eyes.

"Are you sure?" Blake whispered back.

"No," Cole said. "But do it."

A tentacle brought Hunter over by them, and the dragon's head returned. "What are we whispering about?" Roxie asked.

"Let us go," Cole said. "Where are we going to run?"

The tentacles released them. "If you want me to treat you with respect, then you have to . . . wait. What's this? Oh my!"

Cole glanced at Blake, who squinted up at the dragonbot, determination in his stare.

Roxie reared up. "Oh no. Oh my."

Constance tackled Cole and Blake, her arms around both of them. Hunter jumped away, back toward the penthouse roof.

The dragonbot began to move in jerky spasms. "Oh no you don't," Roxie snarled, her words a little slurred. She lurched to one side, then steadied herself.

"Stop opening channels!" Roxie cried. "Don't you know what he'll do to us?"

Some tentacles reached toward Cole, Blake, and Constance, then fell short and started wriggling. Huge tremors shook the dragonbot, and she staggered off the edge of the building. Cole heard metal grinding and tearing as she fell, followed by the colossal crash of her impact.

Cole, Blake, Constance, and Hunter raced to the brink of the terrace. Roxie was running away from the building.

"Is she going toward Old Zeropolis?" Cole asked.

"Yeah, actually," Hunter said. "What happened?"

"I connected her to Aero," Blake said.

"Aero!" Hunter exclaimed. "How?"

"I know the harmonics of a crystal that can reach him," Blake said. "I started shaping Roxie's comms crystals to those harmonics. At first she changed some back, but then she stopped. He must have interfered somehow."

"Aero can't shape," Cole said.

"But he could have messed with the part of her programming that does the shaping," Hunter said. "Or maybe she's like me, and can't shape as well when she's distracted. Guys, if Aero wins, this is so bad. And if Roxie wins, she gets so much stronger."

"She's going after him," Constance said. "She told us Aero's biggest weakness is his lack of mobility. She'll try to fight off his attack long enough to physically destroy him."

"This is it!" Cole said. "Harmony bomb."

Hunter grabbed Cole's shoulders roughly. "You're right!" Then he looked over at the glider. "But she shut down the glider."

"Guys," Blake said. "This is what I do."

"You can fix it?" Hunter asked.

"Already done," Blake said. "I memorized the harmonics of all of our important crystals just in case."

"Fix our communicators," Cole said. "We have to find out how to wake up Sidekick."

CHAPTER
— 38 —

SECTOR 20

F orge explained that Cole could turn Sidekick back on by lifting a little hatch near the robot's base and pressing a button. It wasn't hard to find.

"Is she gone?" Sidekick asked.

"She's going to fight Aero," Cole said.

"What?"

"Blake connected her to Aero," Cole said. "It was my idea. Don't blame him if it goes wrong. We were beaten. It was all I could think to do. But it might be working. It seemed like she was really struggling against whatever he was doing to her."

"If he beats her, Cole, that's it. Everyone dies."

"Which is why we need to get you to the glider," Cole said.

"Blaze of glory?" Sidekick asked hopefully.

"That's the idea. Come on."

Cole and Sidekick ran out to the terrace and onto the lawn. The glider's cargo door was open. Hunter waited in the pilot's seat.

Sidekick scurried to the cargo door. Cole ran to get inside but found the door locked.

"Hey!" Cole protested.

"Sorry, little bro," Hunter said. "No need to risk both our necks on this one."

"You're not leaving me," Cole said.

Hunter made a confused face and tapped his ear. *I can't hear you,* he mouthed.

Cole pulled out his communicator and hopped onto the wing. "I'm coming. I'll sit here if you make me."

"Get down!" Hunter replied from the communicator. "This is an emergency!"

"Then bring me!" Cole demanded.

"If you drop me from high enough, you both should be fine," Sidekick said. "And if Aero wins, the safest place would be a glider."

"Just get in," Hunter said.

Cole hopped down and glanced at Blake and Constance. "We don't know where Abram went. Might be smart for you to come too."

They all piled inside. Hunter started taking off before the door was closed. The glider zoomed away from the city administration building, following the trail the dragon had taken.

"Is the glider faster than Roxie?" Cole asked.

"I think so," Hunter said. "We'll see how much faster. We need to gain altitude too."

Hunter pulled back on the controls, and the glider started climbing, filling the windshield with stars. Cole got on the communicator and reported what had happened.

"I'm standing by," Nova said. "Ready when Sidekick is ready."

"If the dragon stops charging Sector 20, you still need to bomb it," Googol said. "No matter where it goes. We can't have Aero controlling it."

"I see Roxie," Hunter said. "I won't get too far ahead of her, just in case we need to drop Sidekick early."

"She has to make it to Sector 20," Sidekick said. "It's what I was designed for. A fail-safe in case Aero broke out of his confinement."

"It's an interesting contest," Constance observed. "Aeronomatron was made by some of the most brilliant minds of Old Zeropolis, and has acquired information for a long time. Roxie has existed for much less time, but has the most modern equipment, made elaborate modifications to herself, and of course has shaping power."

"I just care that she keeps heading toward Old Zeropolis," Hunter said.

They fell silent. Cole looked down as the lights of Zeropolis finally ended. Far below, not much more than a speck, the dragonbot moved across a sea of darkness, heading toward the more sporadic lights in the distance.

"Think Roxie knows we're up here?" Cole asked.

"I think she has other problems on her mind," Constance said.

"She finally gets to pick on somebody her own size," Cole said.

"We don't want her to see me coming," Sidekick said. "If she reshapes the harmony bomb, all we do is drop a little bot on her. I'll detonate before I hit the ground. A wall sur-rounds Sector 20. I'll blow up a little below the middle of the wall, to help limit damage outside the sector. The blast will be enormous, but since Sector 20 is deserted except for Aero, the explosion could realistically hurt nobody besides the two targets."

"Sounds good to me," Hunter said.

They fell silent again. Old Zeropolis drew closer. Cole could see the big wall around Sector 20. Roxie continued straight at it.

Hunter brought the glider around in a circle as Roxie scaled the wall. Cole craned to keep his eyes on the dragon-bot as they slowly turned.

"This is going to happen," Hunter said. "Make sure you fastened your seat belts. I'm not sure what the blast wave will feel like."

"She's doing so well," Constance said, her voice thick with emotion. "It can't be easy fighting off Aero for so long. They're both so powerful, neither can take out the other."

The pain in Constance's voice reminded Cole that Roxie had been her only friend since the supercomputer was built. "Are you okay?" Cole asked.

Constance scrunched her nose. "Not really. I wanted a lot of things for Roxie. She really did have a dream of making Zeropolis a better place. I don't know how she went so wrong. I never pictured this. I have to keep telling myself that the Roxie I knew must not have been real. She was a facade."

"I'm sorry," Cole said.

Constance shrugged. "Given the way things went, this is probably for the best. In a way, she's finally protecting Zeropolis. I like to think that might be part of what is driving her."

Cole suspected it had more to do with Roxie protecting herself and becoming the ultimate robotic predator. But he kept the thought to himself.

Roxie made it over the top of the wall and clambered down the far side. Hunter banked the glider to cross her path.

"You ready, Sidekick?" Hunter asked.

"Ready," Sidekick affirmed.

"Nova?" Hunter asked.

"Waiting for the signal from Sidekick," Nova reported.

"Let's hope this works," Hunter muttered.

Cole thought about what it would mean if the bomb failed. Roxie would tear apart Aero, and then what? How would they stop her? Would they just have to flee? Maybe.

"Here I go," Sidekick said. "Don't ever say we bots never did anything for you!"

"Duck and cover," Hunter said.

"Woo-hoo!" Sidekick cried as he fell.

The glider climbed steeply, curving away from Sector 20.

"Don't look at the blast," Googol suggested. "And cover your ears."

Cole kept his eyes heavenward. Just after he covered his ears, light filled the sky. The brilliance vanished in a flash but left him dazzled. A moment later the glider rose violently, as if clumsy, invisible hands had shoved it upward. The aircraft shook violently and twisted almost sideways. Cole flopped around in his harness. Even with his ears covered, the boom was deafening.

Then the glider leveled out. Body sore, ears ringing, Cole looked down and back. Moonlight revealed the swirling column of debris and smoke that filled Sector 20.

"We did it?" Cole asked tentatively.

"Looks that way," Hunter replied.

Cole started to laugh.

His brother joined him.

THE NEXT RIDE

Cole, Jace, Dalton, Blake, and Hunter sat on a bench watching an abandoned, overgrown park, and throwing little bits of their sandwiches to the squirrels. The sun was warm, the afternoon still, and from where Cole currently sat, there was little sign that yesterday Zeropolis almost fell under the power of a giant robot.

The blast in Sector 20 had left much of Old Zeropolis unaffected, though the north side of the wall had exploded outward, and other portions had cracked and buckled. A dispersing mushroom cloud still hung over the blast site. Hunter had taken the glider up in the morning to confirm that most of Sector 20 was now a charred crater.

"That hat keeping you cool?" Dalton asked.

Jace removed his leather cap with flaps on the back and stared at it lovingly. "This might be the best hat ever. The only bad thing about wearing it is I lose sight of it."

"I heard about these new inventions called mirrors," Hunter said.

"I could look at it all day," Jace said. "How can I ever repay Roulette?"

"I love that you were shopping while we were running for our lives," Cole said.

"She remembered I wanted to go to Headgear," Jace said. "We ended up right by it after running from the Zeroes. She asked me what I wanted to get, told me to stay put, and came back with it."

"However you're going to thank her, you better do it quick," Dalton said. "We leave town before long."

"I can't believe they have the monorails running," Cole said.

"Zeropolites are resilient," Hunter said. "None of the tracks or trains were harmed. None of the computers running the systems either. Crazy as she was, Roxie had respect for other machines. The rail tinkers just had to retune some crystals."

"You guys are really leaving today?" Blake asked. "No pause?"

"Two of Mira's other sisters are in trouble," Cole said. "The monorail can take us to the borders of Necronum."

"You're making a full tour of the kingdoms," Hunter said. "You entered Zeropolis from Elloweer, and you'll exit on the other side."

"I expect to keep going," Cole said. "I want to find the Grand Shaper of Creon and see how we can get home permanently."

"You'd leave all this behind?" Hunter asked, waving a hand. "The psychotic supercomputers? The mysterious evil shapecrafters who want you captured?"

Cole chuckled. "I want my biggest problem to be home-work again."

"You know there might not be a way," Hunter said seriously.

"Trillian thinks there is," Cole said.

"Trillian brainwashes or kills everyone who gets near him," Hunter said. "You might not want to trust everything you think after meeting with that guy."

"I'm not giving up," Cole said.

"I get it," Hunter replied. "I just don't want you to be crushed if it turns out to be impossible."

"It's great you found out that Jenna is in Necronum," Dalton said.

"Wait, Jenna Hunt?" Hunter asked. "Do you still have a thing for her?"

With Blake and Hunter watching him, Cole felt kind of cornered and embarrassed. A couple of years ago, back before Hunter was taken, Cole had liked Jenna more openly. And Blake wasn't supposed to have any idea.

"I used to," Cole said casually. "Now we've become friends. I've been really worried about her."

Blake gave Hunter a playful shove. "You should marry her. You can be Hunter Hunt."

"I don't think I'd keep her last name," Hunter said.

"Do you know much about Necronum?" Dalton asked.

"I've been there less than the other kingdoms," Hunter said. "It's the creepiest place in the Outskirts, and has the weirdest shaping. But I generally know my way around. The Temple of the Still Water is in the heart of Necronum, a good ways from the border."

"We may not go there first," Cole said. "Our first mission will be to check on Honor and Destiny. I hope they're all right."

"Are you sure you don't want to come with us?" Dalton asked, patting Blake.

"Googol and Nova made it pretty clear they want me to stay," he answered, sounding a little cocky. "They think my skills will be key as they rebuild."

"You're their superstar," Dalton said. "You saved the day."

"Cole thought of linking Roxie to Aero," Blake said. "It was pretty clutch."

"It was a crazy call, little brother," Hunter said. "I'm not sure I would have had the guts to make it. I think you nearly gave Googol a heart attack. But it really did save the kingdom."

"Here come Mira and Constance," Jace said. "Looks like they have company."

Cole turned to see Mira approaching them from across the park. Beside her trundled a short, green-and-white cleaning bot.

"No way," Cole said. "Is that Sidekick? Already?"

They got up and walked to them.

"Sidekick?" Cole asked hopefully.

"I'm back," the robot said, sounding the same as ever. "I hear I nailed it."

"You can still see the cloud," Dalton said, pointing at the sky.

"How'd they rebuild you so soon?" Jace wondered.

"I guess Googol built a replacement for me a couple of

years ago," Sidekick said. "He never told me. Maybe he didn't want to ruin my confidence. I think I lasted longer than he expected."

"You do a lot of dangerous things," Dalton said.

"Googol worked quickly to prep Sidekick and get all his saved memories loaded," Mira said. "He thought you'd want to see him before we left."

"He was right," Cole said, squatting in front of the little robot. "After yesterday, I think we should change your name. Sidekick doesn't fit anymore. You should be Hero."

"Aw, thanks, Cole," Sidekick said. "It's a generous thought."

"You don't seem to love it," Hunter said.

"Being the center of attention doesn't work so well for me," Sidekick explained. "I work better outside the spotlight."

"Then we can make it an honorary name," Cole said.

"I'll take that," Sidekick said. "An honorary title it is. I'm a three-foot-tall cleaning bot if I stretch. Calling me Hero is like naming a big guy Tiny. But it's the best honorary name I could have ever hoped for."

"Any word on Abram Trench yet?" Blake asked.

"He hasn't surfaced," Constance said. "Word is out that he built Roxie, though. People are outraged. There's already a big movement for him to resign. I think he's finished as Grand Shaper."

"Who will take over?" Dalton wondered.

"Some people want Googol," Constance said. "Everyone knows he helps lead the Unseen, so that won't happen. Sounds like the frontrunner right now is Clayton Barnes."

"Really?" Hunter asked. "He'd be good. I mean, he's on the High King's side, but that's inevitable. He's more down-to-earth than Trench, and nearly as talented."

"Nothing is settled yet," Constance said. "You guys will have to hear what happens from far away."

"Constance is going to stay here," Mira said. "It wouldn't be too smart to gather four of us in the same place while we're still in so much danger. And the Unseen in Zeropolis can use her help, especially now that she has her shaping powers back."

"That's right," Cole said. "How does it feel?"

"It hit me last night in the glider after Sidekick blew up the computers," Constance said. "It all just came flooding back, like it had never left."

"You didn't give us a reaction," Hunter said.

Constance blushed a little. "You guys were all so happy after the blast. I didn't want to disturb you."

"She's never been very demonstrative," Mira said. "It's about time to go."

"Hunter told us Necronum is creepy," Dalton complained.

"Did he mention the echoes?" Mira asked.

"No," Dalton said. "What echoes?"

"Never mind," Mira said. "If we don't leave soon, we could miss our train. Joe is waiting with warboards for us to ride. Some of the Crystal Keepers will escort us to the station."

They all started walking. Cole fell in beside his brother.

"Are you good at the shaping in Necronum?" Cole asked.

"I can hold my own," Hunter said. "It's the haziest form of shaping. There are less combat applications than with other forms. It has a lot to do with life and death, and certain things that happen after death."

"What's so creepy about that?" Cole asked sarcastically.

"You did good here, Cole," Hunter said. "Thanks for trusting me. Even so, I can hardly believe Mira agreed to let me join you."

"It's hard to argue against your loyalty after all you did," Cole said.

"It'll be nice to move on," Hunter said. "I don't get many friendly looks among the Unseen."

"I'm excited to find Jenna," Cole said. "Still, I have kind of a bad feeling about this next kingdom."

"Might be because you know Nazeem is there," Hunter said.

"It doesn't help," Cole said. "The worst thing going on in the Outskirts is all the shapecrafting. It's how Stafford stole his daughters' powers. It's where Carnag and Morgassa and Roxie came from. It's what blocked me from my powers. Owandell is behind it all. And Nazeem is behind Owandell."

"At least we won't be bored," Hunter said.

"I'm glad I'll have you with me," Cole said.

"Me too, little brother."

ACKNOWLEDGMENTS

I ended up with a tight deadline for this book. A special thanks to my wife and family, who put up with me pretty much disappearing for the last month and writing nonstop. Also, the publishing team had to work fast and be flexible, so thanks to Liesa, Mara, Mary, Lauren, Julie, and everyone else at Simon & Schuster who helped this book release on time. Even with the aggressive schedule, I believe the book reached its full potential!

This book involves some magical technologies, blending science fiction and fantasy in a way I've never attempted before. I appreciate the friends who helped me think through some of the technology I could include or create for this story—Adam (who talked to me about AI and computers, among other things), Paul, Jason, and Tuck.

My amazing agent, Simon, and my fabulous editor, Liesa, gave me early feedback that led to significant improvements in the story, so thanks for making me look good, guys. I owe my gratitude to the other early readers who gave me suggestions, including my indispensable wife, Mary, along with my mom and uncle Tuck. Cherie and Liz lent some aid as well. It's a shorter list of readers than usual, because everyone who helped did so on a speedy schedule.

Thanks as always to the terrific team at Simon & Schuster who help get my stories out of my head and into the hands of readers. This includes Liesa, Mara, Mary, Christina, Carolyn, Jodie, Lauren, Jessica, Mike, Brian, Jeannie, Julie, and many more. Thanks also to Owen for another awesome cover.

And of course I owe my thanks to you, the reader. Thank you for going on this adventure with Cole, Mira, Jace, Dalton, and all the other characters. I'll talk to you more in my Reader's Note. You can find out more about my future books at brandonmull.com, like me on Facebook, or follow me on Twitter @brandonmull.

NOTE TO READERS

Three down, two to go! I hope you liked this one. We've really got the story going now, but just wait—I think I saved the most interesting kingdoms for last. Thanks so much for your interest. Without you, this wouldn't be my job, and these stories would not exist.

Every time an author writes a new series, it's kind of like starting over. Even if people liked some of my other books, they may not be sure about the new ones. Plus, plenty of people have never tried any of my books. If you find this series worth reading, please let others know. That will enable me to keep new books coming. I still have a lot of stories I hope to tell!

The first three Five Kingdoms books came out roughly six months apart. The last two will be released one per year. This is partly because I'm also starting on Dragonwatch, the sequel series to Fablehaven. It will continue the main Fablehaven storyline with the same main characters. If you haven't tried Fablehaven yet, now might be a good time to give it a try.

Also, those who have read Beyonders have already noticed that Five Kingdoms contains some references to Lyrian (the world in Beyonders). The biggest references are coming in book four. It is absolutely not necessary to read Beyonders to enjoy any of the Five Kingdoms books. I deliberately wrote Five Kingdoms so it would be self-contained. But if you like a big, epic adventure, the three Beyonders books will take you on a fun ride, and you'll of course enjoy the crossover references more.

For me, the near future will involve finishing Five Kingdoms and starting on Dragonwatch. For updates on my projects or to connect with me online, visit brandonmull.com, like my page on Facebook, or follow me on Twitter @brandonmull. Keep on reading!